MARLOTH

A CHILD'S FAIRYTALE WORLD

It's not about creating your own world.
It's about your own world creating you.

CHRISTOPHER W. JOHNSON

SILENT ORB

Marloth
A Child's Fairytale World
First Edition - July 2011

Text copyright © 2011 by Christopher W. Johnson
Illustrations copyright © 2011 by Christopher W. Johnson
Published by Silent Orb.™ Typeset using LuaLaTeX

Edited by:
Kristen Van Tuyl
Scott Pearson
Martha Johnson

ISBN: 978-0615484389 (Silent Orb)

Contents

MARLOTH

A Child's Fairytale World

PRELUDE

The Darkness was spreading. The clouds had gathered thickly above. The landscape was twisting itself closed like a withering flower. In the shadows, they watched and waited. They were growing restless.

For at the edge of the world, a light had broken through the turbulent sky, falling upon a castle that rose above the shadows. Sunlight by day. Moonlight by night. The castle seemed untouchable. They wanted it. Even more, they wanted what it contained. The castle's defenses were strong, but they had plotted for a long time, and soon they would be able to strike.

In one of the tallest towers was the bedroom of a little girl. Her name was Adelle. She was oblivious to the hatred and anguish that had engulfed the land. As she looked out of her window, all she saw was mystery and excitement. The world seemed to be beckoning to her. And in fact, it was ...

Every night, Adelle's mother would come to put her to bed and tell her a bedtime story. She would tell her about heroes and princesses and wars and legends. Everything that made for a good tale and a happy ending. And sometimes, when her mother was particularly moody, she would tell Adelle about ordinary people. She would tell of an orphanage far away, where the children played all day long. She never finished the story. She would always shake herself as though just waking up and move on to the age-old story about the pirate ship that sailed along the ocean floor. She would apologize and say that there were things about the orphanage story Adelle shouldn't hear about. Then, she would kiss her goodnight, douse the light, and disappear behind the door.

Adelle always thought this was funny, and wondered why her mother kept bringing up the story if she didn't think she should tell it. As Adelle would fade into sleep, she would imagine what dreadful things might be in the story. And so she would dream about orphanages and dark occurrences of which mothers never spoke of.

Marloth

PART 1

Once upon a time, nestled deep within the heart of a nameless city, there was an orphanage. Most people would never have taken a second look at the building. Perhaps it was because the surrounding buildings dwarfed it, or because the river which ran through the city passed right beside it, further taking away attention. But most likely it was the wall—a wall that rose nearly ten feet high and completely surrounded the building. Whatever the case, the orphanage seemed to fade into the background so completely, one would almost think an enchantment had been cast upon it, veiling it from the rest of the city. Every now and then, a person walking down the street might pause for a moment, imagining that they had heard a chorus of laughter, carried along the breeze like the ghost of a childhood long since left behind. But it was not imagined, for behind these walls, beyond the touch of the world, the orphans laughed and played.

This was the orphanage of Edward Tralvorkemen. Mr. Tralvorkemen was one of those beings who believed that all one had to do in life was to dispel all of the bad, and naturally all that would be left would be good. And since good is generally considered a rather good thing to possess, Mr. Tralvorkemen was determined to remove every shade of evil from the world.

Or at least from his orphanage.

Thus the orphanage was a separate entity unto itself, completely removed from the bustling city around it. The headmaster was consumed by a hatred and fear for the outside world. He had volumes of written rules to keep the children in line and vehemently forbade them to ever go beyond the wall, as though the orphanage was poised on the very edge of hell. To disobey in the slightest would result in the most severe of discipline.

The children had no interest in Tralvorkemen's vision. They were determined, nay, obsessed with escaping his rule. But they were young and naive and knew little of the world beyond the wall. All they had were their imaginations. So they smiled, nodded, and painfully played along with his rules. But the moment they were out of his sight, their own world would come alive. A world without any wicked headmasters; a world without any of his rules. They would have great adventures and slay evil people, the evilest of them being the dark warlock Tralvorkemen. In their world, they were the rulers, and they could do whatever they pleased.

As for the orphans themselves, it would be helpful to describe some of the most notable of the children.

Miles was the unofficial (and sometimes disputed) leader of the orphans. Not only was he the eldest, but he also possessed the wit, charisma, and determination which caused people of all types to stop and do his bidding. It seemed that no one was immune to his charm. Well, that is not entirely true, for there was one man in the world who was immune to his charm, and that person happened to be their headmaster. Mr. Tralvorkemen identified Miles as trouble and always had an especially attentive eye on the boy.

Nivana was a clever girl. She loved the adoration of her peers, and she had a gift for amassing it. She also loved to identify and remove the flaws in those same peers, though with far less success. Much of her time was spent trying to undermine Miles. Miles tried to ignore her.

George was one of the older boys. He was fascinated by the way things worked, and enjoyed making things of his own. Mr. Tralvorkemen had taken note of this and encouraged the boy to maintain much of the orphanage. While George preferred making new things to repairing existing ones, he still relished these tasks and saw them as an honor. Because of his skills and responsibilities, George had taken on a few illusions of grandeur. None of the other children could construct things like him and he felt that he had the most grown-up talents of them all.

Millamer was something of a prankster. He thrived upon chaos and had the tendency to break things. The odd thing was that he had an uncanny gift for getting out of trouble and laying it upon everyone else. He had managed to get into a strange relationship with George where he would butter up the fellow with praise, be allowed to borrow one of George's latest creations, and then eventually break it due to his manic recklessness. Millamer had found that if he further pumped up George with praise, the boy would forget about the destroyed creation and the process would start all over again.

Brenda was a simple and straightforward person. One of those people who can fly because they don't know that flight requires wings. Some say ignorance is bliss. For her it was a supernatural power. She was the only girl to join in the boy's games of War, which the boys would have found most awkward except for the fact that she was utterly oblivious to any such awkwardness, and somehow that made everything all right. She did not like the world of gossip and pettiness that most of the other girls inhabited; she related to the boys' methods of handling things. If a girl disliked another girl, she would spread unpleasant rumors or drop veiled criticisms. But if a boy disliked another boy, he either punched him or yelled at him, which made so much more sense and was a lot more fun.

Catherine was both pretty and precocious, and was the sort of person one would expect to be loved by all. However, she had one attribute that stunted her status with the other children: she was the only child who sympathized with Mr. Tralvorkemen. Because of this, the girls mocked her and the boys avoided her. She still joined in most of their games, but no matter how hard she tried to avoid it, her interactions with them were laced with unpleasantness. The only girl that treated her with kindness was Brenda, who, even though she did not like the headmaster, saw no reason why a person's opinion of someone should affect her opinion of someone else. She liked Catherine's compulsive honesty, and how their interactions did not require the politics she disliked so much with the other girls.

There was one boy who did not play and scheme with the other children. His name was James. None of the other children knew what had happened to him before he had been brought to the orphanage, but they did know that he had once resided in an institution, and occasionally when he was not around they would speculate as to what sort of dreadful things must have happened to him. He rarely spoke and never smiled. All of his free time was spent in dark corners, reading a large, worn-out, leather bound book. Its name was Marloth.

Within its pages were stories of a world far more magical and wonderful than anything the children could have possibly invented. Tales of heroes rescuing princesses and slaying villains. There were talking animals and surreal landscapes. But what he liked most about the book was that it too had an orphanage. An orphanage that was run by a kindly headmaster who loved the children in his care. A headmaster who wrote fantasy stories and taught the children to grow up to be heroes who were sent into the world and had adventures of their own, facing incredible dangers to rescue those in need.

The other children looked upon James with curious pity. Aside for George, who had little interest in fiction, none of them could read well enough to comprehend all of the large words the book used, and even though they generally enjoyed a good fairytale, they left James to read it on his own. Not only did Marloth use large words, it was also composed of more than one language. James could only read one of those languages, and even then he was only able to do so with a dictionary of Mr. Tralvorkemen's by his side. As he stumbled through Marloth he would look up nearly every other word, and since he did not know most of the words the dictionary used in its definitions, he would have to look those up as well. It was a very slow and laborious process, though it gradually grew easier as his vocabulary expanded.

Aside from James, only Catherine was interested in the book. Whenever Catherine had grown too frazzled by Nivana and the other girls' constant lording it over her, she would retreat to whichever cranny James was curled up in and ask him to read to her from his book. James loved having someone to read to. He took great pleasure from watching her expressions of excitement and concern as he stumbled through the book. Sometimes when she was feeling especially enthusiastic she would assist him in looking up words in his dictionary.

Occasionally, Miles would manage to break James out of his little world long enough to play with the others. The children greatly enjoyed James' company, for he always provided a refreshingly outlandish perspective on things. With Miles' sensibilities and finesse combined with James' rampant imagination, they made a good team and would sometimes host puppet shows. But after a time, James' focus would fade and he'd sink back into a corner and continue struggling through his book.

As for Tralvorkemen himself, he was a man of business and had many ventures by which he supported the orphanage. Whenever he was not overseeing the children, he was busy corresponding, processing paperwork, or meeting with other businessmen. He arranged his operations so that he had to leave the orphanage as little as possible, though occasionally he would need to take extended business trips, during which a nanny would be brought in to watch the children.

*　　*　　*

Chores, lessons, and play. As far as the children knew, this was the routine they would follow for the rest of their lives. But one day, everything started to change.

It began with a monkey. The children were busy maintaining the garden when the creature leapt over the wall and into the middle of the courtyard. It wore a blue shirt lined with glittering buttons and a red cap tied upon its head. On its back was a large satchel filled with papers. The monkey looked at the astonished children with insolent disinterest and, reaching into the satchel, removed an envelope, and set it on the ground. With that, the monkey bounded onto the wall, took one last look at the children, and was gone as fast as it had appeared.

Instantly, the children converged upon the envelope.

"I wonder what could be in it?" said Henry.

"Well don't just stand there, open it!" Nivana cried out.

"Hold on!" said George. "What if Mr. Tralvorkemen is expecting this? If he found out we opened his mail, he'd punish all of us!"

"Nonsense!" said Miles. "The bloke would never have anything to do with a monkey! Could you see him waiting for a chimp to bring his mail? If you all are too scared of the likes of him, I'll open the envelope and catch the blame myself. I'm so bored I'd take a flogging just to get some action around here."

Before anyone else could object, he slit the envelope open with his knife. The children were delighted when he extracted an elegant document printed on a paper that resembled parchment.

"What is it?"

"Let me see!"

"It's got so many words!"

"I can read it just fine." said Miles as he scrutinized the text. "It appears to be an advertisement for 'Jakob Damond's Toy Shoppe.' Here, it has a slogan: 'Where fantasy becomes reality.'"

Shouts of joy burst all around.

"It's opening on Wilkes Street where the old parsonage used to be. Here it has a list of some of the toys."

At this point most of the others were practically climbing on top of him to see if they could catch a glimpse of the paper.

"Tell us! What toys are there?"

"Well, it says there are dolls that can speak to you."

"That's ridiculous!" said George. "Dolls can't talk!"

"I'm just reading what it says. There's more. Here it's got books with pictures that move!"

"Seriously? It must be magic!"

"And pogo sticks that can bounce two stories high."

"Are such things possible?"

"If there's such a thing as heaven, there must be toys like that!"

"I'd give my right arm to see this store!"

"I'd give your right arm too!" said Miles. "Forget this gardening trash! I'm hopping the wall and—"

"Why are none of you working?"

Everyone froze. That is, except for their heads, which slowly turned to gaze up at Mr. Tralvorkemen. None of them said a word.

"I repeat my question. Why are none of you at work?" Spotting the paper in Miles' hands, he reached down and tore it away from him.

"What is this?" he demanded. "If it is another defaming depiction of me I . . . will . . ." His words trailed off as he scanned the paper. His face noticeably paled and when he finally spoke, he was so hoarse they could hardly discern his words.

"Where did you get this?" he asked. The children did not respond, but instead tried to avoid his gaze. Suddenly he burst into shouting.

"WHERE DID YOU GET THIS?" he repeated. Everyone snapped to attention.

"It's hard to say," said Miles quickly. "We think it was probably carried over the wall by the wind."

"The wind! Don't mock me! The only way a document like this could make it into your hands is if—" He stopped again. The anger quickly subsided. For a moment a hint of fear flashed across his face, and then he straightened himself and made an admirable attempt at changing his demeanor. "The wind, yes, of course. There was some rough weather this morning. Blew over the wall. Yes, that must be it."

He turned to go and then, as if suddenly remembering something, turned back to face them and said in a firm tone, "Wind or no wind, under no circumstances are you to ever go near this toyshop. Ever. Under no circumstances are you ever to possess any advertisements from this toyshop. Ever. Under no circumstances are you to ever discuss these toys amongst yourselves. Ever. These are my words, and they are final. Do I make myself clear?"

The children nodded, if begrudgingly. Tralvorkemen likewise nodded and returned into the orphanage, immediately tossing the advertisement into the fireplace.

"Well, he shouldn't worry about seeing such stuff," Miles muttered as he grabbed his spade. "Next time I get my hands on a paper like that, he won't catch a hint of it!"

*   *   *

The next day, the children were spending the mid afternoon on the orphanage roof and watching the goings on of the city around them. The roof of the orphanage was flat and had a two foot wall lining its edges to reduce the chance of a random child falling off. Most of them were sitting around lazily, simply enjoying not having to do any chores at the moment. James sat in one of the corners, reading his book. Miles sat at the edge of the roof, looking at the city through a toy spyglass.

"What are you looking at?" asked Mary.

"I'm trying to see if I can catch a glimpse of that monkey." said Miles. "I figure if I get its attention maybe it will give us another advertisement. I'll give it a banana or something if I need to."

"That would be capital!" said Millamer. "Since yesterday all I can think about is that toyshop! What I wouldn't give to buy something from that place!"

"What would you buy?" asked Brenda.

"That would be so hard to decide! I don't even know what all the store sells."

"Well, imagine something. What would you want the store to sell?"

Millamer thought for a moment and then smiled. "I'd want a gun. A gun that children can play with but fires real bullets. No, not bullets—large balls of fire! Think of it! I could be blowing holes through walls right and left!"

"Give a weapon to Millamer?" said Nivana. "That would be the death of us all! I don't feel safe with Millamer holding a fork and spoon, much less something that could punch a hole through my head! No, if I were to buy something from the toyshop I would buy something much more constructive. For instance, a wand that could make people like Millamer civilized. *That* would be magic!"

She smiled and looked over at Miles. "And what would you buy, Miles?"

Miles did not look away from his spyglass but said, "All of you blokes always think so small. I don't want to buy any toys. I want to find out how he makes them! I've never heard of anyone making things like that before. He must be using something no one else knows about! Some kind of magic or something. If I find out what it is then I could use it too. Then I could make whatever toys I wanted!"

"I don't think it's magic." said George. "I'm sure there's a scientific explanation for how these toys do what they do."

"Maybe so, but either way it's pretty impressive and I'm going to find out what it is. And then I won't need Tralvorkemen or this Damond bloke! I'll be able to open up my own toyshop and then it will be just toy, toys, toys for everyone!"

"Stop it!" said Catherine. "Stop talking about those toys! Mr. Tralvorkemen told us not to talk about the toyshop, much less scheme about ways to buy things from it! This is wrong!"

Nivana gave a brief, icy laugh. "Listen up everyone," she said. "Queen Catherine is here to set us straight! Her first decree is to ban all fun from the realm. Anyone who so much as thinks about having fun will be promptly burned at the stake. Or thrown into the fireplace if no stakes are at hand."

Catherine looked embarrassed. "I never said I was Queen. I was just—"

"Look at those children in the streets!" said Millamer, pointing below them. "They have toys from that advertisement!"

Aside from James, (who didn't seem to hear), all of the children rushed to the side of the roof and peered over the edge. Sure enough, down below were several children running about and playing with shiny new toys.

"That should be us!" said George.

"If it wasn't for Mr. Tralvorkemen that *would* be us!"

"Look at them!" said Miles. "They're spoiled brats! They have all of those incredible toys and they don't even look like they're having fun! They look bored!"

"That's because they're dead." said James.

Everyone turned to stare at him. He was sitting there serenely reading his book.

"What do you mean?" asked Millamer.

James closed the book and walked over to the edge of the roof.

"See, if you look closely, they've all got glazed over looks. Like they're wearing glasses but they're not. And their skin is pale. And they've got a good deal more cuts and scratches than we do. That's because they've been zombified. They died some time ago and then someone went and reanimated the lot of 'em."

"People can do that?" said George.

"Yup. All you need is the right mixture of magic and science."

"So if they're dead, what happens if you kill them?" asked Millamer.

"Nothing, I suppose. You can't be killed twice."

"They'd be invincible!" said Miles.

All of them turned to stare at the street children with new interest, except for James, who went back to his reading.

"Now that you mention it, they do seem rather dead looking." said Nivana.

"I still hate them." said Miles. "If even zombie children can have enchanted toys, why can't we?"

"Because we have something better!" said Catherine. "We have Mr. Tralvorkemen! He protects us! I bet the parents of those children don't care for them at all!"

Nivana looked genuinely amazed. "Tralvorkemen ... better than magical toys? That's the most idiotic thing I've ever heard, even from you! Do you mean to tell me that you actually don't want any of these toys? Honestly, you're a child and you have a pulse; don't you find these toys absolutely fascinating?"

Catherine looked to be fighting inside herself and finally said, "Yes! I admit it! They are very fascinating!"

"And wouldn't you want one?"

"Yes! Desperately!"

"Then why in the world are you arguing with us?"

"I don't know! I want to obey Mr. Tralvorkemen! He's a grown-up, and he reads really big books all the time. He must know more about these things than we do!"

"Like you said, he's a grown-up. He might know tons about grown-up stuff, but what would he know about toys? Nothing! He doesn't understand them! He doesn't understand our need for them! And he *doesn't* care for us. He's never had a stitch of fun in his life and he's going to make sure we don't either!"

"I'm sure he has a good reason." said Catherine weakly.

"Then you really are a tragedy." said Nivana, feigning pity. "When we finally get our own toys just like those children down below, we'll be off enjoying them while you'll be all alone hating yourself for your foolishness. If you don't want to hear people talking about toys I suggest you leave."

There was a long silence. Catherine glanced over at James in the hope of finding some support from him since he was the only child who did not seem to be interested in the toyshop, but he was too absorbed in his book. With her insides turned in knots, she bowed her head in resignation and made her way down stairs, leaving the others to their talk of toys.

*   *   *

Several days passed, and yet the children made no progress toward visiting Jakob Damond's Toye Shoppe. One difficulty was that they were not exactly certain of the toyshop's location. The city in which they lived was vast and they had neither map nor much knowledge of the city's layout. Due to his age, Miles was the only orphan that Mr. Tralvorkemen would use to send on errands, so the boy knew how to navigate to a few locations, and he had a vague notion of where Wilkes Street was, but could not say for sure.

But there was an even more immediate obstacle. The day after the advertisement incident, Mr. Tralvorkemen purchased a dog. None of the children were sure what he did with the dog during the day or where it went, but every night he would unleash it upon the orphanage yard. It was not a friendly dog. Several of the orphans tried to befriend it but the creature seemed unaffected by all of their efforts and would snarl and growl when any of them drew near. It was a truly frightful night watchman that could not be reasoned with.

The third obstacle was Tralvorkemen himself. Despite all of the children's talk of rebelling against the headmaster, all of them, even Miles, harbored a subconscious fear that if they were ever to sneak off to the toyshop, the headmaster would somehow discover their disobedience and be more wrathful than they had ever experienced before. They had no choice but to bide their time and hope for an opportunity to present itself.

*   *   *

It was tradition in the orphanage to spend cold evenings in the living room. Against the main wall of the room there was a large fireplace, and around this landmark various pieces of furniture were arranged. The children would gather all over the room to play games, make crafts, read picture books, while Tralvorkemen would sit in his armchair by the fire, absorbed in a book on religion or metaphysics.

Here is an example of one such evening not long after the advertisement incident. The children were playing with a restrained amount of noise. Tralvorkemen was reading by the fire. Miles was constructing a new puppet, though it was Catherine who was doing the actual knitting of the puppet's form; Miles was overseeing the work and giving commands. James was sitting against the wall by the fireplace, reading Marloth.

In the center of the room a group of the children were playing cards. Normally Miles won in whatever game they played, but his preoccupation with the puppet allowed the others a shot at being the victor. One by one, each player folded until the only remaining children were Nivana and Millamer. They were an evenly matched pair. Nivana was good at analyzing the nature of the game, keeping track of the cards, devising formidable strategies, and implementing them with frightening confidence. Millamer was good at cheating.

George was one of the later ones to fold. He hopped onto a sofa and waited for the current round to end and the next to begin. As he waited, he looked around for something to pass the time. His eyes rested on James, who was still reading Marloth.

"Hey, James! This would be a good time to resume our conversation!"

James looked up from his reading. "What conversation?"

"The ongoing one we've been having."

"I don't remember talking with you."

"You never do, but that's no problem. During the last conversation, you were talking about how your book is actually a series of dreams, and I said, 'If all of it is a dream then it has no meaning,' and then it was time to resume our lessons so we—"

"There's no such thing as *just* a dream."

"There we are! Conversation resumed. So what do you mean from that statement? How is there no such thing as 'just a dream?'"

"When I have a nightmare I wake up scared. When I have a good dream I wake up encouraged. What happens in one world affects what happens in the next."

"Interesting. I agree with you to a point: dreams do have *some* effect on reality, though it's a small effect at best."

"Different kinds of dreams have different effects. A book is a sort of dream; they have an even stronger effect on reality than sleeping dreams."

"I've never thought of a book as a dream before, but I can see the similarity. And I *have* seen the power books have over reality. Many books have influenced my life; some have turned the course of nations."

"Which brings us back to the question that led to this part of the conversation: why don't you read other books than Marloth?"

"Because Marloth is more sincere! Most books—"

"'—try to be something they're not and act like there isn't a world beyond them.' Yes, I know. 'Marloth is a humble book. It knows it's a fairytale. It says so on the cover. It knows there is a world beyond itself.'"

"Wow! That's exactly what I was going to say!"

"That's because you've already said it. I wasn't actually asking you that question just then; I was bringing us back *to* it. I *already* asked it, and you *already* gave your answer to it; we don't need to go in circles."

"I don't really understand what's going on."

"That's all right. I'm keeping track of things for the both of us. The past several discussions we spent working out the background to my question about you reading other books. You've been arguing that Marloth has unique dreamlike properties that other books don't have. However, just now you presented an argument that could be applied to other books as well."

"Fascinating," said Mr. Tralvorkemen. Both orphans stopped abruptly and turned toward the headmaster. Mr. Tralvorkemen was no longer reading. He had set his book down and was was listening to their conversation intently. "James' wild imagination meets George's rigorous mind—what an interesting combination. Don't let me stop you; please continue."

George was willing to resume the discourse, but James did not like talking about Marloth when he knew Mr. Tralvorkemen was paying attention. The headmaster had disciplined him in the past for living too much in his fantasies, and somehow that had been one of the few things James didn't forget. Once it was clear that James did not wish to speak, Tralvorkemen said that it was no matter and turned to the rest of the children.

"I just remembered," said Mr. Tralvorkemen. "Tomorrow we will be receiving a visit from Doctor Hurley. It has been too long since he was last here."

All the children looked at each other nervously. Every so often the orphanage would be visited by Doctor Hurley. The doctor was a broad, husky man with a deep voice and a sharp eye. Though he was a friendly and talkative gentleman, to the children these visits equated to needles and ill tasting medicines.

Even though his chief purpose at the orphanage was to examine each child and ensure their good health, ordinary doctoring was not his normal practice. He considered himself an inventor and spent most of his time experimenting with new medical procedures, some of which he tried on the children. Tralvorkemen was not entirely aware of this.

On this particular visit, when he had finished examining each of the children and sent them outside to play, he mentioned a need to speak with Tralvorkemen alone, as they sometimes did, and they adjourned to the headmaster's study.

"Ah, it's good to be in your study again. The décor, the view of the city, your excellent selection of books, every bit of it forms a cohesive whole. Have I told you how much I admire this place?"

Tralvorkemen assured him he had.

"Yes, well, I'd love to have a study like *this* someday. Currently I have no official location for my work. I am scattered between multiple practices and none of them see fit to provide me an entire room for my labors. Instead I am forced to share space with others, most of whom know nothing about order."

"Perhaps if you focused more on a single field you would have more resources at your disposal."

"But that is my main strength! My knowledge of one science helps me in my pursuit of another. For example, one of my colleagues is a psychiatrist who is studying electrical impulses in the brain. But he's a psychiatrist, not an electrician. As for me, I am both! Thus, he is continually coming to me for explanations on the nature of electricity, and I am happy to oblige."

The headmaster said that was all very interesting and then asked the doctor what subject he had wished to speak about.

"Oh, right," said the doctor. "It's about James. The drug I have been administering is losing its effect. I don't believe there is a problem with the drug itself, but that his condition has degraded beyond its ability."

"And exactly in what way are your drugs 'losing their effect?'"

"The boy's hallucinations have returned. Several of your children told me that just yesterday they found him conversing with his invisible amphibian friend. *And* he has resumed addressing that mangy stuffed toy of theirs as a living person. *And* in my personal questioning of him, he consistently referred to events within that fairy book of his as though they had really happened. Were you aware of any of this?"

"I was. They are, however, nothing to be concerned about. James is simply a child with a very active imagination. He is greatly sensitive to the metaphysical, and I appreciate that more than he realizes. He does have a hard time valuing concrete reality, which is a grave problem, but that is something I am working on. He may be a little foolish, but I can assure you, he's not mad."

The doctor shook his head. "I'm not saying he's mad. I'm saying he's willing to be. He desperately wants the stories within that book to be true. If any chink in his reasoning faculties were ever to develop . . . a hole in logic that would allow him to be completely consumed by his delusions—he would take it, even if he knew it was a lie."

Mr. Tralvorkemen looked hard at the doctor. "I am not sure I agree with you. You have always had a peculiar fascination with that boy, and you have tended to make more assumptions about him than is your custom with other things. In a similar manner, you tend to throw aside your normal skepticism whenever your drugs are concerned. If James really is losing his grasp on reality, how do I know it's not your drugs causing these symptoms?"

"The medication is definitely not the problem! He was exhibiting that behavior before I gave him a single dose! And for a time the symptoms subsided. All of the evidence points to the medication being beneficial."

"I'm not sure I fully agree with you, but I will hear you out. Let's say that James is on the brink of delusion and your drugs are no longer able to restrain him; what would you recommend I do?"

"Deal with that book! Right now his mind is unable to completely turn its back on reality, but I think his continued reading of Marloth could change that. It's feeding his fantasies. I think that book should be examined and, if it contains even a tenth of what I think it does, permanently removed from his presence."

"If that book is indeed the line between sanity and madness, then I would heartily agree with such a course of action, but I will not do so rashly. I will observe him closely and if his symptoms continue to degrade, then I will act."

The doctor conceded that to be a reasonable approach. After a little more conversation, he then asked how Tralvorkemen's business was faring.

"Not good." was the weary reply. "More stock was stolen last week. I was forced to close another outlet."

"That certainly isn't good! Is your business in jeopardy?"

"Not yet, but it cannot sustain much more of this. I may need to consider a new direction."

"But that can't be the answer! Whoever is perpetrating these crimes must be stopped! Do the authorities have any clue as to who is behind it?"

"No. I do not think there is much they can do."

There was silence for several moments, and then Tralvorkemen said, "Have you heard of this new toyshop that recently opened its doors?"

"Ah, yes. I heard of the place. Jakob Damond's Toye Shoppe. I hope you aren't begrudging its arrival; they say it's quite a marvel!"

"Marvelously devious, more like it. Jakob Damond has my children utterly captivated!"

"Right then, a *little* begrudging. Maybe it wouldn't hurt to give the children some newer toys?"

"They already have the best I have to offer, yet it's not good enough; they only want *Jakob Damond's* toys. You speak of drugs losing their effect? Everything I do is losing its effect! I have never seen the children so rebellious in unison. No matter how much I instruct and discipline them, they are completely distracted with no apparent remedy. I fear that they may actually attempt to seek out that toyshop regardless of all I have said."

The headmaster expressed something between a chuckle and a sigh. "The grand irony in all of this is, despite everything you have said about James, he may be the only child in this orphanage who is contented with what he already has. He clings to his book and looks down on every other toy. Of all the children he is the most harmless."

"I wouldn't be so sure of that." said the doctor. "Even though James may not care for this toymaker's merchandise, his interest in that book is still rooted in discontent. Remember, he wants things to be different! Radically different. Who knows, James' fascination with this book may be indirectly fueling the other children's fascination with this Damond fellow's toyshop. I've heard the man's slogan: 'Where fantasy becomes reality.' That is the sort of thing James lives for. He may not be consciously encouraging the children toward discontent, but I think his book is."

Tralvorkemen sighed. "I will keep what you have said in mind, though I do not honestly think it will make much difference. I fear circumstances are already out of my hands."

"Come on, old friend, pull yourself together! I was just airing a few concerns of mine. Valid concerns, mind you, but all the same, you're doing an excellent job caring for these orphans. I tend to get a little over excited when talking about patients, and should have used more reserve. It sounds like you have more on your plate than ever, and I forget you've always tended to go about this business as though . . ."

" . . . as though no matter what I do, this entire world has conspired against me?"

"Yes, that's what I was talking about."

Tralvorkemen made an attempt at smiling along with Hurley. "Sometimes I am more convinced than ever that it is."

At this, Hurley started to laugh, and before long Tralvorkemen had joined him.

*   *   *

James awkwardly climbed the ladder and pushed open the door to the attic. He had expected to be greeted by a cloud of dust but instead found the air relatively clean, as though the door had been used recently. James did not think much of it and climbed the rest of the way into the room.

Like most of the rooms in the orphanage, the attic was far larger than it looked like it ought to be. And like most attics you would find in a story, it was filled with old furniture and the remains of wooden objects that had once served some purpose. And cobwebs; there were lots of cobwebs.

After scanning his surroundings, James' focus gravitated to a mirror that stood at the far end of the room, just to the right of a small window. It was a large, old mirror—so old that James wondered if it could be one of the mirrors in his book, the kind that reflects ages far beyond the horizon of man's knowledge. But it was quite an ordinary mirror. All it reflected was the image of an ordinary little girl. It was the image of Catherine, to be precise, for she was sitting in front of the mirror intently with her back to the rest of the room.

James was surprised to find the attic anything but empty. His first thought was to turn around and forget about the whole matter. But then some ill used part of his mind thought it would be fun to be curious for once. What was Catherine doing up in the attic, staring at that mirror? She was so absorbed in whatever it was that she had not noticed James' entrance.

It bears noting that James was in no way a person of details. To him, his surroundings were a constant blur, so that while some people need glasses for their eyesight, James would have benefited from glasses for his general perception, especially when it came to any sort of thing a girl might find interesting. For example, James was oblivious to things like hair. At that moment Catherine had her hair pulled up into a makeshift bun, a style she never wore. Also, James was oblivious to things like makeup. Whatever it was that Catherine had put on her face, it was *not* makeup, but it was the closest thing to makeup she could find, and in a pinch may have actually looked better than not. As for her posture, she normally carried herself with either her shoulders slumped, as when she was sad, or with her shoulders loose, as when she was happy; but at this moment she was working very hard to keep her shoulders back, her neck straight, and her chin high.

But the most striking feature of her conduct was the way she kept tilting her head back and forth as though politely looking from one person to another and was speaking out loud in a manner more firm and regal then any she had been known to use.

"Now, now," she was saying. "Duke Henry made a very good point and I think if the rest of you would consider it in its proper context you would see why the delegation would be prudent . . ." And then she would pause and nod thoughtfully as though paying close attention to several peoples' observations. "I understand your concerns," she said, "but realistically we will have to compromise . . ."

"Who are you talking to?" asked James, looking over her shoulder.

Catherine shrieked and nearly knocked over the stool she was sitting on. "What are you doing here!" she hissed, trying to catch her sudden outburst and keep her voice down. Her powdered face was now quite red.

"Are there people on the other side of that mirror?" asked James, who had stepped closer to the glass and was examining it curiously.

Catherine covered her face in exasperation. "Of course not! I was just . . ."

She waited, hoping she could leave it at that, but when she looked up she found James waiting expectantly. She felt compelled to give a response.

"Well . . . I was just . . . practicing."

"Really?" said James, turning back to the mirror. "Practicing what?" He still didn't completely believe her about the mirror and was trying to see if he could see a glimpse of some supernatural third person in its background, or catch the boy and girl inside the mirror doing something contrary to what the Catherine and James on their side were doing.

"It's none of your business!" said Catherine, and then in a desperate bid to change the subject, "What are you doing here anyhow?"

She had an accusing tone that made it sound like he was doing something wrong, which annoyed James because he knew he had as much right to be in the attic as she did. (In other words, neither of them should have been there.)

"I'm looking for cloth." he replied, and, after a moment's pause, realized that that was in fact what he had come to do . . . and began looking about the room to see if any pieces of cloth would leap out at him.

"Cloth? Why in the world would you be looking for cloth?"

"Brenda sent me. She's patching up Fugue and needs cloth to make him a new left arm. I think Millamer said 'Look! Fugue can fly!' and it all went downhill from there."

For anyone who may be wondering, Fugue was not one of the orphans. Fugue* was a cloth animal. Or at least something like that. One day Mr. Tralvorkemen had brought to the orphanage a box filled with shredded pieces from a variety of stuffed animals and dolls as a gift for the children. Other children might have thought such a gift to be silly, but the orphans eagerly pooled together the best pieces in the box and sewed them together to form a single creature of cloth: Fugue. Even though every part of its body from its eyes to its legs were mismatched in their color, material, and species, it was beloved by all of the orphans and had become their mascot.

Normally, Catherine would have said something like "Poor Fugue!" but at the moment she was unusually preoccupied. She was back looking at her reflection in the mirror, and the more she looked the more discouraged she became.

"James, do you think I'm pretty?"

James looked over at her in surprise. Ideas like 'pretty' were hardly in his vocabulary. "I suppose so," he said at last.

"And do you think I'm childish?"

James shrugged. "I don't know exactly what childish is. Do you want to be?"

---

*Pronounced similar to 'fewg' or 'fee-oog'

"Of course not! People don't like people who are childish! They like people who are mature and sophisticated and say clever things all the time!"

James shrugged again. "If you say so." He spotted an old quilt and pulled it out from behind a hutch. Once he had it out in the open he began to turn it over to see if some part of it would work as an arm.

A surge of anger rose up in Catherine, but she pushed it back. She wished James would pay her more attention, but she needed to be a lady and treat James with respect even if he didn't respect anyone else. And despite his total lack of social skills, he was one of the closest things to an ally she had in this place. Perhaps he could help her with some other things she had been weighed down with.

"James, there's something I've been thinking about, and you may be the only person who would understand. It's about Mr. Tralvorkemen. I know most of the time he seems mean and unpleasant. He's switched me more times than I know how to count. But it's almost like he is two different people. I could swear I have memories of times when he was kind to me. We had conversations where I felt sure he was sincerely interested in me as a person. But those memories are so fuzzy . . . more like memories of memories."

"That's nothing special," said James, "I deal with that sort of thing all the time. My memory is a total fog. You're probably just getting mixed up between Mr. Tralvorkemen and the headmaster in Marloth."

"No! It's not just me! Some of the other children have told me they have similar dreamlike memories, though they would never admit it in public."

James thought for a moment, and then shrugged. "Maybe Mr. Tralvorkemen is a nice person; maybe he isn't. He's not the headmaster from Marloth, so it doesn't matter either way."

"It matters to me! It matters to the other children!"

"Then maybe you should be talking to them instead of me."

That was it. The dam broke. Catherine stomped her foot in frustration. "You are so heartless! Don't you care about anything other than that book? Don't you ever think about the people around you? What we might be thinking and feeling?"

"I have feelings! Just because I don't go bubbling out every thought that crosses my mind like you doesn't mean I don't feel anything. I love Marloth because it makes me feel. It makes me care about things."

"But not about things that are real! You read about people sacrificing their lives for their friends, but you don't sacrifice anything. You read about adventures, but you don't even join in the boys' games of War. You read about heroes rescuing princesses, but I don't see you rescuing anyone!" By now Catherine was on her feet, poking James in the chest with her index finger.

"I don't think you really like Marloth! You talk about wishing it were real, but you would never *really* want that. You would *hate* being in Marloth! That would mean running around and getting tired and hungry and hurt! In Marloth you would need to actually become *attached* to people. To not only risk your life, but your heart as well! Those are all things that are *very* un-James-like."

James was speechless. He stood there for several moments. Then he stepped back, gathered the quilt, and left without saying a word.

Catherine watched him go, sat down, and then burst into tears.

*   *   *

The next day, Catherine found James in one of the many corners he inhabited, and apologized for her outburst from the previous day. While she was still hurt by his lack of interest, she was more hurt by the thought of hurting him.

James received this without a hint of resentment and said he didn't remember much of the conversation. This was hard for Catherine to hear, but she said she understood and did her best to continue on with her day. She was not sure whether or not he had really forgotten, but if he had, she had the unnerving suspicion that his mind had consciously blotted the event from his mind, like a white blood cell blots out a virus.

*   *   *

It was not uncommon for Mr. Tralvorkemen to spend much of his time in his study, but the day following Doctor Hurley's visit was an unusual one in that Mr. Tralvorkemen spent *all* of his time in his study, to the point of missing breakfast, lunch, and dinner. The children were accustomed to preparing the meals for themselves, but not to that degree, and it felt surreal to go through the entire day attending to themselves without the headmaster's supervision. They did not mind it by any means, but at the same time there was a growing apprehension amongst their ranks as to what this absence could mean.

As usual, the children spent their evening gathered in the living room. Millamer eagerly volunteered himself to build the fire and before long a fire was raging three times larger than anything Mr. Tralvorkemen would have allowed. While there was some amount of games and similar activities, the children utilized their current freedom to talk about the inexhaustibly fascinating subject of Jakob Damond's Toye Shoppe.

"Hey, where's James?" asked George. "I haven't seen him since dinner."

"Oh, he somehow managed to lose his book." said Brenda. "He's been looking all over for it."

If you were to have looked on at that orphanage that night, you would have first noticed that all of the rooms were very dark except for three lights. One of the lights was large and flickering, and illuminated a room at the bottom floor. That was the living room. On the third floor, an old brass lamp illuminated one of the smaller rooms. That was the headmaster's study. Then there was the light of a frail candle. That light was moving frantically from room to room and floor to floor.

If you were to have watched the orphanage for a long enough time, you would have eventually seen a fourth light, also from a candle, leaving the large, firelit room and traveling upward and along through winding stairs and hallways until its light met up and merged with the other candle.

"James, it's too late to look for Marloth now." said Catherine. "Why don't you come downstairs and join the rest of us? You can look for Marloth tomorrow when it will be easier to find."

"Just give me a few more minutes. I'm sure I'll come across it any moment now."

"Miles said you've been searching for hours! You're not going to find it 'any moment now'. Here, if you come with me right now, I'll help you look for it tomorrow. I'm sure some of the others will be glad to help as well."

"They won't need to. I'm going to find it any moment. I can feel it."

"Ugh!" Catherine groaned. Taking advantage of James' preoccupation, she suddenly leaned forward, blew out his candle, and leapt back. James turned to find himself in a very dark room with the only source of light being the candle Catherine was holding several feet away.

"Give me that candle!" James growled.

"If you want the candle, follow me!" said Catherine. James lunged at it, but Catherine gracefully dodged through the doorway and down the hall.

"Come back here!" James shouted, charging after her. From outside the orphanage, you would have seen a single frail light hurrying about from room to hallway, hallway to room, gradually making its way downward until it merged with the large light of the living room. You also might have noticed that by then the living room was the only lit room in the house.

Laughing and gasping for breath, Catherine rushed into the living room with James on her heels. The laughter immediately ceased. In the center of the room, outlined by the raging fire, stood Tralvorkemen. In his hand he held James' prized possession: Marloth.

The other children were very still, and very quiet. They hardly even noticed Catherine and James' entrance. All eyes were on Mr. Tralvorkemen.

"How many of you have heard of the headmaster in this book?" This was said by Mr. Tralvorkemen. He waited for a response, but none of the children spoke a word. "This book tells of a headmaster," he went on. "Have all of you heard its account?"

The silence continued. He did not appear to be angry, but he definitely wasn't happy. He seemed as though all the energy had been wrung out of him and then suddenly shot back into him with painful inspiration. The children had never seen him so agitated.

Miles looked like he was preparing a clever answer when Catherine said, still trying to catch her breath, "I think we all have at one time or another."

Mr. Tralvorkemen slowly nodded. "And can anyone tell me what sort of a person this headmaster is? What are his qualities?"

More hesitation. "He's a nice fellow?" hazarded one of the children.

Mr. Tralvorkemen nodded. "What else?"

"He doesn't spank his children!" said Miles.

"No. That is incorrect. Clearly you have not attended to your studies of fairytales. This headmaster *does* spank his children. He employs many forms of discipline."

"But it always pains him to do it!" said Catherine. "He cares deeply for his children, even when he is disciplining them. Even though it hurts so much, he does it for their own good!"

Tralvorkemen turned toward her and smiled, although it was not a happy smile. "Very good! In fact, everything he does is for other people. He is utterly selfless! Everything he does is always exactly the right thing a person should do. He never makes a mistake!"

He began to move around the room, facing each child in turn. "Wouldn't you want a headmaster like that?" he asked. Several hesitant nods. "Someone who would always put you before himself?" More nods. "Someone who would tell you fantastic stories of far-away places?" The nodding grew more enthusiastic. "Someone so fun and wonderful that you wouldn't even care about magical toys?"

All nods abruptly stopped. Tralvorkemen looked about him with morbid satisfaction. "Oh, but of course not! You're not content with me; you still want magical toys! And why is that?"

As he spoke his pitch and condescension had risen until it reached a crescendo that now hung in the air atop his rhetorical pause. But it did not rest there long before it came crashing down and landed in their midst with a crash.

"Because I'm not that man!" he shouted. All of the children jumped back in surprise. The wake of his outburst hardly settled before he charged onward at full speed. Gone were the dark humor and condescension. Now his fury was unleashed.

"I decided to examine this book because I suspected that it had been encouraging your desires for that toyshop. I wish it had! For now I find myself fighting discontent not from one direction, but two! On one side I have a toymaker who would accuse me of being too good, and on the other, an imaginary headmaster who would accuse me of not being good enough! This toyshop would have me be something my conscience cannot allow, while this book would have me be something nature cannot allow! I am human! I am not perfect! I am flawed and the first to admit it! But through this book you expect of me a state I cannot attain!"

He paused to regain his breath. He slumped into his armchair near the middle of the room. Every eye of every orphan remained fixed on him.

"I can't do magic!" he moaned. "I can't dazzle your senses and capture your minds! But this Toymaker can! I can't compete with that! I can't compete with magical toys! Nor can I compete with a perfect headmaster that is solely fictitious!"

Timidly, Catherine approached him and put one of her small hands on his arm. "You have done so much for us!" she said hardly above a whisper. "You don't need to compete with anyone!" For a brief moment, a genuine smile crossed the headmaster's face. "Catherine," said he, "I hope you never lose your innocent compassion."

Then the gloom returned to his face. "But fate is not that simple. Nor kind." He rose from his chair. Most of the anger had left him. Now was not the condescending Tralvorkemen, nor the vengeful Tralvorkemen, this was the more familiar battered Tralvorkemen, the rational intellect curiously pondering its own imminent doom. Almost casually, he turned to James and said "I wonder if you understand even a tenth of what this book says. I've spent all day studying it and I have hardly pierced its surface. Have you even read all of it?"

James thought for a moment and then shook his head.

"I figured that was the case. You don't seem frightened enough to have read the whole of it. Then again, I doubt you understand what little you've already read. Do you have any idea what this book really says? What it really means? If this book is true then I am a lie. This book I hold in my hand claims that the world we inhabit is naught but an illusion! And not simply an illusion, but an evil one! To this book I am not simply a lie, but a perversion; a malicious perversion of your perfect headmaster!"

At this he put his hand to his head as though his brains were aching. "This is absurd! How can I even be quoting such rubbish! This book is twisting my mind! I can't imagine what it has done to yours ..." (That last part he addressed to James.) He pounded his fist atop the book in an attempt to regain his substance. "I ... am ... *real!*" he shouted. "This book ... is ... *fantasy!* It is the lie, not me!"

Once again his voice had risen to a crescendo, and once again both voice and man slumped into his armchair. He sat there some time, grimly cogitating. The children were too frightened and confused to stir an inch. The only motion in the room was the flickering of the fire, which cast the brooding figure of Mr. Tralvorkemen in solid black. Finally he spoke.

"One thing is certain. The book must be destroyed."

Instantly all of the nerves in James' body snapped into tension so violently he felt he would explode.

"What!" he blurted. "You can't do that!"

Mr. Tralvorkemen looked as though he were trying very hard to contain his temper. "Have you heard nothing of what I said? The book must go!"

"But I need it!

"What you need is submission! Need I remind you, little boy, that if it were not for me you would still be in that horrid asylum, if not dead? Or that this is my house, and you are my charge? It is only by mercy that I am not punishing you this instant! If you display any more defiance you will experience discipline like never before."

"You can beat me and starve me and lock me up and beat me some more, but I must have Marloth!"

Tralvorkemen's temper finally snapped. "So be it! If you're so obsessed with the accursed book, fetch it!"

With that, he turned and hurled it into the fire.

"*NO!*" James screamed, and before the book had even landed, he jumped into the fire after it.

"The devil! You're possessed!" the Headmaster shouted. Time seemed to freeze as everyone watched in horror as James struggled to reach the book, for the fireplace was quite large and very deep. The headmaster was so stunned that it took him a moment to gather his wits and pull the boy out of the fire.

"No! My book!" James shrieked. He flailed around as he was torn from the furnace, sending glittering embers around the room.

"Get me Doctor Hurley!" Mr. Tralvorkemen ordered Miles, who straightaway ran out of the orphanage and climbed over the wall. Tearing a blanket from under one of the children, Mr. Tralvorkemen quickly put out James' burning clothes.

"Everyone out!" he commanded. As all of the children piled out of the room, he left James on the floor to get some water from the kitchen.

All alone, James quivered on the floor and watched through blurry eyes as Marloth turned from embers to ash. He did not feel the pain of his burnt flesh. He did not feel the tears streaming down his face. All he felt was emptiness.

*   *   *

Doctor Hurley was quickly brought to the orphanage and James was ushered to a facility where he was treated for his burns. He was transferred to the sick room of the orphanage the next day, bandaged like a mummy. There he spent the next several weeks in fitful sleep.

"Do you think he will recover?" Mr. Tralvorkemen asked the doctor.

"He should pull through. There's nothing fatal. He'll have a number of scars, but he won't look disfigured. *Striking* ... that's probably the word I'd choose."

Mr. Tralvorkemen walked over to the bed and watched the boy. James was tossing and turning in agony. All the while, he was muttering and whispering to himself about zombies and evil toys.

Suddenly, he stopped and opened his eyes. It took him a while for his eyes to fully open and adjust to his surroundings. Then, he spotted Tralvorkemen.

"I hate you!" he shouted hoarsely.

The headmaster stood there motionless.

"I hate you!" James repeated, and then went into convulsions.

The doctor rushed to the boys' side and began to inject him with medicine.

"This behavior has nothing to do with any physical damage," he said. "Whatever he's going through is in his mind."

Before long, the drugs took their effect and James drifted back into deep sleep.

"We'd best leave him alone." said the doctor.

Mr. Tralvorkemen nodded and the two men walked out of the room.

"Why did you have to go and destroy it?" said the doctor, once they were in the hall. "There were less violent ways to detach the boy from the book, and I would have liked very much to have seen what was inside it."

"I am glad you didn't."

"What do you mean? Are you trying to hide something from me? You know that if I am to fully help James, I will need every scrap of information about this whole Marloth business."

"James? Honestly, I don't think there is much more you can do for him. As long as I can remember things have never felt quite right, and I'm starting to realize why. No, I think things are going to get much worse and there is nothing you can do about it."

"Your paranoia is reaching a whole new depth! Does everyone who reads that book go mad?"

"I'm leaning toward the affirmative."

"I didn't mean for you to answer that!"

Tralvorkemen brushed the comment aside. "I was simply thinking how I've been going about life trying to fill in the pieces of a puzzle, and that book provided many possible pieces, and when I perceived the puzzle near completion I suddenly found myself wishing I had not put any pieces together at all."

"For someone who just burned the foul thing, you certainly are fascinated with it!"

"I know. It haunts me from its grave, and for more reasons than one."

The doctor looked at Tralvorkemen in a very peculiar way. "Next time I visit," he said, "I may bring a little something for you to take as well."

"As to that, the next time you visit, and possibly many visits after that, you will be conducting your business through a—hold on . . . what was her name . . . a Miss Perry, I believe, or something like that. Whatever her name, she will be overseeing the care of the children until I return. I have no idea how long I will be gone."

"And where ever will you be?"

"Abroad. On business."

"Business? I would not have expected you to have a reason to travel for several more months."

"Correct. This business is not of my normal kind."

"Well, are you going to at least tell me where you are going?"

"No, it doesn't look like I am."

"Why the sudden mystery? What end are you pursuing in all of this?"

"If you must know, from here on I have but one object in mind: to find out who wrote that book."

*   *   *

No one was more distressed by the fireplace incident than Catherine. The other children did not sympathize with her. Before, they had mocked her devotion to Tralvorkemen, now they hated her for it. She had never felt so separated from everyone else. She no longer tried to fit in. If the children were playing outside, she would be inside, and if the children were playing inside, she would be outside.

One morning Catherine was in the yard by herself when who should appear but the monkey, looking down at her from the top of the wall like some furry gargoyle.

At first Catherine tried to ignore the monkey, for she was conflicted about the creature. On one hand, she felt that it was at least partially responsible for setting in motion all of the mischief that had befallen the orphanage. But on the other hand, it seemed so intelligent and was so remarkable in both apparel and manner, she felt rude ignoring it.

She turned to face the animal and was about to speak when she spotted an envelope lying at her feet. She looked up at the monkey and back down at the envelope. The creature did not appear to have moved from its perch on the wall.

Hesitantly, she reached down and took the envelope. She could not read as well as James, but she could read just well enough to see that it was addressed to her. She looked up at the monkey in surprise, but gained no information from the monkey's steady smile. Deciding that there was no mistaking the monkey's intention, she opened the envelope and took from it a single piece of paper on which was written the following:

Why is your heart so sad, little girl?

Jakob Damond

She looked up in puzzlement. "How am I to respond to such a letter?" she asked, looking at the monkey but addressing no one in particular. "I can barely write, and Mr. Tralvorkemen would never allow me to send a letter to Jakob Damond of all people!"

She thought about it more and shook her head in frustration. "I don't even know why I'm sad. I don't know what to think anymore! Well, that's not entirely true. I guess part of what irks me is that all these years I defended Mr. Tralvorkemen and now he's gone and thrown Marloth into the fire! It wasn't only James' favorite book, it was mine too! And even though it was James who decided to jump into the fire, I can't help feeling like that was Mr. Tralvorkemen's fault as well! And now the others treat me worse than ever! They accuse me of thinking they're not good enough for me when all I want is to be their friend!"

By then Catherine had worked herself into quite a frazzled state and collapsed to the ground in a pitiful heap. But she was not there long before she felt an envelope gently land on her lap. She looked up in surprise to see the monkey maintaining its steady post on the wall as though nothing had happened. Turning over the envelope, she saw that it was addressed to her just as the one before it. Brimming with curiosity, she quickly tore it open and examined the paper inside. This one had far more words than the previous paper, and it took her much longer to make any sense of it. The letter went something like this:

I know how you must feel. I too am frequently misunderstood. So often I try to help people and in return they slander me. All I want to do is make the world a better place.

If you came to my toyshop I could solve all your problems. I have toys that would cause your friends to love you and Mr. Tralvorkemen to respect you. Right now you are a child, and will be for ever so long, but I could make you a Lady right now, so that you would have all the wisdom, admiration, and pleasures that adults experience. Unfortunately, I have heard that your headmaster has forbidden you from visiting any toyshop, so I guess there is nothing I can do for you.

Jakob Damond

She did not know what all the words meant, but she understood enough to see that the headmaster's commands were in question. Without thinking, she automatically looked up and said "No, not any toyshop! Just yours. He said if we went to your toyshop he would throw us out of the orphanage! I know that must sound a little severe, but I'm sure he has good reason for it."

She had hardly finished saying this when the monkey lightly dropped down from the wall, reached into the bag slung over its shoulder, and handed Catherine yet another letter. Catherine looked and behold, like the ones before it, this letter was also addressed to her.

Ah, I think I understand what is going on. There are many people who are envious of my magical goods, and it sounds like your headmaster has heard some of the lies these people spread to spite me. I fear your headmaster is sadly misinformed as to my character. I want to help him by helping you.

The fact of the matter is that your headmaster has never actually seen my toys. If you were to acquire one of them and bring it back to the orphanage, he would be so amazed by it and so enraptured by you through its influence that he would never even think about punishing you.

Jakob Damond

Along with the letter there was another piece of paper in the envelope. A colorful one. She took it out and found herself staring at a second advertisement to Jakob Damond's Toye Shoppe. This advertisement had pictures and descriptions of even more wonderful toys than the first one.

"These toys are so amazing!" she gasped. "But I don't know if I could do the things you are asking of me. I don't know what to think. What you say is so different from what Mr. Tralvorkemen has said!" By now she was not sure who she was addressing, but she didn't really care; she was wholly caught up in the conversation. She did not think anything of it when the monkey once more dropped down and handed her another letter. She didn't even bother checking to see who it was addressed to before opening it.

Believe me, the headmaster and I both have your best interest at heart. I am not forcing you to do anything. Whether or not you accept my offer is the difference between everyone being miserable, and everyone being happy. The choice is yours.

Jakob Damond

When Catherine had finished reading the letter and looked up, the monkey was gone. She stood there for some time after that, staring at the pile of envelopes and letters at her feet. Part of her was frightened at the idea of disobeying the headmaster and venturing beyond the confines of the orphanage, but she found that part of her becoming fainter. She felt alive in a way she had never experienced before; ready to take chances she would have never considered. All her life she had done everything she had been told to do and all it had brought her was disappointment.

"It's just like the toymaker said! All I've done is try to be kind to people and in return they've just walked all over me. I'm tired of being made fun of! I'm tired of being manipulated! And I'm not going to take it anymore."

She reached down, gathered up the papers, and looked toward the orphanage.

"I'm tired of being the good girl."

*   *   *

Over time, the burns healed, leaving only faint scars over James' face and arms, but his soul did not fare so well. He withdrew even more from the other children, and no longer did he have his book to turn to. Instead, he spent his time sitting alone in the sick room, staring darkly into space. The children frequently visited him and tried to include him in their games, but to no avail. He was consumed.

One day, there was a knock at the infirmary door. Before James could say "Go away!" the door opened and in stepped Catherine.

"Go away!" said James.

"I'm doing fine, thank you." said Catherine. "How are you to-day?"

James didn't respond. Catherine pulled up a chair and sat down beside the bed.

"I'm sorry about what happened to Marloth. I can't imagine how hard it must be for you not to have it anymore." She paused to give James an opportunity to comment but he didn't say anything.

"Anyhow," she continued, "I've been trying to come up with a way for you to get another copy of Marloth."

"There are no other copies of Marloth! It was one of a kind!"

"You don't know that! Marloth did not look like a handwritten book; I think it was published. For all you know there could be hundreds of copies throughout the world."

An ember of hope flickered across James' countenance, but he wasn't ready to leave his gloom. "Even if that were true, how could I ever find such a book?"

"Well ... we *could* start by looking in Jakob Damond's Toye Shoppe ..."

The irony of such a suggestion coming from Catherine was completely lost on James. "Marloth wasn't a toy; it was a book."

"Didn't you pay any attention to that advertisement? The toyshop sells books! Magical ones! Books of fantasy even!"

James sat up. "Seriously?"

Catherine reached into her pocket, took out the advertisement she had received from the monkey, and laid it out before James. "If you don't believe me then just look at this."

James was amazed. "I thought Tralvorkemen burned this!" he said.

"This is another one." said Catherine. "I found it in the yard."

James scanned the paper and sure enough, there were several fairytale books.

"It doesn't mention Marloth." he said.

"But you do agree that it could be there, don't you?"

"It looks possible..."

"So would you like to go?"

James thought for several moments. "Yes. I would."

"Terrific!" Catherine beamed, and then paused. "Now that just leaves one other issue: I don't know how to get there. I'm not good with maps, or finding places, and I wouldn't be good at finding a way to sneak out of the orphanage and back. But you're really smart; I was hoping you could find a way..."

"I can do it." said James.

"Really? That *is* good news! When do you think we could go?"

"I don't know. I'll need some time to think ... and gather information. I'll let you know when everything is ready."

*   *   *

They didn't have to wait long. The next day Mr. Tralvorkemen set out on a mysterious business trip, leaving the children under the care of a nanny. While she was just as watchful and conservative as Mr. Tralvorkemen, she was not as bright, and near the end of the day James told Catherine that he had worked everything out and they would be visiting the toyshop that night. Catherine was thrilled.

Night came, and after everyone had gone to bed, James slipped on his clothes and pocketed the bag which contained the few shillings he possessed. Before he left the room, tied his sheets together and rolled them into a ball. With the bundle tucked under his arm, he carefully crept to the girls' bedroom, where Catherine was waiting outside. Without saying a word, they proceeded downstairs.

They found the nanny in the living room, fast asleep. They tiptoed past her, and to the back door.

"Wait a minute," said Catherine. "What about the dog?"

"I took care of it." said James.

With much care, they slipped outside and closed the door behind them. James locked the door with a key he had procured from the nanny.

"You have the keys?" Catherine whispered. "That means you can unlock the gate!"

"I considered that, but the gate makes too much noise."

"Then how are we going to get over the wall?"

"That's what the sheet is for." said James.

In explanation, he unrolled the sheets, grabbed a corner in each hand, and tossed the middle over the spade-shaped spikes that lined the top of the wall.

"Here, you can climb up using the sheet. I'll help push you up."

As it turned out, Catherine was far more athletic than James, and needed less help then he did climbing up. Once they were both sitting on top of the wall, James looped the sheet over the outer side of the wall, and each of them lowered themselves into the alley below. Leaving the sheet hanging for their return, they set off down the street in the direction of the toyshop.

As they walked along the streets, they were surprised at how many people were out and about after dark, and at how many lights were still lit. However, they did not see any children wandering about unattended, and some of the grownups were eyeing them curiously.

"Are you sure we are going the right way?" Catherine asked him.

"Yes." said James. He had the advertisement with him, which contained the toyshop's address, and he had a map of the city he had acquired from Mr. Tralvorkemen's study.

It wasn't long before they turned a corner and saw the sign which said, "Jakob Damond's Toye Shoppe." Above this crouched a statue of a monkey with a cymbal in each hand. It was posed in such a way that it was looking directly at them as they passed underneath it and into the shop.

The children gasped in awe as they beheld the splendor before them. The inside of the shop was overflowing with more toys than they could have ever imagined. There were tables and counters stacked with toys. Toys were neatly piled along the floor, forming narrow paths that wound through the store. From the ceiling were hung many more toys, all of which were slowly rotating above their heads. Everywhere they turned there were colored lights glittering like fairies. The noise and bustle from the city outside failed to penetrate the little world they had entered. All was quiet and peaceful. They could see no other people in the store.

"Why, it's just like Christmas!" said Catherine.

"Like no Christmas I've ever had." said James.

"Look at this!" said Catherine, pointing at a teddy bear which slowly turned its head back and forth.

"I don't know . . ." said James. "These toys almost seem alive. It's as if they were watching us."

"And so what if they were alive? Just think how much fun it would be to play with toys that could play with you! I could have a real tea party with my dolls, and they'd carry on conversations with me!" She lifted the bear off of the table and set it on the ground. Immediately it stood up and began to blindly walk around.

"I don't see any books." said James.

"Don't worry, I'm sure they're around here somewhere."

James felt something hit his ankle. Looking behind him, he found a shiny red fire truck the size of a shoebox which had driven up and was raising its ladder. At the end of the ladder was a toy little man holding a little hose. James bent down and peered into the nozzle of the hose. The craft was so detailed it almost looked real!

"This is so fascinating!" Catherine laughed. Looking around the corner, she spotted a giant jack-in-the-box.

"James, come quick!" she called. James who had been examining a wheel which was perpetually rolling along the floor, wall, and ceiling, went over to see. "I wonder what could be in it?" she said.

"Jack, I suppose. But seriously, I don't think we're supposed to be messing with all this stuff. What if someone finds us? Please don't open it!"

"What are you talking about? It's *meant* to be opened!" Grabbing the crank, she tried to rotate it, but it wouldn't budge.

"Could you give me a hand?" she asked.

"If it was meant to be opened, I think they would have made it easier to turn." said James.

"Come on!"

James begrudgingly took hold of the crank. With one forceful tug, they managed to yank it free, throwing them onto their backs. The crank continued to make several rotations, all the while playing a cute yet slightly off-key tune. Suddenly, the top burst open, and a man shot into the air, nearly landing on top of them.

"Welcome to Jakob Damond's Toye Shoppe!" said the man. "Within these walls you will find everything you could ever desire! I guarantee that I can make your wildest fantasies come true!"

He reached into his coat pocket and revealed a long slender whistle, upon which he gave a sharp blow. Instantly, the room came to life. Every toy began to move. Dolls danced. Trains zigzagged across the store along winding tracks. Board games began enacting battles. Fountains of water shot into the air, reflecting the multicolored light.

"This place is too incredible! I must be dreaming!" Catherine exclaimed.

"So what is it you desire?" the toymaker asked, turning back to the children.

"Oh, yes. We're here to find a book for James."

"A book? Well you're in luck, for I happen to have a wide assortment of rare books in stock!" Follow me toward the back of the store!" And so they set out deeper into the toyshop. As they went, the toy maker maintained the conversation.

"So where are you from?" He asked.

"Oh, no place of much consequence. A small orphanage. That's all"

"Dear, dear! Do you mean to say then, that you have both lost your parents?"

"I suppose so," said Catherine. "Though I don't think about that much. Parents are things that other people in other places have. In a way, I guess Mr. Tralvorkemen has always been our parent."

At the mention of the headmaster, a brief shadow fell over the toy maker's countenance, and Catherine noticed it.

"Do you know him?" said Catherine. "Do you know Mr. Tralvorkemen? You remind me something of him in your stature and dress."

The toymaker turned on her and for a brief second anger burned within his eyes. "I am not anything like Edward Tralvorkemen! He lives in a cold, lifeless world filled with rules and self-induced labor. He thinks he is better and wiser than everyone else, which is farthest from the truth. In short, he is a miserable man who scorns all forms of fun."

Then his familiar smile returned. "But as for me, I am the father of fun!"

Catherine was puzzled. That sounded very different from what he had said in his letters to her. She was about to question him about that discrepancy but she couldn't think of any way she could politely bring it up and decided to overlook it.

The man gestured and one of the rows of toys slid aside to reveal a massive bookcase. "I have every great fairytale and fantasy ever written!"

"Do you have Marloth?" James blurted out.

The toymaker halted.

"What was that?" he asked.

"*Marloth.*"

"No, I'm afraid I've never heard of that one. What sort of book is it?"

"It's a fairytale book full of villains and heroes! And adventures! Many of them!"

Mr. Damond scratched his chin thoughtfully. "Hmm. I'm not certain, but I think I may have just what you're looking for. Follow me!"

Mr. Damond led them past the bookshelves and through the maze of toys. The toyshop went far deeper than they had imagined. When he stopped, they had reached a darker corner of the shop where there was a thick glass case with several expensive looking objects behind it. The toymaker took a key from his waistcoat pocket and unlocked the case. After perusing it for some time, he pulled forth a shiny, leather bound book and carefully handed it to James.

"Here it is! This is one of my most valuable pieces of merchandise! With this, your dreams can *really* come true!"

James opened the book and flipped through the pages carefully. It did not take him long before he had read the entire book.

"Is this some kind of joke? All of the pages are blank!" he exclaimed.

"And why shouldn't they be? If the pages were already filled with words, there would be little room for you to write your own!"

"Me?"

"Yes, you! Is there anyone who could write a more perfect book for you than you? And the stories you write here will not be mere fantasies, they will be *real!*"

James was not thrilled about the idea of purchasing a blank collection of paper, but surely Mr. Damond knew what he was talking about. He was an adult, was very intelligent, and seemed to know things few other people knew about.

"If it's all right sir, I'd like to consider this for a while."

"A wise call! We'll leave you to think things over." Taking Catherine's hand, he led her back toward the front of the store.

"Now, my dear, what sort of wonder would you wish to buy?"

"I fear that I shan't be able to decide! There are so many marvelous things here; I wish I could have them all!" Then her shoulders slumped as reality set in. "But I have very little money to spend!"

"Don't fret! I'm positive we shall find just the right item for you! Tell me, what are your interests? What do you aspire to do with your life?"

Catherine pondered this for a moment and then said "There is one dream of mine, but it's rather silly."

"Come now! Even silly dreams are worth making real!"

Catherine blushed and dug her foot into the floor. "Well, when I grow up, I want to be a queen!"

"There's nothing silly about that! You're already a princess, where else can you go?"

Catherine beamed.

"Though, I must admit," Jakob Damond continued, "becoming a queen can be a tricky business. It usually helps to marry a prince. But you know you're a queen when everyone says you're a queen; that's what really matters. So I think I know just what you need . . ."

After digging through the toys, he unearthed an elaborate golden box. He carefully raised the lid, revealing a plush velvet interior. Inside rested a slender diadem. As Mr. Damond lifted it from the box, it appeared to glimmer with its own light. The gems which encrusted the front seemed to reflect the histories of kings and queens within their depths. With a courtly air, the toymaker solemnly placed it upon Catherine's head.

"I'm sorry," said James as he walked up to them still examining the book. "I just don't think that—"

He halted abruptly as his eyes fell upon Catherine. She looked . . . different. She seemed more mature. More graceful. And possibly even . . . alluring?

"It's wonderful! Catherine squealed with joy as she looked in a nearby mirror. "Absolutely wonderful!"

James shook his head violently and tried to think of something else. Wow. It was amazing how apparel can alter people.

"So you'll buy it?" asked Mr. Damond.

"I couldn't bear not to!"

"And how are you faring?" he asked James. "Have you found what you're looking for?"

James didn't say anything. His mind was spinning with a million different thoughts, all of them conflicting with each other.

"You like the book, don't you?"

"Yes. Yes, I like it very much. It's just that—well..."

"I'm sure you'll love it, James!" Catherine said. "What if there are no more copies of Marloth? Could there be anything better than a book of your own creation? You *are* very clever!"

James looked at Catherine. He was starting to like the crown.

"I'll buy it!" he said.

"Splendid!" The toymaker performed some quick calculations and told them the combined cost of the two items.

Both James and Catherine were terribly disheartened. James explained to the toymaker that they did not have anywhere near that much money. They were about to turn toward the door when the toymaker beseeched them to wait.

"Hold on! There's still hope! I have already grown attached to the both of you. I normally don't do this, but I'm feeling especially generous tonight and want to offer you a special deal. How about I give them to you for free?"

"For free?" said James. "Are you serious?"

"We wouldn't have to give you a single coin?" Catherine asked.

"That is correct! Just follow me to my desk!"

He shoved several toys aside and climbed behind the counter. After digging about in various drawers, he pulled out two official looking documents and laid them out before the children.

"All you have to do is sign on the dotted line and then the toys are yours!" he said, setting a pen beside the documents.

Catherine turned to James. "What do the documents say?" she asked.

James examined the paper. He was horrified to discover that even though he knew many of the words, he couldn't make head or tail of it. Reading was his expertise, yet he had never seen words so elaborately twisted together.

"It just says that the toys are ours." he told her.

"That's all?" said Catherine. "It has a lot of words just to say that."

"It also mentions that I am not responsible for anything that you might do to yourselves with the toys you are receiving." Mr. Damond added helpfully.

"Oh, that makes sense." said Catherine. She picked up the pen and wrote out her name on the paper in front of her. She handed the pen to James, who likewise signed. Strange, even though the pen was clearly filled with black ink, the ink came out crimson when used on the document. The toymaker took the documents and put them in a book of contracts.

"Well there you are!" said Mr. Damond. "The toys are yours! And here, James, you can have this pen! Now I assume it's well past your bedtimes, so you'd best be on your way."

"Thank you ever so much!" said Catherine.

"Yes, thank you." said James

"My pleasure!" said the toymaker, and then, just as the children were stepping outside, "Oh, and James, I wasn't joking about what that book can do. Be careful what you write."

As the children stepped into the street, the door closed behind them and the toyshop suddenly dimmed. Now the city was far more quiet than it had been. Only an occasional person walked by, staring at them disconcertingly.

"I don't like this." said Catherine. "We are just children and who knows what sorts of people could be out at this time of night."

"I'll protect you." said James.

"Oh, *sure*. I am more fit than you are! All you do is sit and read."

"Whatever the case," said James, trying to ignore that, "we had best stay out of sight as much as possible."

James led the way through the twisting alleys, doing their best to stay within the shadows.

"Don't tell the others about this." said James as they navigated through the city.

"Why not? You don't think they'd tell Mr. Tralvorkemen, do you?"

"They might, but that's not my main concern. They'd probably be jealous."

"And why shouldn't they be? They deserve nice toys too. We aren't any better than they are."

"It's not a matter of who's better or more deserving. They don't have any excuses to sneak out in the dead of night and buy toys."

"*Oh?* And what's *your* excuse?"

"I'm mad."

"You're not mad. You're just eccentric. I like you that way."

"I'm mad. I know I am. And I love it like a drug."

"Stop talking like that! You're unnerving me!"

"I hate reality." James continued. "It's all wrong. Terribly wrong."

"Well there's nothing you can do about it." said Catherine.

"Yes, there is. I've been thinking about this book and the more I think, the more I like it. When we get home, I'm going to write in it. I'm going to write a new Marloth. But this Marloth will be *mine*. And it will get back at all of the Tralvorkemens and street children and doctors and everyone else who's screwed up my life. They sit there watching me and analyzing me and trying to fit me into neat little boxes and label my problems and then write out nifty drugs for me. Okay, the drugs are sort of fun, but that's not the point. I'm going to create a book like they've never seen before! They want to know what makes me tick? Well, they're going to find out!"

Catherine was very quiet. He was starting to scare her.

"Welcome to My World." said James.

The children climbed back over the wall and into the orphanage without incident. They parted in the hallway between the bedrooms, where Catherine slipped into the girls' bedroom as quietly as possible. James, however, had no desire to go to bed. Slowly, he turned about and made his way for Mr. Tralvorkemen's study. It was more cluttered than usual. At the far end was a window through which faint moonlight glided inward, casting a bluish hue over the room. Beneath the window and near the center of the room there was a desk. Even though the desk was loaded with volumes of papers and writing equipment, all of this was somehow organized with such precision that it looked more like a small city had been built upon the desk than a mess of stationary.

James circled the desk and climbed up onto Mr. Tralvorkemen's chair. He carefully lit the lamp that hid amidst the papers. After several attempts, the wick finally burst into flame and illuminated the room with its golden glow. After pushing aside enough papers to make a little valley, he was able to lay out his new book upon the desk and gather his thoughts to write.

He could picture Mr. Tralvorkemen standing beside him with a shallow smile creeping over his face. Mr. Tralvorkemen was saying, "So the little child is going to write now, is he? I wonder what silly things he'll write? Whatever it is, I'll probably have to throw it into the fire too."

"Oh, *you will!*" said James. Taking the pen in hand, he wrote down the first thing that came to his mind. Below is a much embellished version of what he penned:

Somewhere in the myriad of dimensions, there rose a hill. It had once been a cemetery. It even looked like a cemetery. It had all the right tombstones and that creepy atmosphere clinging to it that just reeks of foreboding. But it was no longer a cemetery, for it had no bodies, and cemeteries always have bodies.

On top of the hill stood the church. Well, what had once been a church. So many pilings and attachments had been hammered into it that it was next to impossible to distinguish any of the original walls. From inside the building came the hum and hammer of machinery. The eccentric inventor Otto Marecchian had turned the church into a factory. Now, instead of praying to God, he was playing God. And loving it.

For the product of his factory was nothing short of reanimated dead persons. He had dredged the grounds of all its occupants and, with science and black magic, brought them to life. The best thing about his system was that once he got it rolling, the zombies had been given control of the machinery, allowing him to tinker with other projects. The dead were reproducing.

Suddenly, James was awoken from his writing by the sound of several objects within the room clattering to the floor. He couldn't see over the desk, but whatever had caused that sound, it hadn't been him.

"Hello?" he whispered

The room was silent.

Slowly, James stood up on the chair and peered over the piles of papers. In the far corner of the room, he could see one of the smaller cabinets lying sideways on the floor. Papers were strewn all around it. Somehow it had fallen over. As quietly as he could, he dropped to the ground, made his way to the fallen cabinet, and set it upright. He had just begun to stuff the papers back inside when he suddenly had the feeling he was being watched. Slowly, he turned around.

Right beside him was a boy about his own age. Except that this boy was far paler and was covered in sutures. The boy stood there nearly motionless, staring at James vaguely.

"Hello." said James. "What are you doing here?"

The boy did not respond, but looked about the room with mild curiosity. It appeared to be harmless enough.

"Where did you come from?" James asked.

The boy just shrugged and began to walk about the room as though looking for something that would keep his attention for more than half a second.

"So what is there to do around here?" asked the boy.

"Hmm?" said James. "What do you mean?"

"You know, for fun!"

James wasn't accustomed to thinking of things in terms of fun. He liked to read Marloth and occasionally play with the other orphans, but he had never consciously pursued *fun*. Fun was something that just happened every now and then.

"I used to read." he said. "But my book was thrown in the fireplace. Now I'm working on a new one."

"Sounds boring." said the boy.

"Actually, it's quite exciting. I was writing about a mad inventor named Otto who lives in a mutated church."

The boy nodded. "Oh yeah, that guy." he said.

"You know him? But I just made him up!"

The boy again nodded vaguely and then focused on the lamp. He picked it up and began to swing it around.

"Stop it!" James shouted. He immediately regretted this, because he was positive everyone in the orphanage had heard him. But it didn't seem to bother the newcomer. He just turned the lamp upside down. The oil and flame fell all over him and instantly fizzled, sending the room into darkness.

James stood there frozen. All he could see was solid black. The moonlight which had illuminated the room had abandoned him. He waited for a long time, listening carefully for the sound of footsteps along the hall. But several minutes passed and no one came. After a time, it occurred to him that he hadn't heard anything from the boy either. Even though he had been even less talkative than James, James was surprised the boy hadn't destroyed something else. Feeling about with his hands, he managed to locate the desk. After more groping he found that the lamp was resting on it. At least the boy had put it back. But James had seen the boy drain all of the oil.

Now it was useless. Desperate to escape this deafening blindness, James tried the lamp anyhow.

It flickered on. It was still full of oil.

James looked around him. There was no sign of the boy. Frantically, he searched every shadow of the room, trying to discern if the boy was hiding. But he wasn't there.

Now James was thoroughly unnerved. He climbed back into the chair and looked at what he had written.

For the product of his factory was nothing short of reanimated dead persons.

Could it be? Had that been a zombie child? Did his writing it make it come to life? James glanced over the room again. At first he was frightened. But after a while, fear gave way to a rush of power. He had to write some more!

With new energy, he set to work creating an entire world. A world populated by a variety of demented denizens and mysterious locations.

As the heroes made their way through the dark and haunted library, they were alerted by a scream to the presence of a skeleton splayed out on the damp ground and half concealed by moss.

"What happened here?" cried one of the girls.

"Oh, that was poor Philip." said Mr. Mosspuddle. "He died of starvation."

"Did he get lost?"

"No. He read a book. Something in it took away his ability to eat. No one was able to figure out how the book had caused it, which was due in part to everyone being afraid of reading the book and following in his plight. So he died. There are two kinds of wizards in the world: the careful ones and the dead ones."

James reviewed his work with pride. This was what he was made for! While the text he penned was written in a childish manner that would have been unintelligible to most people, it made perfect sense to him. In his head his writing was very professional.

Throughout his narrative, he also added sections documenting various details of the world. Much of this was taken from Marloth, though he mixed in some of his own ideas as well. For example, Marloth had occasionally contained references to ogres, but it did not say much about their nature. James thought it would be fun to fill in the gaps and imagine how they functioned. When translated into more refined and educated language, it went something like this:

It is a common belief that ogres are slow and stupid. There is some truth to that belief, and some misunderstanding. Ogres are creatures of momentum. Aside for their unparalleled strength and constitution, an ogre's base ability, both physically and mentally, is quite limited. However, the longer an ogre pursues a given task, the more proficient it becomes at that task, with no measurable limit. They are capable of almost anything if given enough time.

For example, when an ogre decides to devote itself to crafting a weapon, it begins without knowing a thing about weaponry. As the ogre begins to think about weapons, and tinker with metal, it gradually grows in understanding. During this period the ogre does nothing but work on that craft. It does not eat. It does not sleep. It simply works. After several years of this, the ogre will have reached astonishing mastery of weapon crafting. This is how ogres, despite being initially simple and brutish, wield the most advanced and deadly weaponry in existence.

After so many years, the ogre will eventually need to rest from its labors. This generally requires hibernation for nearly as long as the period of labor.

Aside for a special process of frozen hibernation, if the ogre is ever interrupted from its craft for more than a few minutes, the bulk of its development will be lost. Thankfully for ogres, this rarely ever happens. It is not easy to interrupt an ogre.

As he continued writing, James' thoughts turned to Catherine. He liked the idea of having her in the story. He wrote of a princess that would eventually become queen. That was a good start, but after some review it didn't seem very interesting by itself. He liked that Catherine was sweet, but she was a little too sweet. He made his princess gradually grow edgier. Her parents died horrible deaths. She was constantly having to fight for her place on the throne. To aid in this struggle, he gave her special magical powers. But the magic also corrupted her mind. She grew bitter and broken. Before long, she was the Fallen Queen of Marloth; brazenly dazzling and dangerously beautiful.

Then he wrote of an orphanage. An orphanage ruled by a wicked tyrant known as Tralvorkemen. He punished all of the children for the most trivial of offenses. He even took their beloved book of lore and destroyed it. But one day the children rebelled. They slew the evil headmaster and went out into the world to learn and grow and become powerful heroes.

The night seemed to stand still and go on forever. He was able to work unceasingly as page after page of story flew from his pen. But finally sleep did catch up with him, and he slipped into slumber, his head resting atop of the book.

*   *   *

"Wake up! Wake up! Big things are happening!"

James cracked his eyes open just wide enough to see Miles shaking him violently.

"Leave me alone." James mumbled and rolled over. Which was a mistake because he had forgotten that he wasn't in his bed, but propped over the desk. His head lost its perch and he landed on the floor.

"James, you've got to see this! A duke is downstairs!"

James simply groaned.

"Come on James! Everyone's already having breakfast! And then this fellow comes along with servants and everything! You've got to get up and see it!"

Before James could form the proper sort of retort for someone trying to sleep instead of think, Miles had lifted him to his feet and was shoving him out of the room.

By the time they reached the bottom floor, James was fairly awake. He was also very out of sorts. Miles had taken too much pleasure in pushing him down the stairs.

"I don't know what you were doing in Mr. Tralvorkemen's study, but you should be thanking me for getting you out of there before he found you." Miles said as they entered the dining room.

There was, in fact, a Duke.

The room was chaos. More than a dozen children, halted in the middle of their breakfast and as excited by the incident as rapidly shaken soft drinks, were desperately trying to leave their chairs and run around the room. Mr. Tralvorkemen was desperately trying to keep them from doing so. Several attendants stood like statues along the wall. Though they were not moving, they were taking up much of the already limited space. And in the middle of this sat the Duke, surveying the surrounding activity with cool composure.

"Come!" said Mr. Tralvorkemen. "Why don't we step into the parlor where we can more comfortably talk?"

"Lead the way my good man." said the Duke. The two of them left the room, followed by the Duke's attendants.

The children had no sooner been left alone than the room exploded with voices.

"You went to the toyshop last night, didn't you?"

"Yes, I heard Catherine sneaking into the bedroom!"

"And look how tired you are! You must have stayed up all night!"

James was speechless. All eyes were on him and Catherine.

"All right! I admit—we did go last night!" said Catherine.

"Did you get anything?"

"Let us see!"

"They had to have bought *something!*"

"I would have."

While James was feeling increasingly uneasy, Catherine was thrilled by the attention. Reaching into one of her dress pockets, she took out the diadem and placed it upon her head.

The children did more than simply ooh and ahh. They were stunned.

"It makes you look older!" said Henry.

"It's so beautiful!" said Mary.

"That's what I want!" said Nivana.

"And what about you, James? What did you buy?"

James glanced about nervously. "Well .... I did buy a book."

"Really! Is it like your old book?"

"Sort of. Actually, it's more—"

Suddenly, Mr. Tralvorkemen threw open the door and stood staring at all of them. He looked confused and rattled.

"Catherine," he said. "You need to pack your things. It appears that you are to leave with this man immediately!"

"What? W-Why?" Catherine stammered.

"It turns out that you are in fact—" he stopped. His brows furrowed as he noticed the crown. He took off his glasses and wiped his face with a handkerchief.

"Where was I? Oh, yes, the Duke. Anyhow, the Duke claims that you are of royal blood. Yes, I am quite serious. He told me that your parents were killed in a revolt and you were placed here so no one would know who you are. (Apparently they didn't even tell me!) Now, after many years of warfare, the throne has been taken back by your uncle. He sent Duke Philip to escort you to your new home ... in Castle Elington!"

Silence. All eyes were on Catherine.

One of the attendants courteously entered the room and bowed.

"The Duke wishes to know when the princess will be ready to embark?"

"Oh, yes—well, within a quarter of the hour!" said Mr. Tralvorkemen, turning toward Catherine. "It would be good if you could hurry!"

Catherine paused for a moment and then raced out of the room. Since the whole of her earthly possessions could be fit into a bag, packing would not have taken long, except she was delayed several times by her sentimentality as she would pause to reflect on the memories she was leaving behind.

When she came downstairs everyone was gathered to say farewell. Most of the children had not treated her kindly, and yet she still found it hard to say goodbye. She could not spend time with anyone without her heart gradually forming attachments. When she came to James she paused.

"I owe you so much." she said. "Without you none of this would be happening! Even though I may never see you again, I'll always remember what you've done for me. I know you keep saying you have a muddled memory, but please tell me you won't forget me?"

James looked at her. He *did* have a hard time remembering things, especially names and faces, but Catherine was one of the kindest people he had ever met. She was a ray of light in a sea of black. "I'll never forget you." he said at last.

"Thank you!" said Catherine, and after a few more farewells, she was through the gates, into the carriage, and gone.

*   *   *

Tralvorkemen stood in the doorway for a long time, gazing at the closed gate that Catherine had disappeared through. The children watched him curiously, waiting for some reaction, but finally they all gave up and went about their day. Only James remained. He sat at one corner of the entryway curled up and watching the back of the headmaster. Somehow he knew something was happening here, something everyone else was missing.

"You went to the toyshop, didn't you?" said Tralvorkemen. There was no hint of accusation. He sounded mournful. Now James wished he had left with the others.

"No! Of course not!" said James.

"It makes no difference." said Tralvorkemen. "Catherine is gone. She's a princess now, just like she wanted. I saw her crown. I know what is happening."

"Okay, so we did go to the toyshop! What do you care? You don't care about us! You threw away my favorite thing in the world!"

Tralvorkemen slowly shook his head. "No it wasn't. And I didn't really throw it away."

James was stunned. "What do you mean? I saw you throw it into the fire! I saw it burned into nothingness!"

"That is what you say now, but it is not what you would have said yesterday. Everything has changed. I know what you purchased from the toyshop. You purchased a writing book. And you've been penning all sorts of stories in it. Some of them supernatural; some of them about the orphanage."

James felt a growing uneasiness in his stomach. He had not been expecting anything like this. "How do you know all of that?" he asked; a mix of accusation and fear. The Headmaster passed over his question.

"What you seem to be missing is that Jakob Damond really meant what he said. Whatever you write in that book *does* come true. That book alters reality. But even more than that, it is not a neutral book that can be used for good or evil. It is inherently warped by the will of the Toymaker, and will only accomplish his vile ends."

"No!" said James. "That can't be true! He is a nice man while you've been a bully to us all this time! I have no reason to believe you."

"You are right, that is certainly how things look. But what if—*what if*—things weren't this way? With this orphanage and this city and *everything*? What if *you* were different? What if *I* were different? What if I were really a kind, fatherly man and all of you children loved me?"

"But that's silly! I don't remember anything like that."

"Of course not! When you change reality, you change *every-thing.* Not just the present; not just the future; but the past as well. However, the reason I know what I know is because the changes were not consistent; after all, it was written by a child. There are still fragments of how things were before. Part of me knows I never would have thrown away that book, though I do not know why. I did throw something into the fire, but now I'm beginning to recall it being a different sort of book, though I don't remember any details about it. I have vague memories of how things should be, and I think you do as well, but that is all we have left."

James was frightened out of his wits. His mind had always been on the brink of one reality or another, and now he didn't know what to believe.

Tralvorkemen looked off into the distance. "What if the world had shattered? Shattered into a myriad of dreams within dreams that dream of the dreams which dreamt of them?"

Slowly, he rose to his feet and made his way up the stairs. Before he had reached the top he paused to look back at James.

"There is one hope. The Author of the original Marloth. He is bigger than all of this, and he is the only one who can make things right. He is the only person the Toymaker fears."

He thought for a moment and then added, "However, before things can get better, they are going to get much worse."

With that, Tralvorkemen disappeared into the twisting hallways, leaving James with the impossible idea that things could get any worse.

* * *

James felt weak. He wanted to go find his new book, but at the same time he was now afraid of it. His lack of sleep, the rush of the morning's events, and Tralvorkemen's otherworldly speech had sapped all of his energy. Dragging himself up the stairs, he limped into the boys' bedroom and fell into an exhausted sleep.

*   *   *

When James finally awoke, the sun was just setting. His first thought was that of regret. He liked Mr. Tralvorkemen a lot more after seeing him fall apart. It was the first time he had seen the man appear out of control. And there was something about what the man had said that intrigued him. He wanted to ask him more about it.

Painfully, he climbed out of bed and made his way to Tralvorkemen's study. He peered in but didn't see anyone. He went a few paces down the hallway and knocked on the door of the headmaster's quarters. There was no reply. It was then that he heard the sounds of laughter. The children were playing outside.

Still groggy, he stumbled downstairs and made his way through the front door. Sure enough, all of the children were outside playing around the yard. Here he could see more clearly the sun dropping behind the buildings. It was soon to be evening. Mr. Tralvorkemen always had them inside before now.

He walked up to a group of them who were playing in the earth; digging tunnels and building hills of dirt. They had torn up much of the yard. The headmaster would be furious when he saw this.

"Where is Mr. Tralvorkemen?" he asked.

"Oh, he's not here." said Nivana.

That was odd. Mr. Tralvorkemen must have been more shaken than James had thought. The headmaster never left them alone. Perhaps he really had gone over the deep end.

"James!" said Miles. "Where have you been? Niv came up with the darndest play!"

James noticed Miles was holding several hand puppets.

"Where did you get those from?" said James.

"Oh, I've always had these," said Miles. "Come on and help me out, will you?"

"Maybe in a little bit." said James. He noticed several robots milling about the grass.

"What are those?" he asked.

"I made them!" said George. "Out of spare parts!"

"Wow!" said James. "I didn't know you could do anything like that!"

"Well I helped him!" said Millamer.

James nodded vaguely. As he looked about the yard, he kept spotting things he hadn't seen before."

"Where did you get all of these toys?" James finally asked.

"Where did you get your book?" said Nivana.

"You all went to the toyshop?" James said in surprise.

"Yes! Isn't it thrilling!" said Mary. "Mr. Damond gave all of them to us for free! All we had to do was sign our names on some papers!"

"But Mr. Tralvorkemen will whip the lot of us when he finds out!" James shouted. "He already knew Catherine and I had gone to the place, and he was literally raving at me! We've got to hide these toys before he finds out!"

"Don't worry, he won't be around for a *long* time." said Miles.

"Why?" James demanded. "Where is Mr. Tralvorkemen?"

The children turned to look at him as though they were the adults and he was the child.

"If you must know," said Nivana. "You're standing on him."

*　　*　　*

James looked down at the large mound of dirt below him.

"He was going to take away our toys!"

"We couldn't let that happen!"

"He was such a mean old man!"

James couldn't believe what he was hearing.

"You mean to tell me that he's *here?*" he said, pointing at the mound. "You *killed* him?"

"It was the only way!"

"He didn't want us to be happy! He meant for us to be miserable!"

"And besides, he was the most wretched man. Now he's at peace."

James couldn't take anymore. He ran into the house and up the stairs. Climbing floor after floor, he fled into the study and closed the door behind him.

His heart still beating a million miles per minute, he crossed the room and sat down behind the desk. The book was still open right where he had left it. Had Tralvorkemen been right? Were the toys really evil? Either way, the headmaster was gone now. Suddenly James felt all alone. He was frightened of the other orphans. His vision fell upon the open book. This was all his fault!

But what if Tralvorkemen had been wrong about the book *only* producing corruption? Now that he knew the danger, maybe he could fix things . . . Rushing over to the desk, he took up the pen and began to write fervently, trying to conjure up the happiest images he could think of.

Knock! Knock! Knock!

James ignored it and continued writing.

Knock! Knock! Knock!

"Go away!" he shouted. "You're all possessed!"

Knock! Knock! Knock!

James slammed the pen against the desk so hard it snapped, spewing ink all over him. Furious, he stormed over to the door and threw it open.

"That's it!" he screamed. "Now you're—"

He stopped. There were three children standing in the hall, but they weren't any of the orphans. By now the sun had set, and there was no light to reveal their faces, but he knew they weren't anyone he had met before.

"Who are you?" he demanded.

"We want to play with you!" said the children, as they shoved their way into the room.

"I'm sorry, but—what am I saying? I'm not sorry! I don't know who you are, but you need to get out of here at once!"

"He doesn't like us!" said one of them.

"I don't like anyone right now!" James shouted. "I've got a lot of stuff crammed in my mind and I need some time to think! Just leave me alone so I can write in peace!"

"That's not fair!" said another. "We like him. He has no right to go hating us!"

James' temper snapped. He grabbed one of the children and spun them around.

For the first time, he had a good look at their faces.

The children were badly disfigured and covered with stitches. Their skin was pale. What at first he had thought to be spots of dirt were actually splotches of dried blood. The children immediately stopped and looked at him, hurt expressions on their faces.

"He hates us! I can see it in the way he's looking at us!"

"He only hates us because we're zombies!"

"The spoiled brat!"

"I-I d-don't hate you!" James sputtered.

"Well he most certainly won't want to play with us!" said one of them. Without hesitation, she shattered the glass front of one of the cabinets with her fist and pulled out some of the business instruments within it. She examined one of them and then hurled it at James, who barely managed to dodge it.

"Don't hurt me!" he shrieked.

"Hold on!" said one of them. "I know how we can make him like us and play with us!"

"How?" asked the others.

"If he was a zombie!"

"But Mr. Otto couldn't make him into a zombie because he's alive! Mr. Otto can only..."

And then it dawned upon them. The heads of the children turned in unison to stare at James, who had slowly inched around the desk so that it stood between him and them. Slowly, the children began to circle the desk.

"Get away from me!" James cried. "Miles! Niv! Help me! *HELP ME!*"

But none of the orphans replied. As far as he knew, they were in a whole nother world.

The zombie children leapt upon him. Each of them snatched his flailing limbs, and with one stomach lurching swing, hurled him through the window. It shattered into a myriad of spinning shards glittering about him like pixies, carrying him along as he floated into the air. For a moment, the lamp lit streets were stretched out before him. Time seemed to freeze. And then, he began to fall. He left his stomach far above him as he picked up speed, falling mile after mile after mile. Then, he looked down and saw the ground hurtling upward, rushing to meet him faster and faster until

Part 1

Part 2

Adelle was wakened by her own screams. Embarrassed, she wiped the tears from her eyes and looked about her. Rays of early sunlight drifted through the window and settled on her bed. It was morning. Still a little dazed, she climbed out of bed, got dressed, and set out for the kitchen.

*   *   *

Far below the tower that Adelle was then descending, the gates of the castle were being opened for the King and his entourage. They were returning from a very manly hunt. The King would go on a hunt whenever he was frustrated with affairs in the castle, and he went hunting regularly.

As the King made his way along one of the elegant hallways of the castle, an attendant hurried up to speak with him.

"Your majesty! I've been hearing the strangest reports of late!"

The King looked back in annoyance. He was a stout man with broad shoulders, strong arms, and a thriving beard. And little patience. With a faint growl, he continued down the hall. The attendant gave pursuit like a loyal gnat and eventually caught up to him, struggling to maintain stride with the King's sweeping gate.

"Sir, a number of farms have been attacked! The occupants were gruesomely killed and the buildings razed. But there has been little sign of looting, just senseless destruction. The rangers do not know what to make of it."

"Did they find any tracks? That's what they do, isn't it? Track things?"

"Yes, they found footprints. Small footprints. But they aren't certain what sort of creature could have left them, and the trails always disappear."

"If there is something my rangers can't track then they are over-paid. Find me better rangers. You can start right now."

"Yes, your majesty. Except I had a few errands I was in the middle of running. Can I do those first?"

"You talk of people being butchered and yet have more impor-tant things on your plate? What errands do you speak of?"

"They're mostly regarding the queen, Milord. I need to go and deliver a gift from the governor of Rhumeveld to the queen and then I need to review this list of items she said she—"

"A gift from the governor? To the queen? Well I guess I shouldn't be surprised. Things have reached the point where I only hear of these things in passing."

"If you would like, I could inform you whenever—"

"Don't be a fool. Well, at least try not to be." The King sighed. "Clearly being King isn't everything it used to be. The queen can do whatever she wants."

"That is very noble of you! You know how the queen is adored by everyone!"

"That's just it, isn't it? *Everyone* loves the queen. Especially men."

"I'm sorry, I don't quite grasp your—"

"Just shut up."

They rounded a corner and were met by Adelle, who was just leaving the staircase. The King's face brightened at the sight of her.

"Ah ha! And how is my little beauty this morning?" said the King.

"Hello father!" said Adelle. "I had the most unbelievable dream last night, and you simply *must* hear about it!"

The King reached down and hugged her, lifting her right off her feet. "All in good time, my dear! Right now there is some boring old politics I have to deal with. I have to prepare to meet some delegates that should be arriving at the castle some time later today. Which reminds me, there were supposed to be some young people with the group."

"Young people? As in *children*? People my own age?"

"I think so. If you like you can accompany me to the gates when they arrive."

"Oh! I would love to!"

"Excellent. And then once they are settled and that business is out of the way, then you can tell me all about your amazing dreams."

"Thank you, Father; though could I at least tell you a little bit now?"

"I'm sorry, but I am already running late. I will see you soon. Why don't you go find Miss Bethany?"

Adelle watched her father round the corner and waited until he was out of sight. She was grateful he had only suggested the idea. The last thing in the world she wanted to do was find Miss Bethany. Instead she continued in the direction of the kitchen.

*   *   *

Miss Bethany was a large woman. Large in size; large in personality. She was taller than most men and maintained an equally considerable girth. While she was not considered the most pleasant occupant of the castle, she got things done, and people knew it. Miss Bethany held many roles in the castle, and one of them was Adelle's nanny. Adelle believed that she herself had grown too old for a nanny, and perhaps her parents thought so as well, but Miss Bethany still saw need for a nanny, and that was the end of it.

Adelle didn't have to find Miss Bethany; Miss Bethany found her. She grabbed the girl by the ear and led her down to the kitchen. Adelle had tried to explain to the woman that she had already been going to the kitchen, but it was a futile endeavor. Every time Adelle tried to speak, the lady pulled her along harder.

"You try my patience, young lady. Why do you *always* try my patience?"

"Ouch!" was all Adelle managed to say.

"Well it won't get you anywhere. I have more patience than your little head can hold. I'm a waiting woman."

That was Miss Bethany's common refrain. "I'm a waiting woman. Always waiting. The patience of Job and I'm still waiting."

"Waiting for wha—ouch!"

"None of your business, young lady. Suffice to say, I can easily out-wait a waif like you."

Despite the pain of nearly having her ear torn off, Adelle managed to smile inside as she thought to herself, *"she can easily outweigh most anyone!"*

After feeding Adelle, the lady took her up to her room and made certain she was properly cleaned and dressed to meet their guests. Adelle wouldn't have minded this so much except that she had very different ideas about what it was to look pretty, and fights always ensued over her wardrobe and the arrangement of her hair. Adelle felt that Miss Bethany's sense of fashion would be better applied to dressing viking warriors than little girls.

It was not much later that it was announced to Adelle that the delegates had been sighted approaching the castle. Adelle hurried to the entryway and took her place beside her father just as the carriages drew up.

The delegation was smaller than had been expected. There was only one nobleman: Duke Francis of the Green Halls. Accompanying him were four children: three boys and one girl, all of them members of powerful families. The children were on holiday and the Duke had agreed to bring them along and act as their chaperone. As the children stepped out of the carriage Adelle's focus was drawn to one of the boys in particular. He was older than the others and nearly a head taller. He did not appear particularly happy and eyed his surroundings with disinterest. He was also very handsome.

Above all, he had the natural ability to make simple actions like walking and standing look profound.

For a moment, Adelle was struck by a sense of self-consciousness. She didn't know why she suddenly felt inadequate, and she tried to fight it away. She reminded herself of her position and beauty and was soon rejoined by her normal confidence. She moved closer to her father and followed him to greet their guests.

"Welcome to Castle Elington!" said the King. "I know you'll find your stay a pleasant one."

"Thank you." said the Duke. "I am honored to be your guest."

The King motioned toward his daughter. "Allow me to introduce my lovely daughter, Princess Adelle!"

"Also an honor." said the Duke, bowing again. He was about to compliment her appearance when the doors to the entry room opened and in strode Adelle's mother, the most beautiful woman in the world. Time seemed to slow as all present turned to stare at her. The queen did not demand attention. She did not have to.

She glided down the stairs and spoke some words to break the spell. The Duke shook himself, found something akin to a smile, and replied to her greeting. After further exchange of pleasantries and introduction the adults proceeded down the halls of the castle, the boys ran into the garden to play with swords, and Adelle was left with the girl. Adelle watched the boys leave with a tinge of longing. She wanted to follow them, particularly the older boy, whom she had learned was named Bobby. But she felt responsible to entertain the girl and was also excited at the prospect of having a female companion.

Adelle went up to her and beamed warmly. "Hello, Ivy! As you already heard, I am Princess Adelle. I'm so glad to make your acquaintance. I'm certain your stay here shall be a wonderful time for the both of us!"

"That's nice." said Ivy.

"Here, let me show you around the castle!"

"Why?" said Ivy.

"I don't know. Aren't you curious to see the sights of Castle Elington?"

"No, not really."

"Then would you like to take a walk in the garden? It's especially beautiful this time of year!"

Ivy shook her head. "Gardens aren't really my thing."

"Well what do you want to do?"

Ivy looked here and there as though searching for something. "Do you have any entertainers?" she asked.

"Entertainers?"

"Yes, musicians, acrobats, magicians. People who can add zest to any occasion."

"Oh! Of course! Music! Dancing! Magic tricks! I love all of that! To have parties and fireworks and endless excitement!"

"Yes, yes! That's what I'm talking about."

"We don't have any of that here." said Adelle. "But I've read about them, and would love to experience such things someday."

Ivy sighed wretchedly. "I knew it. This place blows."

There was silence for a few moments and then she said "Fine, I'll take a walk in your pretty garden."

Adelle led the way to the middle of the castle and into the court-yard. It was very large, and most of it was occupied by a luscious garden. Sloping lawns, clusters of trees, a winding stream, and a wide variety of flowers were just some of the gems that made the castle's crown.

In the distance Adelle could see the boys dueling at the top of a hill. They were remarkably agile.

"So, where are the other children?" asked Ivy.

"It's just me." said Adelle. "No other children live in the castle."

"You must be kidding!"

"No. It can be rather lonely. But now that you're here, I'm sure we'll have lots of fun!"

"What about boys? Surely there must be some boys!"

"Like I said, I'm the only child that lives here. Unless you count Samantha, though she's somewhat older than me."

"Who's Samantha?"

Adelle held up her doll. "Samantha, this is Ivy. Ivy, Samantha. Now that you're introduced I'm sure you'll be best of friends."

"Ugh!" Ivy moaned. "I'm more interested in bigger dolls." She looked over at her traveling companions. "Though I'd prefer ones I haven't gotten bored with."

"So you don't like Samantha?"

Ivy looked back at the doll and shrugged. "Samantha's fine. I've had stiffer company. But like I said, I've grown into older tastes." she paused for a moment and then added, "But I do love my stuffed animals Bipsy and Boppin."

She looked at Adelle critically. "I think you could use a Bipsy and Boppin of your own."

Adelle wasn't really paying attention at this point. Her attention was drawn toward the other side of the garden where the boys were fighting with their swords. She was amazed at how agile they were. Particularly Bobby, who had a flair for acrobatics. She had seen the soldiers practicing outside the barracks many times, but she had never seen one of them block multiple blows while somersaulting through the air.

"You're *already* smitten? We just got here!"

Adelle turned to her companion in confusion. "What do you mean?"

"I mean that over there you have Osmond, the klutzy essence of anti-charm, Harris, the obnoxious prig, and Bobby, God's gift to preteen girls. I have three chances to guess which one you're ogling."

"I wasn't—whatever you just said. I was simply intrigued by the maneuvers the boys were performing."

"Yes. Good save. For a moment you almost had me thinking you found boys appealing."

Adelle was at a loss how to reply to this and they walked for some time in silence. As they proceeded, Adelle went out of her way not to look in the direction of the boys, though she desperately wanted to. By the time they had circled the fish pond and were passing under one of the many arbors, she had regained enough courage to ask Ivy something that had been bothering her from the moment they had met.

"Forgive me if this sounds impertinent, but aren't you a little embarrassed to be walking around like that?"

"Like what?"

"I can see your legs! And your shoulders!"

"Oh, you mean my clothes? Why should I be embarrassed? I'm proud of my body. I wear more revealing outfits than this."

"My father told me that only women of ill repute wear such clothes."

"Your father? That must have been a weird conversation. Well maybe your father is the expert on irreputable women, but what could he know about girls' clothes? Is he the expert on fashion as well?"

Adelle was too confused to respond.

"As for me, I'm not a woman of ill repute; I have a grand reputation. And what I'm wearing is normal these days. You're the first girl I've seen to wear such a frumpy dress as that. I'm surprised *you* aren't embarrassed."

Adelle looked down at her dress. She thought it was beautiful. It had taken quite a struggle with Miss Bethany to be allowed to wear it. (The woman had wanted her to wear something gray. Gray!)

Ivy noticed the slightly hurt look in Adelle's face and hastily tried to patch things up. "Not to say that it has *no* taste. A lot of money definitely went into its creation, and people always have respect for a person wearing money. I'm just saying that you could turn a lot more heads if you wore something closer to what I'm sporting."

Adelle was aghast at the thought of being seen in public wearing such attire, and she said so.

Ivy sighed. "I hate to think that you are beyond hope. Here, you don't like my dress, and I don't like your dress. Seeing that you and I are roughly the same height and figure, why don't you lend me a few of your dresses to try on, and I'll lend you a few of mine. You'd only have to test it out in your room; no one would have to see you but yourself. Would you at least wear one of my outfits in the privacy of your own room? You could look in the mirror and see how it feels."

"No." said Adelle. "I'm never putting on anything like that."

"Well, at least you know your own mind." said Ivy, and she promptly changed the subject back to boys.

*   *   *

Adelle tried to remember where she had left her swan doll. She had been playing hide and seek with her dolls the day before and had forgotten where the swan had hid. She checked one room after another but could not find the swan. Then she strode into one of the spare bedrooms and stopped in surprise. Bobby was there. His things were all over the bed. This must be where he was staying. She was in his bedroom!

"Excuse me!" she said, blushing. She turned to leave but then her attention was arrested and her mind went tilt.

Bobby was throwing knives into the wall.

"What are you doing!" she said in horror.

Bobby threw another knife into the wall. "Just killing time."

"And the room! Look at what you've done to the beautiful mahogany!"

Another knife buried itself into said mahogany.

"And where did you get those knives? You should be more careful: knives are very dangerous! Last year Miss Bethany cut one of her arteries and it was shooting out all over the place! She told me she had to plug it up with a cork!"

Bobby stepped across the room and extracted the knives. "No more knives in the wall. Happy?"

Adelle looked unsure. "What are you going to do with them?"

"Here, you can have them." He held them out to her. Adelle didn't know what to do.

"Take them." said Bobby. "It's a gift."

"But I'm sure I wouldn't be allowed to—"

"Nobody has to know."

"But—"

"Do you have to make *everything* so difficult? Just take them!"

Adelle struggled inside. She didn't want to even touch the wicked looking things and she was certain her parents wouldn't want her to either, but she felt wretched to refuse his gift.

"I'm sorry but I can't!" she said at last, backing away toward the door. "I have to go!"

"Whatever!" said Bobby, clearly offended. As she left the room, he turned and hurled all four knives into the dresser.

*   *   *

"I do not trust those children." said the King. He said this to his wife, who was on the other side of the bedchamber. It was just before dinner time and she was touching up her appearance before rejoining their guests. The queen looked back at him through the reflection in the dressing table mirror.

"They are only children! Children are harmless."

The King's face grew sterner. "Not all children."

"Don't be silly! From what I've seen of these children, they are very charming."

"Charming or not, I would sleep more soundly if Adelle was not associating with them."

"You know that would not be good! She should do everything in her power to befriend them. They are all the children of very important people; people who are very pivotal to the future of the throne."

"Our daughter's safety is more important than any throne." said the King.

"And she is safe! Remember the rules. No one can harm her."

"We threw out the rules. Are you picking and choosing which rules still work?"

"Yes." said the queen.

"I don't think that's possible! We are in over our heads!"

"We always have been." said the queen.

*　　*　　*

Every evening the royal family would dine with the company of the most prominent members of the court, such as the chief counselor and his wife. Any politically noteworthy guests would also dine with them, which included Duke Francis and his charges. Normally Adelle sat with the adults, but on this night, due to the number of children, a separate table was designated for the youths.

While Adelle had spent much of the afternoon with Ivy, it wasn't until dinner that she was able to really converse with the boys and form an idea of what they were like.

Just as Ivy had said, Harris really was full of himself and his own self-importance, though some of this was possibly justified. He was knowledgeable about a great many things and had a demeanor that bespoke of power. People looked at Harris and knew they were beholding a future ruler under whose feet their own lives might one day rest.

It was Harris who spoke the most to Adelle. More than anyone else there he saw Adelle as a politically beneficial friend and wanted to know all about her.

Then there was Osmand. He was a very distinct character. He *could* have been handsome. But his manner of dress and carriage did violence to that possibility. For one thing, his clothes were absurdly fit for his frame. They would cling to him in one direction and hang from him in another. Osmand tripped over himself.

As for his manners, every one of his actions seemed unconsciously calculated to bring the maximum amount of discomfort to anyone in his vicinity. He may have been smart, but he was so self-conscious he avoided independent thought for fear of inciting disapproval.

But he did possess one attribute that made people feel comfortable around him: it was universally agreed that he was the most harmless person in the world.

Adelle felt sorry for him and the way the others ignored him. She tried to counteract the way they treated him (and the way he treated himself) by doing her best to make him feel welcome and put him at ease. But Osmand was such an inconsolable being that it was hard to tell if this had any effect on him. If anything, her attentions only made him more awkward.

But no one had Adelle's attention more than Bobby. Bobby was a puzzle to her. His every move was so confident and full of careless abandon. He exuded effortless style, and yet was it really effortless, or was it all just an act? Adelle couldn't decide. Either charismatic rhythm ran through his very veins or he was a poser. Adelle may not have admitted it to herself, but she enjoyed watching him either way.

Bobby was also very reserved. When he spoke, his words flowed like street-wise poetry, but Adelle found it difficult to get him to say much. It was almost as if he was subtly teasing her, perceiving that she desired more conversation and yet holding it just beyond her reach.

Throughout the meal, the King periodically glanced over at the children's table suspiciously. Whatever he was looking for, he never caught it.

In a desperate attempt to get more people talking than just Harris, Adelle steered the conversation to asking about each person's families.

"My father is Lord Jasper of Harrington Weigh." said Harris. "We too have the blood of kings, but it is a different line than yours."

Osmand made a nearly indiscernible comment about his father, who was also a duke, and something about his family being pivotal in a long list of wars.

"My family doesn't claim anything special about our blood." said Bobby.

Adelle looked at him curiously. "And yet I have heard that your family has much influence over the affairs of the world. How is that so? Is your family rich?"

Bobby shook his head. "No. Not particularly rich either. Let's just say that anyone who goes against my family's wishes tends to regret it."

Adelle wanted to learn more about Bobby' family but she noticed that Ivy had not yet spoken since they had sat down and wanted to include her in the conversation. "What about your family?" she asked her.

Ivy's face went sour and she said. "Please, let's not bring them up at the dinner table! My family does not agree with anyone's palate, especially mine."

"But what about your family?" said Harris, looking at Adelle. "I'm guessing they are struggling very hard to maintain the court's relevance."

"What do you mean?" she asked him.

"Simply that there is a growing movement to disband the aristocracy. Kings and queens are a thing of fairytales. We are moving into a modern age of merchants and lawyers. Many people think there is no longer any need for the pomp and extravagance aristocracy demands. That is why Duke Francis was invited here. Your parents are trying to convince him that being aligned with the throne is still his best option. But I'm not sure he thinks that anymore."

Adelle was appalled. "And what do you think?" she asked him.

"I am very pragmatic. I will go with whatever works."

"And what about you?" she asked, turning to Bobby.

"I'm not into politics one way or another. I leave that to the wigs. But it does pay to keep an eye on which way the games are going."

"And which way do you think they are going?"

"I think Harris is probably right. When you reach adulthood there may no longer be a crown for you to wear."

*　　*　　*

The next morning Ivy spent some time with the boys, became upset with them, and set out in search of her young hostess. After looking about and asking many people she finally found her in a large hall near the back of the castle, and to her utter amazement, the princess was on her hands and knees, washing the marble floor!

"What horror is this? The Daughter Heir of Marloth ... scrubbing floors?"

Adelle squeezed out her rag in a nearby bucket and continued scrubbing. "Miss Bethany makes me do it. She says I need to appreciate women's work."

"Do your parents know about this?"

"Maybe. Maybe not. It's Miss Bethany." She said this as though that was a full explanation in itself.

Ivy watched Adelle and shook her head sadly. "We need to get you out of here!"

After some time Adelle finished her chores and the two set off to explore the castle grounds and talk. While they were conversing, Adelle brought up the subject of Bobby.

"He seems so distanced from me." she said. "I'm afraid I hurt Bobby's feelings!"

She expected Ivy to say either something like, "No, I don't think you offended him," or "Now that you mention it, he did seem a little miffed," but instead she simply said, "Bobby doesn't have feelings."

"Oh, but he does! I've seen it! I think he just keeps them buried."

"If in buried you mean *entombed*, then yes, perhaps."

Adelle didn't say it out loud, but she suspected that Ivy either hadn't seen that side of him or simply wasn't sensitive enough to notice.

"Anyhow, it's not a big deal. I was just curious what you thought."

"You're right: it's no big deal. You're just one more of the countless girls who have fallen for his charms. He charms the wits out of people he doesn't even know exist."

"I haven't fallen for anyone! I simply would like to be on good terms with him. I *do* like him. He just doesn't seem to like me."

"You're not his type. And that's a good thing."

Adelle considered herself and wondered what exactly made her not his type. She debated about asking what *was* Bobby's type, but decided to wait on that. Instead she asked Ivy how well she knew Bobby.

"We used to date. I suppose that's worth something."

"Date? Aren't you a little young to go out on dates?"

"No."

"But you aren't dating him anymore?"

"No, we are not, and yes, he is available. But take my advice: I fought to get out of that relationship, and you should fight to stay out of it."

"But why?"

"Because Bobby is one of those people who is strong enough to get just about whatever he wants, and he knows it."

*   *   *

Dinner that night was much like the previous one, though Ivy spoke a little more than before. Bobby was still enigmatic. Harris was starting to get on Adelle's nerves. He dominated every conversation he was associated with. Adelle had experimented with several different tactics, but had yet to find a way to shut him up. As for Osmand, it was hard to tell if he was basking in their presence or pained to be in their society.

After dinner, Adelle visited Ivy's room and brought the rest of her dolls to show her.

"My parents have been so generous in all the wonderful things they have given me, particularly my dolls. Though I have to say, while I love my dolls dearly and am very grateful for them, I can't wait until I become a mother and can have real, living dolls instead."

"Really? That's the first time I've ever heard anything like that. You actually *want* to be a mother?"

"But of course! Don't you?"

"Never! I'd be too afraid of ending up like my own mother!"

"Why? Don't you love your mother?"

"My mother is an arrogant bore whose only concern for me is that she remain in full control of every aspect of my life! I hate her!"

Adelle was shocked. "I'm very sorry for you. I wish you could experience what it is like to have a mother who loves you. My mother loves me very much. She has given me so many wonderful things! And sometimes at night she sings to me and tells me bedtime stories!"

"Singing? Bedtime stories? Did I just step into a nursery rhyme? I guess so if this dream of yours actually has loving mothers. All mothers are the same! They kick themselves for getting pregnant and kick their daughters for being born!"

Adelle was shocked. "My mother is not like that! She is a good person!"

Ivy looked up and scrutinized Adelle curiously.

"You don't know much about your mother, do you?"

"What do you mean by that?"

"I mean... It sounds like you haven't heard any of the rumors..."

Adelle looked concerned. "What rumors?"

"Oh, nothing. I shouldn't have even brought it up."

"Please tell me! What are the rumors?"

"Well . . ." said Ivy as she feigned pondering the moral ramifications of her situation. "I don't want to cause any distress, but if you insist . . . *One* of the rumors is that the queen is actually much older than she looks. Supposedly she made a deal with the devil so that she'll live at least three times longer than normal people and always look beautiful."

"But that's silly!" said Adelle.

"Maybe so. But if it's true, you'll die an old woman long before she does. You'd never be queen!"

"That's even sillier! Even if my mother did live that long, she would eventually step aside and give me the crown."

"Why would she? Why would any sane woman choose not to be queen?"

"Because she loves me!"

"Perhaps. But there are also rumors about how she's afraid of you. Afraid that when you come of age you might somehow try to take the throne from her. You know, slip a little something in her tea or stir up the people against her. Stuff like that happens all the time with royalty."

"That's terrible! Those are all terrible things to say!"

"Hey, you wanted me to tell you about the rumors."

"Well I've heard enough!" said Adelle, and she stormed out of the room.

"That's probably best." said Ivy under her breath. "Those were the nicer ones."

*   *   *

That night, as with every night, the queen crossed the hall to tuck her daughter into bed. During the day she was the Queen of

Marloth, but when she kissed Adelle goodnight she was simply the mother of a little girl who loved her very much.

"Can you tell me the story of the orphanage?" Adelle asked her, as her mother sat beside her on the bed. "The *whole* story?"

"No dear. Not tonight. Maybe when you are older."

"It seems like everything is after I am older."

"Many good things usually are. But many hard things too. Be happy where you are; it will pass by so fast and before you know it you will be facing grown-up problems."

Adelle tried her best to accept this, but she never seemed to get the hang of it. After a few more moments, she decided to bring up something that had been weighing heavy on her.

"Mother, do you love me?"

"What a question to ask! Of course I love you! You're my little angel! What could make you think otherwise?"

"Oh . . . nothing." said Adelle, now feeling embarrassed for even bringing it up. "Just rumors."

"Rumors? Is this from your talks with Ivy?"

Adelle idly played with her hair for a moment before nodding.

"Oh, Adelle! You will come across many people like Ivy. You can be nice to them and humor them and it is even useful for them to like you, but don't ever believe a word they say."

The queen hugged her daughter close to her and they talked for some time more. Adelle loved her mother so much. But at the same time, in the back of her mind she wondered if her mother was one of those people.

*   *   *

The next morning Adelle was weighed down by her conduct toward Ivy the day before. She felt guilty for the way she had shouted and walked away from her. Agitated by this burden, she searched throughout the castle for her new friend. She knocked on

Ivy's bedroom but there was no answer. She asked Duke Francis but he replied that he had not yet seen Ivy that day. Finally, she checked in at the room Harris was staying in and, to her surprise, Ivy answered the door.

"Why, hello Ivy!" said Adelle.

"Oh." said Ivy. "Are you looking for Harris?"

"No, actually, you're just the person I wanted to see. It's about yesterday evening. I'm sorry for my outburst when we were conversing. I don't know what came over me! I hope I didn't hurt your feelings, and that we can still be friends. Will you forgive me?"

Ivy was not sure how to take this. Apologies were a foreign creature to her.

"Um, yeah. If it makes you feel better. But really, you didn't do anything wrong. You have fire in you, and that's a good thing."

Adelle wasn't certain if that was a compliment, but she was glad to get her sins off her chest. "Thank you," she said. "So we're still friends?"

"Of course."

"Wonderful! Would you like to play jacks with me?"

"You know, I really appreciate the offer but I *think* I'll pass. Maybe some other time."

"That's not a problem. We can do something else!"

"No, you go on ahead. I've got some things I have to do by myself."

Ivy closed the door and Adelle was left to her own means of entertainment. It was strange that even though she had spent most of her life diverting herself, it wasn't the same anymore. She wanted to be with *people*. She sighed and decided to go see what her father was doing.

*   *   *

Adelle put her ear to one of the large doors and listened. From inside the courtroom she could hear her father conferring with his counselors and the people of the court. She tried to understand what they were saying, but the bits and pieces she picked up were so dreadfully dull that she couldn't concentrate. Giving up, she sat on the ground with her back against the door and played with her jacks, all the while humming a tune she had heard the soldiers singing while they drank in the castle barracks.

She had not been long at this when a raven glided into the castle through a nearby window and rested on the ground beside her. Adelle tilted her head and gazed at it curiously. She almost thought she could see through the bird to the wall behind.

"What a ragged looking bird!" she said

"Where is the king?" The raven demanded, ignoring her.

Adelle dropped her jacks in surprise. "Why, it talks!" she exclaimed.

"Why, she talks!" the bird replied sarcastically. "Off course I talk! Now tell me where the king is or I'll peck your eyes out!"

Adelle looked affronted. "That's not a very nice thing to say. Don't you realize who you are addressing? *I* am Princess Adelle!"

"Good. Then you'll know where the king is."

Adelle sighed in exasperation. "Well if you must know, my father—*the King*—is behind those doors. But he's busy."

"So am I." said the raven.

With a quick bow, he spread his wings and took off through the window. Adelle hastily sprung to her feet and darted to the window, just in time to see the bird drop out of sight.

"Fancy that. Talking animals." said Adelle. "Next thing you know, even the dead will be speaking to one another."

She had just returned to her jacks when she heard several frantic shouts from inside the courtroom. That was it. She simply *had* to see what was going on. Taking hold of the door, she pushed it open just far enough to peer inside.

The courtroom, which was very dark and dreary due to a lack of lights and its windows being tinted, was packed with a great variety of official looking people, all of who were talking or yelling at one another. Beyond all of the heads, and at the far side of the room, Adelle could just make out the throne upon which sat her father. He was shouting for everyone to be silent, but no one seemed to hear him, or care. All of their attention was focused up at the ceiling.

"So, finally a little excitement around here?" whispered Ivy over her shoulder. Adelle nearly jumped out of her skin she was so startled. Quickly she closed the door and turned to face Ivy.

"You scared me!" she whispered loudly.

"What's the matter?" Ivy asked her. "Let's go inside and see what's happening!"

"We can't do that! Children aren't allowed in the throne room!"

"Let me get this straight: You're a princess, right?"

"Yes."

"And you are to be the Queen one day?"

"Yes, of course I am!"

"Well then, what kind of a queen are you going to be if you've never even seen what goes on in the royal court?"

Adelle didn't know what to say.

"I'll make this easier for you." said Ivy. She opened the door and pushed Adelle inside. Adelle made no resistance.

Everyone was far too busy to notice the two girls. After a few moments looking around, they climbed onto the base of one of the pillars so they could see over the top of the crowd.

There, in the rafters, perched the raven, sternly studying the chaos. Gradually, the voices dimmed and then died altogether. The raven dropped to the floor before the King and continued to look about.

"So this is Marloth." it said. "It's even darker than I imagined."

"What devilry brings a talking beast to the Court of Elington?" the King demanded.

"Much devilry." replied the raven. "I admit, you have reason to be angry, for I bring dark tidings. Your wickedness has finally caught up with you!"

"Enough! Guards, shoot him!"

The men raised their muskets and fired but the volleys passed through the raven as though it were a ghost. The bird stood in the center of the room unharmed, cocking its head sideways to lock eyes with the King.

"Weapons cannot silence your doom. Only turning your course can perform that feat."

"Oh? And what course is that?"

"You welcomed the doctor Otto Marrechian into this land, and have provided him with many valuable resources. The rules specifically forbade the support of individuals who tamper with evil, and you know that is exactly what he is doing!"

"I know the rules, but they were meant to help us, not shackle us to the ground! Our current science is stagnating and we need geniuses like Doctor Marrechian to lead us into the future!"

"Where is the book of rules? If you had bothered to read it you would have seen that the rules are there for your own good."

"We don't have the book anymore, and we don't need it. The rules may have been good for us once, but our needs are different now. Times are changing. The world is changing."

The raven hopped up and down in feathered fury. "Details change! Names change! But the underlying reality stays the same! That's what the book was all about!"

"I am the King of this kingdom, not you. So even though I apparently have no power to silence you, you have no power to do more than babble."

The raven calmed down to a simmer and kicked a nearby pebble. "I don't really know why I would expect anything else. No one ever listens to me. My entire existence has been spent handing people their fate and watching them stomp on it, only to have Fate eventually stomp on them. Why do I always get so worked up about these things? It's not my problem. You've dug your own grave, who am I to kick you into it?"

The crowd began to murmur. Once again, the court was thrown into a chaotic thrall of panicked voices. As Adelle tried to adjust her spot, she thought she heard a familiar voice.

"Hello Adelle."

Adelle was so surprised she slipped off her perch and fell onto the floor. It was her mother. Ivy inched further around the column to make certain she was out of sight. So far the queen had only spotted her daughter.

"I thought you were downstairs with Miss Bethany." said the queen.

Adelle quickly got to her feet.

"Don't worry about her, mother, she won't get into trouble."

"You're in no place to jest! You know well enough that you should not be here. This is no place for a child!"

"But mother! Am I not to be Queen one day? I should think I need to know all there is of royal life—*you know*—things like politics and intrigue!"

"Politics is learned through schooling. As for intrigue, no—"

"Excuse me, your majesty," said an attendant, "but this raven is causing a serious disturbance. The King needs your support immediately!"

The queen glared at Adelle. "Go find Miss Bethany at once!"

As the queen disappeared into the crowd, Adelle decided that it would probably be best to do what her mother commanded.

Right after the rest of the raven's speech.

By the time Adelle had returned to her station beside Ivy, the commotion had once again died down, largely due to the presence of the queen. Ivy said something about wanting to get a better view and stole along the edge of the room behind the crowd. Adelle wasn't feeling nearly so bold and remained at her post at the base of the pillar.

"Very well." said the King to the raven. "You have succeeded in casting turmoil upon this court. Now begone before I seek out some sorcery that can do more harm to you than bullets!"

"I am the voice of Destiny. I will not depart until I have said everything you are to hear."

"What more is there to say?" spoke the Queen. "You have given your warning, and we have heard it!"

"You think I came simply to speak of your doom? No, that was only my greeting. The fate of the whole of Marloth lies upon the knowledge I bear.

"For the situation is thus: The eyes of darkness are not upon your castle. It cares little for you or your pretty queen. Its eyes are upon the only thing left for it to feed upon. The only thing it has left to desire, and to fear."

The raven fluttered about and turned toward the back of the room. The crowd followed his gaze to the pillar beside the entrance.

"In short, It seeks your daughter."

All eyes turned to Adelle. As she felt the full attention of every-one in the room and the eerie words of the raven echoing between her ears, she found herself more frightened than ever in her life. Leaping to the ground, she fled from the room.

The King could take no more. He hurled himself at the raven in a blind rage. But just as the bullets, the King passed through the bird as though it were never there. With a painful thud he landed upon the floor.

The raven ignored him. He was watching the little girl as she ran away. For a brief moment what might have been sorrow fell across his countenance. When the girl had gone, he turned once more to the King.

"There is still time for you to mend your ways, but that time is growing short. Already the forces of evil are gathering, and soon they will come to take every life in this castle. But enough doom. I do bring with me one piece of good news ... I'm getting out of here!"

And with that the bird leapt to the window and was gone.

* * *

At around that same time in another dimension of Marloth, the city of Rhumeveld was on the verge of a surprising visit. Its guests turned out to be an army of children. Unruly little children with knives and clubs and all sorts of objects that were never meant to be weapons. They swarmed over the city like a plague, quickly slashing apart any defenses it might have had.

In the center of the city there was a rather magnificent mansion that was the residence of the governor. He was one of the most rich and powerful men in Marloth. Powerful, that was, until his army of guards found themselves beset by creatures that could be shot, stabbed, and beaten and yet keep on biting you. The defenders were helpless.

The governor's house had no sooner been captured than a short, battered looking goblin made his way through the spacious doorway of the mansion with about a dozen of the children trailing behind him. The goblin crossed the threshold of the lobby and stood before the governor himself, who at the moment was being held down by five more of the children.

"Hello." said the goblin. "My name is Deadwick. What's yours?"

"Joe." said the governor.

"Well, Joe, I've heard that you've got a mighty powerful relic hidden somewhere in this place. Something that could change the world! Know what I'm talking about?"

The governor shook his head.

"That's okay. I'll refresh your memory for you."

The goblin hit the fellow over the head. The governor slumped to the floor unconscious.

"Aren't you supposed to just hurt him?" said one of the children. "People can't speak when their eyes are closed. It's called being asleep or dead or something."

"Oh well," said Deadwick. "I never was good at moderation. We'll just forget about him and find this powerful relic on our own. Search the place for anything that looks really powerful. You'll know when you see it. They usually have colorful glowing auras or ancient inscriptions or disintegrates the first bloke who steps into the room. Something like that."

"What about the governor?"

"We're done with him. Take him outside and kill him."

The children split up into several groups and began to scour the mansion. The goblin went about the rooms, overseeing their questing.

"How about this!" said one of the children. It was carrying a small red fire truck.

"That's nothing but a stupid toy!" said Deadwick.

"Well, it's shiny looking."

"Pull yourself together! We're looking for items of *power!* Things that can blow people up or tell the future or turn day into night!"

A group of children returned from the eastern wing with piles of

"Junk!" Deadwick moaned. "You're bringing me piles of junk! We already live in junk! You zombies are practically made of it!"

"Look what I found!" said another child, as it came rushing down the hall. "I found a book! And it's got words in it!"

"Books?" Deadwick said. "Who wants books? All they do is mess with your head!"

He grabbed the book and threw it out the window.

"We're not here for a bedtime story! Somewhere around this place is that relic of power, and I mean to find it!"

*   *   *

No one noticed the dead governor. The people were too focused upon the destruction around them, and the zombies were too focused upon causing it.

Except for one. The zombie child with the straggly hair. He had thought nothing of the death of the governor, as the two children had taken him outside and stabbed him repeatedly. But then something had fallen from the sky and landed next to the body. He had been about to continue on his way, trying to find his next victim to play with, when he jolted backward. That was odd. It grabbed all his attention. Not the governor, but the item that had landed beside him. There had been something familiar about it. Slowly, gears began to turn within his mind. An ember flickered to life for just an instant. Walking into the middle of the street, he awkwardly bent over and looked at the object.

It was a book.

He reached down and picked it up. It was bound in tattered leather. On the cover was written in large, golden letters, Marloth, and below that, A Child's Fairytale World. With dull fingers, he picked open the book and sat down in the mud. There, surrounded by the carnage and horror of a city being strangled to death, he began to read.

He read of a wonderful fairytale world, full of adventures and happy endings. Of beautiful landscapes and fascinating creatures. Of a boy who rose from obscurity to save a princess. Of a noble headmaster who protected his children from the darkness and loved them dearly.

A tear. A genuine tear formed in the zombie child's eye. It rolled down his rotted cheek and landed on the page. How could a heart of stone and eyes of glass form a tear? He tried to continue reading, but he couldn't. The pages were too blurry. For once in his existence, he felt emotion.

Emptiness. He could feel his numbness to the world around him. He had caught a glimpse of joy. A joy he would never experience. Now he saw just exactly what it was he didn't have. Even now, he could feel his body slowly disintegrating. He was naught not but an illusion. A carcass animated by dark sorcery and string.

For once in his life, he felt Dead.

*   *   *

Ivy found Adelle cowering in her bedroom.

"Wow!" said Ivy. "That was one of the most exciting shows I've seen in a long time! To be honest, I was figuring the court would be a bore, but that talking raven sure spiced things up!"

She stopped and took a closer look at Adelle. "What's the matter with you?"

"This is awful! Didn't you hear what it said? Dreadful things are coming to get me! And everyone saw me in the courtroom! I shouldn't have been there! My father is going to be furious!"

"*Please!* When are you going to grow up? That raven was babbling nonsense and you're a fool to even think twice about what it said! And if either of your parents try to make an issue about us being in the courtroom I'll give them a piece of my mind!"

"No! Please don't! I—"

There was a knock at the door. Ivy went over and opened it to find one of the duke's attendants standing before her. The attendant bowed and said to her, "Miss Ivy, I have been asked to escort you to Duke Francis at once!"

"Why? What's happening?"

"I do not know. But if you come with me he can tell you himself."

Ivy followed him out of the room while Adelle pulled herself together and hurried after them. They were brought to the spacious room that had been provided for the duke and wherein the duke himself was presently stationed, rapidly giving orders to his servants as they came and went. He saw Ivy and quickly approached her.

"What is going on?" she demanded.

"It is time we were leaving this place," he said. "The servants are already packing your things. We will be leaving in an hour."

"Is this a joke? You aren't actually scared of that scene the raven made?"

"By no means. I assure you, the timing of this gloom and doom is purely coincidence. My business here is done and it is time we were elsewhere."

It was then that the King also arrived on the scene. He took stock of the situation, noting the hurried packing and his daughter's presence, and then strode up to the duke.

"I have just been informed that you are leaving us." said the King. "I am sorry we do not have further time to talk. I was hoping we could come to more of a resolution."

"There is no need to worry on that account. I have made my decision, and in your favor. The queen convinced me to continue my allegiance to the throne. Her arguments were very ... persuasive."

The King was taken aback by this. It was evident that he was not sure whether to be happy or glare. But he didn't say anything.

"And you should be glad I am hurrying. I am off to speak to Lord Dominicus. Last I heard from him, he was preparing to side with the Merchant's Guild. I am going to try to sway him back to the throne. Then I will speak with the Lady Mediev. If she can support you then you will be in a very good position. But I do not know what she will say. Things are still very precarious right now."

"Thank you for all your efforts." said the King. "I don't know where we would be without you."

"Please! There is no need to thank me. The pleasure is all mine!"

They spoke for a short time more before the Duke resumed his preparation. Once he and the children were ready, they gathered in the entryway and said their farewells. Ivy stood with Adelle for several moments before managing to speak.

"I'm not going to lie: I won't miss this place. But I will miss you. I've never met anyone like you before. I feel like I don't need to worry about you stabbing me in the back. It's as if you care about me."

"I do care about you! You're the first friend I've ever had! Except for grown-up friends; that's not exactly the same thing."

"No, they aren't. But listen, you need to come to the City of Orphans soon. You could stay at my house and then I could show you what a *really* good time is like."

Adelle said she would love to but did not know if her parents would ever allow her. Ivy said a few more choice words about the King and Queen and then the rest of the children said their farewells. Harris gave her a very warm parting, Bobby finally did say something about enjoying her company, and Osmand didn't say anything at all. After that, the group climbed into the carriages and disappeared through the gates. Adelle was already missing them before they were out of sight.

*   *   *

By the time the zombie child got to his feet, the carnage had ceased. Ceased, that is, simply because there was nothing left to destroy. Most of the other troupes had already left to find new things to torment. Only a few zombie children remained to scour the debris and ensure that they hadn't left anything alive.

The zombie child closed the book and began to walk about. There was something familiar about this place. As though walking through a dream, he passed through the smoldering architecture. Bodies were strewn everywhere. The embers of what had only moments before been roaring fires were now shriveling away because there was nothing left to burn. Though the landmarks were all but gone, the zombie child was certain it had once read of this place.

This was Rhumeveld, the City of Wonders. Or a mockery of it. Sinking back into the debris, the zombie child opened the book and flipped through the pages, eventually reaching the spot that described the city of wonders. It was a beautiful city of marble and crystal, all of which reflected the light in a dazzling manner, but no one could see any of that now. Depressed, the zombie child dropped the book and collapsed into the mud.

After a time, Deadwick the goblin came around the corner, trailed by several zombie children. They had not found any legendary relics of power, but they had found a big gun, and Deadwick considered that worth the trouble.

"Hey you!" Deadwick called out, "What are you doing sitting? We're clearing out. No time to hang around."

The zombie child did not look up. It merely lay there with its face in the mud, staring at the book that rested before them.

"Is it dead?" asked one of the others.

"Off course it is!" the goblin muttered. "You all are! Now get up, you stupid zombie!"

The zombie child sat up and looked at him dumbly. "Don't call me zombie," it said. "I have a name you know."

"No you don't. And don't talk back to me!"

"Well now I do. My name is James, like the character in this book."

"That's ridiculous! Zombies can't read!" Deadwick picked up the book and looked at it as though it were poisonous, not that he could be affected by anything like poison.

"Well I can. This is a wonderful book. All of the stories are vaguely similar to our world, just happier. And the children in this book are alive!"

At this everyone began to laugh.

"Who ever heard of children who were alive?" said one of them.

But Deadwick wasn't laughing. Things weren't right. This zombie was acting far too smart for a zombie. He examined the book more closely. He sensed trouble. There was something very bad going on, and he had to deal with it at once.

"I don't want to hear any more of this! It's just a bunch of stupid fairytales!" he shouted, throwing the book at the zombie child. It hit him square in the head, knocking him back into the mud. "We're leaving this instant! We've got work to do!" More zombies gathered around them, curious about the commotion. The fallen zombie child quickly picked itself from the ground and took hold of the book.

"Well I'm not going!" it said. "I believe this book is real! I don't believe we were meant to be dead and go about killing people who weren't!"

That was it. Inside the goblin's mind, books were balanced and accounts were settled.

"Kids, I have an idea of how you can all have more fun!" A cruel smile spread across his face as he turned toward the zombie child. He began to speak slowly and methodically, like the caress of a torturer.

"Let's . . . play . . . with . . . *James*."

*   *   *

Once again, Adelle was alone. All of her new friends had been torn away from her. Her initial fear of the raven was gone. Now she hated it. What right did that knavish bird have to force himself upon the court and do nothing but rant and rave? If she were queen, she would have all ravens put to death. What nasty things to say! They were ugly creatures to begin with, and talking in no way improved them. And now it had scared away the duke, and her friends with him. It had humiliated her and revealed her disobedience to the whole court and her father had been furious and had scolded her severely. She had never seen him so upset. But worst of all, ever since the raven incident her parents had begun openly fighting with each other. She had suspected in the past that there had been arguments, but she had never heard them before. Now she was covering her head with her pillow in a pathetic attempt to block out the shouting. It wasn't working. Everything was going wrong.

Finally the shouting died down and was replaced by the silent trickling of tears across her pillow.

"Hello little girl."

Adelle lifted her head and looked behind her. There was a man in her room! A man she didn't recognize.

"Who are you?" she exclaimed, putting several pillows between her and the man.

"What? You mean you actually don't know who I am? I am Jakob Damond, the Toymaker! Surely you've heard of my toyshop?"

Adelle nodded warily. "Ivy talked about it. She said your toys practically come to life."

"And they do! I have the power to make a child's most wonderful dreams come true! Just the other day I met a boy that was lame in both feet. He wanted to walk. But I did something better than that, I gave him a flying carpet and now he is soaring over the heads of those who once looked down on him."

"That was very kind of you." said Adelle.

"Yes, well, it's what I do. Which brings me to why I am here: I couldn't help but notice that you were in great distress, and I was wondering if there was anything I could do to help you?"

"Forgive me, I was being selfish. All my friends have gone and my parents hate me and a raven came and caused such a stir that now the entire castle is talking about me, and not in a flattering manner."

"Your parents don't realize how lucky they are to have such a daughter as you! You deserve their love!"

"I think deep down they love me." said Adelle. "But I'm not so sure anymore."

"You are so underappreciated! But they aren't to be blamed, really. The world has not yet seen what you are fully capable of, but

I can see it. You are intelligent, noble, bold, graceful, and above all, the most beautiful creature I have ever beheld!"

Adelle wiped the tears from her face and attempted a smile. "Thank you." she said timidly.

"For what? I'm merely stating the obvious! You have so much potential! The world just needs to see it!"

"But I don't know that it ever will. All my life I've been imprisoned within this dreary castle; and I will be for so much longer."

The man's smile broadened. "But I can change that. I have the power to make a child's most impossible dreams come true. Would you like to break free from these walls and experience Marloth? I could make it so! Do you want adventure? I'll have adventure fall from the sky like rain! Do you want to be adored and respected as the royal grace you are? I'll open the eyes of the world to your elegance!"

"That all sounds most enchanting, but how can you do such things?"

"Ah, that is my little secret. Through toys mostly. Toys are far more powerful than people realize. Only children seem to have any idea as to their real value."

"But how could I ever repay you for such things?"

"Don't worry about it. Down the line I may need you to dust a certain piece of literature for me, but for now you—"

Before the man could finish, the voice of Adelle's mother could be heard calling from outside the room.

"I had best be off," said the man. "But before I go, I must inform you that there is one item you'll be needing before I set to work. A crown. A symbol of royalty and beauty!"

"But where am I to find—"

"Adelle!" her mother shouted as she stepped into the room. "Who in the world are you talking to?"

"Mother, allow me to introduce Mr. Jakob Damond!"

"But there's no one here!" said the queen.

Adelle looked about her in surprise. They were alone.

*   *   *

James slowly opened his eyes and looked around him. He was lying on a stretcher in a room filled with many other stretchers on all of which were many other persons. He had the fairytale book tightly clenched in his hands. Aside from James, the only other person moving was a strongly built nurse. She was currently occupied examining the other people and one by one tucking them to sleep. She did this by pulling the covers over each person's head.

As James lay there watching the nurse, a nearby door flew open and in stepped the King, followed by two attendants.

"So this is the only survivor?" he said, looking at James.

The nurse continued on with her work. "If you like." she replied, thumping one of the people on the head to see if he responded and then tucking him into bed. "I myself wouldn't call him a survivor. Hasn't done anything but moan and whine in his sleep."

"Well, he's staring right at me." said the King.

The nurse turned to look at James. "Oh. So he is." she said, returning to her work.

The King approached James. "Tell me, boy, what was it that leveled Rhumeveld to cinders?"

James didn't know what to say. He just looked about him blankly.

"Don't be afraid. I'm your King. I'm here to protect you!"

James didn't respond.

"Drat it, boy! This is of the gravest importance! What the blazes happened there?"

"He's still probably in shock or some such." said the nurse. "He needs some peace and quiet."

"Fine. I'll be back tomorrow. Notify me immediately if he says so much as a word."

The nurse wagged her head about as if to say *"who cares?"* and ushered the King out of the room. After a while, James sat up for a better look at the room. For once the nurse paused long enough to actually look at him. She wasn't an official nurse really. All of the real nurses in the castle had caught some flu and keeled over. While her main profession was that of seamstress, she was also the castle Jill-of-All-Trades and had been chosen to fill their place. She was a Tough Old Byrd, and it was said that if you gave her barbed wire, she'd weave it into a dress. She didn't know enough about nursing to take a pulse, or she would have noticed that James had none. All she knew about nursing was that if someone was full of holes or had an arm ripped off, you sewed them back together, just like any old garment. But she did know a thing or two about children.

"I bet what you really need is some fresh air and a good time." she said. Picking him up by the scruff of his neck, she carried him over to the window and pointed below them.

"See that garden down there? Just go through the door behind us and follow the stairs to your left and you'll be right in it. Go frolic about or whatever it is you kids do."

James felt compelled to obey her. Leaping to his feet with surprising ease, he bolted through the door and down the stairs. Sure enough, after descending several flights of stairs, he found himself standing before the most wondrous garden he had ever seen.

*   *   *

As James walked about the garden, he came upon a girl sitting in the grass, looking idly at the birds flying overhead. James stood there for a long time, studying her curiously. There was something vaguely familiar about her. After some time had passed, the girl happened to look about her and spy the boy.

"Why hello!" she said in surprise. "Another child! Where ever did you come from?"

James didn't know how to reply to this and resorted to an ambivalent shrug of his shoulders.

"You look hurt!" said the girl. "Are you in much pain?"

James shook his head.

"Here, why don't you—" Adelle suddenly stopped. "I almost forgot; my parents do not want me to be alone in the company of a man, or a boy. Except for my father, of course; I can be alone with him. But I am supposed to be very cautious about boys. They can appear nice but have very inappropriate intentions." She said this as though she had some idea what that meant.

"Okay." said James, and he turned to leave.

"Wait!" said Adelle. She quickly examined the grounds around them. "On second thought, this garden is in the middle of the castle; anyone can see us. Surely there is nothing to worry about in such a public place. Look, Miss Bethany is staring at us right now."

Sure enough, from a distant window the castle nurse could be seen eyeing them suspiciously.

Adelle motioned toward the trees. "What I was going to say was 'Why don't you come sit in the shade?'" After some timid deliberation, James crossed the lawn and sat down a little ways from her.

"There", said Adelle. "No harm." She pulled several loops of colored string from one of her pockets and proceeded to weave pretty patterns by stretching the loops across her fingers. It appeared to take every ounce of her concentration, but she didn't need concentration to talk.

"In case you're wondering, I am Princess Adelle. My parents are the King and Queen of Marloth. I live here all by myself, and I've been so dying for company! Well, I did have company for a while; Ivy was here, and a few boys. But they had to leave, and now I'm more lonely then ever! Well, now I'm not, since you're here, but I was just a moment ago. Can you believe that I'm the only child who lives in this castle? I'm a princess! You'd think that I of all people would have friends! But where are my manners, going on and on about myself! What about you? Exactly who are you?"

"My name is James." said James. "I'm just a boy."

Adelle nodded as though that was in some way profound and as if to say that she had suspected as much. "So, what do you do for fun?" she asked.

James furrowed his brow and tried to think. He couldn't recollect ever identifying things in terms of "fun". But as he mulled over the concept, an unfamiliar idea began to surface.

"I like to read." he said at last.

"Ah, yes! Like the book in your hands."

James looked down at the book and nodded.

"What sort of book is it?" she asked.

"It's a book of fairytales."

"How fascinating! What are some of the fairytales?"

"They're all about a distant land full of magic and adventure. Most of the stories involve a man named Edward Tralvorkemen. He was a very good and wise man. He was the headmaster of an orphanage, which was a sanctuary from the darkness. The headmaster and his children would frequently enter the world to fight evil and help people in need. They are very exciting stories!"

"My mother used to tell me bedtime stories." said Adelle. "But she doesn't much anymore. Once she told me a story about an orphanage, but I don't think it was as happy as the one you describe."

"A lot of it isn't happy. But all of its stories have happy endings."

"I like happy endings." said Adelle.

There was quiet for a time. Then a thought struck the princess.

"You are new here! That must mean you've been beyond the castle walls!"

James nodded.

"What is it like out there? Is it truly exciting?"

"Yes," James replied slowly. "It is exciting. But I don't think you'd like it."

"And why is that?"

"It's sort of ... well ... unpleasant."

"Unpleasant? What could make it unpleasant?"

"Well ... there's a lot of death for one thing ..."

This didn't register with Adelle. "What sort of places have you been to?"

"I've been to Rhumeveld."

"The City of Wonders! I'd love so much to go there! What is it like?"

"Not much is happening there right now."

Adelle nodded. "I'm sure its major events are seasonal. What about the City of Orphans? My friend Ivy lives there and she says it's the most lively place in Marloth! Have you been there?"

"Yes," said James. "But it's always changing. I don't know what it would be like now."

"How fascinating! I can't wait to see it! My parents won't let me leave the castle, not even for a holiday, but things are going to change. Soon I'm going to leave this place. Then I'll see the world far away and have adventures just like in the fairytales!"

"Maybe your parents have good reason to keep you here." said James. "People who have adventures in this world tend to end up dead."

"Oh James! You always did have a morbid air about you."

Both of them turned to look at each other in surprise. "I'm sorry!" said Adelle. "I know it's silly but I feel like we've met before. But the thought is so hazy."

"Probably just a dream." said James.

Adelle shook herself slowly and looked about in agitation. "It's getting late." she said. "I'd better be getting back to my room now. It was nice meeting you. Will I see you again?"

"I'd like that." said James. Adelle smiled and made her way out of the garden.

James' gaze was frozen upon her. Even after she had left, he could still see her there, smiling and talking and playing with her string. He couldn't get the vision of her out of his mind. Perhaps she had been able to set aside any idea of seeing James before, but he couldn't. He *had* seen her before. He was sure of it. But the details were as rotted as the rest of his memories. Exactly where had he seen her? Where had he read that book before? Who had he been before he died? He was sure his memories were all wrong because they were nothing like the hellish world he was now trapped in. Shaking his head, he set off in the direction of the infirmary.

"Dying sucks." he said.

*   *   *

James returned to the infirmary only to find that the nurse had gone and he was all alone with the sleeping people. They slept very soundly. Walking over to his bed, he hopped up and leaned against the windowpane to gaze at the garden below.

"Are you the boy named James?" said a voice.

James turned to see one of the sleeping persons stirring under its covers.

"I repeat: Are you the boy named James?"

"Yes." James replied uncertainly.

"Good, for I bring you bad news."

Now James was puzzled. "How can a sleeping person bring anything? You just lie there."

"Stupid fool!" it shouted. From beneath the covers burst forth a jet black raven.

"I am the Doombringer!" said the raven. "I have come to foretell the darke tidings of thy future!"

Oh. James was used to this sort of thing. "Very well. Let's have it."

"Your doom is thus: very soon you shall die!"

"Sorry, won't happen."

"What do you mean, it won't happen? I'm the prophet here, and I say you're going to die!"

"Well you're a little late. I'm already dead."

The raven hopped up to James for a closer examination.

"You're a zombie!" it shrieked, more out of anger than fear.

"Yup. Must be some mistake."

"I don't make mistakes!" the raven screamed. It began to jerk its head back and forth violently, apparently its method of thinking.

"I can be destroyed." said James. "But it's not exactly dying. Technically, I don't have a life to lose. I'm little more than a machine powered by magic.

"Well that's just great. So now I'm conversing with a machine. What is this world coming to? Since the beginning of time I have borne the doom of endless souls, and my words have never proven false! It has to be this fouled world. Everything here is twisted!"

The raven calmed down enough to study James. "Prophecies are complicated things. There's often some kind of trick to them. Maybe you'll come back to life and *then* die. I'd love to hang around and see how this plays out, but I have more doom that needs to be delivered before nightfall."

And with that, the raven flew out the window. James sat around for a moment and then decided he'd explore the castle and see if he could find that girl again.

*   *   *

At the same time, one of the royal attendants was hurrying through the castle. It was a daily ritual for attendants to be scurrying about the castle in search of the King. Normally one would expect to find a King on his throne, but the King was rarely in the throne room. He preferred to be on his feet and on the move. After a frantic dash, the attendant finally caught up with him along one of the corridors.

"Your majesty, the rangers say they've found the source of all this mischief that's been going on throughout the kingdom!" piped the attendant. "They say its little children. No ordinary children, but demons!"

The King half nodded as he and the attendant passed through the halls. "Yes. That's what I figured it was."

"You know of them, sir? Then it's true?"

"Of course. They're zombie children. What do you think me and the boys have been hunting all these years? There's no deer. There's no bears. There isn't even a chipmunk anymore. Just zombie children."

"Sir, surely you jest!"

"What was that?"

"I said, 'that sounds like such a dangerous pastime,' sir! From what the rangers say, these children are bloodthirsty!"

"And jolly good sport at that! Nearly indestructible! You just about have to reduce them to base components before they'll stop trying to kill you! But not to worry, we're keeping abreast of their growth. If you haven't noticed, we go hunting nearly every day. You should come along some time. You could use some excitement."

"Forgive me, sir, but I cannot even imagine myself attempting to hunt murderous, undead children!"

"Suit yourself. We're going to be heading out within the hour. Looks like we have our hands full."

"But what about Rhumeveld? Do you think it could have been attacked by zombie children as well?"

"It's not very likely. Rhumeveld was a heavily fortified city. Nothing short of an army could have breached its walls. Zombie children are too scattered and disorganized to compose such an army. It's possible that zombie children were involved, but they alone couldn't have plundered Rhumeveld. Have you found me any better rangers?"

"Not yet, sir. But the best of the rangers we do have are already exploring the ruins and should be arriving back from Rhumeveld sometime tomorrow with more information."

"More information? Dare I hope for better results than what you and these rangers have been giving me?"

The attendant took a chance that the King was speaking rhetorically, and attempted to change the focus of the conversation. "And what about the boy? The boy they found in the ruins? He was an eye witness!"

"He's either stunned or an idiot. Maybe he'll snap out of it, but I wouldn't put my money on it."

"Doesn't it seem a little suspicious that he *was* the only survivor and that he *is* a child? What if he's one of those . . . *demon children?*"

"I thought the same thing, but I looked into his eyes, and I could see life in 'em. Some children it's hard to tell, but it was pretty easy to see that he's at least *alive* if nothing else."

*   *   *

Somehow, James makes a wrong turn and winds up in some alternate dimension. (This is Marloth; things like that happen.)

The dimension within which James found himself was an endless maze of bookshelves that stretched both horizontally and vertically in all directions until they vanished into the darkness. Water cascaded down from these bookcases to such an extent that if there was a floor, it was so flooded as to be completely hidden from view. But there were many things to stand on. There were floating bits of furniture and occasional spots of dry, mossy land that rose above the murky water, and there were also pilings and the tops of shorter bookcases that barely rose above the water.

Several paces in front of him there floated a desk behind which sat a short, fat little man. Except that on close inspection it wasn't a man at all, but a toad. The toad was wearing a tweed vest that was tightly buttoned about his waist. Upon his flat nose rested the largest pair of glasses James had ever seen. Through these the toad was carefully examining an ancient tome that was stretched open upon the desk. As he read, strange misty forms consisting of vivid colors rose from the book and then faded into the darkness.

Every now and then, the toad would close the book while keeping a webbed thumb between the pages he was reading and dip the book several times into the water.

The toad didn't seem to have noticed the boy's presence.

James looked down at the book of fairytales and then back at the toad. That had to be Mr. Mosspuddle, the librarian. And that meant that this was the Great Library!

Suddenly there appeared in front of the toad a shimmering, water-like figure. Its form was as that of a human, except featureless. It had no distinct legs and, instead of walking, it floated in the air.

"Hello." said Mr. Mosspuddle. "It's good to see you again." Though he did not sound like he meant it.

The figure did not return the greeting but instead spoke in an echoing voice: "Why do men seek to play and chortle, when just like men all fun is mortal?"

Mr. Mosspuddle looked perplexed. "I don't know."

"Nor do men." said the figure.

"That's all very interesting," said Mr. Mosspuddle. "Though I doubt that's why you are here."

"I am here to review your performance. Or lack of it. But first, we are not alone." James jumped in surprise as the figure turned and looked at him even though he was standing in the darkest of shadows.

"Come forward." said the figure. James' mind bounced back and forth frantically. Should he run away or go along with this strange creature? He wanted to run, but he was curious and the creature had a very commanding presence. Timidly, he stepped into the dim light.

"A visitor!" exclaimed Mr. Mosspuddle. "I can't remember the last time we had a visitor! The glory days have returned!"

"This entity does not belong here!" said the figure. As it moved hints of color rippled across its surface.

James gathered some of his courage. "The Great Library was always a public place! Who are you to be saying who does and doesn't belong here?"

"I am Message, the collective voice and ear of the Wizard's Council. You had best be grateful I am merely a creation of the Wizards and not a Wizard myself, or I would disintegrate you for your impudence. How is it that you are here?"

"A door. I went through it."

"Yes, and how did you find this door?"

"Well, I was talking to this girl, and then I met this raven, and then—"

"You mean the princess?"

"Why, yes. How did you know?"

"Because she is the only girl."

"What do you mean? Is everyone else boys?"

The figure shook its head. "There are no boys in this world. There is only one girl. Period."

"Well then what am I?"

"Clearly you are a zombie." said Message.

"I hoped it wasn't so obvious. But I'm still a boy, just a zombified one." Then, as the rest of what Message had said caught up with him. "Are you saying that there are no other living children? I could have sworn I heard of other children, like in the City of Orphans."

"No. Everyone else thinks there are children, but they are all zombies. It's just that nobody wants to admit it. Stupid people."

Message turned to the librarian. "There is still a doorway that has not been sealed. You were supposed to seal all of them!"

"I'm sorry! I'm sorry! I'll seal it right away! I promise!"

"Your incompetence is astounding. Don't forget, we are still looking for someone to replace you." (A thought that clearly frightened the librarian.)

"No one could replace Mr. Mosspuddle!" said James. "He's the best librarian in the world!"

"I could replace him." said Message. "I am fully capable of performing all of his duties, and I would perform them better. But there is only one of me and I have more important things to do than shepherd books."

"What duties could you perform better?"

"I do not need to convince you. But since the toad is present and may be harboring doubts of my superiority as well, I will provide at least one example: Mr. Mosspuddle requires a catalog to keep track of the complete inventory of this library. I already have its entire inventory within my memory banks. Which is an impressive feat considering that the Great Library contains every book ever written."

"Really? I didn't know that. Does it have Marloth?"

"This is a library, not a cosmotory. It holds books, not worlds. Of course, every book is vying for a piece of reality, but that's a different subject."

"No, I don't mean the world of Marloth, I mean the *book* of Marloth."

"There is no such thing as a *book* of Marloth!"

"Actually," said Mr. Mosspuddle. "I've read accounts of such a book. I don't know if any of those accounts are accurate, but if I were not constrained by my duties to the library I might be out searching for such a book."

"The book of Marloth is real! I have it with me!"

At this the voice that came from Message rose in pitch. "Nonsense! Let me see this book of yours!" Message stretched forth its hand and motioned toward James. The book flew out of James' grasp and was caught by the figure. Message did not open the book but instead passed its hand through it as though absorbing the words through osmosis.

"It is nothing but a child's fairytale!" said Message. "It's not even a real book!"

"Of course it's a real book? What else could it be—a *fake* book?"

"Behold!" said Message and threw the book open wide. "It has no power! Real books alter the world around them when read! They redefine reality! This doesn't do anything. It merely sits there."

"You're wrong!" said James. "There's something different about this book. There's some deep magic about it that none of this world can understand!"

James slumped down in dejection. "I just don't completely understand it myself."

"You are not governed by reason." said Message. He turned and dropped the book on the librarian's desk. "You have expressed an interest in the idea of this book. That is not healthy. You are forbidden to read it. In fact, I order you to destroy it. And to remove this cretin from the Library."

And without any warning or further words, the apparition disappeared as suddenly as it had appeared. Mr. Mosspuddle looked at James miserably.

"I don't want to turn out anyone from the Library, especially a *visitor*."

"Don't worry; I'll leave. But it didn't say anything about you having to remove me right away."

The toad thought about this and then nodded. "Message *is* a stickler for precision. It would probably agree to such a technicality."

James looked at Marloth, which was still resting on the desk. "Are you going to try to destroy Marloth?" he asked. James only asked out of curiosity; he wasn't about to let the librarian destroyed it.

"No." said Mr. Mosspuddle. "I will be in grave trouble if I don't, but I cannot destroy it. I cannot destroy any book. It is against my nature."

James walked over to the desk and picked up Marloth.

"Well at least that Message guy didn't destroy it himself."

"Message can order me to destroy a book, but it cannot directly destroy books itself. The rules are complicated as to what Message can and cannot do. The wizards carefully limit its abilities and autonomy to keep Message from becoming independent and rebelling. But they are equally concerned of my rebelling. They keep close watch over me and the Library, and I'm afraid they will know if I don't follow through with their wishes! Just take the book and please keep it out of their sight. Don't let them know it still exists!"

"Why do they care so much about you and the Library?"

"Because books are an essential part of the wizards' magic. They would be at a loss without them."

"Are you saying that without the Library they would simply be ordinary people?"

"Very smart ordinary people, yes. They may still have a few books of their own, but mostly they pooled their resources here so they could share each others' knowledge."

"That doesn't sound like the wizards I've read about; they were a lot more competitive."

"Wizards are still competitive, but not in the way they used to be. The older wizards made more sense to me: they were always trying to outdo each other in their knowledge and abilities. But these new wizards have a far more communal idea of competition. They are less concerned about knowing more than other wizards and more concerned about ensuring that other wizards don't know more than they do. So they forced each other to pool all of their resources into the Library to ensure that no wizard has access to information another wizard doesn't."

James looked around. "That's strange. If that was the case I would expect there to be all sorts of wizards walking around the Library."

"The wizards rarely visit here. If they need a book, they just summon it. Which is annoying because such power and convenience makes wizards very careless about due dates."

James frowned. "None of this is how it's supposed to be! Wizards shouldn't be controlling the Library. And there should be visitors everywhere reading the books!"

"You keep saying things like that. Where are you getting all of these ideas about the Library from? And you speak like you know so much about me. How is that?"

"Because you and the Library are in this book. It tells of how you were the leading expert in interpreting it."

"Interpreting what?"

"The book."

"The book I am in?"

"Yes."

"But that doesn't make any sense!"

James shrugged. "I don't know. I can't even read the whole thing. It's written in many different languages and I only know one of them."

"This I have to see!" said Mr. Mosspuddle and then abruptly stopped. "No. I can't. The Wizards Council told me to destroy it—which I'm already disobeying—and not to read it—which would only add further condemnation—so I need to restrain myself."

"Why do you care what they say? They don't own this library! The headmaster does! *He* made it!"

"I don't know what headmaster you are referring to. No one knows who built the Library, and there is no official owner of it. But a large number of people who can hurl fireballs and turn people into salt have taken a keen interest in it, and that makes them as good as owners."

"That's not the way it's supposed to be. The headmaster is supposed to be in charge."

"And who is this headmaster you keep speaking of?"

"He's one of the most powerful and upright men in the world. It talks about him in my book."

"Again with your book! Stop using arguments from it! I can't read it and so I can't address whatever ideas you have from it!"

"But if you looked at it you'd understand what I'm talking about!"

"I can't do that! Stop tormenting me! Go! Go back to the castle! I need to seal that doorway, and you can't stay here."

"But—"

"Visiting hours are over." said Mr. Mosspuddle. By this point he looked thoroughly frightened, and it was fear that drove him to take hold of James' coat and forcefully guide him to the doorway. James wanted to stay, and he could have easily picked up the toad and tossed him into the murky gloom, but Mr. Mosspuddle was one of the legendary characters from his fairytale book, and his respect for the librarian caused James to oblige him. Once James had stepped through the doorway and was back in the castle hall, the librarian bid him farewell and promptly shut the door.

James stood there for a moment, staring at the door. Out of curiosity, he took hold of the knob and turned it. To his surprise, the door opened, but not by its hinges. Instead, it fell forward on top of him as though it had never been attached to anything, revealing a solid stone wall behind it. One more doorway to the Great Library was now closed forever.

*　　*　　*

The King was just about to leave his bedchamber when the queen hurried into the room.

"Did you hear the news about Duke Francis?" she asked him.

"No. What is it?"

"He's dead. Murdered. They found his body just yesterday."

"Murdered? But how?"

"The messenger didn't know. But he made it clear the duke did not die from natural causes."

"Was the duke able to speak to Lord Dominicus before he died?"

"No. I don't think so."

The King slammed his fist against the wall. "Everything is falling apart!"

"It's not over yet. There is still hope." the queen said, though she sounded like she was trying to convince herself as well as him.

The King straightened. "I don't know about hope, but I'm not one to go down without a fight. I need to get to the bottom of this Rhumeveld business. The darkness out there is spreading, and I need to know what we are dealing with. I'll try that boy again to see if I can get anything out of him."

He left the queen sitting on their bed, trying her best to pull herself together. She tried to keep a firm countenance around the King, but internally she was struggling to keep herself from falling apart like the kingdom around her. She needed to relax. Considering all of her options, she decided upon a bath. A bath would help a lot. She called for one of the servants.

*   *   *

Adelle left her room and as she was heading for the stairs she stopped by the royal chambers to see if the queen was inside.

"Mother?" she called, "are you there?"

After receiving no answer, she was about to leave when something caught her eye. There, resting atop of the dresser was her mother's diadem. This was the first time she had seen it away from her mother's head. It was slim and elegant, silver like moonlight and nearly as ethereal. In an instant, all of the millions of times her mother had ever scolded her passed through her mind. She knew she should leave at once, but the diadem was mesmerizing. Slowly, she tiptoed across the room for a closer look. The closer she got, the more attractive it looked. She had to try it on. There was the mirror right in front of her. She could put it on, take it off, and leave. Her mother would never know.

She eagerly took hold of the diadem, lifted it into the air, and set it upon her head. Instantly, she felt more mature and sophisticated. She was Queen Adelle. Her mother had no right bossing her around. Well, the queen was going to have to make do without her crown for a while, for Adelle wasn't about to give it up.

She stepped out into the hallway and bumped into James.

"Oh, excuse me!" she said, straightening herself.

James didn't reply. There was something different about her. He suddenly felt much younger than she.

"Are you all right?" she asked.

"That crown." James murmured.

"Oh, yes! Isn't it lovely?"

"Where did you get it?" asked James.

"Oh, I've always had it. I only wear it on special occasions."

Zombies don't know fear. They have nothing to fear. But contrary to popular belief, they do feel something. They feel happy, or at least something close to it. It comes from being completely animated without the need of things like glands, nerves, and organs. If they had anything to worry about, they didn't know about it. But James was not happy. He hadn't been happy since he had found the book. And now he was terrified.

"The toymaker." he said breathlessly.

Adelle looked at him in wide-eyed surprise. "How did you know? I'm meeting him tonight! He's going to take me away from this dreadful place. Promise you won't tell anyone?"

James didn't move. Except that his mind was moving. It was tearing backwards at a pace of a million miles per moment. Bits and pieces of his rotted brains were connecting themselves back together again, and they didn't like what they were seeing. Fragments of an age old story of an orphanage were surfacing. A story full of dark occurrences of which mothers never spoke of.

"It's happening all over again!" he shouted.

"What ever are you talking about?"

"Except that this time it's not me, it's you!"

"Come now, you can make more sense than that! Tell me what's going on!"

119

But before James could respond, the door flew open and the two children found themselves staring up at the queen. And she was furious.

"Adelle! What are you doing with my crown?" she roared.

Adelle looked at her mother, looked at James, looked back at her mother, and then shot across the hall and into her room. The queen lunged after her, but Adelle had already bolted the door behind her.

"Adelle!" The queen shrieked. "Open this door at once! You hear me? Every additional moment this door remains locked is only increasing the punishment that's awaiting you!"

Pausing for breath, she noticed James. Her eyes narrowed. "You must be her accomplice." she stated coldly.

James didn't like the way this was going at all. Following Adelle's lead, he bolted down the hall and disappeared into the stairway.

*   *   *

The King looked around the infirmary. There was no one there but sleeping people.

"Where's that blasted boy?" he growled.

"You Highness!" called the attendant as he rounded a corner. "One of the rangers just arrived with news about the city!" The attendant and a ranger came up the hall and stopped in front of the King.

"Well it's about time! You had better be of more use than that half-witted boy."

The ranger managed to shrug this off and proceeded with his report. "I was over the city like a fine tooth comb and I think I know what attacked the place. Children. Zombified children. A whole army of them, I reckon."

"Zombies? An army of them? But that's impossible! Where in the world would an army of zombies come from? What would keep them from killing each other and wandering off?"

"It was hard to say. There was definitely a vast number of them, and they appeared to have approached the city from all directions. I smelled magic. It was everywhere. Something is helping them; channeling them. Maybe a wizard."

"Wizards? This is getting worse and worse! Where is this army now?"

"That's the worse part. Their tracks just disappeared. I have no idea where they could have gone. They are still out there, and they are probably on the move."

"An army of zombie children." the King muttered. "Rhumeveld is not very far from here."

"Do you think they would actually attack the castle?"

"I've heard of stranger things." said the King. "They leveled a whole city."

"Our forces are already positioned in the two passes that lead from Rhumeveld to Castle Elington. It would take several days for this undead army to circumvent those passes. Our scouts should be able to locate them within that time, and then we can directly engage them."

"That sounds promising, though it all hangs on whether or not we can find an army that has so far eluded us. If these enemies are using magic, who knows what we are up against. They leveled Rhumeveld! And you said—"

The King suddenly froze. Slowly, he wheeled around and looked one more time into the infirmary. As he did so, the nurse came back to cart away the sleeping people.

"Nurse!" the King shouted. "What sort of state did you find that boy in?"

"Why, he was in pretty sore shape. I had to sew back a couple limbs and patch up his innards a good deal, but I'm good at that sort of thing. Before long, he was up and about as though nothing had happened!"

The King's face contorted with rage.

"Have you lost your wits? That was no boy! It was a bloody zombie!"

*   *   *

Once the sounds of her mother's ranting faded into the distance, Adelle relaxed and backed away from the door. What she needed now was some real company to talk to. Aside from that weird boy, she was the only child her age in the castle, and all of the adults had their heads on backwards. There were only one other group of people she had left to turn to. Searching about her room, she gathered her favorite dolls.

"What would you like to do?" she asked them.

"Let's have a tea party!" she spoke for them.

*   *   *

The queen stopped her shouting and leaned against the wall. She was suddenly struck by a wave of weakness and nausea, as though she were coming down with a fever. She started to make her way back to her room. She was having an increasingly difficult time walking. Her skin felt clammy and was beginning to itch. She stopped half way across the hall to look at her hand.

Her skin was cracking and folding over. Her back grew heavier. Her form began to sag under the weight. Frightened, she rushed back to her room as fast as her failing body could take her and stopped in front of the mirror. And nearly had a heart attack. She was aging. Aging before her increasingly blurry eyes.

"How is this happening?" she moaned, as she watched the color slowly drain from her hair.

Her hands shaking, she rushed to her dresser and rummaged through its contents, throwing one drawer after another onto the floor. Eventually she found what she was looking for: a large box of Jillybons. Without missing a beat she tore the lid from the container and began to eat them in rapid succession.

*　　*　　*

James had no sooner reached the bottom of the stairs then he found himself surrounded by several guards.

"Going somewhere?" said the King.

James instinctively tried to pass between the guards but they closed upon him tightly and grabbed his arms.

"So, thought you'd have a look around? Spy a bit? Perhaps even try to get the gates open?"

"That's not true!" James shouted. "I wouldn't do anything like that!"

"Of course not!" said the King. "After all, you're a civilized dead person! It was coincidence that you were in the middle of a recently desecrated city. Just passing through, no doubt."

The guards snickered.

"But here's the situation. We need information, and we need it now. Tell us where this army of yours is, and what it's up to."

"I don't know anything about them!" said James. "They beat me and chased me away!"

"Ha! Perhaps I should rephrase things. Tell me all about the undead army or I'll cut you up into pieces the size of olives. I know a thing or two about zombies, and I know they can't do much harm when they're comprised of a million separate pieces!"

"No!" James screamed. "Please don't cut me into little pieces!"

"And I'll oblige you. Just tell me where's that blasted army!"

"If I knew I would tell you! But I don't!"

"So you choose the hard way! Then again, cutting you up may take some time, and we don't have much of that. Search him first.

Maybe he's carrying some information that will save us the trouble of persuading him."

While three of the guards held James tight, a fourth began to search his person.

"Not much in his pockets, just needle and thread. But here! He has a book in his knapsack!"

"By George!" said the King. "It's the book of rules!" He grabbed the book and briefly skimmed its pages. Then he bent over so that he was eye to eye with James and growled, "So you're the thief who stole our book!"

"No!" said James. "I didn't steal it! I found it in Rhumeveld!"

"A likely story!" said the King.

"It's very likely!" said James. "It's like the story in the book!"

"Say what?"

"The King finds a knight with the magical book!"

"You are no knight."

"I know, but everything else is just about the same. If you read it you would—"

"I have read it!" the King interrupted him, and then said in a softer tone, "And I know the story you are referring to."

He paused for a moment to take in the full depth of what was before him, and then said, "So you've read this? Have you read the parts about zombie children? How it condemns them? How I am supposed to destroy them?"

"Yes!" said James. "But there is also a zombie child in the book named James that does good things. I named myself after him." The King marveled.

"Put away your weapons." he ordered his men. "Don't hurt him."

The guards looked at the prisoner nervously. "Then what should we do with him?" one of them asked.

"Place him in the dungeons for now." said the King, as he set off down one of the hallways. "I need to think. Alone."

*   *   *

The queen stumbled toward her mirror and saw an old woman staring back. A blurry old woman. Everything was blurry now. How could this be? She was not *that old*. Where did all of her years go? And yet the back of her mind pointed out to her that she had never really known what the rules were.

The queen's thoughts flitted to Adelle.

"It's all your fault!" she screamed.

Somehow, she knew that putting on the crown again would not bring anything back. This was it. This is who she would be for the rest of her life. She bent over and began to weep bitterly.

She loathed herself.

*   *   *

The King stood alone in his throne room, warring with a past he had thought had been put to rest. He considered his throne, and then sat beside it. In his hand he held the book of rules. After some time, he opened the book and began to read. As he read, a man walked up and sat beside him.

"You didn't hurt the zombie child." said the man. "Why didn't you?"

The King didn't turn to look up. He just continued staring at the book and said "That boy. I have seen many zombie children, but never one like that. I can't imagine that he is innocent, and yet he doesn't appear to be bent on malice either. He actually read the book of rules! What zombie child would ever do that? And he did not appear to flinch at the harsh truths it speaks about his kind. I find myself wondering if he could actually be telling the truth."

"He is. He's one of my orphans, though he doesn't remember it."

"I can't shake the idea that all of this seems so familiar. The boy was right about one thing; this reminds me so much of the stories in this book. Though not exactly; the stories in the book were more ideal. But this is madness! They were just fairytales! Why am I even worrying about them! I am so confused! Nothing makes sense anymore! I feel like everything is slipping away from me. My queen, my daughter, my kingdom, everything!"

"It is slipping away because of what you've become."

"What do you mean? It's the world around me that has changed, not I."

"No. There was once a time when you were a different sort of man. You were strong and stood for what was right even when the people were against it. And they followed you despite themselves because I showed you favor for upholding my book and rules."

"That's strange," said the King. "You are right; I completely forgot that there was such a time. It feels so long ago, as though it was someone else's life."

"In a way it was."

The King reflected on his past and he smiled briefly. "Those were good days, weren't they! Whatever happened to them?"

"You probably don't even remember, but you were once in love with a young woman who lived in one of the neighboring towns. She wasn't particularly handsome. She wasn't educated nor was she of noble birth, but she was honest and kindhearted and fiercely loyal, things you rarely experience in the claustrophobic world of politics you grew up in, and you found those attributes attractive. Many rich and powerful people tried to dissuade you from any interest in her, but they never succeeded. The rules did not forbid such a union and you were determined to marry her. But then someone new entered the scene. Someone who was beautiful and clever and of royal blood. A person everyone fell in love with, including you. I think you knew she was danger, but that didn't stop you."

"You're referring to my wife. I admit, she has led me down paths I never thought I would tread. I should have been stronger."

"She was able to lead you where you are because she had your heart. There was a time, long before you ever met her, when she wasn't all that different from the peasant woman that once caught your eye. She was ignorant of avarice and manipulation, and she loved my stories. But then she turned away from them and me. Once you were joined, it was only a matter of time before you turned your back on them as well. If I were to counsel you—which I already did through my book—I would have told you not to marry her."

"But I love her! She's my wife! I would gladly give my life for her!"

"And those are all good things. In the grand scheme of things you were meant to marry her. It is part of the story. But that is something you will never fully understand in this life. Suffice to say that in the end, Good will triumph over Evil, as it does in all good stories."

The King paused, deep in thought. "Everything the raven said in the courtroom; it's true, isn't it?"

"Yes." said the man.

The King continued to look at Marloth. "Now that I have the book, is there anything I can do to right the wrongs I have made? To help Good triumph over Evil?"

The man did not immediately reply, and when he did his voice sounded pained. "Everything will be made right," he said at last. "But you will still need to reap the consequences of your actions."

The King sighed. "I understand." And then he rose to his feet and set out toward the door saying, "There is one thing I can do."

*　　*　　*

James was growing agitated. He had a growing apprehension that terrible things were about to happen and there was nothing he could do about it from within this prison cell. He hated prison cells. Elusive memories began to surface of being in such a place before. Memories that made his lifeless skin crawl.

But the strangest thing was the looking glass on the wall. Why in the world would anyone put a mirror in such a place? For a moment he forgot about his anxiety and reflected on the stories he had read of people stepping through looking glasses into alternate realities.

Suddenly there was a clattering outside and the door to his cell was pulled open. The King stood in the doorway and beckoned to him.

"Come out! You're free!"

James warily stepped outside of the cell. The King and several guards were standing around him.

"What happened?" James asked. "Why are you letting me go?"

"Because I trust you. And because I want you to do something for me."

James had anticipated many different possibilities, but this was not one of them. He did not know what to say. The King could see the confusion in James' face and tried his best to explain.

"The time for the queen and I has come. There is no longer any hope for us, at least not in this world. But there is still hope for Adelle. She is still innocent. I have tried so hard to keep her from the taint of this world. But I can't do that any longer."

The King looked straight into James' eyes.

"Will you protect her? Protect my little girl?"

James froze. Now he *really* didn't know what to say. He already felt willing to give his life for Adelle, but he was overwhelmed by the intensity and weight of the King's manner. James didn't like making promises, and he didn't know how something as tainted as him could keep anyone from evil. But he couldn't say no. He had to do what he could.

"Yes." he said at last. "I'll protect her."

"And I don't mean any casual attempt," the King went on. "I mean giving everything you have to keep them from her."

"I'll give my life, not that it's worth much."

The King smiled. "Thank you!" he said, and then engulfed James in a massive bear hug. "It's been so long since I have come across anyone who valued this book. I wish we could sit down around a pint of beer and talk of its stories, but we have no time. We need to hurry to the front of the castle. He motioned for his guards to follow him.

"We're all pawns in this game of life." said the King. "There's no going back. But we can move forward."

*   *   *

Few souls know how to get there, but if you were to travel past the bleeding edge of technology and make a U-turn at morality, you would find yourself standing before the arcane laboratory of Dr. Otto Marrechian.

Rumor had it that the doctor had once been a prominent figure in society, but whether or not such rumors were accurate, now he spent most of his time within his sanctum of science, forgotten by much of the world.

He was an inventor. He did not use most of his inventions, or at least not directly. Mostly his inventions used his inventions. He wasn't even sure what most of his creations were doing. That wasn't his concern. They did what they were designed to do, and usually a lot more. If things ever got really ugly he would just create a new invention to clean up the mess.

One of his latest obsessions was the idea of teleportation. Teleportation was very easy in Marloth since its spacial reality was already so inconsistent. The hard part was consistency, especially when it came to destinations. He was trying to refine a teleportation system that would allow a large group of people to move from point A to point M. So far, the closest he had gotten was a mechanism that transported a large group of people randomly along points K, L, M, N, O, etc. This wasn't very useful at first, but his latest version had been able to narrow the range of these random destinations to a more reasonable distance. The subjects would still appear within a mile radius and need to be rounded up, but that was a lot better than the first version where they could end up anywhere in Marloth.*

At the moment, these latest teleportation devices were being used to ferry a large quantity of creations past a host of soldiers and into a region not far from an equally large fortress.

* * *

The captain of the castle guard lit a cigar, drew in deeply, and slowly exhaled. With one waft he painted the air with a tapestry of ashen strokes that idly danced for his amusement. Life was good. He was in possession of a job that required next to no effort, and he had just requisitioned a practically endless supply of tobacco in the name of the King. He leaned back in his chair and watched the smoke wreath up to the ceiling.

"Captain! Captain!"

The captain groaned. Why of all people did that fool have to come bothering him? He ought to be bothering the King instead.

"Go away!" he growled, not looking at the gatekeeper who lurched into the room.

"But this is urgent! Someone is outside the gate and wants in!"

"Then tell them to go away too! You know the policy. That gate is just for appearances. We never open it for anyone. Especially at night. I wouldn't even open it if the King was out there." The captain smiled pleasantly.

"But sir, it's a child!"

The captain looked up in surprise. "What in blazes is a child doing out there? It's dangerous as hell!"

---

*Most of those subjects have yet to be found.

"That's what I said! The sun is setting, and we can't leave a child out there all alone in the dark!"

The captain rose to his feet and headed for the door. "Fine. I'm coming. But if you're wrong about this, I'm gonna kill you."

"Yes, sir!"

The two of them climbed down the stairs to the top of the gate room. The captain grabbed a lantern and leaned out one of the windows to peer downward. Sure enough, a little girl was standing below them, staring at the massive gates.

"Why, the girl's all beat up! She's bleeding!" said the captain.

"Is she?" said the gatekeeper. "It's hard to tell in this light."

"Well don't just stand there! Get these gates opened and let her in!"

"As good as done, sir!"

The gatekeeper quickly ran off and gathered together a group of guards. After much effort with the levers and pulleys, the portcullis was lifted and the doors pushed open.

The captain stood at the entrance and ushered the little girl inside. She was very pale and her body was covered in cuts and sutures. Yet despite her condition, the girl smiled eagerly and skipped into the castle. Immediately, the gates slammed shut behind her.

"Terribly sorry for the delay, miss. How bad is the pain?" the captain asked.

The girl shrugged vaguely and looked about her at the various guards. It was then that the captain noticed that she was rather round about the waist. That was odd. She had looked much thinner from outside.

"Perhaps she doesn't speak." said the gatekeeper.

The captain didn't reply. He had continued to examine the girl, and now he was convinced that she was expanding. The child was swelling up like a balloon. He needed some answers, and he needed them now.

"What's going on here?" he demanded. The girl had her back turned to him and did not respond. "Where are your parents?" he shouted. "Are you an orphan?"

Suddenly, the child turned around and smiled right at him. "I'm not an orphan! I'm a bomb!"

*   *   *

The King turned in horror. With a deafening boom, the castle shook so violently he was thrown clear off his feet. Raising himself to a window, he was just in time to watch as the gates were enveloped in a towering ball of smoke and flame.

"What happened?" shouted one of the guards.

The King gritted his teeth. "The gates have been blown wide open."

"What! How?"

"Clearly someone wants inside." the King muttered, and then turned to James "Don't worry about the castle. Find my little girl. And if you remember, tell her I love her."

Then the King called for his sword. His sword bearers had been following closely behind him, and the fearsome weapon was promptly handed to him. It was a massive sword. Few men were strong enough to carry it, much less wield it. The King did so through muscle and momentum.

"To the gates, men!" he bellowed, leading the charge down the hall. As he gathered speed it was impossible to tell if he was wielding his sword or riding it.

*   *   *

"I think your mother is in need of a spanking!" said Mrs. Gingersmile.

"Now Mrs. Gingersmile! You know you shouldn't say such things!" Adelle scolded the doll, though she couldn't help smiling. "My mother had a very troubled youth; that's all."

"Well, it's not right for her to keep you cooped up in here." said Miss Perrywinkle.

"It's not that bad." said Adelle. "Why, I'm having a splendid time in your company!"

"All the same . . ." said Mrs. Gingersmile.

"Now, now! Why dwell upon the negative?" said the stuffed animal swan. "You should try one of these crumpets, they are sensational! Tell me Samantha, how did you manage to make them so light and fluffy?"

"Oh, it's no trick really. I just added this white powder instead of flowers."

Adelle leaned back in her chair, closed her eyes, and smiled. She enjoyed playing with her dolls. They were her only friends. As she sat there, thinking of nothing in particular, it began to dawn upon her. She frequently talked for her dolls. She had different personalities for all of them and would pretend that they were alive and talking on their own. But now she had her eyes closed. She wasn't thinking about what the dolls should say. Her mind had drifted onto other things.

The dolls were still talking.

Adelle jumped up and looked about her. She was no longer pretending. The dolls really were sitting there drinking tea, carrying on a lively conversation.

"You're alive!" she exclaimed.

"Of course, dear!" said Mrs. Gingersmile. "Why ever why shouldn't we be? You've been talking to us all this time."

"But, but, you're just dolls! You never talked by yourselves before!"

"Silly girl!" said the swan. "Here, why don't you have another crumpet? Oh, forgive me, it appears we've eaten them all!"

Adelle looked at the empty basket. *Dolls can't eat!* she moaned.

"Don't worry about that." Samantha told the swan. "I'll go down to the kitchens and make some more!"

"Why don't we all go?" suggested Miss Perrywinkle.

"That's a splendid idea!" said Mrs. Gingersmile. The dolls hopped down from their chairs and hobbled over to the door.

"Are you coming?" Mrs. Gingersmile called back to Adelle.

"No, I'm all mixed up right now and—" Adelle jumped to her feet. "What! You can't leave! If someone saw you, who knows what trouble I'd be in!"

"Now dear, we appreciate your concern, but there's nothing an honest explanation and good old fashioned reason can't sort out. This is a royal castle, and occupied by only the most civil of persons!"

With that, the dolls stepped out into the hallway. Adelle tried to think for a moment, gave up, and ran after them.

*   *   *

There were no gates. But there were zombies. Hundreds of them rushed through the hole, slashing and bludgeoning anyone in their path. By the time the King and his entourage arrived, the majority of the castle guards had already been pushed back into the center of the castle. The zombies broke off into groups that began fanning out throughout the castle, searching for anything alive.

The King charged into the midst of the zombies, swinging his broadsword like a giant, cleaving zombies in half by the dozens. No one knew how to slay zombies like the King of Marloth. But there were too many of them. They climbed up the columns and dropped on him like flies. It was only a matter of time before the deluge engulfed him. A million knives were fed upon royalty. The King was dead.

*   *   *

The queen found herself laughing uncontrollably. The Jillybons were having their effect. But then she started careening between laughter and crying. Her misery was too great to be masked by enchanted candy. She was hysterical. She had no concern with sadness or old age or the sounds of carnage coming from the lower parts of the castle.

Eventually both laughter and crying abated. The queen sat for some time in a motionless stupor. Something resembling peace slowly crept over her.

Suddenly everything was clear. The queen arose. She knew what she had to do. Trying to maintain as noble a gait as possible, she stumbled across the room and out onto the balcony. The moon was out. It was a very beautiful night. Hers was a very tall tower, and from it she could have seen the whole castle stretched out below her and bathed in moonlight, cradled in a sea of clouds and stars. But she didn't really notice that. She didn't notice the screams of the dying or the flames that were lazily spreading across parts of the castle. She was numb to all of it. Peacefully, she walked up to the edge of the balcony.

And kept on walking.

*   *   *

Things were happening far too quickly for James. He needed room to think. Jogging to the nearest window, he climbed out and onto the roof. He felt at home on the rooftops. From there, he could see all of the towers rising around him, the garden sprawled out in the moonlight below, and the lights hurriedly passing throughout the halls. He didn't know exactly what was going on, but whatever it was, it was big, and it probably involved zombie children. James sat down and began to frantically scan through his book.

He was not there long when the raven flew out of the night and dropped down beside him.

"It's happening!" said the raven. "Fate is finally dishing out the king his sentence. All of your siblings are here to pay the dear soul a visit! And that's not all. Practically the whole of Marloth is converging upon this place! People are coming from the City of Orphans and everywhere! There's even been talk of the toymaker himself coming this way!"

"But they aren't here for the King. They're here for the princess."

"Yes, but if it wasn't for the king they'd—wait a minute! How would you know that?"

"It's all in my book."

"And what book is that?"

"A book I found. It's a collection of fairytales."

"Well that makes sense. I ought to have realized you were getting all of your wisdom from a fairytale book."

"It has the same story as what's happening right now, even though a lot of things are different. The castle, the King and queen, the forces of evil, it's all there. All that's missing here is a hero. But there's no knight; only me."

James frowned with determination and set off for the edge of the roof.

"Where are you going?" asked the raven.

"To rescue Adelle."

"Have the maggots gotten to your brains?" shrieked the raven. "You can't go back there! If the zombies don't destroy you, the toymaker will!"

James turned around and stared the raven straight in the eye.

"Look at me!" he shouted. "I'm nothing! I'm not even alive! The more my memory comes back, the more I realize how much I threw away! I have nothing to gain; I have nothing to lose. But down there is a little girl with everything to gain, and everything to lose. She's sweet and beautiful and innocent! Yet they want to take that away from her! They're going to make her like me, or something even worse! I can't let that happen."

"You're on the verge of making sense. But there's nothing you can do about any of this. Events have been set in motion that cannot be changed. Trust me, I know about such things."

James continued toward the roof edge and shouted over his shoulder, "But do such things know about me?"

*   *   *

"I wonder where everyone is?" said Adelle.

"It sounds like there's quite a commotion coming from downstairs," said Samantha. "Let's hurry so we can see what it is!"

It wasn't long before the group reached the bottom of the spiral staircase and stepped into the room at the base of the tower. There, stretching across the arched opening into one of the halls of the castle was a steel door.

"What? I didn't know there was a door here!" said Adelle.

"It looks like it descended from the ceiling." observed the swan. Several of the dolls tried to lift it, but it didn't budge.

"We might as well try moving one of the walls!" said Miss Perrywinkle.

"And the shouting is coming from the other side! It sounds like a war!"

"Oh, I do wish we could see what was going on!"

"Forget about wars. However are we to make more crumpets if we can't get to the kitchens?"

The more Adelle listened, the worse the sounds from outside became. There were screams of pain, and the sounds of weapons and flesh and nasty things she didn't know about and didn't want to.

"I'm going back upstairs!" she exclaimed. "I can't stay here another moment!"

"No you are not!" Mrs. Gingersmile scolded. "By the sound of it, things could be getting pretty dangerous around here! You need to stay with us so we can protect you!"

"Oh, shut up! You're just a bunch of dolls!"

"Watch your tongue, young lady! That's no way for a princess to speak!"

"I can speak as I like! You're not my mother!"

"And I consider that a blessing!"

Adelle was infuriated. It sounded as though dreadful things were taking place within the castle, and she was not accustomed to being talked back to by her dolls. As she stormed up the stairs, the dolls were preparing to light a fire with a lantern and burn their way through the wall.

*   *   *

From behind the flood of zombies came Deadwick the goblin, furtively eyeing the chaos with growing enthusiasm. He had his new gun at the ready. Its barrel was so large it shot round the size of his fist! He was a little peeved that the children were so efficient in killing everyone; he had not yet had an opportunity to use it. But he wasn't too worried; war had a way of beating on his door.

"Master!" said one of the zombie children. "Ogres have tunneled under the castle and are coming out of the cellars!"

Deadwick nodded. "Tell the other children not to fight them. Simply stay out of their way. The brutes are so slow, we'll be done with our chores and away before they cause much trouble. Any news of the princess?"

"No one has seen her yet." said the child. "But there is an entire tower that is blocked off by a heavy door."

"Yes, she could very well be behind it. Go get more explosives and see if you can't rid us of that door."

Part 2

James entered the kitchen and looked about him. He needed weapons, and this was the place to find them.

"This is madness!" cried the raven. "I'm beginning to sense dark forces accumulating about the castle! I may be immune to ordinary death, but there are supernatural powers in this world that even I have reason to fear!"

"Then hurry up and get away from here!" James said as he began opening cupboards and dumping shelves onto the floor. Near the middle of the shelves he found what he was looking for: row after row of knives.

"I'm no longer proud of it," said James, "but I have had an eternity of experience with such devices." He grabbed one, sheathed it, and screamed in agony.

"What's the matter?" said the Raven. "I thought you'd had an eternity of experience with such devices?"

James tore out the knife and clung to a table for support. "I used to just stick these through my waist and use my insides as a sheath," he gasped, "but ever since I found that book I've become increasingly aware of pain. Now I've reached the point where I must be as sensitive to pain as a real person would!" He looked at the knife in bewilderment. "I'll have to figure out some new means of carrying these things!" And then, as if the full weight of his situation was just then dawning on him, he added slowly, (and you could hear the tears in his voice), "This is going to hurt . . ."

"Well, I assume you are at least one of the more capable of the children, and can outmaneuver the lot of them?"

"I am neither as fast nor strong as my siblings." said James as he began tearing strips out of old sacks and using them to tie knives to various parts of his person. "My only hope is that what this book of Marloth says is true."

"So if it is, you will defy impossible odds and miraculously defeat an entire army?"

"No. I will be soundly beaten. But that will not be the end of it. In the end the princess will be saved." He pulled forth a stout broom and, with one forceful lunge, broke the feathered end across his knee. Then he threw the beam over his shoulder and strapped it to his back with a belt.

"And what about you?" asked the raven.

James gave a weak smile. "I don't know if there's any hope for me."

"Then why are you doing this?"

"For many reasons." said James as he headed for the door. "Everything is pointing to the same thing: this is what I am supposed to do."

*　　*　　*

Adelle was becoming agitated. It was growing late and the toymaker still hadn't arrived. To make matters worse, there had never been a time when she wished to leave this place more. The screams were growing less frequent, but there was still a great commotion coming from all directions of the castle, as though the walls were crawling with rats. She had no idea how long she had been sitting patiently in her room, but it felt like ages.

As she listened, she noticed that a new sound was growing amidst the others. It was a low hum. Gradually the sound became louder, until it sounded like a thundering motor. Something was moving toward the castle, and by the increase in volume, it was approaching at a frightening speed.

Suddenly, the window exploded inward with a shower of glass. Pieces of the surrounding rock and wood were blown across the room, tearing holes into the adjacent wall. Yet despite all of this,

Adelle was not touched. In fact, she was not nearly as shocked as she knew she should be.

The debris settled to reveal a solid black coach resting in the middle of the room. It was sleek and constructed of pure metal. Even the wheels were metal, like that of a train. At the back of it was strapped a huge rocket engine from which smoke was still billowing. At the top and toward the front of the contraption was a bench upon which sat a monkey, who was apparently driving the thing.

A door along the side of the vehicle swung open and out stepped Jakob Damond.

"Greetings, fair princess!" said the toymaker, removing his hat and bowing. "A thousand apologies for being late. You would not believe what we had to go through to get here!"

"What a bizarre device!" said Adelle. "It looks dreadfully dangerous."

"Oh, not to worry! You and I will be safe inside. But tell me, how are you enjoying your dolls?"

"So it was you behind my dolls coming alive!"

"Naturally. That's what I'm best at. Making things come to life."

"Well to be honest, they haven't behaved themselves at all."

"Of course not! Do you want them to just sit all day and speak when spoken too? What would be the fun in that? No, people need foibles to be truly alive. Now, if you don't mind, we need to hurry! I've already kept us too late!"

"Yes, by all means! I think the castle is under siege or some such!"

"Well then that makes it all the more urgent that we get you away from here!" said the toymaker as he motioned for her to step inside.

"Is there no other means of transportation?" she asked nervously.

"Trust me, it's just like floating. You won't even notice whether or not it's moving!"

Adelle had barely stepped inside when the bedroom door was pummeled to the ground by a rush of zombies that quickly flooded the room. The toymaker slammed the door behind Adelle just as Deadwick waded through the mass of zombies and stopped before the machine. Both the monkey and the toymaker looked at him with dull interest.

"Hey!" said the goblin. "Where do you think you're going?"

"Excuse me?" said the toymaker. "The princess and I were just going for a short jaunt. Is there a problem?"

"Ha! You think this is funny, do you? Who do you think you are, trying to stand in front of me and my army?"

"What's happening?" Adelle called out as she tried to see through the small windows of the coach.

"Oh, I'm no one in particular," said the toymaker. "I just promised this fine young woman a midnight drive through Marloth, and have come as good as my word. But who are all of these fine young children? I just so happen to have a few toys that I've been meaning to give to such sweet children as you!"

The zombie children clapped their hands in excitement. Reaching into a large burlap sack in the back of the vehicle, he pulled forth several toys and proceeded to hand them out to the closest zombie children.

"You must be mad!" said Deadwick. "Don't you realize that me and my army of the undead have just overcome and slaughtered every inhabitant of this castle except for the princess?"

"Well I'm sorry to hear that. This always was such a cheery place! But I haven't the time to dwell upon such things. I'm on a tight schedule and should have already departed a quarter hour ago!"

"You'll depart right now!" Deadwick bellowed. "KILL HIM!"

But the zombie children were far too busy fighting over the toys. One group was struggling over a toy fire truck when it suddenly made a noise like a siren. The children were so surprised they dropped it on the floor. As they all watched, the fire truck awkwardly lifted its ladder into the air until it halted nearly two feet from the floor. On top of the ladder clung a motionless toy fireman who was holding a shiny hose. Suddenly, it shot out a jet of blue-white flame into the room, completely engulfing several zombies. At the same time the other toys began to also do unpleasant things. A jump rope attempted to strangle several zombies while the teddy bear started feeling sick and vomiting glowing green acid.

Suddenly, there was a crash of glass as a shadowy figure dropped down from the upper window and landed right between the two men. For a brief instant, both of the grown-ups stared in surprise at the small, unimposing figure of James. Then, before either of them could react, he whipped out his staff and with one circular blow knocked both of them off their feet.

"KILL HIM TOO!" shouted Deadwick. Fresh zombies materialized from every nook and cranny, all converging upon the machine. Quickly, James leaped onto the coach and alongside the monkey. The monkey was preparing to bring the contraption around but was interrupted when James slammed his staff into the controls. The two of them barely had enough time to duck before the vehicle lurched forward at a gut wrenching velocity and exploded through the facing wall like a cannon ball.

The monkey turned the vehicle sharply along the hall and barreled down the winding stairway. He tried to shut it off but James had broken the lever that controlled the speed. The machine was at full throttle.

The contraption crashed through the outer wall of the tower and flew into the midnight air. For a brief moment, time seemed to stand still. The moon outlined the machine as it flew through the sky, the wind whistling past their ears. Then, it crossed over the courtyard and, with a collision that nearly shook the entire building, it crashed into the midst of the castle below. Bricks and mortar showered the sky. The machine bore straight through the roof and continued on down a corridor.

And so they bore onward, shredding stone from steps and walls like a wave of water, all the while accompanied by Adelle's screams from inside.

Through all of this, James had barely been able to keep his grip on the top of the machine and was hanging on by his fingers. The monkey didn't fail to notice this. Reaching back, he pried James' hands loose. Before James could grab a new grip, the monkey made a sharp turn and threw James straight into a pillar.

After falling to the ground and lying there for a few moments, James rose to his feet and watched as the machine disappeared into the labyrinth of corridors.

For a brief moment, all was quiet. But it wasn't long before a noise began to rise from the distant outskirts of the castle. He heard them long before he saw them. Scurrying, creeping, climbing, and running. It sounded as though every zombie child in the castle was converging upon the spot he now occupied.

They were. From all directions, zombies jumped into view and rushed him. But just before the swarm could smother him, he slipped through the railing of the balcony beside him. This was only possible due to the fact that several of his bones were broken and he was only partially relying upon them for animation, thus making him triple jointed and flexible as a sack. He fell two stories down and hit the floor rolling, possibly breaking more bones, but still managing to leap to his feet and break into a run. From far above a cascade of zombies followed suit, crashing upon the spot where he had landed and continuing pursuit along the ballroom floor.

James was determined to catch up with that monkey. But by now his limbs were broken in several places and he was not able to move as quickly as before. He still had a rhythm to his movement, but now it was a heavily syncopated one. And he didn't know where the monkey and that bizarre machine were. What he needed was a good vantage point. Turning a corner, he entered a long hall and nearly ran straight into another group of zombies. Screeching to a halt, he threw himself against the wall and proceeded to scale it.

It was a rough stone wall, and he was able to shoot up it almost as fast as he could run. The top of the wall was lined with stained glass windows. One of these he shattered with his staff and climbed outside. After crawling up several more stories outside, he reached the roof and once again commanded a view of the whole castle.

Even though he could not see the toymaker's machine, he didn't need to. It wasn't hard to pinpoint its location from the rumbling of its motors and the sounds it created as it bore through walls, furniture, and an occasional zombie. Based upon the ruckus, he estimated that it was heading for the main keep, the largest and second tallest building of the castle. The moment James ascertained its location he rushed onward, for he could already hear his fellow children climbing up the wall in pursuit. Leaping onto an adjacent rooftop, he dropped through an open window and back into the castle. After several turns, he found himself somewhere in the middle of the keep. He could hear the machine two stories above him. Climbing several flights of stairs, he reached a long hall, made a right, and found himself in the massive throne room. At the other end of the room, right beside the throne was the machine, finally halted. The monkey was busily fiddling with its engine.

Adelle threw open the door of the coach and fell out onto the ground in a dizzy heap.

"That was the worst experience of my life!" she moaned.

James could hear the zombie children approaching in the distance. He had to get her out of there. The monkey also heard the commotion. He tried feverishly to get the machine going again, but was only met by the complaining of sputtering gears.

"James!" Adelle called out in surprise. "What's happening?"

James quickly rushed over to her and helped her to her feet. "We've got to get out of here!" he said. "An army has taken over the castle!"

"That can't be!" said Adelle. "The castle is invincible!"

"That's not the half of it. The toymaker you were going to meet, he's evil! He can only mean you harm!"

"How can you say such things? Mr. Damond is a very good man. He would never hurt a soul!"

"That is perfectly correct." said Jakob Damond.

Both of the children turned in surprise. The toymaker was standing beside them. Taking off his hat, he gave each of them a cordial bow.

"Forgive me for all of these mishaps," said the toymaker. "But I'm afraid there are some rather unpleasant characters afoot. It appears that the castle has been infested by a legion of zombie children."

"Zombies?" said Adelle. "You mean dead people who get up and walk around? My mother told me stories of such creatures! She said they stumbled about and slobbered all the time and that if I wasn't good they would come and eat my brains!"

"Well then all the more reason to get you out of here!" James shouted, grabbing her hand.

But the toymaker had been eyeing James suspiciously.

"Wait a minute, you're no ordinary boy!" he said.

"Come on!" said James to Adelle. "We've got to get away!"

"What are you talking about?" Adelle demanded, trying to pull James back.

"You've got to listen to me!" Jakob Damond shouted. "That's no boy! It's a zombie!"

Adelle stopped and looked at James. James looked back, a tinge of fear flickering across his face. In the background, the machine suddenly sputtered to life. Encouraged, the monkey took hold of one of the knives James had dropped and began to sneak around the group.

"But that's ridiculous!" said Adelle. "He's not a zombie! He's too smart and nice!"

"And deceitful! I don't know what his game is, but I'm telling you the truth. I know a zombie when I see one, and that there is a zombie!"

Suddenly, the monkey rushed toward them from behind, brandishing the knife. Before James could react, the monkey lunged at him and sunk the blade deep into his back. It passed clean through and burst out of the boy's chest. Adelle cupped her mouth and screamed.

For a brief moment, James stood there, stunned. But then all of his senses snapped together with a rush. He spun around with lightning speed and hit the monkey with such force that it flew across the room. The monkey managed to catch onto a chandelier in mid air and drop to the ground, only slightly dazed.

James turned back to look at the toymaker and Adelle. It wasn't until then that it dawned upon him. The knife was still lodged inside of him, the blade protruding from his chest. Adelle was so shocked and horrified she had fallen to her knees. Suddenly he felt unclean. Contorting his hand behind his back, he ripped out the knife and threw it from him.

"Look at the creature!" said Jakob Damond. "He isn't hurt at all! And why? Because he isn't alive! He's a rotting corpse!"

Adelle burst into sobs. James could see the fear in her eyes. Fear of him. James cringed with self-loathing. He wished he could die. To die right then and be gone from there. But he wasn't allowed even that luxury.

It was then that the others arrived. Smashing doors and shattering windows, they flooded into the room from all angles. The monkey brought the machine sharply around and headed straight for the middle of the room. He pressed a button and the front of the contraption opened like a mouth. Before James could react, the contraption scooped Adelle off of the ground and once again swallowed her inside the coach. By then the zombie children had already reached the center of the room and were swarming around it. James vaulted into the air and grabbed onto the rafters. Several of the others followed after him.

As for the toymaker, he casually passed through the crowd without a care in the world. They seemed to be unconsciously avoiding him like a boulder in the midst of a foaming river. He strolled out of the room, heading upstairs.

The machine made several circles, flattening a weaving path of squished zombie children. At the same time, James had been tackled by several of the children and the lot of them fell from the rafters in a giant tangle of writhing bodies. They landed squarely on top of the machine as it maneuvered through the crowd. The monkey tried to fend them off, but was overwhelmed. He lost control of the craft and before he could stop it, one of the children had kicked the accelerator lever and the machine's rockets were sent into full throttle. The machine was launched toward the far wall and exploded through it. With a shower of bricks, the group of zombie children who had been on top of the machine found themselves hurtling into the twilight sky. An endless abyss of nothingness stretched out before them. The monkey had likewise been thrown from his perch and was floating some distance ahead. James twisted about in midair just in time to watch as the machine rocketed, into the horizon, quickly lost in the misty haze. Gradually, their horizontal velocity dissipated. With shrieks and screams, they began to fall, hurtling into the inky darkness below them.

*   *   *

The toymaker climbed out onto the roof of the tallest tower and looked out over the misty expanse surrounding the now burning castle. Smiling to himself, he began to whistle a happy little tune.

"Who the (many colorful expletives) are you?" Deadwick screamed, climbing after him. "You've ruined absolutely everything! My boss is going to have you melted into goo when I tell him how you've meddled with our plans!"

"What's that?" said Jakob Damond, spotting the goblin as it stumbled beside him. "Silly fellow, I've ruined nothing."

"The princess has escaped, I've lost who knows how many kids, and some of them are even fighting me! I bet that's your doing!"

"My, it's a beautiful night." said the toymaker, looking out over the moonlit cloudscape. "I do so love this world."

"And there goes your monkey. I can see him falling into the abyss with a bunch of my kids."

"He can take care of himself."

"Arggh! If you don't quit with that mindless optimism, I'll tear that smile off you face and make you eat it!"

"You need to calm down, good fellow. All the things you've been scheming will work out in due time."

"Due time just came and went, you idiot! It's all over now!"

"On the contrary," said the toymaker, as he straightened his hat and turned to descend the stairs. "It's only just begun."

Marloth

PART 3

Nighttime. It was very dark. The moon and stars were shrouded in cloud, and the city had few streetlamps. But there were several lights moving about the orphanage, both inside and out. These were the lamps of men; men who are searching the orphanage grounds.

"I found someone!" a voice called out from the yard at the side of the house. The voice was answered by other voices, and before long the lights drew toward the side yard. There, lying on the ground, was a boy. He was unconscious. His body was covered in scrapes and bruises, and limbs were arranged at slightly unnatural angles. From the dew on his skin, he must have been there for some time.

A man stepped to the front of the group. It was Doctor Hurley. "It's James!" he said. "He's one of the orphans!" He kneeled beside the boy and began to examine him critically.

"He is badly injured." said the doctor. "We need a stretcher."

As two of the men set out to procure a stretcher, the doctor noticed something lying on the ground beside the boy. It was a book. Without anyone noticing, the doctor took the object and tucked it into his coat.

A stretcher was soon brought and before long, James was being carried out of the yard and onto the street. In the middle of the street was a carriage with two men standing beside it. The stretcher, Doctor Hurley, and one other man somehow were squeezed into the carriage. As the carriage set off, James was jostled about in the stretcher, causing him to moan and thrash about. He cried out something about a princess being in danger.

"Don't worry about a thing." said the doctor to James. "We're taking you to a place where you can leave all of the pain and confusion behind."

Deep within the farthest reaches of the most devious of minds, there was a room. It was a narrow, dingy room with a tall ceiling. Its only source of light was a small upper window through which a narrow beam of light managed to trickle. Within this room there was a little boy. He was just waking up from a long, dark dream.

He groggily opened his eyes; he was having a hard time detaching his mind and body from sleep. After a time, he forced himself up with his elbows so that his head was just raised enough to look around. The room was relatively empty aside for the sink and toilet near the bed. There was also a mirror across the room in which he could see a bewildered little boy staring back at him. In the distance, he could hear what sounded like muffled moans and an occasional scream. There were many people around him, just beyond the walls. Tormented people. But he only half heard and half saw any of this. For the most part, his mind was clouded by fading dreams, both good and ill, but mostly ill. As he looked about the room, he had a growing apprehension that he ought to be very scared, and that even though he currently was not scared in the slightest, it would be only a matter of time before the emotion caught up to him in full. He was in a foreboding place, with foreboding memories clinging to him. The sort of memories people try to forget.

He clumsily climbed out of bed. He felt as though he hadn't used his feet in ages. Carefully, he hobbled over to the mirror for a closer look. It was large enough that it covered most of the wall, and there were a few cracks running along it diagonally, greatly distorting the room he saw through it. He raised his hand and waved at the boy. The boy waved back. He began to hop up and down. The boy likewise, hopped up and down. And yet something was telling him that they weren't quite the same. For one thing, he just couldn't imagine himself making the sort of face the other boy was. It was too . . . well . . . *wicked*.

Suddenly, the reflection lunged forward. *"BOO!"*

The boy screamed. The scream of a child who has woken up from a nightmare only to find that it is still the dead of night, and that morning is a long, long way away. Except in this case, the morning was more than far off. He knew it would never come. All around him, people beyond the room joined in with his screams, forming a numbing chorus of shrieks and wailing that flooded his ears and forced him to the ground. He could take no more. Now he knew where he was.

The Asylum. He was mad.

The door flew open and a young woman dressed as a nurse rushed into the room. She took one look at the boy and then put her arms around him, trying desperately to comfort him. He was shaking so violently he was near convulsions, and his screams had grown hoarse as though the life was being ripped out of him by some unseen force. The nurse held him and wiped the sweat from his brow, whispering to him soothingly. Finally, he seemed to run out of energy and went limp, nearly passing out in her arms. Still writhing about weakly, he was carried over to the bed and carefully laid on his back.

Before long, a man came hurrying through the door and took in the scene critically. James was not certain, but he thought the man looked familiar.

"He's awake!" said the man.

The nurse nodded. She backed away toward the wall and the man stepped over to the bed.

The boy was tossing his head back and forth, his eyes half closed. "Get me away from here!" he moaned.

"James!" the man said sternly. "It's all right! You're awake!"

The boy looked back at the mirror. The reflection boy smiled and waved to him, a sinister gleam in his eye. Somehow he had acquired a wicked looking knife, and was casually holding it in his other hand.

"He's going to kill me!" James screamed.

The nurse turned to look at where James was staring. She didn't see anything but the cell wall.

"There, there, James," said the man. "We're here with you. Whatever happens, we will do everything in our power to protect you."

The nurse motioned toward the man and whispered something into his ear. The man nodded and whispered several words in return. The nurse looked shocked, and then resigned. She left the room and soon reappeared with a tray laden with several metal instruments. The doctor took up one of the objects, a syringe, and then took a small vial from inside his coat pocket. The vial was filled with a green liquid. The doctor shook it, and the liquid began to glow, weakly illuminating the room and turning their faces pale green. Filling the syringe with the vial's contents, he grabbed hold of James and emptied the syringe into his arm.

The whole room began to become green and hazy. It looked like everything was underwater; thick, phosphorescent water. The man and the nurse began to move slowly and shakily toward the door, as though time was being rewound and sped up erratically.

"Don't leave me with him!" James moaned.

The man looked back and said something. His voice reverberated in the distance, so thick with echoes as to make them unintelligible. Before the door had closed behind them, the green had completely enveloped the place, and then faded into nothing.

*   *   *

Adelle opened her eyes and looked about her. It was so bright she was nearly blinded. The sun was filling the sky with golden light. She squinted to the east, where the sun was already setting. Or was it the moon? The color of the sky kept shifting; she could not tell if it was morning or evening.

She stretched out on her bed and tried to focus on the sky above her. That was funny—she had never been able to see the sky from her bedroom before. And what was more, her bedroom had never been so unstable. Her bed was rocking back and forth.

"Ahoy Matey!" shouted Samantha.

Adelle sat up in surprise. The dolls were there on her bed! And the bed, as it turned out, was in the middle of the sea. Suddenly, every muscle in her body tensed and she clung to the mattress for dear life.

"Samantha!" Miss Perrywinkle scolded. "You speak as though you were a primitive!"

"But that's the sort of thing one is supposed to say when one is out at sea." said Samantha. "I even read it in a book once."

"You're making things up again!" said Miss Perrywinkle.

"Well if you don't believe me, look at this! The book is right here!"

The doll reached over the edge of the bed and pulled a book out of the water.

"Now that's what I call a coincidence!" said Miss Perrywinkle, taking the book.

"Not really." said Samantha. "Probably just about every book must be out here."

And she may have been right. The sea was strewn with hundreds of books, casually floating along the surface.

"What are we doing here?" Adelle said with a strong pitch of urgency.

"What do you think?" said Samantha. "We're sailing!"

"But where's my bedroom? Where is the castle?"

"It's hard to say." said Mrs. Gingersmile, who was baiting a fishing rod with a candy cane. "I think it exploded."

"We're very fortunate really." said Miss Perrywinkle. "It's a miracle that we are safe."

"Safe?" said Adelle. She was staring at the water suspiciously. Or was it water? The more she looked at the stuff, the less it looked like water. It was too wispy and rose up and down too much.

"Are we in the sea, or are we floating on the clouds?" asked Adelle.

"I'll go with both." said Samantha.

Adelle gathered her courage and reached her hand into the water. It was the strangest sensation. It was too thick to be clouds. She cupped her hands and was able to lift some of it into her bed. Yet it was too light to be water. Most of the stuff was caught in the breeze and blown from her hand, and yet even as it was dissipating through the air, it still caught the sunlight and glittered just as water would.

Miss Perrywinkle closed the book and waved it at Samantha. "I can't find any passage in this book that talks about the sea!"

"I'll show you!" said Samantha, taking the book and sitting beside her.

"Look, the swan is back!" said Mrs. Gingersmile.

As she spoke, the swan glided toward them and landed in the cloud water beside the bed.

"Ah, she's awake!" said the swan. "It was about time. I was beginning to wonder if she wasn't under a spell."

"No spells." said Mrs. Gingersmile. "What did you see? Any sign of land?"

"No, I saw no land. But I did come across a few people here and there."

"Anyone interesting?"

"They're all interesting. Downright mad, for the most part. As are most people outside of the castle."

"But we're outside of the castle!"

"Ah yes. That is why I said most people. We, of course, are the exception."

"But that's ridiculous!" said Adelle. "If that were so, then the castle would be like an asylum turned inside out!"

"Come to think of it, there was that zombie child." said Mrs. Gingersmile. "He was inside the castle, and he was clearly mad."

"What zombie—" Adelle began, but was cut off by Samantha.

"Look!" she said. "There's a toad out there!"

Sure enough, a toad wearing a tweed jacket and thick glasses was swimming about the sea of clouds, feverishly collecting the books and piling them onto a small desk that was likewise floating in the water. The pile was already several yards tall, and was swaying about precariously.

"A toad! I'm sure he would be loads of fun to converse with!" said Miss Perrywinkle. "Say, Mr. Toad!" she called out. "Why don't you tarry a bit and relate to us your business!"

The toad looked up for a moment with a slightly startled expression and then went back to his work, muttering something derogatory about a bed full of women.

"Never mind then." said Miss Perrywinkle. "Clearly he has no sense of manners."

"Here it is!" said Samantha, pointing at the open book. "Here's the passage about the sea! See right here? The doll says 'Ahoy mate!'"

Miss Perrywinkle looked at the book. "You're right! She does say 'Ahoy mate!'"

"And see here? She says it again!" said Samantha. "And then another doll says it on the next line!"

"Well." said Miss Perrywinkle. "You're a good deal sharper than I give you credit for."

Adelle leaned over their shoulders and looked at the book curiously. It looked familiar.

The clock struck 10 o'clock. The nurse promptly closed the book. Her break was over and it was time for her to make her rounds among the patients.

*   *   *

James groggily opened his eyes as best he could, but his vision was too dark and blurred to make anything out. He tried to move, but he could hardly feel the rest of his body. He suspected that he was in a bed. Not the nicest bed he had slept on, but he was in no condition to care.

That was the strangest thing: he didn't care. He could never recall being in such a state. He had always been deeply concerned about *something.* For once, he had no idea where he was, or what was happening, and he didn't care. Nothing mattered anymore. Was he dead? Who cared.

He liked it. He felt invincible. For once, no one could mess with him. No one could hurt him. After all, what could they do to him? Any vulnerability had been killed. He was finally free from it all.

After a time, possibly minutes, possibly hours, the gloom opened up and a figure appeared. Some faint talking sounds came from the crack of light, and then it was engulfed by the darkness and he was left alone with the new figure.

"Hello, James." The voice echoed hollowly and seemed to come from far away, even though James was sure that it was coming from the figure beside him, who looked to be close.

Hmm. It speaks. Thought James. *Perhaps it does tricks too.*

"How are you feeling?" asked the voice.

I suppose it wants me to say something. Stupid figure thing.

"Do you remember me?" asked the voice.

No.

"Do you remember anything?"

No. Thankfully.

The figure looked to be paused deep in thought.

"The drugs are working almost too well."

Not if I can still see you.

The figure lowered several feet. Perhaps it had pulled up a chair and sat down.

"You spoke a good deal in your sleep," it said. "Dreadful, really. I can't imagine where a boy of your age would have ever acquired such horrific ideas. Zombie children and the most gruesome acts of violence. I wish I knew what happened back in that orphanage. Nobody seems to know."

Orphanage?

"But that's all behind you. Now, I know you and I have had our differences in the past, but Edward was a good friend, and I feel responsible to do everything within my power to help you."

James suddenly recognized the figure. It was Doctor Hurley!

"But I have to warn you, it's going to mean giving up a few things that I know you've clung to in the past. But it will be worth it."

The doctor looked at his watch.

"I wish I could talk to you more, but I need to check on another of my projects. Before I go, there is one question I would like to ask you. Has anyone gone out of his way to save your life?"

James thought about that for a moment and then shook his head. Of late most people had been trying to achieve the opposite.

"Thank you." said the doctor, and then he left James to himself.

*   *   *

Somewhere in the swirling mists of Marloth, just at the crest of a setting sun, there was a bed, floating along the clouds as though it were on the sea. It was an elegant bed, with golden posts rising from each corner, and a large headboard across the top on which was engraved an elaborate depiction of an ocean shore. The bed was lined with embroidered linens and pillows. In the middle of the bed a little girl was curled up and sleeping peacefully.

All about the bed were flitting little lights which, if you looked more closely, would have turned out to be fairies. The fairies were very excited, and were carrying on a conversation that went something like this:

"What is it?"

"It is hard to say. Everything looks so similar when they are asleep."

"I think it must be an angel!"

"Do not be silly! It is a girl!"

"A girl? Like us?"

"No, this is a real *girl! I know it! I saw a picture of one in a book!"*

"You mean she is really real*? She can actually do things?"*

"Yes! She is made from the earth! She is like a woman, but smaller."

"Oh, yes, I remember now! I have *heard about them! And see that object on her head? That means she is a princess!"*

"How wonderful! This is a day to be remembered!"

And the bed continued on. Presently the fairies began to drop out of sight. Night was falling, and they were growing sleepy. (Though where the fairies sleep, only they know.) The shadows thickened. Here and there through the fog could be caught glimpses of buildings and people, all of which were staring at the girl curiously before sinking back into the mist. No longer was she in a world held together by things like longitude and latitude, but by mere ideas. It was impossible to tell whether the mist hid land and mass, or if there was nothing behind it at all. And in a way, it did not really matter; all that mattered was that anything *could be behind it, for this was not a world of actualities, but of possibilities.*

The bed gradually followed the current under a low bridge that crossed the mist.* As the bed passed underneath, a small carriage paused atop the bridge and an elegant woman peered down at the boat. She made a comment to no one in particular, and then motioned for the coachman to continue on his way.

A few zombie children swam out to the bed, but were eaten by alligators before they could reach it.

The nurse flipped back several pages and looked at what she had read the evening before. That was strange, from the best she could tell he had written two versions of the same scene. She wanted to read more but she heard the doctor approaching and she was sure he would not be happy if he found her reading that book. Besides, it was almost time for her rounds again.

*   *   *

---

*Although, considering that the mist was not simply below the bridge but everywhere around it, saying it crossed the mist is not entirely accurate.

The tragedy of Life.   Everyone, at one point or another, is dropped in the middle of it.   They all try to cope with it one way or another.   The popular choice is denial.   Fortunately for these people, there's a whole world created just for their amusement.

It's affectionately called the Asylum.

Each one of its residents is an individual.   Each one of them is special.   Each one of them is a separate reality unto itself.   And each one is equally true.   So walking the halls of the Asylum can be likened to exploring an interdimensional observatory.   Not one of these worlds conflict with each other, because none of them interact with each other.   And all of this is made possible by the wonderful invention of the prison cell.   But only a narrow-minded person indeed would call such a place a prison.   It is an environment where people can freely express themselves with no negative results.   A place where their expressions are not imprisoned by such outmoded ideas as reality.   This expression takes many forms.

When the nurse entered James' room, he was huddled in the corner, shouting at the wall.

"Good morning!" she said.   James grew quiet and glanced at her warily.   She looked far too young and pretty to be in such a place. "I've brought you some breakfast." she continued.   She set down the tray she was carrying on the bedside and watched for a moment in the hope that he would somehow respond.

"It may not be the most nourishing, or even the most tasty, but I'm sure you're starving."

James looked at the tray.   He was starving.   His insides felt hollow and shriveled.   Like a machine, he awkwardly walked over to the bed, sat down, and began to eat.

The nurse sat down beside him on the bed.   James just ignored her.

"I remember you," she said.

James looked up at her, puzzled.   He did not recall seeing her before.   He returned to his eating.

"You know, when you were here before."

Now he stopped, and did not start again. "Before?"

"Yes. You were so little; I didn't know they put people so young in here."

"I don't remember."

"Well, it was a long time ago."

"I don't remember anything."

The nurse seemed to look off as though she were seeing beyond the walls and into a more beautiful world.

"I used to hate working here. This is not the place for the hopeful cases. This is not the place people come to get better. Many of our patients are violent, or shout perverse and horrible things to me. We have patients who are in constant torment, and there is so little I can do to help. And much of what the doctors do, and require me to do, has greatly troubled my heart. I fear we are more villain than healer. If I could have left, I would have, but times were hard and I had nowhere to go. So I stayed, all the while cursing my existence. Until the day you left. That day changed my life."

Then she checked herself and smiled reassuringly at James. "Not to say that it was *because* you left. On the contrary, I missed you more than words can express. Everyone here is so hardened. You were different. You were a little child. You were fragile. Every day you would cry and cry. Nothing would make you stop except for fitful sleep. They said you had all sorts of mental disorders, and that it was hopeless. There was nothing we could do."

James returned to his eating. He wasn't fragile anymore. He had made sure of that. No one was going to mess with him anymore. He was invincible.

"Then one day, a man came to the Asylum. He was a tall, kind looking man. I don't know where he came from, or even on what business he was allowed into the Asylum, but he must have had some sort of authority, for my employers told me to take him to your cell and let him talk to you. I did as I was instructed, and when we arrived in this same room, you were in that same corner, except then you were moaning and screaming. When the man saw you, he looked sad, and yet there still remained a glow to his countenance. Then, he reached into his coat and pulled out a large, weathered book, and gave it to you.

"I can't begin to express how your eyes came to life and your face brightened. Then he picked you up in his arms and carried you out of the place. He may have had the authority to take you. He may not have. Somehow, I wasn't worried about that. All I had to do was look at that man's face, and I knew you were in far better hands than anyone could ever find."

The nurse shook her head. "My recounting doesn't do the scene justice. I can't even explain why, but I never looked at life the same way since."

She reached over and gave James a gentle hug. James had stopped eating again, and didn't move at all. The nurse rose to her feet and moved toward the door. Before she left the room, she turned back to James and smiled again.

"We could use more men like that in this world." she said, and then closed the door behind her.

*   *   *

Somewhere in the City of Orphans there was an open square. In the middle of the square, there was a bed. In the middle of the bed there was a little girl, curled up and sleeping peacefully. She was very beautiful, and there was a crown on her head.

Around the bed were many creatures. Some were human. Most were children. A few were beasts from myth and legend.

One of the bystanders was a goblin. He motioned for the children to grab her but none of them acknowledged him. They were too captivated by this angel who had descended to them from the heavens.

The girl began to stir. The crowd began to disperse. Except for the goblin. He railed for his children to come back. But they didn't, and once he was the only bystander remaining, he likewise disappeared into the labyrinth of streets.

The girl yawned, stretched, and sat up drowsily. After she had rubbed the sand from her eyes and opened them, she found herself in a sprawling city. She suddenly felt very self-conscious and pulled the covers more closely over her. She was in public view, wearing nothing but her nightgown! After the initial shock passed and her awareness settled on the square around her, she realized that there was no other person in sight. She was alone.

At first she was overwhelmed by apprehension, though the longer she sat there it was slowly replaced by curiosity. There was not much light where she was, but there was a great deal of light further ahead in the city. And noise. There must be something big and exciting taking place. Possibly even many big and exciting things all at once.

And that's when it really dawned on her; she was outside the castle! Out in the real world! She was free! This was her golden opportunity to see the world—she wasn't about to spend another moment of it sitting in her bed!

Cautiously, she slipped out of the covers and onto the cobbled surface of the street. Despite her newfound sense of freedom, she felt vulnerable with just her nightgown, so she took one of sheets from the bed and wrapped it around her. Thus attired, she embarked down one of the streets.

It was very dark in her part of the city. A full moon cast its beams through an opening in the clouds overhead, and the street was dotted with lamplight. But any place beyond the rays of these light sources was pure black. There were far more shadows hiding about than ordinary nighttime should be capable of.

Adelle didn't mind. She set off down an avenue and was practically floating along the cobbled streets. All about her, pleasant music could be heard being played from who knew where. At first she didn't see any other people but, as if the City were gradually growing accustomed to this new princess in its midst, she began to come across more and more people. People who were laughing and swapping tales and having a grand time. And children! Many children, every one of them running about and playing games, though oddly never on the section of street she was on. It was as if she were walking through a series of tableaux, or a haunting memory that was only to be witnessed. Part of Adelle wanted to interact with them, but part of her was also fearful. She felt so out of place, walking about in her sheet and nightgown. For now she was content simply being an observer of this new world.

The further she went, the more fantastic the sights became. Occasionally, two men would draw their swords and have a duel on a rooftop. Or an ogre would lumber by, towing a cart piled so high with goods that a person could have stepped atop of it from a second story window. And then there were the fairies. Throughout the City could be seen the glowing trails of pixie dust as they flitted about the city, causing who knows what sort of mischief. Every now and then, one would fly right up to Adelle's face and look at her curiously. Adelle could feel the warm yellow light radiating from the tiny creature, and it was very soothing.

Every now and then Adelle would see a billboard advertising some fancy new product that everyone ought to buy. Most of them advertised clothes, especially girls' clothes. It looked like most of the female articles were modeled by the same person. The model was very beautiful and Adelle couldn't help feeling a tad bit envious, especially considering her present wardrobe.

Suddenly Adelle did a double take. It was Ivy! She was the person in the billboards! Adelle had always thought that Ivy was pretty, but she had never seen her so glamorously presented.

She was staring at this revelation in amazement when she was suddenly disoriented by a flash of light so intense she felt like she had just stared into the sun. Adelle turned dizzily to see a short, greenish creature. It didn't have any eyes, but it did have razor sharp teeth and a magical device in its hands. The creature held up the device and there was another flash.

"What *are* you?" Adelle asked. But the creature didn't hear her. Adelle didn't know that Query Gremlins can only hear answers to questions.

"So what brings the princess heir of Marloth to the illustrious City of Orphans?" asked the gremlin, as it again flashed her with its device. (That was its means of seeing.)

Adelle thought this rather rude, but she didn't want to follow in like manner, so she took the higher path and replied, "I am here to see and experience the many wonders of Marloth."

"What do you think of the City of Orphans so far?" This question came from behind her. Adelle turned to see another Query Gremlin. She opened her mouth to speak but was interrupted by yet another question, this time from a gremlin to her left. More and more Query Gremlins were appearing around her. And more flashes from magical devices. She was sure she was going permanently blind from all the explosions of light.

"I asked my question first!" said one of the gremlins. Which, of course, none of the other gremlins heard. This didn't prevent them from spiraling into a fierce argument. The deluge of questions made it impossible for Adelle to answer every one of them, and there is nothing a gremlin hates more than an unanswered question. One of them grabbed Adelle by the arm. Then another gremlin grabbed the other arm. Pulling ensued. And more flashes.

Suddenly, Adelle was lifted into the air, wrenched from their grip, and thrown backwards. She floated through the air at a furious pace before being dropped inside an open coach on a street that was a level above the street she had been on. She landed beside a tall, austere woman who was looking at her with cold calculation.

"What in the world do you think you were doing?" asked the woman.

"Excuse me ma'am, but I truly don't know! I don't normally fly through the air like that! I swear!"

"Not that! I'm talking about those infernal creatures! You were feeding them!"

"You must be mistaken. I have no food with me. What could I have possibly been feeding them?"

"Information, for one thing. Query Gremlins only do two things with little girls: ask them questions, or eat them. Once they had finished with the former, they would have proceeded to the latter."

"They were going to eat me?"

The woman rolled her eyes and motioned for the driver, a little gnome with a coachman's cap larger than his head, to set off. He gave the reins a good tug and the two emus that were harnessed to the coach lunged forward, catapulting the coach along with them.

Adelle looked at her clothes. The sheet had been torn from her by the gremlins, and her nightgown was in considerable disarray. She felt more uncomfortable than ever, but she was the daughter of the King, and she was determined to maintain whatever shred of decency she could muster.

"I am Princess Adelle." she said as pleasantly as she could manage. "Who are you?"

"What is a princess like you doing in the City of Orphans all alone?" the woman asked.

Adelle paused for a moment, trying to maintain her composure. "I'm trying to get a taste of life. Learn all I can about this fascinating place. See the wonders of the world!"

"Good Author of Everything!" the woman moaned. "You should just be grateful I got a hold of you when I did! You are evidently even more clueless than you look!"

"What do you mean?"

"You think this is a pleasant, happy little fairytale world? Well I'm sorry to burst your bubble, your highness. This is the dregs of insanity! This is Marloth! Welcome to Hell."

She certainly is the most disagreeable of women! Adelle thought to herself. *I wouldn't be surprised if she can't get out of bed each morning without having some poor soul to spank!*

It was then that she noticed the two children sitting behind them, a boy and a girl.

"Who are they?" Adelle asked.

"My children." said the woman. "The little devils."

Adelle thought they looked rather disheveled and sickly. Each of them was holding an armload of toys and candy, and both of them were glaring at her in unison.

And those are certainly the most disagreeable of children! Adelle noted as she sat back in her chair and looked straight ahead.

"Where are we going?" she asked.

"Why, to the Theatre. I own it. I am the Lady Mediev, Keeper of the Fine and Mysterious Artes. I own most of the more elegant establishments here in the City of Orphans. While the rest of this city tries to sink into the mud, I try to bring a little culture to the world."

As she spoke, one of the children leaned forward with a stick and poked Adelle viciously.

"Ow!" said Adelle.

The Lady Mediev turned to look at her children and frowned. "Now now, my dears. You really shouldn't bother royalty. They're liable to go and have you executed."

"You make me out to be some kind of monster!" said Adelle. "I wouldn't go about executing people! I believe in kindness and consideration! Besides, I—"

The Lady Mediev motioned for silence. "We're all monsters!" she said, and then smiled, pinching each of her children on the cheek whimsically. "Aren't we, now?"

The children smiled with her, and then one of them chucked a toy at a gawking passerby.

The streets were rather haphazardly thrown together, rising up and down and crisscrossing like a labyrinthian roller coaster track. The strangest thing about it was that the streets genuinely appeared to be moving and changing course around them, shifting from one side of a building to another, suddenly deciding to double back against themselves, or throw themselves across one of the many canals. Yet the coachman proved to be a brilliant driver, and before long they came to a magnificent structure at the edge of the main waterway. There were several barges making their way across the water to the Theatre, and crowds of people were scurrying along the streets and into the Theatre.

As they drew nearer and Adelle saw the crowds of people, a new fear struck her. "I can't go to a play dressed like this!"

The Lady looked at her—something she hadn't done in some time. "While it's not the most amazing dress I've ever seen, I'm afraid it will have to do, your Highness."

Adelle was shocked by such a callous display, and was about to further protest when her eyes looked downward. She was no longer wearing her nightgown. Instead, she was clothed in an exquisite dress of a deep ruby hue.

"Where did this—I wasn't wearing—Did you—"

"The main entrance is far too crowded," said the coachmen. "Even with my sharpest wheels, there's no way we'll be able to get through them."

"Then take us to the top." said the Lady Mediev. The coachman nodded grimly and motioned for the emus to make a sharp turn. After winding their way up one street after another, Adelle realized they were heading back toward the Theatre, but this time at a far higher level of the city. The carriage tottered along a twisting street that wound high into the air and finally connected with the top of the Theatre. The coach rode onto the roof and came to a halt. There were several more emus on the roof, all of them wandering about and grazing on tile. Several of these migrated to the side of the coach and formed a stairway for its occupants to descend.

"Welcome to the Theatre of Fine and Mysterious Artes!" said the coachman, who had dropped to the ground and bowed.

With the coachman at the lead, the group made its way down-stairs and into a spacious entry room filled with crowds of people all trying to get into the Theatre. The din was nearly overwhelming for Adelle; she had never heard so much sound in her life. As they followed the coachman again, he led them through a maze of halls and passageways. The further they went, the louder the din became. When they finally emerged out onto a balcony that overlooked the Theatre, the commotion was so deafening that Adelle felt as though the air itself was pressing against her. She couldn't hear herself think, much less imagine how so many people could be attempting conversation in such a state. The Lady did not seem affected by the noise. Her attention was on the rows of seats that lined the balcony and to the people who were occupying them. Several well-dressed men and women rose to greet her as they approached.

"Allow me to introduce Princess Adelle." said the Lady, motioning to Adelle. "She will be staying at my manor for the next few days."

"I am?" said Adelle in surprise, though no one seemed to hear her.

"That's splendid news!" said one of the gentlemen. "It has been far too long since we have had royalty stay here in the City."

"Yes," said one of the ladies. "It was beginning to look like the royal family thought they were too good for us. Especially the King."

"May he rest in peace." said a second gentleman.

"What?" Adelle exclaimed.

"There's someone I would like you to meet," said the Lady Mediev. "You've already met my younger children; my eldest is right over here." Just beyond the group of adults there were several girls seated and talking with great energy.

"Princess Adelle, allow me to introduce my eldest daughter, Ivy."

Ivy spotted Adelle and abruptly rose from the middle of her conversation with an enthusiastic exclamation of "Adelle!" She went over and hugged the princess. "It's so good to see you again! I had no idea you would be coming to the City so soon!" She paused and stared at Adelle curiously. "You look so much older."

Adelle was struggling to keep up. "The Lady Mediev is your mother?" Ivy's countenance shriveled as she looked over at the Lady and said "That's what they say." There was an awkward pause before Ivy rallied herself. "But what does that matter? What's important is that one of the greatest plays ever is about to begin. We've all been waiting months for it to be released."

"What's it about?" asked Adelle.

One of the children Ivy had been talking to—a chubby girl with curly hair—said, "Don't you know anything? This is 'Deminox Farinoi', 'The Darke Dream'! The whole world has been waiting for this evening!"

"Not the whole world." said Adelle. "This is the first I've heard of it."

The children were taken aback. "I always knew royalty was a little sheltered, but not that much!" said one of the girls.

"How many plays have you been to?" asked the chubby girl.

"This is my first." A few of the girls backed away from Adelle.

"Who cares about the past?" said Ivy. "Now Adelle is here and will be able to see it with the rest of us." She gave Adelle a reassuring look. "I'm sure you'll love it!" She squeezed Adelle's hand and then said "It's strange, but I had a feeling you were in the City; I had just figured it must be fancy."

She looked like she was going to say more when everyone started to return to their seats and the Lady Mediev motioned for her to be quiet saying, "There will be more time to talk later. The play is starting!"

Once Adelle had been seated, she took her first real look at the inside of the Theatre. It was huge. Cavernous. The ceiling rose far above them, and endless rows of seats curved out in both directions below her. To her surprise, nearly all of the audience members she could distinguish were children. Well that was encouraging. She had been made nervous by the Lady and her views, causing Adelle to wonder if the play would be just as stuffy. But all of the children Adelle could see appeared very excited, and she was certain that whatever was showing would be designed with their young tastes in mind.

The story revolved around a group of children that wandered into an abandoned orphanage and found themselves trapped inside by a cruel and odious undead hunter by the name of Edward Tralvorkemen. The undead hunter proceeded to systematically track down the zombie children through the orphanage and exterminate them. While he was not as agile as them, he was equipped with an array of deadly weapons and devices to assist in his genocide, and the orphanage itself was filled with booby traps. But in the end, the few remaining zombie children were able to catch him in one of his own traps and escape.

It took Adelle some time to realize that they were not ordinary children in the story, but were actually zombies. At first she was shocked by the fact, but after seeing the way the undead hunter would gleefully ignore their pleas for mercy and dispatch them in gruesome ways, she found herself increasingly sympathetic to the poor creatures. By the end when the man was slashed to pieces by his own trap, Adelle was horrified, but also relieved. The nightmare was over and the children were free.

After the play had finished several people asked Adelle what she thought of it. She said she wasn't sure. Ivy recommended that Adelle see it a second time, and also said that what they had just seen was only the first part of two, and that the second part would be presented in a few weeks and that Adelle simply had to see it. Adelle replied that she would consider it.

Meanwhile, far above the audience, a maddened goblin was pummeling his head in frustration. *What were they thinking?* The princess was surrounded by his kids and they weren't doing a thing! Why wasn't she captured yet? Why weren't they at least hurting her?

As the play ended and the crowds began to file out of the auditorium, Deadwick decided he needed to deal with the princess himself. He waited at the back of the lobby and eventually the

Lady Mediev and several children appeared, one of them being the princess. As the owner of the establishment, the Lady was in no hurry to leave and began mingling with some of the more prominent members of the crowd. This left Adelle alone with the other girls and Ivy's younger siblings (their names were Phyllis and Loury). Deadwick moved in.

He stopped in front of the princess and bowed. "Good evening, your highness. I am Deadwick the goblin, an ambassador from the venerable doctor Otto Marrechian. Would you be so kind as to spare a few minutes of your time?"

Deadwick nearly put his hand to his mouth in shock. Did he just say all that? He didn't even know what some of those words meant!

Adelle gave him a polite smile. Even though Adelle was slightly put off by his unkempt appearance, she was impressed by his manners. "Yes. I should be able to afford a few minutes. What matter do you wish to speak of?"

"My master—I mean, my *boss*—is a dedicated philanthropist. In his efforts to benefit humanity, he has created a machine that . . . heals people. But so far it can only heal children. Otto has tried and tried to make it also work on adults, but with no success. I don't understand the details, but apparently you are the only person who can help him fix his machine so it can heal everyone. You are the key."

"I'm very flattered." said Adelle. "What would I need to do to assist him?"

"All my master—I mean, my *boss*—needs is for you to visit his laboratory. I could escort you there this very evening."

"This evening? I just arrived here today! No, I couldn't do it so soon. Perhaps in a few days. Or next week. I'm sure the doctor can wait that long."

"But—"

Ivy stepped forward. "She's already given you her answer, and your time is up."

Deadwick glared at Ivy. He knew who she was, and who her mother was. Adelle tried to smooth things out.

"I really would like to help your master, but if it means my leaving the City of Orphans, I already have prior engagements and am simply not free to go with you right now."

Deadwick stood there for a moment, smoldering. Enough of this. It was time to resort to tried and true violence. Deadwick reached for his gun.

And found himself standing outside the theater. He turned around in confusion and stared at the doorway behind him. Did he have a vague recollection of saying farewell to the princess and leaving? Yes, he did.

What was wrong with him? Was he going insane? He needed to barge back inside and take her captive!

But he didn't. Instead, he set off down the street, wondering why in the world he was doing it.

*   *   *

The Mediev Manor was not far from the Theatre, and this was where they eventually stopped for the night. It was agreed that it was too late to prepare a room for Adelle, but that she would sleep with Ivy. There was also talk of her attending school with Ivy as long as she was there. Adelle was hesitant about that idea, but the Lady insisted, and Ivy wanted it as well, so she said she would try at least one day of it.

Phyllis and Loury proved to be a handful, even for Ivy. She was constantly yelling at her siblings to give her space. At one point she locked the door to her room but they managed to climb in from one of the windows and proceeded to run around like little savages. Adelle thought this feat of gaining access to the room was rather impressive, but Ivy wasn't amused one bit and chased them around the house. It wasn't until the two pests finally ran out of energy and crashed in their respective rooms that Ivy and Adelle were really free to talk.

"You've shown me some of your toys, now I'd like to show you something of mine," said Ivy. She reached across the bed and grabbed two small objects of cloth.

"These two are my favorites!" she said. "They help me catch boys!"

Adelle looked at the stuffed creatures in puzzlement. They were both very pink, fuzzy, and round. Somehow they made her think of bunny rabbits even though they didn't have much in the way of ears. While she thought they were cute, from the little she had seen of boys, she could not imagine them being attracted to such things.

"I bought them at the toyshop." said Ivy. "Their names are Bipsy and Boppin."

Adelle said they were very cute and then, after Ivy showed Adelle several other of her things, (all of them very expensive), the girls proceeded to catching up on what had happened to each of them since they had last spoken, though for Adelle the details were surprisingly fuzzy. She couldn't even recall exactly how she had arrived at the City. But that didn't bother her.

They stayed up late into the night talking. Adelle wanted to know everything about life in the City of Orphans, and Ivy was happy to flaunt her knowledge of it. Adelle also felt more free to talk about boys with Ivy than with anyone else she knew. Adelle had caught a glimpse of Bobby at the Theatre, and she asked if he would be at school the next day. Ivy said he usually was. This intelligence both excited Adelle and made her even more nervous about the next morning. When she finally did fall asleep she had humiliating dreams of what her first day of school would be like.

*   *   *

In a back corner of a seedy bar somewhere within the City of Orphans, Deadwick the goblin was waiting for one of his many informants. Time passed. Deadwick drummed his fingers against the table impatiently.

Suddenly there was a shift in the light and the goblin's informant was sitting in front of him. The informant was a shade; a creature of the night that appeared as little more than an indistinct humanoid carved from blackness, gulping down a mug of beer.

"There you are." said Deadwick.

"There I've been." said the informant.

Deadwick muttered something indiscernible under his breath.

The informant continued draining its mug. "So what would you like to know?" it asked.

"What I want to know is why everything gets weird when the princess is around. Everyone starts acting funny. My kids don't do what they're told, I can't even touch her, people start using big words, so on and so on. It's getting ridiculous! Do you know anything about any of that?"

"Yes, I do. But that is particularly valuable information."

"Here, I'll give you six lollipops."

"Even more valuable than that."

"You're killing me! Okay, I'll throw in a handful of jawbreakers."

"Deal." The informant took the goods and they disappeared into shadow. Then he drew closer for the proper mode of divulging skullduggery.

"Earlier this evening I overheard an exchange betwixt a representative of the Wizard's Council and the Lady Mediev. Supposedly the Lady has a peculiar knack for spotting enchantments. The representative—he called himself Message—said the wizards knew there was some kind of spell surrounding the princess but they couldn't figure out what it was, and this Message fellow was demanding she tell him all about it. She plays dumb for a while, but he threatened a good deal, you know, the typical wizards 'we'll curse your bowels and burn your dog' kind of stuff. Apparently she is sort of a member of the Wizards Council herself but it's complicated since she's a dame, and she says they should go to hell and they say she needs to obey them and she says they should get haircuts and they say—well, you get the idea. So after more threatening and fuss she finally says the reason why the wizards have had such a hard time figuring out what the deal is with the princess is because there is not one, but *two* spells surrounding her, and those spells are mixing to strange effect. The first is an aura that protects her from evil."

"Like us." said the goblin.

"Right. It's basically a magical shield around her. The Lady said the princess got it from her parents, but she didn't say how. I never knew either of them to do any magic."

"You said there were two of them. What's the other one?"

"The other spell has to do with some kind of amulet. It's magical. She used a lot of fancy magic lingo that I didn't catch and you wouldn't have either, but I was able to gather that this amulet has something to do with making people fall head over heels for whoever wears it. She said it affects guys differently than girls."

"In what way?"

"She didn't go into detail there."

"Did she say what the amulet looked like?"

"No, except the girl must be wearing it most of the time."

"Every time I've seen the princess, she was wearing a crown. I bet that's the amulet."

"She's got a crown? Yeah, the crown might be the amulet, though I'd expect such a thing of power to be better hidden."

Deadwick scratched his gnarled chin pensively. "So whatever this amulet is, all we have to do is snatch it from her and that should deal with one problem. The only hitch would be making sure that whatever gets nicked is actually the amulet." Deadwick smiled wickedly. "Looks like the best means would be to completely strip her!"

"Taking it won't be that easy. From the way the Lady talked, it sounded like she wants the amulet as much as she wants the girl, but can't pinch it yet 'cause of both spells together. She said if it was only a matter of one or the other, she'd already have the amulet, but the two spells are an overwhelming combination. If the Lady can't take the amulet even with all her magic, you'll probably have an even harder time."

"Then what about the shield thing? Did she say how to get rid of that?"

"She said it could be chipped away. But she didn't say how. That was the limit to what Message's threatening could accomplish. At that point the Lady put her foot down and said she had given more than enough information and if the wizards still needed more than they should go find someone else to hold their hand. Then she did some threatening of her own. It was very entertaining."

"Is that all?"

"For you, yes."

"I don't think that was worth all that candy."

"Feel free to come and get it back." said the shade. And then it faded out of sight, leaving behind for a few seconds longer the sound of slurping alcohol.

*   *   *

Doctor Hurley entered the medical room to find the nurse curled in a chair by the operating table, her attention wrapped up in a book. He no sooner arrived than the nurse hurriedly jumped up and began fiddling with several metal implements. The doctor stood there for a moment, looking stern.

"Found a good book?" he asked.

The nurse tried to act nonchalant. "I was just glancing at it for a moment."

The doctor walked over and examined it. His brow furrowed.

"This looks like the book that boy wrote." he said.

"Yes, I suppose it is." said the nurse, not looking up from her work.

"How did you even get a hold of this? I thought I had it locked away upstairs. You know how much trouble is wrapped up in this book?" the doctor asked.

The nurse didn't immediately reply. "All I know is that it's a good window into the boy's mind."

The doctor hadn't expected that. "What do you mean by that?" he demanded.

"Well, I've grown to care a great deal for the child, and I wanted to get to know him better. I listened a good amount to him when he was delirious, talking in his sleep and all. He was talking about similar things as are in that book. The last chapter I was reading told about a little girl who was becoming famous. He talked a lot about a little girl in his sleep. He said she was in trouble. There's something strangely consistent about it all. I can't help wondering if there really is a little girl who is in trouble."

The doctor pulled up a chair across from the nurse and looked straight at her. Her sight remained focused on the medicines she was preparing.

"You don't actually believe he's sane, do you?" he asked.

The nurse looked up, eyes wide.

"Because if so, we'd be happy to give you room and board here. I think there's even a vacancy in the room across from him. You two could keep each other company."

The nurse looked shocked.

"Oh, I'm sorry!" said the doctor, seeing her expression. "I was only joking!" he patted her on the shoulder. "Come now! You're as sane as I am."

The nurse began to breathe again. "So you're not angry about the book?"

The doctor smiled. "Of course not! If you had been reading the book the boy had before, I would have been rather alarmed, but this is the one he wrote. I've read through it myself, and while it's as bizarre as a drunk nun, I don't think it could cause any harm."

"Thank you." said the nurse.

"Think nothing of it. You've worked here so long and hard, you deserve a few liberties. Besides, look at you! You're already preparing for your six o'clock rounds, and it's only five!"

The nurse looked confused. "But this is for—" She looked at the clock behind her. "Lord help us!" she exclaimed. "It's five o'clock! All of the patients! Their medications! Oh, Mr. Hurley, please forgive me!"

"Whatever for?"

"Time has slipped past me! I was not preparing for the six o'clock rounds, but for the three o'clock rounds!"

The doctor looked concerned. "Maybe this book *is* trouble, if it could cause someone like you to actually miss a round. From what I can recall, you've never missed *anything* in all the years I've worked here." and then, after a moment's thought, "But I thought most of the patients weren't on the three o'clock round."

"Only a handful are! And one of them is the boy! His medication has surely run out by now!"

She grabbed the tray of medical instruments and hurried for the door.

"I fear the madness has already returned!"

*   *   *

James sat up and looked around. He thought he'd heard something.

On the other side of the mirror, the boy was holding a picture of a little girl and staring it up and down.

"She is so beautiful!" the reflection exclaimed. "She's the most beautiful creature in the world!"

James stared at the poster. That was the girl. The girl in his dreams. The boy on the other side saw James' fascination and his smile broadened.

"You like her, don't you?" he asked.

James didn't like the reflection boy in the least. He hoped that if he ignored him the boy would go away. Or at least go back to mimicking him like any proper reflection should.

"But she'll never give us the time of day, will she?" the boy continued.

James turned away from the mirror and faced the other wall.

"And why? Because we're *dead!* Tough luck, falling in love with a girl who's alive. Tragic, really."

James spun around. "I'm not dead!"

The other boy shook his head patiently, as though trying to convince a baby that not everything in the world should go in your mouth.

"Don't you remember the castle? How she looked at you when she realized who we were? Don't you remember her face? She was horrified! And why not? We're an abomination!"

Images flashed across James' vision. He felt jabs of pain and clasped his hands to his head as though someone were stabbing his mind. The other boy returned to the picture.

"I must admit, for how seemingly perfect she is, she does have one flaw. But it's a flaw that can be amended."

"If she has a flaw, it's not seeing how screwed up this world is!"

"No, her flaw is far simpler than that. But so is the remedy. The remedy is love."

"You're crazy!" said James.

"Of course we are!" said the boy and then, looking back at the picture, "All that the girl needs is love. All we need to do is love her with all our soul. To love her like this!"

Leaping viciously across the room, he pulled out a knife seemingly from mid air and buried it into the center of the poster.

"Don't worry my love," he whispered soothingly, leaning against the wall. "Don't cry. It will only hurt a little bit."

"Stop it!" James screamed. He slammed his fist against the mirror. It had no effect. He hit it again. He kept hitting it until both his hand and the mirror were covered in blood, but still the mirror remained. The reflection boy was still in the same pose as when he had stabbed the poster, except now he was slowly tearing the picture up with his knife.

"And then, you will be born again. You will be a new person, and see us through new and kinder eyes." the reflection went on, not seeming to notice James' desperate attempts.

James took hold of the chair and began beating the mirror with it. Legs splintered off the chair and flew bouncing off the walls. By then his rage had blurred into sobbing.

"And then, for once, you will love us."

James' soul broke in half. When the nurse finally came rushing into the room, she found him collapsed onto the floor in a pool of his tears and blood. He lay huddled and twitching, deliriously begging for more drugs.

"I am so sorry!" she said, as she knelt beside him. Taking the syringe, she hurriedly administered the shot, and then took some gauze out of her apron to tend to his bleeding. The medication worked quickly. By the time she had turned to his wounds and was bandaging them, he was already fine. He no longer felt the pain. He no longer cared.

*   *   *

Adelle awoke the next morning with much apprehension. Today was her first day of school. It was not in a completely official capacity; she was simply going to visit the school and accompany Ivy through each of her classes, but still, it was a radically new experience for her, and she felt ill prepared.

After breakfast they were about to walk out the door when Ivy suddenly stopped.

"Oh, I almost forgot!" said Ivy. She ran upstairs and quickly returned with Bipsy and Boppin. Then she stuffed each of them beneath the front of her dress.

"There!" she said. "Now we are ready!"

They went outside where a carriage was waiting for them. Ivy spotted her mother inside. "What does she think she's doing?" Ivy grumbled. "She never accompanies me to school."

"Good morning." said the Lady Mediev as Ivy and Adelle stepped into the carriage. "I trust you slept well?"

"Yes, I did, thank you." said Adelle, and then, after failing to think of anything better to ask, "What are you doing today after you drop us off at school?"

"I'm not dropping you off. I'm going to the school as I do every week day."

"Oh, but Ivy said—"

"Silly, we have many carriages!" said Ivy, feigning a joke. The Lady was not clear as to what her daughter meant, and simply continued.

"It would be very remiss for me not to be present at the school, considering that I am a member of its faculty."

"What? You mean you teach?" said Adelle.

"Yes, among the million other roles I shoulder in this society."

"It's a wonder she finds the time to raise a family." said Ivy.

There was an awkward pause until the Lady resumed speaking. "And what is the sum of your education so far?" she asked Adelle.

"In the castle I had a tutor. He taught me geography, history, science, arithmetic, how to read and write several languages, and court etiquette."

"Is that all?"

Adelle reviewed her lessons for a moment. "Yes, that covers all my major courses, though my tutor always said that the most important thing he could teach me was wisdom. He was a very good teacher and very patient."

"It sounds like your education has been neglected."

"Neglected? What do you mean?"

"I mean that the limited selection of subjects you've been exposed to explains much about your behavior."

Adelle struggled very hard not to be put out by this and asked, "What subjects do you teach?"

The Lady drew herself up even straighter (if that was possible) as though she had been waiting the whole time to answer that question. "Some schools slave away at bestowing children with wisdom, but wisdom is so overrated. Every philosopher throughout history is dead and what good did it do them? No, I bestow more practical things like style and sex appeal. But most importantly, I give classes on class."

"I'm not sure I follow you . . ."

The Lady frowned. "Clearly your education has been gravely neglected. *Class* is what makes the world go round. The more of it you have the more people you can look down upon."

"And that's . . . *good?*"

The Lady rolled her eyes. "You are barely ready to suckle milk, much less be conversed to about the foundations of life. Come back to me in five years and then we'll be able to resume this lesson."

When they arrived at school and entered the school grounds, it was as if Ivy was a different person. She smiled and laughed and waved to all her friends. She went from the despondent cynic to the bubbling socialite. She and Adelle entered one of the many school buildings and started down a long hall filled with students.

Halfway down the hall they came across a group of children who were each friends of Ivy to varying degrees. Osmand was among them, and so was the chubby girl from the night before. (Her name was Sandy, though everyone called her Sandwich.)

The first person in the group to notice them coming was a pretty looking girl by the name of Wendy. Her clothing and makeup were also a little creepier than the other children. As the two girls approached she laughed and said, "So Ivy, I see you're finally not the only one with a fetish for color."

That's when Adelle first noticed. She and Ivy were the only two children whose clothes had vivid hues. For everyone else there were occasional muted patches of color, but they were mostly clothed in shades of black and gray.

"But the princess is even beyond Ivy!" Wendy continued. "Look at her skin—it's all pink and rosy! Honey, nobody has colored skin anymore. What was that called again . . . ?"

"Flesh tones?" said Sandwich.

"Yes! Flesh tones! That is *so* passé! Chalk white, ash gray, or coal black—those are the complexions of choice."

"But I can't change the color of my skin!"

The girls smiled wickedly. "Oh, there is a way . . ."

"Oh look!" said another girl. "Her cheeks are getting even redder!"

Adelle was about ready to sink into the floor when a voice said behind her, "I think her skin looks cool. It's unique. Maybe she'll start a new trend."

Adelle turned to see who had spoken. It was Bobby! He and two of his friends had approached the group from the side.

"Yeah right." said Wendy. "They'd call it 'Royal Flush.'"

"I'm going to be late for class if I don't hurry." said Ivy, grabbing Adelle's hand and moving past the group and on to Ivy's first class of the day.

"Don't worry, they're just teasing." she said to Adelle. "You easily outclass them, and before long they'll see it."

"What were they going on about my skin for?"

Ivy looked embarrassed. "Well it sort of proclaims that you're . . . that you've never done it before."

"Done what?"

"It! You know . . . *died*."

Adelle looked confused. "Of course I haven't! Is this more of your city slang?"

"Yeah, yeah. It's just a . . . manner of speech."

"What does it mean?"

"Right now we have class." Ivy said as they stepped into the classroom.

*   *   *

Adelle was having a difficult time concentrating on the different classes she was in. She had heard much from the other students, and the more they spoke to her, the worse she felt. She looked out the window. The sky was overcast and gray. She didn't like gray.

At one point the Lady Mediev entered the classroom and stood near the back. The teacher asked her if she would like a seat, but she said she was merely checking on how each of the classes were going and would only be staying for a few minutes. Adelle breathed a little easier when the woman finally left the room. That was how the entire morning had been: no matter where Adelle was, the Lady always seemed to be close by.

"So how is your first day of school so far?"

Adelle turned to find Jakob Damond sitting in the seat next to her. No one seemed to notice either his person or his speaking. Most of the students seemed to be zoned out as it was.

Adelle sighed. "It's alright, I guess. I'm intrigued by the different subjects being offered, but it is hard the way most of the children are treating me. They mock my hair, my clothes, my skin, the way I talk, everything! No matter how nice I am to them, they somehow manage to use it against me! One girl told me she wore clothes like mine . . . when she was *five!* I don't understand; this isn't anything like what you said it would be!"

"Don't give up yet. Everything I said was true, you just need to tap into your own abilities."

"The only ability I have is the power to make people laugh ... *at me.*"

"Don't disparage yourself so. Your abilities are vast. And that crown is the key to unlocking them. But it will do little unless wielded."

"How does one wield a crown?"

"It's an intuitive process. The crown follows your desires. Feed your desires and make them grow. Channel your passions and the crown will follow suit. The instinct is already in you, it's just a matter of practice."

"I don't know ... that doesn't sound like me. I'm—"

"Excuse me, little miss princess, but are you talking in the middle of my class?"

That was the teacher. He looked as pleased as he sounded. Adelle's stomach twisted itself like a wet rag and she turned to the toymaker for assistance but—as seemed to be the usual case—he wasn't there anymore.

"Hello? I asked you a question." the teacher continued. Adelle didn't know what to say. She felt about ready to burst into tears. She wished the teacher wouldn't treat her like all of the students.

"I'm sorry," said the teacher. "I shouldn't have lost my temper. I really am glad to have the future Queen of Marloth in my classroom. I hope you enjoy the lesson."

The teacher resumed his lecture and Adelle was left staring at him in amazement.

*   *   *

After school Ivy and Adelle hit the town to engage in some much needed shopping. While Adelle did not have any money, Ivy attempted to explain to her the magical thing known as "credit", and how there was no greater and more widely accepted line of credit than the royal coffers. Adelle did not fully comprehend these explanations, but it was not hard to accept the giddy freedom of "buy whatever you want without care."

Adelle was astonished at how many shops there were. And so many things to buy that she had never imagined before. Dresses that made what she had worn in the castle look like potato sacks. Cosmetics, ribbons, hair dyes, jewelry, exotic foods and drinks, and an endless variety of other novelties.

One particular thing Adelle fell in love with was a gem studded music box that sounded like it had an entire orchestra inside it. She promptly purchased it and for the rest of the day its music accompanied their exploits.

"That is a nice music box," said Ivy. "But I've seen more fantastic at Jakob Damond's Toye Shoppe."

"Oh! I would love to see that place! Why don't we shop there next?"

Ivy shook her head. "It's not here right now. It moves from one place to another. Personally, I suspect its movements aren't for any geographic reason; he's just trying to increase the rarity of his goods."

"When will it be in the City again?"

"No one knows. It could be any day."

Adelle was also amazed at how many interesting people she met in the city. Everyone was so friendly and gracious to her. All of the shopkeepers were eager to give her discounts. The query gremlins had published many articles with pictures of her so that many people recognized her on sight and would wave and call out to welcome her to the City of Orphans. The query goblins were still following her, but in the public crowds of daylight they were much more discreet and limited their activities to flashing their strange devices from a distance.

Adelle wished the day would last forever, but eventually the sun set and it was time for dinner so the two girls hurried back to the Manor with the spoils of their conquest.

As was mentioned before, the Lady Mediev owned some of the more elegant establishments in the City of Orphans. The two grandest of these was the Theatre and the Globe. The Globe was a dome-shaped ballroom poised on a hill at the far end of the City. The Globe's outer surface was made almost entirely of magically enforced glass. After dinner, Adelle accompanied Ivy and a group of her friends to the Globe to hang out and dance.

While so far Adelle had been impressed by all that she had seen of the City, she had also been slightly shocked by how much wilder everything was. The drinks had more alcohol, the games had more violence, and the music had more rocks in it. Everything had to be always newer and bolder. By that point she was starting to see a pattern.

Her education had included instruction in all the forms of dancing that appeared in royal court, but Adelle was afraid she would find the City's idea of dancing far more wild and aggressive than anything she knew or particularly wanted to know. But it turned out that dancing was the one remaining bastion of antiquity in the City of Orphans. The music was smooth and majestic, and so were the movements that accompanied it. The flavor of dancing was so tame compared to the rest of the City that it almost felt out of step, but Adelle didn't mind. She had never felt so at home since she had arrived there. This was something she knew, and she was pleased to find so many young men who also knew the forms of dance she enjoyed most. From then on the Globe became her regular place to visit every evening. While between her and Ivy she was normally the more responsible one, when it came to the Globe it was Ivy who was always pulling Adelle away from it and begging to get home and to bed.

Adelle soon learned that the magic which controlled the Globe's appearance was not presently running at full capacity, which she found hard to believe. The Globe was already breathtaking, but apparently even in its present state its lights were not as brilliant, the sound was not as loud, the magical flourishes of color not as vibrant as they could be. This was for two reasons. One, because it was too costly to run the Globe at full power every night, and secondly, because the full display of power was reserved for the Grand Ball that was held once a year. The Lady Mediev made sure to maintain a contrast between the Globe's everyday operation and its appearance on that special night. That was always the most anticipated night in all of Marloth. They said that when the Globe was raised to full power it provided light for the entire City. And what was more, Adelle learned that the Ball was only a handful of weeks away. She could hardly wait!

*　　*　　*

Never before had the nurse looked forward to her breaks between rounds as she did now. She was finding herself morbidly fascinated by the book the boy had written, and read it every spare moment she could find.

The marble hall was far longer than the boy had realized. It seemed to continue on forever. But at least he could easily run twice as fast as his pursuers, and before long they were little more than a pinprick of torchlight in the distance. The raven was easily matching his pace, soaring above him.

James stopped for a moment to look around.

"This hall seems to go on forever!" the raven moaned. "I could swear this place didn't look so big from the outside!"

"If I'd known it I would have gone through one of those doors back there." said James. "But it appears that they've stopped. The last door we passed was at least a good mile behind us."

"Well let's not go back." said the raven. "Unless my keen eyes are failing me, that crowd is growing in number. Those stuffed coats have turned into a throng! There's something not right about all of this. I sense magic. Dangerous magic."

"Well come on, they're getting closer." said James. *"Let's keep moving!"*

It wasn't much longer before they came across a small table in the middle of the hall, around which were gathered a handful of characters, all huddled closely together. As James drew nearer he saw that they were playing a rather unusual sort of card game.

"Hello." said James. No one acknowledged him. Apparently they were in the middle of a particularly intense round.

"I'll play a skeleton and the toymaker." said one of the players, laying two cards on the table. He was in a white gown, and James guessed that he was a patient there.

"I'll double that." This was a doglike creature beside him, who appeared to be made out of faded pieces of patchwork crudely sewed together.

"Ha, well I've got both a king and a queen, so you can just save yourselves the trouble and kick the proverbial bucket!" This was a zombie child.

"What about you? Are you going to fold?" asked the dog creature of the player on his left, a monkey.

The monkey did not reply, but placed a single card on the table. Upon the card was depicted a giant person sneezing and laying waste to a small city.

The zombie child threw down his cards in disgust. *"Not again! There's only one of those cards in the whole deck! How in the world do you keep drawing it?"*

"Excuse me, gentlemen," said the raven, landing in the middle of the table, *"but do any of you know a way out of this endless hall we're in?"*

"Now I'm seeing talking birds!" said the patient. *"Shoo, talking bird! I can only take so much of this at one time!"*

"Do you know what the test for madness is?" asked the dog creature, shuffling his cards back into the deck.

"No, what?" asked the patient.

"If you can see me, you're crazy." said the dog creature.

The monkey began to laugh quietly. It was vaguely unsettling.

James looked back and once again saw the ominous torchlight appear at the end of the hall. For a while they had gotten far enough ahead that it was out of sight, but now their pursuers were catching up to them.

"How do I get out of the Asylum?" James asked.

"That's a bit complicated." said the dog creature. "Much more complicated than me simply giving a few directions. You have to fight to get out of here."

"Wait a minute," said the zombie child, who had been eyeing the monkey for a good while. "I think you're cheating!"

The monkey made a face and went back to his cards.

"I'm positive! That little devil is cheating!" the zombie child shouted, pointing at the monkey.

"So what?" said the dog creature. "We're all cheating."

"That mob is getting closer!" the raven crowed.

"Can you help us get out of here?" James asked.

"Depends. Why do you want to get out?"

"Because they want to lock me in a cell and keep me there!" James moaned. "They think I'm crazy!"

"Well, can you see me?" asked the dog creature.

James thought about this.

"Can you see yourself?" he asked.

The creature screwed up his face for a moment and then laughed. "I never thought of that. I must be crazy too!"

Sometime later the nurse put down the book. This was getting too surreal. She looked over at the doll that was resting on the table before her. Then she looked back at the book and read the passage again. The similarity was creepy.

Finally, she grabbed the doll and went to James' cell. She found him curled up on his bed, though he wasn't asleep. The nurse drew closer and said to him. "I don't know how it got there, but I found this in one of the halls. I thought you would like it."

She handed him a small, mangy looking cloth animal. James did not say anything, but he took the object and held it close to him.

"Have you seen this cloth animal before?" she asked him. James nodded. "What is its name?"

"Fugue." said James.

*   *   *

The next day of school went much more steadily. While Adelle still saw much of the Lady Mediev, the woman was no longer hovering over her as she had been before. And after the initial shock of having the heir of Marloth at the school, the children began to adjust to her and the teasing diminished. The crown may have had something to do with that.

Between two of her classes she passed by the field where all the major sporting events took place. There she saw multiple teams competing in some game that involved a rubber ball. She knew little about such things, but she knew enough to tell that Bobby was exceptionally good at what he was doing. Later on she learned from the other children that he was the strongest and fastest youth in Marloth, and the champion of every major athletic competition. But as she watched him, all she could think was not how impressive his record was, but how wonderful it would be if he talked to her.

After the rest of her classes, Adelle met outside the school with Ivy and several other children. She was starting to get a sense for who Ivy's usual crowd was. Sandwich and Wendy were there, and so was Harris. There was no sign of Bobby though.

Adelle noticed Osmand in the back. She felt sorry for him. He looked so lonely and no one seemed to care. She went out of her way to catch his eyes and say, "Hi Osmand!" Osmand was amazed that she would acknowledge him and after gathering his wits, he timidly waved back at her.

Ivy linked arms with her and said to her eagerly "After school some of us are going over to the Candy Castle to eat Jillybons. You want to come?"

"Oh! I'm not allowed to eat Jillybons."

"What's not allowing you?"

"My parents; the King and Queen."

"And where are they?"

Adelle opened her mouth to reply and suddenly hit a gap in her mind. Everything having to do with her parents was so fuzzy now. She'd half forgotten she had parents. How were they doing? When had she last seen them?"

"I don't know." she said at last.

"You don't even know where they are? Do you want to come or not?"

"I would love to, but I can't disobey my parents!"

"Fine. It's your life."

As Adelle watched her friends set off for the Candy Castle, she forlornly turned her mind to wondering how she was to get back to the Manor. She had heard that large cities like this contained many forms of public transportation, but she was not sure how to employ them. It was while she was considering this predicament that she heard a voice beside her say, "You know, you always could ride with me."

Adelle turned to see Jakob Damond standing by her side like an out of place shadow. She wasn't surprised anymore. He had become like some footnote to her life that followed her around.

"My memory is unclear about the last time I rode with you," she said. "But I have the impression that it was rather uncomfortable."

"Pshaw! Where's your sense of adventure? But if you want comfort, then we'll drive in comfort!"

Adelle looked and there was a coach in front of them. It was similar to the one Damond had used before, except this was lower and longer. It had shiny black paint and rubber tires. The windows were also painted solid black, which Adelle thought rather silly.

One of the doors opened, beckoning them to enter. Adelle found the inside of the coach far more luxurious than any she had seen before. The interior was so plush with velvet that it resembled a padded cell. And it turned out that she could see clearly through the windows from the inside; it was only from the outside that they appeared opaque.

"The world is your oyster." said the toymaker. "Where would you like to go?"

"The Mediev Manor would be good." said Adelle.

"Hmm. Not the most exciting destination, but no worry. Your whim is my demand."

As they journeyed to the Manor, the toymaker asked how she was getting along with the crown.

"I think I'm starting to understand what you were speaking of the other day." Adelle replied. "People have been increasingly civil to me since our talk." Then she sighed. "But I'm still a long way from being a queen."

"Not as far as you may think. You've already taken your first step toward becoming a queen. You are outside of the castle and experiencing the wide, magical world of Marloth for yourself. And not just that, you've also taken a second step too: the people are already talking about you right and left. You've managed to make a big impression on a populace that is so accustomed to the extraordinary that it takes a lot to grab their attention; yet you've done it."

"The next step is to transmute interest into idolatry. This present age is very skeptical about things like nobility. They would prefer to see more qualities in a leader than a lucky birth. What they want are tangible attributes they can witness firsthand. Your face is a good start; it was made to be on the front of every paper and magazine. But you need more than a pretty face; you need to *do* something with it."

"I'm guessing you already have something in mind?"

"Yes. The best thing for you would be to sing."

"To sing? As with music?"

"Exactly! A performance could be arranged at the Theatre. The entire City would show up to hear your lovely voice, and every one of them would fall in love with you!"

"I'm sorry to disappoint you, Mr. Damond, but even though that sounds absolutely amazing—and, I confess, a little scary . . . I can't sing."

"Nonsense! You're a princess. Of course you can sing!"

Adelle was not entirely convinced by this, but she decided to approach the idea from a different angle. "But even if I could sing, and showed the world that I could, so what? What does singing have to do with being a queen?"

"Everything! Music is inspiring. These people need someone to inspire them. You're the one to do it."

"I don't feel very inspiring."

The toymaker laughed and told her not to worry. She had everything she needed. Queenhood was just around the corner.

It was not much later that they arrived at the Mediev Manor. Before Adelle left the carriage the toymaker expressed how great his delight would be if she could again visit his toyshop sometime soon.

Adelle looked perplexed. "I would love to visit your toyshop, though I've never actually been there before."

The toymaker laughed again and said he had no idea what he had been thinking of. After thanking him for all of his encouragement and the use of his carriage, Adelle entered the house.

*   *   *

Ivy returned that evening looking very cheerful. It was not long after her arrival that Adelle and the rest of the Mediev household sat down at the table for dinner. While they were eating, the Lady brought up an idea she had been contemplating.

"Adelle, a thought occurred to me today. While you have been seen around the City on a number of occasions, it would be good for you to have a more official public appearance. I considered many ideas, but one keeps rising to the top. How would you like to sing at my Theatre?"

Adelle was astounded. After some thought she said she would like that, though she was not as certain as she acted. The Lady beamed at her and further explained the many benefits such a concert would render to the princess. Then the conversation shifted to the matter of selecting a repertoire and practicing it. The Lady had a number of vocal instructors under her employ and knew of just the one for Adelle. Her training would begin on the morrow.

*   *   *

The problem that faces doctors in a mental institution was the same problem that faces doctors in any other medical field: if there is something broken inside a patient, how do you get inside to fix it? How do you pass through all of the parts of the patient that stand between you and the part that is broken? Do you take the direct approach and cut your way to it? Do you introduce foreign chemicals into the patient? Or do you try to fix them indirectly by manipulating the patient from the outside?

Doctor Hurley was convinced that all of these methods were insufficient. He wanted to get to the root of the problem. To climb inside his patient and rearrange them from the atomic level. To determine the fundamental essence of human life and take control of it. What he was presently experimenting with looked like the medicinal route, but the stuff he was filling his syringes with was far more complex and intelligent than any chemical. If even one of the other doctors discovered what he was doing, he would be fired. Or maybe arrested. But they were never going to find out. They would not have understood even if they had seen it. He was attempting to tame forces that few people know of.

As he passed the rows of patients, he didn't pay them much attention. To him most of the people in the Asylum were hopeless. He was not going to waste his time on them. Even if they could be cured, they would never be of much use. They weren't part of the big picture, and were simply draining resources from an establishment that didn't really understand what it could be doing. It wasn't enough for Doctor Hurley to simply return patients to functioning roles in society. People could function in society and yet still harbor gross delusions. He wanted to slay *all* the fantasies. He wanted to reach into the minds of men and mold them until they clearly saw reality for what it was. Or at least what he thought it was.

As he passed through the rows of cells, one of the patients who was just then being escorted back into his cell turned and called after him, "For someone who deals so much in death, you sure are afraid of it!"

The door to James' cell was opened and in stepped Doctor Hurley. While James was not in a particularly attentive mood, the doctor did his best to explain to him a recent turn of events. To begin with, James had been progressing very well. So well, in fact, that an examination was being arranged to determine if James was cured enough to leave the Asylum. The examination would consist of James' appearing before a panel of doctors who would judge his sanity. The exact date of the examination had not yet been solidified, but Doctor Hurley was certain it would be within a few days.

As the doctor explained these things to James, he was not sure if the boy was hearing any of it. But when he finished James showed that he had not been utterly inattentive by asking if he would still need to take the doctor's drug. Doctor Hurley replied that James would always need to take the serum. James was not sure what he thought about this. Most of his sense of feeling was no longer with him, but what little feeling he did have told him he was missing something. Missing a part of his heart. He could hardly feel any pain, but he could hardly feel any good either.

Now such questions only lived short lives in his mind, because now he also lacked much capacity for questioning. For the first time he found it easy to follow the prescriptions of others, simply because it was the path of least resistance. Before the doctor left, James told him that he would be ready for the examination, and thanked him for his miraculous elixir.

*   *   *

As the days passed, more and more advertisements began appearing for Adelle's performance. But so did advertisements for the upcoming Ball. And then there appeared advertisements for the return of Jakob Damond's Toye Shoppe. Each spectacle seemed determined to eclipse the others. The managers of all things publicity were at their wits end about this. So much great fanfare was in danger of being wasted through competition. But after much struggling and beating of heads against walls, the query gremlins and the merchants and the doctors of all things that rotate were able to merge the multiple upcoming events by summarizing the present time as, "The Most Important Days in the History of Marloth!"

Adelle had never worked so hard in her life. Every day she spent countless hours practicing for her performance. By the time the first weekend came around, she felt in need of a break. And the weekend provided. That evening the second part of 'Deminox Farinoi' was being presented at the Theatre. After dinner Adelle, all her new friends, and just about everyone else in the City of Orphans flocked to the Theatre.

It was even more spectacular than the first part. In this second installment, Tralvorkemen rose back to life to continue his scourge upon the children. But this time he had a much larger scheme; he wanted to destroy the world. But a noble toymaker appeared on the scene and rallied the remaining children to fight the crazed undead hunter. After an epic battle, Tralvorkemen was slain once and for all and the world was saved.

When it was over there was little else anyone could talk about but the play. Once again, Adelle left it feeling somewhat disturbed, and yet she was at the same time fascinated by it and relieved that it had ended happily.

Instead of taking a carriage to their next destination, the group of children thought it would be fun to walk. Bobby was with them, something which made Adelle nearly dizzy from delight. Except that he hardly acknowledged her. She noticed he talked more to the other girls. Was he avoiding her? She couldn't tell. Eventually he did speak a few words to her. She was so startled from of her own thoughts she fumbled what could have been a graceful answer. Now she felt like an idiot. Why couldn't she read him? She was good at reading everyone else. It annoyed her that she didn't know what sort of things he thought about. She especially wanted to know what he thought about *her*.

She imagined what it would be like if one day Bobby came to her and told her that he had always had feelings for her but had not known how to express them. Oh the rapture! Oh, what splendor! Oh what a day! Then they would go on dates and she would help him learn how to express his emotions and slowly he would bare more and more of his heart to her. She would work hard to be patient with him, and not expect too much from him too quickly.

"What did *you* think of it?" Harris asked her.

Adelle started. "Think of what?" she said, though the words came out too fast and too loud.

"The play. That *is* what we were all just talking about. Did you like it?"

"I think I liked it." said Adelle, doing her best to regather her wits. "It certainly was very captivating. I completely forgot where I was through most of it. I don't think my mind has completely left the Theatre yet."

"That's the way it is with all good plays."

"I sometimes wonder about that." said Sandwich. "There's so many fascinating things outside of the Theatre; why do they always feel dull right after a play? What if someone were to make a play that, when it was over, you were eager to leave the Theatre?"

"It's already been done," said Ivy. "They're called flops."

"No! I mean—plays that roll right into the next course, like a meal rolls right into dessert. A play that inspires people to live their lives!"

"This play inspires me to slay headmasters; does that count?" asked Wendy.

"Possibly, but in such an encounter you probably wouldn't be the one doing the slaying." said Harris.

"Which isn't going to happen one way or the other," said Ivy. "Tralvorkemen is just a myth."

"Are you certain of that? Some people say there really was an Edward Tralvorkemen. Some even say that he is still alive, roaming the world looking for helpless children."

Sandwich shook herself. "Don't say that! Just even the thought of that monster gives me the creeps!"

"We could take him." said Bobby.

Adelle felt a tinge of guilt, but she didn't know why. "I remember there being an Edward Tralvorkemen in the stories my mother used to tell me. While he was an easy person to misunderstand, he was a very good man that protected children."

"How perverse!" said Wendy. "Dressing up a monster as a nice person? That's just not right!"

Ivy wanted to say that she had also heard stories like the ones Adelle spoke of, but decided to hold her tongue.

"If Tralvorkemen is real, then he is evil." said Harris, and then he turned toward Adelle. "You don't actually believe those stories your mother told you, do you?"

Adelle hesitated. "No." she finally said. "No, I don't."

"Good." said Harris. "Because if you ever come across anyone calling himself Edward Tralvorkemen, toss whatever he's offering in his face . . . and run!"

As they walked they passed by a man who was standing on the edge of the street and looking down at them sadly. As they passed, the man spoke quietly,

"What happened to the little girl who defended me when no one else would?"

*　　*　　*

The nurse entered James' room. She did not appear as happy as she should be considering the occasion.

"Today is the day," she said. "The day of your examination. The doctor asked me to get your prepared for your hearing."

She had all of her regular collection of instruments with her. One of them was a syringe. The other was a bottle of the doctor's serum which she used to fill the syringe. She did this very deliberately, as though with every step she debated whether or not to continue. When she finally was ready, she further delayed administering the drug and instead made an attempt at talking with James.

"This is very hard for me," she said. "For a long time I have wrestled with the rightness of my position. I cannot say that I agree with Doctor Hurley, or any of the other doctors here for that matter."

James didn't really care one way or the other. He was basking in the effect of the serum. The nurse sighed.

"Recently there have been several events that have made me question this place more than ever. Many of them have involved you. And your book. I have read all of it. It is very disturbing. That poor girl! Could a little boy truly imagine such horrors? But at the same time I could see something more. There are echoes in it. I think you were mimicking something else. Something better."

The nurse bent over James and, with a voice barely over a whisper, said to him "He's alive! Mr. Tralvorkemen is alive! Or at least, either he is alive or I am mad, for I have seen him. And not only did I see him, but he spoke with me. I talked with a man who is supposed to be dead!"

James made no response. Her words did not appear to have any effect on him.

"You do remember Mr. Tralvorkemen, don't you? He was an integral part of your life! Don't you remember anything about him?"

James shook his head.

"He was a good man!"

James simply stared at her blankly. She stared back with growing distress. And then looked at the syringe.

"It's what I feared! This drug . . . it's not simply taking away the bad; it's taking away the good as well!"

She held the syringe away from her as though it were a venomous reptile. "I can't do this! I can't be a part of this anymore! It is wrong!" Without further hesitation, she emptied the syringe into the sink. Once she had finished this and had put the syringe away with the rest of her instruments, she turned back to James.

"I don't know how much time I have; the men will be here any moment to take you to the examination. Before you leave, Mr. Tralvorkemen wanted me to give this to you." She held out a piece of paper to him. "He said you might need it." James was still too disoriented to pay much attention to the paper so she placed it inside one of his pockets.

"And one other thing." she added. She reached into her bag and took a satchel out of it. She showed him what was inside the satchel but he was still too disconnected to notice its contents. "I'll be honest." she said. "I wish I could keep it for myself. But he said one day he would give me one of my own, and for now you should have it." She placed Fugue inside the satchel, and then she slung the satchel over his shoulder and strapped it down. "There. Now you are ready for any kind of adventure."

She had barely finished when two orderlies entered the room. The nurse abruptly straightened and tried her best to act calm and professional.

"Is he ready?" one of them asked the nurse.

"Yes." she said, hoping they did not detect the hesitation in her voice. The men brought James to his feet and escorted him outside the room, one on either side. They did not seem to mind the satchel strapped to his back.

He was led down one corridor after another. Most of them were so dark it was hard for him to see anything. As he went he could hear a patient scream, "Don't let the shadows get us! They are everywhere!" and another, "Burn the book! Burn the book!" and then another cry out "The End of the World is coming!"

Eventually they arrived at their destination. The orderlies took their post on either side of a doorway and opened it for James to enter. The place he stepped into seemed to defy understanding. Maybe it was the lighting, or the drugs, or the way the lighting played with the drugs, but James was in an infinite expanse of black with only a dusty beam of faint light descending some distance ahead of him. Instinctively, he stumbled to the patch of light and stood in the center of it. He had a suspicion that the room was quite large, and yet due to the narrowness of the light, he felt tightly pressed by the blackness on all sides.

As he stood there, his visual awareness of this place slowly expanded. The first thing he noticed outside of the shaft of light was what might have been a podium. It was some ways in front of him and a little to his left. After a little longer he thought he could see a wall of wood on his left and on his right. It was a low wall, barely taller than his shoulders.

"Is this the boy named James?" boomed a voice that seemed to come out of nowhere. James had a suspicion that it had originated from the podium, in which case he figured that the owner of the voice must be a Judge.

"Yes, your honor." cowered a second voice.

"And is it true that we are gathered here to test his sanity?"

"Yes." said the second voice.

"Very well then. We will now proceed with the examination."

The more James stared into the darkness, the more he thought he could see people just beyond the light. People sitting behind the wall of wood. And a man coldly looking down at him from above the podium.

"Well, to begin with, our records are a little confusing regarding the boy in question. It's actually somewhat mysterious. Apparently, the boy was here before, but there is no mention of him leaving. Any indication of his being here simply trails off with no mention of why or how he left."

The Judge spoke up, sounding angry. "Acquitting a resident is a serious matter, and should always be recorded with the greatest detail!"

"Yes, your honor. It is a grievous occurrence, indeed! But whatever the case, he eventually was taken into the orphanage of an Edward Tralvorkemen, where one of the doctors of this place examined the boy from time to time."

"Really?" said the Judge. "Is that said doctor present?"

"Yes, your honor. I am here." came a voice. James recognized it as that of the doctor.

"And is it true that you examined this boy while he was in the orphanage?"

"Yes, your honor."

"And did you have any idea that he had formerly been a resident of this establishment?"

"No, your honor. Even now, this is only one of my practices. I am a very busy man, and do not know half of the patients here."

"And do you have any idea as to how the boy arrived at the orphanage?" asked the Judge.

"No, your honor. I do not."

"This matter as to the boy's origins is most important if we are to release him back into the world. I will not allow this establishment's methods to fall into disarray! I believe it would be expedient to summon the owner of this said orphanage so that we may question him."

At this the second voice spoke up. "I'm afraid that that will not be possible, your honor. The owner of the orphanage died nearly a month ago. He was found dead around the same time that we found the boy unconscious. The boy had fallen out of a second story window. The other orphans claim they have no idea what happened."

"I declare, this is growing to be the most peculiar case I ever heard of!" said the Judge.

"It is most mysterious." the second voice agreed.

"Well, I deem it best that we move on with the examination and return to this question of the boy's history later." said the Judge. There was a pause and the sound of shuffling papers. "Exactly what is the summary of the boy's illness?"

"Over the course of his history here, including both before and after his disappearance, he has been diagnosed with schizophrenia, chronic nightmares, masochism, amnesia, violent tendencies with possible sadism, paranoia, Cotard's syndrome, and multiple delusions. Most of these revolve around a book of fairytales and an inability to distinguish between dreams and reality. As to the book, it was recently destroyed, which may have been a trigger to some of his recent symptoms; he was closely attached to it."

"The little mad boy with his book of fairytales." said the Judge, ponderously.

"Looking at all of the symptoms at once, it does make one wonder what we're doing here."

"If the boy can't distinguish between fantasy and reality, then clearly he doesn't belong outside." said the Judge.

"But he has been cured!" said the doctor.

James could imagine the Judge raising his eyebrows in surprise. "How so?" the Judge asked.

"With a serum I have been developing over the past several years. With this serum, I have been able to cure the particular madness of this boy. He is now sane!"

At this, a great murmuring arose all around them. James was frightened by the number of voices he heard, all whispering to one another, some elated, some scoffing, others outraged. By the sound of it, there had to be dozens of men beyond the edge of the light, all sitting in their pews, watching him intently, all of them just beyond his view.

After some time, the Judge silenced the gathering and proceeded. "I think I recall hearing of your experiments. But I was under the impression that they had all failed with, shall I say, dismal results?" he asked the doctor.

"I admit, in the past there have been problems, but this boy is a special case, and since I began administering the drug to him, all of the delusions have vanished and he has become a normal person! It has to do with his particular strain of madness. Now I may be able to alter the serum to work on other patients as well."

"Very well. Despite the bizarre nature of this case, it appears that the boy may be capable of living a normal life. But first, we must question him in detail to test if he truly has his wits in full."

All of this time James' vision had been growing clearer and the range of the light expanding. At this point it had spread far enough to reveal the Judge and the first row of people. From there the light still gradually faded into shadow. Now he recognized the doctor amongst the people. He also saw sitting beside the podium a man with a handful of papers scattered in front of him. That must be the second man that had been speaking.

The Judge himself reminded James of Mr. Tralvorkemen, except that the Judge was far older, almost ancient, and had the battered look of a general.

"First," said the Judge, looking straight at James, "Tell us in your own words about this book of yours."

"Its name was Marloth. I don't remember much about it anymore."

"Whenever you speak, boy, address me as Your Honor."

"Yes, your honor."

The Judge nodded. "Do you believe this book was real?"

James looked around him dismally. "No, your honor," he said. "I don't believe it could have been."

Yet he had no sooner spoken then he saw a monkey dodge in and then out of the light, smiling at him menacingly. James' eyes, which up to that point had been slightly groggy, bolted wide open.

"Good." said the Judge. "Would you say that you believed in it before?"

James looked back at the Judge. "I wanted to believe it."

"But not anymore?"

The monkey was followed by several pale looking children, all creeping along the edge of the light, trying to stay away from the view of the people.

"Now I want to believe that it *wasn't* real!" said James. He was beginning to feel dizzy. He closed his eyes and opened them again. All he could see was the Judge and the people standing in the pews.

"May I remind you to refer to me as *your honor*!" said the Judge.

"Yes, your honor."

The light was still slowly expanding, and by now, James could see the wall directly behind the Judge.

"Did anyone in your delusions ever go out of their way to keep you from harm; to preserve your life?"

"No."

"Describe your delusions to the court. What sort of things did you see during your madness?"

On the wall, there was a large mirror.

"I could see myself." said James.

The Judge didn't seem impressed.

"In a mirror," James hurriedly added. "Except I don't believe the mirror was really there, your honor. And the reflection of me wouldn't do what I did."

The reflection waved at James.

"A mirror that didn't mimic you?" said the Judge. "How intriguing. What sort of things did it do?"

"It waved at me." said James.

The reflection began to dance up and down.

"And it danced up and down." he continued.

"Did it do anything violent?" asked the Judge. "Or anything against the law?"

"Once it stabbed a picture with a knife." said James. As he said it, he found himself glaring at the mirror. The reflection only laughed silently.

"A knife? *Did you have a knife?*"

"No—no, your honor! Sometimes he had things I didn't, and other times, he only had what I had."

"So are you saying that his possessions varied from yours?"

"Yes, your honor! Right now he doesn't have anything!"

Dead silence. Not even a breath could be heard.

The Judge, after a long and stunned pause, regained his composure. "What did you just say?" he demanded.

James was horrified. "It-t was a slip of the tongue, your honor! I'm just a boy! I'm so terribly nervous!" The reflection began to tremble in mock terror.

The Judge looked straight at James. "You don't see any mirror by any chance, do you?"

"No!" said James. "I haven't seen it or anything like it since I started taking the medication!" He could feel the tension twisting up his insides. He wished he could run from the place. Run from that mirror. Run from everything. But then he thought about the nurse. Somehow he felt like he would be betraying her if he did not face what was before him. Something told him that this was important.

"As you say." said the Judge, not sounding convinced. "What other things did you see in your madness?"

"I had a long dream that seemed real at the time, but I hardly remember any of it now."

"What *do* you remember?"

James searched his memory. Everything seemed so far away. "I remember a girl. Her name was Adelle."

As he spoke, a gust of wind blew through the court, even though no one seemed to be affected by it. The wind carried a piece of paper which caught under James' foot. He looked down to find that it was the tattered picture of the girl. He looked up and saw the reflection in the mirror wave at him again.

"Is something bothering you?" asked the Judge, a strange expression on his face.

"No, it's just that—" He looked back at the picture. "It's just that I—" He looked again at the picture. It wasn't quite as he had remembered it. For one thing, the girl wasn't smiling anymore. Her eyes had lost their sparkle. She looked empty. No, worse than empty. Lifeless. Almost cruel. Such an expression looked so unnatural on her.

"Yes?" said the Judge. "You were saying?"

It was then that the doctor rushed over to James and turned to the Judge. "Forgive me, your honor, but I fear his medication is running out! I should have clarified that for the sanity to remain, he will need to continue to take the serum, though we hope with time that he will be able to be weaned from it. But for now, if you don't mind, I will quickly go and administer the drug to him and he should be normal within minutes." He took hold of James, who at this point was beginning to sway back and forth, and started to drag the boy away from the center of the courtroom.

"This is not good." said the Judge. "You should have clarified that fact in the beginning!"

"Your honor, at least now you can see the distinction between the boy with and without the drugs, for at the start of the session he was fully under the effects of the drug and he was perfectly fine."

The Judge did not seem satisfied, but the doctor continued half-guiding, half-dragging James until they were out of the room. By then, a great commotion of voices had risen behind them.

The doctor reached into his black bag and pulled out a syringe and a bottle of the serum.

"It's a good thing I came prepared." said the doctor. "I thought I had the nurse administer the serum right before the examination, but it looks like she must have given it much earlier. No problem, I'll have a talk with her later. Now here, give me your arm."

James backed away. "I don't know if I want it!" he said.

The doctor was astonished. "What? Are you crazy or—*what am I saying?* Come here and stop playing games!"

"No! Just wait a minute! I need to think!"

"What is there to think about? Things are not going well and the Judge is growing impatient! Look! I'm giving you the opportunity to start over; have a new life. Are you going to turn your back on that? Go back to your cell and stay there 'til you grow old and die?"

"No, but—"

"And there's more! If things don't work out here, they probably won't allow me to continue giving you the drug!" As the doctor said this, he filled the syringe with the liquid, and shook it until it was illuminating the hall with its greenish glow. "That means it will be back to all of your nightmares! Is that what you want? *A lifetime of merciless torment?*"

"No! I hate the nightmares! But the kind of life you want me to live; I don't think that's me! That drug isn't me! You can't cut me off from my dreams! I wouldn't be *me* anymore. I wouldn't be *anything.*"

Somewhere in the distance, James swore he could hear a girl scream. Not a scream for help. Not a scream of pain. It was a scream of helpless surrender.

"She needs me!" James exclaimed. "I can't stay here! I've got to find her!"

The doctor looked at James with cold resolve. "The madness has you! It's too late to reason with you: you're past reason!" The doctor thought for a moment and then suddenly sprang to life. He lunged forward and took hold of James' arm with one hand, the loaded syringe poised in the other.

"No!" James shouted. "Let go of me!"

The doctor ignored him and sunk the needle into the boy's skin. "You'll thank me in a minute!" he said.

But before he could finish, James swung at the syringe with his free hand. He hit it with such force that it shattered, sending glowing green liquid all over the doctor. The doctor let go of James and fell backwards, stunned. James stood there for a moment, nearly as stunned as the doctor. He looked at his arm. The needle was still lodged inside. He quickly yanked it out and threw it from him as though it were a viper that had sunk its fangs into his veins.

By then the commotion from inside the courtroom had grown quite loud, and there were people calling to see if the doctor and the little mad boy would be coming back soon.

"Well that does it, boy!" the doctor growled. "There's no way you're going to pass the examination now!" He managed to get to his feet and began to stagger away. "Your madness can take you for all I care! I've done so much for you, gone so out of my way to help you, but it means nothing, doesn't it? Well, I've done my duty, probably more than Edward would have done himself." He paused to grab his bag and continued on down the hall. "I'll look forward to seeing you tomorrow morning, cowering in your little cell again, moaning about all of the nasty things your dreams are doing to you!"

James watched him go and then turned back to the courtroom. He had no idea what he was doing. All he knew was that he was walking back into the room, and there was a new resolve to his stride.

The voices quickly died down as he stepped into the middle of the room. By now the light covered the entire room, and he could see the rest of the rows of people and the walls behind them. Suddenly, the room looked far smaller than it had before.

"What was that shouting back there about?" the Judge demanded. "Where is the doctor? What is going on?"

"I'm leaving." said James. "I'm going to find Adelle. She is in danger, and I may already be too late."

The Judge almost looked amused. "I'm sorry, little boy, but you aren't going anywhere unless I say so, and I don't appear to be in the saying mood."

James was nonplussed. "I am *going* to rescue Adelle," he said, "and anyone who gets in my way will either wish they were dead, or wish they were still alive."

The audience gasped. The subject was definitely suggesting violent tendencies. The Judge, however, looked as calm as James. He leaned over the edge of the podium and examined him coolly. Men began to enter through the two doorways and cut off any possible exits.

"Will you now? And all because of a girl?"

"Not just for her! Because it's all true! It has to be!"

"And what about this drug of Doctor Hurley's? Without the drug your nightmares will eventually find you."

"They will find me," said James, "because I'm running straight toward them."

One of the men called out something about the only place James running toward being a padded cell.

"If you had read Marloth you would know that's not what's going to happen."

The Judge suddenly spoke up, contempt dripping from his voice. "And exactly what *is* Marloth?" he demanded.

James turned and looked the Judge in the eye. Any hint of fear and doubt was gone. Now all that remained on James' countenance was determined resolve.

"*This* is Marloth." said James. "We're in It."

The Judge began to shout. Everyone began to shout. The insane began to shout from their myriad of quarters deep within the Asylum. The door through which James had entered burst open and dozens more men burst into the room, some of them carrying clubs, all of them heading for James. Somehow, the book was dashed against the podium, showering the room with papers. Several of the men drew knives and pistols. A window was shattered. Wind swept through the place like a haunted spirit.

James leapt into the air and landed within the rows of officials. They were far too disoriented to grab him. Running across the benches, he suddenly shifted direction and charged straight for the wall of men pursuing him. Just before he reached them, he ducked down and slid under their legs, arriving back in the middle of the room. By this point several people had stood up from the benches on the other side and were trying to box him in. He jumped to his feet with only a moment's pause to gather his wits in the rapidly changing circumstances. Deciding fast, he turned to the podium and slammed all of his weight against it. There was the sound of nails being ripped from board as the podium's foundation was torn from the floor. It shook threateningly for a moment, and then crashed into the midst of the pursuers. Leaping atop of it, he ran its length and threw himself into the air, passing over the crowd and landing in a roll directly in front of the main doorway.

Within moments, he was out of the courtroom and racing down the corridor. He could hear shouting not far behind him and knew they were close. He hurried down the corridor and turned a corner. The entrance to the Asylum stood before him. He sprinted forward, took hold of the large double doors, and pushed with all his might. The doors opened and red light flooded the hall. For a moment, he was nearly blinded.

The city stood sprawling around him, the streets filled with so many people they looked more like canals then streets. The steps of the Asylum entrance rose high above the street, high enough for him to see the buildings stretching on and on in the distance before him. For a moment, he suddenly remembered sitting with the other children atop of the orphanage, watching the sun set over that same city.

But he did not have much time to enjoy the thought. He could hear the Asylum officials flooding out of the stairway and rushing down the hall. Quickly, he descended the steps and dropped down into the teeming masses. No one seemed to notice him. All of their effort was bent just trying to keep moving forward past everybody else.

He looked back to see several of the officials emerge from within the Asylum and look about the sea of people in bewilderment. But despite the fact that he was a good several feet below the top of the crowd, they somehow managed to spot him and immediately set out in pursuit through the sea of people.

Navigating blindly, James pushed his way down one street after another, unsure as to whether he was losing them or if they were a mere step behind. After a time, he found himself next to a lamppost, and decided to climb it so he could collect his bearings. Like a jungle animal climbing through the canopy, his head popped out over the crowd and looked about him. As it turned out, he was at a junction where the streets went off in all directions. In one direction, he could make out the top of the looming Asylum. Two of the other directions had no indication of where they might lead. But in the fourth direction he could see a large sign hanging high above the crowds that read, "Journeyman Train Station."

Suddenly he heard a loud ruckus overhead and looked up to see a monkey directly above him! The creature was likewise holding onto the lamppost and was screeching and pointing down at him.

"There he is!" he heard someone shout. Turning about, James spotted the officials, one of them pointing at the lamppost he was on. Quickly, James dropped back into the crowds and made his way toward the train station. This time he was more certain as to their position, for he could hear the commotion of people being shoved aside and random curses following in his wake.

As he drew nearer the train station, the crowds thinned out, so that by the time he reached the main gates, there was no one immediately around except for the steward. James could see the train just behind the gates, and it looked like it was about to embark.

"Next stop, the City of Orphans!" he heard a raspy voice shout. That must be the conductor, thought James.

"Ticket, please." said the steward, grabbing James as he attempted to rush through the gate. James tried to resist but was surprised at how strong the man was.

"But I don't have a ticket!" said James.

"Then you'll need to go back and purchase one." said the steward.

James looked back. The officials hadn't yet burst from the crowd, but he knew they would any moment.

"I don't have time!" he said, and then suddenly he remembered something. Reaching into his pocket, he found the piece of paper the nurse had handed him. Taking it out, he found it to be a train ticket.

"Here!" said James.

The officials burst from the crowd and rushed toward them, just as James slipped through the gate. The officials tried to follow after him, but the steward forcefully held them back.

"Tickets, please." said the steward.

By the time James reached the boarding platform, the train had already lurched forward and was gradually gaining momentum. Running along the tracks, he threw himself into the air and caught onto the railing, pulling himself into the train.

And so it was that James set off for the City of Orphans, leaving sanity far behind him.

Part 4

Dear Sir,

It has come to my attention that you have destroyed my ledger of contracts. You know the rules; you know the forces at work here: whoever nullifies that ledger will himself be nullified. In this case, even though they do not know that rule, your children are unwittingly eager to fulfill it. But I don't want to see you dead. I am a very merciful person, and am willing to make an exception in your case. If you never return to the children, I will forget about the whole thing.

*So please heed my advice: do not go back to your orphanage. Your children hate you, and if you return, they **will** kill you.*

Best of luck,
Jakob Damond

*   *   *

For such a late hour, the train was surprisingly full of passengers. *"Don't people ever sleep around here?"* James wondered to himself. Seeing that there was no room in the car he had boarded, he starting making his way up the train to find an empty seat.

It was a very long train.

After crossing several cars, he paused between two of them to look out at the passing view. They had left the city behind them, and were in open country. It was now full night, and the hills looked blue in the moonlight. The train itself was raised far off of the ground on a wall that rose high above the ground. Eventually, the wall was replaced by a tall platform, and James realized that the tracks were gradually rising higher and higher. Before long, the tracks were so far off of the ground that the train popped out and over the clouds, a new level of bluish-white hills stretching into the distance. And yet there was still another, thinner layer of clouds overhead, so that this new view didn't look much different from when they were on the ground, and for that matter, James began to find it hard to tell whether he really was looking at rolling clouds or if they were still beside the rolling hills.

As he continued along the train, he found that many people were sleeping. He couldn't imagine how they could manage it, seeing that there were so many people still up and talking to one another. For most of the passengers it was a regular social gathering. A group of people would be debating over politics and then a passerby would stop to give his opinion. In one car there was a boxing match, with all of the walls lined with men shouting enthusiastically. James had a difficult time getting past that car. (Partially because he went *through* the match, and one of the contenders tripped over him.) Every now and then he would pass a peddler selling various wares. Some were selling souvenirs. Others were selling evening meals and tea. One looked to be a postman, delivering mail to the passengers. At one point, he passed a man who had somehow managed to bring a piano on board and had several violinists to accompany him.

The train was like a late night village.

James eventually came upon a car near the front of the train that had only a few people occupying it. James took a seat in one corner and spent some time staring out the window at the rolling hill-clouds.

Eventually he lost interest and looked a second time around the cab. There was a gentleman sitting not far from him who was reading a newspaper. On the front page James saw the following headline:

CASTLE ATTACKED BY ZOMBIE CHILDREN. PLACE UTTERLY DESTROYED.

Below that was a vague article depicting the night's events and a picture of the castle in flames. He wished he could walk over to the man and ask for a closer look at the paper, but he felt it would be better to keep a low profile.

It was around then that it occurred to him that he was wearing a satchel. Curious, he slid it off his shoulder and examined its contents. It had some food and needles and thread and a handkerchief. And then there was a book. Too afraid to hope, he quickly pulled the book out and looked at it.

It was Marloth. The *real* Marloth. He couldn't believe it. With joy inexpressible, he opened the book and began to read. He read about a little boy who was trying to escape from an Asylum. The boy was running through a labyrinth of corridors while being accompanied by a raven. Behind them a crowd of angry people was giving chase. Then they came across a card game being played by a monkey, a zombie child, a cloth animal, and a madman. A bizarre conversation ensued. Eventually the cloth animal agreed to help the boy escape from the Asylum.

"I don't know what you think you're reading," said a voice. "But that is *not* how it went down."

James lowered the book to find Fugue staring up at him. "I'm serious." said Fugue. "I don't even talk like that."

"I knew you were alive!" said James.

"And I knew you were alive too!" said Fugue, whatever that was supposed to mean. They sat back down on the bench and talked about old times. Fugue was much larger now. He was still shorter than James, but not by much.

"So what are you doing now?" said Fugue. "Please tell me you're on a quest! I'm starving for a good adventure!"

"Well, I suppose I am on a quest of sorts."

"Awesome! What's the gig?"

"Right now I'm trying to find a princess. And rescue her."

"More Awesome! I love rescuing princesses! What are we rescuing her from?

"Most everyone." said James.

"Us against the world, huh?"

"That's about the gist of it."

"Most Awesome! Trying to save the world or fighting against it, either way works for me."

As they were speaking, a new passenger entered the car and sat down across from them.

James' eyes widened. "That's Mr. Mosspuddle!" he exclaimed to Fugue.

"Who?"

"The custodian of the Great Library! I wonder what brings him here?"

James and his cloth companion went over to the toad, who had been too preoccupied to notice them.

"Hello." said James. Mr. Mosspuddle looked up in surprise.

"Why hello." he said in return. "We spoke once, didn't we? I don't think I caught your name."

"I'm James." said James. "What are you doing outside the Library? Are you gathering new books?"

"No. Never again. I was fired."

"Fired? From the Great Library?"

"Yes. For the first time in as long as I can remember, I am unemployed."

"But who could fire you? The wizards can't do that!"

"Yes, they can. And they did. Somehow they discovered that I had not destroyed your book. They were furious. I am fortunate to be alive." (Though his tone did not sound very fortunate.) After several moments of quiet, Mr. Mosspuddle pulled himself together.

"I'm sorry. You don't need to be dwelling on my problems. How have you been?"

"Great." said Fugue. "We just escaped an Asylum."

"That's nice." said Mr. Mosspuddle.

"And now we're trying to find Adelle." said James.

"You mean the princess?"

"Yes. We're going to rescue her."

"Rescue her from whom?"

"Most everyone. Do you know what happened to the castle?"

"Yes, I read about it in the paper. Most dreadful! They say the king and queen have been presumed dead! Without their leadership, I fear this world might lose what little sense of order it still claimed. But what of the princess? Each paper says something different about her situation; I don't even know if she is still alive!"

"She's alive. I think she's in the City of Orphans."

"The City of Orphans? That is one of the most dangerous places in Marloth! What makes you think she is there?"

"I can sense her. At least I think it's her."

"That's kind of creepy. How in the world can you do that?"

"I don't know. I wasn't able to sense her in the castle. But now I can. It's not so much a sense of direction as an idea that Adelle is somewhere within that city. I think it might be a zombie thing."

"That's even creepier."

"Would you like to come too?" Fugue asked him.

Mr. Mosspuddle looked surprised. "I don't know that I could be of any use! And the City of Orphans; I probably wouldn't survive more than a few minutes! If the princess really is in the City, I would be willing to give a great deal to get her away from that place, but I don't think I have anything to give."

"You know a lot about books, and all of our hopes lie in this one." said James, and he put Marloth onto the table. The librarian jumped as if James had just set the table on fire.

"That book! It's what got me fired!"

"You never got fired. The only person who can fire you is Edward Tralvorkemen, not the wizards. He created the Library. As far as I'm concerned, you are still and always will be the head librarian of the Great Library."

"I can't say I share your ideas of this Tralvorkemen, but I have to agree with your assessment of the wizards. And I am dying to explore this book you have."

"If you come with us you'll be able to read it all you like."

Mr. Mosspuddle rubbed the back of his bald head nervously.

"You can count me amongst your number." he said at last. "Not that I will be of much use, but I will do what I can. I just hope you are misled about Princess Adelle's whereabouts. If she truly is in the City, I don't know what any of us can do."

"I think this will answer a lot of your questions." said James, and he handed him the book. The toad hesitated, and then eagerly took it and began to read. He read all the way to the City of Orphans.

*　　*　　*

After much work and practice, the evening of Adelle's perfor-mance finally arrived. She was preparing to leave for the Theatre for her final rehearsal and passing by Ivy's room when Ivy popped out and called out to her.

"Adelle, we need to talk."

Adelle looked back in surprise. "Okay, but I don't have much time. I need to be at the Theatre for my final rehearsal." She fol-lowed Ivy into the room and Ivy closed the door behind them.

"Please have a seat." Ivy said. Once they were both seated on the edge of Ivy's bed Adelle asked her what she wanted to talk about. Ivy had been thinking about how to introduce this for some time, but she still considered a moment longer before beginning.

"I don't completely know why, but everyone is nicer when they are around you. Even I feel more gracious when I am with you."

Adelle beamed. "I'm glad I can be an encouragement to you."

"Yes, well, that making-people-act-nicer-thing . . . it goes for Bobby too. When he is around you he is more civil than I have ever seen him."

"Really? I was wondering if I could be a positive influence on him."

Ivy grimaced. This wasn't exactly the direction she was wanting to go. "But that's the thing: you aren't really changing anyone. When Bobby is out of your sight he is just the same as he always was. The good you've seen is only on the surface. You've never seen his darker side."

"I don't believe in giving up on people so easily! Maybe he does have a darker side, but I think I can help him. He just needs someone who understands him."

"I don't want you to understand him! In order to truly do that you would need to experience things … do things … that you could never reverse. I like you the way you are, and I don't want you to lose that. Please, *please* don't get too close to Bobby."

"Well then, which boy do you recommend? Harris? Thome? Or maybe Osmand?"

"No. None of those. Not even Osmand."

"Well then once again I ask, which boy do you recommend?"

"No one. None of the boys are good enough for you."

"But they are good enough for you?"

"Yes."

"I hope you don't think I'm better than you."

"It's not like that. You have something I don't have. Something I don't think I ever had. You have hope. I look at you and I almost begin to wonder if the fairytales really are true; if there really can be happy endings."

"I do believe in happy endings! And I think those can happen to anybody, even Bobby. Why are you so down on him and the other boys?"

Ivy thought for a long time and then finally said, "I'll tell you why, but first you have to promise never to repeat it to anyone."

"I promise!"

"It stays between you and me. No one else can know!"

"I won't say a word of it to anyone. Cross my heart and hope to die!"

Ivy winced. "Okay." she said at last. "Here I go. I've never told this to anyone before. Do you know why I'm so popular? I'm not a princess like you. Sure, my mother is a bit of a celebrity, but being her daughter draws more negative attention than positive. I have money and decent looks, and that helps, but so do hundreds of other girls in this city, and most of them are hardly even heard of. Do you know why I'm so popular? It's because I'm everyone's slut. Everyone I've ever known has used and abused me. Everyone except you."

Ivy paused as though she expected Adelle to comment, but Adelle was very quiet. And wide eyed. Ivy sighed and then continued.

"I don't understand myself. I love boys. I can't stop thinking about them. They define me. And yet all they've ever done is hurt me. I keep throwing myself at them, and I keep getting crushed into the ground and the rare drops of good in me stolen away. I hate to say it, but they are stronger. Even when it's all a matter of magic, somehow they are still stronger. No matter how nice they act at first, deep down they are all thugs. My mother is the only woman I know who is more powerful than men, and look what she had to become to reach that? I don't want to be my mother!"

It was at this point that they were interrupted by one of the servants, who came to tell Adelle the carriage was waiting to take her to the Theatre for her preparations before the show.

"I'm sorry, I have to go!" Adelle said to Ivy once the servant had left.

"No worry. I shouldn't spend all day boring you with my problems."

"What you are saying is *not* boring! I'm so honored that you would share your heart with me! Hopefully we can continue this after the show!"

"I can't say that I share that hope. But we'll see. Now hurry along or you'll be late."

Adelle rose and hurried to the door, but before she left, she turned and said, "I don't believe the world is nearly as bad as you think it is."

"And I want you to keep believing that. You're the best drug I've ever had."

*　　　*　　　*

The train slowed to a stop on the outskirts of the City of Orphans. The three heroes looked to be the only passengers getting off at that destination.

There were not many people out on the streets. Here and there could be seen a lone peddler pushing his cart or a woman of questionable virtues standing on a corner or a group of children moving from one bar to another. Silhouettes could be seen through many of the lit windows. After brief conferring, they set off down one of the streets.

"I see you're still dead."

James looked up to find the raven resting on a signpost above them.

"Why, hello." said James.

The raven scanned the party, paused for a moment at Fugue, and turned back to James. "What are you doing with one of the Jakob Damond's minions?"

Fugue gave a flawless expression of innocent surprise. "Who? Me? I'm no minion. I'm Fugue!"

"You're an enchanted toy. There are few enchanted toys in this world who haven't escaped his taint."

"Well I'm one of them that did."

"The odds are against it."

"Well they're not against me. I'm as odd as they get."

"I like your thinking." said the raven.

"Who is this Jakob Damond you speak of?" asked Mr. Mosspuddle.

"The toymaker." said James.

"The Toymaker!" cried the raven. "That is what he calls himself, but that is a gross misnomer! The *'Toymaker'* doesn't make anything. He can't! Despite his imaginative appearance, he is the most uncreative person in existence! All he does is steals other people's creations, curses them, and then sells them to clueless people he wants to control! Look around us! We have already passed several toyshops, all of them closed. They were driven out of business because they had no more merchandise to sell!"

"Fugue was not made in any toyshop, and he was never stolen by any toymaker." said James. "He was made by children. Real, live children. Fugue is one of the good guys."

The raven looked back at Fugue. "Very well. Maybe you aren't an agent of Jakob Damond. But even so, you can't be very useful. You're just a fluffy collection of scraps."

"You would not be saying that if I had my equipment! Every one of the rare artifacts I collected throughout my travels possessed awesome powers! But alas, I do not know what happened to them. At the moment I am more bare than dog." And then his face grew sterner. "But even without my equipment I am still a force to be reckoned with."

The raven chuckled in an unaffirming way and turned to the toad. "And what's this creature?"

"Hello, Mr. Raven. I am Mr. Mosspuddle, former custodian of the Great Library. It is a pleasure to meet you."

"If you are pleased to meet me then you are a fool." said the raven.

The librarian was shocked. "That's not a very nice thing to say!" he told the raven, who rolled his eyes.

"It's humor. Softens the blow. Makes people laugh. 'Service with a smile', that's my motto." Then he turned back to James.

"So what are you all doing in the City of Orphans?"

"We're here to rescue Adelle." said James.

"You're still after the princess? Getting stabbed and thrown into an endless abyss wasn't enough for you, eh? Well good luck with that. What makes you think she's here in the City?"

"I can sense her." said James. "Somehow I know she is somewhere around the City."

"That's kind of creepy."

"Unfortunately I'm having a hard time figuring out which direction she is. Do you have any idea which part of the City I could find her?"

"No, I do not. Aside for the messages of doom I have delivered here, I know very little about this world. Except that it is dark. And it smells bad."

If James' had possessed a watch, he would have been looking at it. "While this is an interesting conversation, we really need to get moving."

The raven dropped down and landed on Mr. Mosspuddle's head.

"Ouch." said the toad.

"You are the most curious band I have ever met." said the raven. "I am dying to see what trouble you are going to get into. And how James croaks."

Thus the four of them continued down the foreboding avenue. By then the streets were even less crowded than they had been earlier. Before long, the four of them were the only people traversing the streets. All of them had grown rather quiet. Even the raven had not spoken for some time, which was in itself unnatural.

"I don't like this!" whispered the toad to James. "There must be some form of a curfew! And we're trespassing against it!"

"There are no signs that mention anything like a curfew." said James. "Though I must admit, there must be *some* reason why we're the only people outside."

"Not the only ones." whispered the raven, who was still perched atop Mr. Mosspuddle's head. "Don't look back, but we're being followed."

"By what?"

"By a monkey."

James stopped. "Did it have a wicked grin?"

"All the time." said the raven.

James continued walking, now at a faster pace.

"Exactly what is going on?" the librarian demanded. "I think I have a right to know how much trouble we are in!"

"That monkey works for the toymaker." said James.

Mr. Mosspuddle's already large eyes grew even wider. "You mean the Jakob-Damond-Toymaker?"

"Yes."

Fugue sidled up to James and spoke to him, saying, "I'm a little embarrassed to ask, but do you happen to have any weapons to spare?"

James replied that he didn't have any weapons at all.

"Then this is a fine pickle!" said Fugue.

"But aren't you still a force to be reckoned with?" James asked him.

"Yeah. I am. But I would require even more reckoning if I had a sword!" After some quick searching Fugue was able to find a stick, and he said that would help a great deal.

Eventually they came across a confusing looking sign that may have been some sort of map. In the midst of all its complicated circles and boxes, there was an arrow with the inscription scrawled above it: "You might be here."

"I think we should split up." said James. "We can cover more ground that way."

"But won't that make us more vulnerable to all of the dangers around us?" asked Mr. Mosspuddle.

"How about this, you and Fugue can stay together. The raven and I will split up and keep looking for Adelle separately."

"Who said anything about me looking for Adelle?" spoke the raven.

"Do you have anything better to do?"

"No."

The group split up. As the raven took to the air and the amphibian and cloth animal set off down a nearby street, James mulled over which way to turn. He knew nothing about the City's present layout, which was understandable since it had probably already changed within the short period they had been there. Where should he go to get information? He had no idea where the right place was, or if he was already at the right place, or if there even was a right place. After making a round of the block, he spotted a nearby sign with the words "Happy Little Inn" written on it. Inns were good places to get information, or so he had heard.

Stepping through the doorway beneath the sign, he found himself in a tea house filled with half a dozen tables. The front of the room was one large glass window with pretty designs painted along the edges. The back wall of the room was lined with a bar and stools. Behind this stood a stout woman who was vigorously wiping teacups. It was the nurse from the castle.

The nurse turned around and spotted James. "Have a seat!" she commanded, motioning to one of the tables by the front window and then returning back to her work. James approached the table and found that it was ridiculously small. James was not big, even for a child, and yet he had a terrible time trying to squeeze between the chair and table. When he finally managed to reach a position that could be considered sitting, he found himself longing for the days when he could feel no pain.

After waiting there for quite some time, a door to the side opened and out came what James could only surmise was a child's doll. She came skipping out with a notepad in one hand and a platter with a napkin and utensils in the other.

"Hello!" she said, curtsying. "My name is Samantha! What's yours?"

"James." said James.

"How nice to meet you!" she said, setting the platter's contents onto the table. "What would you like to eat?"

"What is there to eat?" asked James.

"Well, there are crumpets!"

"And what else is there?"

"Well, we also have crumpets!"

"Do you have anything besides that?"

"If none of our other wares interest you, there's always crumpets!"

James frowned. The doll smiled eagerly.

"Well then, I guess I feel like a crumpet." said James.

"What a wonderful coincidence!" said Samantha. "That happens to be all that we have! And tea, of course!"

"But of course."

"I'll bring you both!" she said. With that, she curtsied and retreated back behind the door.

The nurse continued to work with her back to James. It was hard for him to discern what in the world she was actually doing, if anything, but she certainly appeared to be busy, whatever the case.

The door at the other side of the room swung open and what looked like a stuffed swan waddled through and began to dust off the tables with its wings. James was watching this and wondering just how sanitary the creature's wings were when he remembered that his primary intention in coming there was to get information, not food. He didn't even need to eat, seeing that he was dead. *I couldn't starve if I wanted to*, he noted to himself.

"Hello, um, do you know anything about a princess from a nearby castle?" he asked. He had no sooner said this than he realized just how stupid it sounded. He never had been very good at asking for help.

"Oh, you mean Princess Adelle!" said the swan.

"Why—yes," said James, surprised. "You know her?"

"Doesn't everybody? It's the biggest news around here! A few nights ago the castle was attacked by an army of those dreadful zombies! But she's a very resourceful girl! She managed to escape the lot of them!"

"Oh dear!" said Samantha, who had just returned with a platter of crumpets and a pot of tea. "Don't even mention those terrible creatures! If a zombie ever came around here, I'd probably faint!"

"Don't worry," said the swan. "Miss Bethany can handle any number of zombies that come this way!"

The nurse half turned from her work and glared about the room as though to testify the fact, and James swore he heard a growl.

"Did I hear someone mention Adelle?" said a doll with a ginger-like smile as it stepped through the doorway.

"Why yes," said the swan. "This nice young man is an acquaintance of hers!"

"That's wonderful!" yet another doll said as it stepped through the doors. "Any friend of Adelle's is a friend of ours!"

"*Egad!*" thought James. "*They're multiplying!*"

"But I do have to say," said Miss Perrywinkle. "That girl has something of a temper about her. She still has a lot of growing up to do!"

James grabbed one of the crumpets and took a bite out of it. Now he was glad he had no need to eat. The things tasted like plastic.

"Do you know where Adelle is now?" James asked, pushing the platter aside and trying the tea.

"She's probably at the playhouse. That's where most everyone is right now!"

He knew little of such things, but the tea tasted an awful lot like tap water. At least it had a neutral flavor.

"And where may I find this playhouse?" he asked

Samantha shrugged. "It's not in here! I know that much!"

"Do any of you know of someone who could tell me?" he asked.

"The Enchantress should know. You can find her at her business." said Mrs. Gingersmile.

"And what is her business?" James asked.

"She owns the playhouse!"

By this time, any doubts in James' mind had been thoroughly bludgeoned to death: this was clearly *not* the place to be asking for help. James tried to get out of his chair, fell onto the floor in the process, and finally managed to get to his feet.

"Thank you for everything." he said. "What do I owe you for the food?"

"Why, you have to kiss us, of course!"

"Kiss you?"

"Yes, each of us!"

James stood there for a moment.

"I have a little money." he said.

"Who needs money in a fairytale world?" said Mrs. Gingersmile. "Now be a good boy and stop trying to gyp us!"

And thus it came to pass that James went around the room and kissed each of the dolls on the forehead. Then, turning to the nurse, who still had her back to them, he motioned toward her inquisitively.

"I wouldn't if you want to live." Samantha whispered to him, rather loudly.

James nodded, and then, deciding that this was his chance to get the hell out of there, burst through the door and peeled down the street.

The dolls gathered at the doorway and merrily waved goodbye.

*   *   *

After James had run a few blocks, he eventually stopped to listen to a particularly loud ruckus that was nearby. He turned a corner to find Mr. Mosspuddle surrounded by several zombie children, all of them circling the librarian eagerly. A few of them were brandishing torches and were shouting something about baked frog legs. Mr. Mosspuddle was cowering in their midst, tightly clinging to his books and desperately trying to explain that he was not a frog, but a toad.

Suddenly Fugue burst from the shadows, hurled something onto the ground that enveloped everyone in smoke, and whisked the toad away. James was far enough from the action to see past the smoke and follow the two of them to a safe place behind several buildings and alongside a waterway. They were soon rejoined by the raven, and then all four of them shared the results of their searching. Since Adelle was currently *the* hot topic of the City each of the heroes had been able to find at least some idea of Adelle's whereabouts, but the raven held the most comprehensive intelligence.

"She's at the Theatre. She's giving a big singing performance. That's where most everybody is right now."

"Wait, Adelle can sing?"

"She's a princess. Of course she can sing."

*　　*　　*

After a final rehearsal, the patrons were allowed to start taking their seats. Adelle watched through the edge of the curtain as hundreds of people began to fill the auditorium. In a remarkably short amount of time every seat was occupied. It was a sea of people. A sea of eyes. Hundreds of minds, ready to take in every move she made, every word she spoke, every note she sang. She was like a person with vertigo who knows that they shouldn't stare down the edge of the precipice but are unable to pull themselves away. The more she thought about it, the more her anxiety grew until it was gorged by her own insecurity.

Then the moment came. As the curtains were pulled back, she felt like she was being disrobed before the entire world so that every one of them could see her nakedness. But they did not see anything to be ashamed of. Everyone applauded as she was revealed before them, and then the applause gradually descended into a hushed silence.

The silence hung for some time, every moment creating more and more tension. Adelle knew she should begin, but she was frozen. She could feel every one of those eyes staring at her, as though they were boring through her and dissecting her and discarding everything they found lacking.

Then, a hint of peace fell upon her like a warm blanket on a cold night. She did not know where it had come from, except that it had come from outside of her. It felt foreign, and yet familiar. It was not of considerable size, but it was enough for her to begin.

She sang a note. Timidly. Her voice quivered and the word itself was nearly unintelligible. Probably some critic near the back of the crowd auditorium snickered. Then she sang another note. And another. Each syllable developed more and more strength, more and more confidence. Each tone grew clearer, each note more pleasing to the ear and piercing to the heart. Before long the warmth had engulfed her and she had forgotten about the people and she was in the moment and singing with all her might.

Déjà vu
Do I know you?
Have I been here before now?
The days pass me by, and slip away

Forever why
Can I not cry
For the loved ones who've faded?
Am I truly so jaded within?

As my heart begs to melt
Ice turns to tears
Foes turn to friends

Hope replaces fear

When she hit the chorus her voice soared, and the audience soared with her.

Please don't tell me that I'm dreaming
I so want to believe that the fairytale is true
I've never been so happy before
I stand before the stranger that I've always known

Far above the audience and near the back of the auditorium, a raven, a toad, a cloth animal, and a zombie boy were watching the performance from the rafters.

"I've never seen the princess before." said Fugue. "She's very beautiful."

"How can you tell?" asked Mr. Mosspuddle. "I can barely discern her figure from this distance."

"I can tell." said Fugue.

The raven snickered. "She's dressing more conservatively."

"Conservatively?"

"Yeah, she's conserving material."

James was the only one who did not say anything. He just watched and listened, not missing a detail.

Though I desperately try
To imprison my eyes
The visions still course through my mind
Shivering and afraid
I gaze up in surprise
As I hear someone calling my name
And then I am drowned
By the million sounds
Of memories long since thrown away
The morn of my birth

The taste of first love
And the wondrous face of God

Everyone rose to their feet as she sang the final chorus.

Please don't tell me that I'm dreaming
I so want to believe that the fairytale is true
I've never been so happy before
I stand before the stranger that I've always known

When Adelle finished, every person in the room was leaping up and down and applauding until their hands were ready to bleed. Within less than an hour, a little girl had inspired the world.

After the performance, Adelle attempted to meet her endless fans. There were people everywhere she turned, and many Query Gremlins and questions and flashes of blinding light. The performance had gone so well that the Lady Mediev asked Adelle if she would be willing to sing at least one song at the upcoming Ball. Adelle said she would love to. Eventually the Lady felt that Adelle had performed enough of the required socializing (something which Adelle readily agreed with), and the princess was discreetly escorted through the top exit and into a carriage which spirited her away. Not to be thwarted by such an easy escape, crowds of adoring fans gave pursuit behind the carriage. Among these was the band of heroes, who tracked Adelle all the way to the Mediev Manor. They gathered on a nearby rooftop that provided an excellent vantage of the Manor and kept them free from the mindless throng below. There the heroes planned their next move.

First they argued over whose house they were looking at, and then they argued over whether Adelle was a prisoner or willingly residing there. James was adamant that she was in danger either way.

"We need to find a way into that building." said James.

"We? I'd rather have no part in that." said Mr. Mosspuddle. "I'll leave the breaking and entering to you."

The raven shook himself as though being zapped by currents of electricity. "That place is crawling with enchantments! I can sense them clear over here! What need does she have for so much magic?"

Fugue looked down at the crowded street. "It's crawling with people, too. It won't be easy to gain entrance with all of those bodies running around. They look like they're ready to break into the house themselves, and that's probably making the people inside that place extra defensive. Maybe we should come back later when this isn't the hot place to be."

James shook his head. "We don't have that kind of time! For all we know, terrible things could be happening to her as we speak!"

"Okay, then can you tell me how we are going to get in there? Beside this noble stick, I don't have any weapons, while there are at least four well armed guards patrolling that building—no, make it six ... seven ... oh, and there's another one over there. Egad! That place's defenses have defenses! We couldn't get close enough to even look for an opening! At least not now."

James turned to the raven. "What about you? Could fly around it and get a good lay of the land?"

"Did you hear nothing about enchantments? That place is riddled with them! Magic is one of the few things I have reason to fear, and this is *the Enchantress* we're talking about. Magic is her breakfast cereal!"

"But if you detect the enchantments, can't you also avoid them?"

"Yes. Staying away is how I do that."

"But what do the enchantments do?"

"I don't know. Maybe they make flowers grow; maybe they turn intruders into mud. I'm not going to find out. If you want to rescue your princess, then by all means do so, but don't try to get me killed!"

James was getting frustrated. He started talking about going into the Manor on his own but Mr. Mosspuddle begged him not to be so rash. Tempers were growing increasingly heated when Fugue grabbed James' sleeve and, with much excitement, pointed down at the street.

"Look! It's a carriage just like the one Adelle rode in! It even has another of those gnomes driving it. I bet you candy it's heading to that building!"

"So what's your point?"

"We need to get under it! It will take us right through the gates and into the dragon's lair!"

"Is that safe?" Mr. Mosspuddle asked.

"Are you kidding? None of this is safe!"

And without further deliberation, he threw himself into the crowd. James glanced at Mr. Mosspuddle, who looked like he would prefer a little more deliberation, and then the carriage, which was about to pass them by. James followed after Fugue.

He landed on the heads of several zombie children and then on the ground just as the carriage passed directly over him, knocking pedestrians in all directions. James and Fugue were both able to catch onto the underworkings of the carriage, where they found several other zombie children already clinging onto it as well. Fugue quickly disengaged these from their holds.

The carriage sliced a path through the rest of the crowd and, just as Fugue had predicted, passed through the gates of the Manor. The carriage stopped briefly in front of the main entrance to deliver its sole passenger, which was Ivy. She stepped out of the carriage looking altogether bored, sleepy, and of a mind to stay up even later.

Once she was inside the Manor, the carriage proceeded to a nearby carriage house that was connected to the rest of the building. As the servants focused their attention on parking the carriage and unharnessing the emus, Fugue and James disengaged from their hiding place and slipped into the halls of the Manor. They decided to split up and explore the building.

Fortunately, there were many children running around the Manor, so the few times James was spotted no one thought anything of him. His sensing of Adelle was growing stronger, but he still had a hard time pinning it down to a particular direction. He was at least fairly certain she was near the front of the Manor. After searching for some time with no success, he was rejoined by Fugue, who came hurrying toward him with a look of great excitement.

"I have important news! The Lady Mediev employs ogres!"

James didn't understand his excitement. "I don't remember much about ogres." was all he said.

"Ogres are always armed to the teeth! They hoard weapons! Massive weapons of destruction!"

"So why are you saying this? Should we keep our distance from them?"

"No! We need to take their weapons! Find their stashes! Stock up on firepower!"

James made some noncommittal comment and Fugue, like a child on Christmas morning, again left him, this time in search of the armory. James wasn't entirely happy about Fugue's prioritizing weapons over the princess, but he was too preoccupied with his own searching to dwell on that.

After further exploration, James came across an unlocked door that led to a second story room at the front of the house. As he opened it just enough to peer inside, he was rewarded to find Adelle sitting on a bed and taking off her slippers. Overjoyed, James opened the door the rest of the way and stepped inside.

Adelle saw James, froze for an instant, and then screamed with all of her might.

"Wait!" said James. "I can explain, I'm just—"

The door again opened and in stepped the Lady Mediev.

"Now what is the matter?" she demanded.

Adelle scrambled backwards, frantically pointing at James. The Lady looked at James, and then back at Adelle. "Yes, I can see him. And your point is . . . ?"

"He's a zombie!" Adelle shouted.

Once again, the Lady Mediev looked back and forth from Adelle to James.

"And that's a problem because . . . ?"

"He's a zombie! Zombies are evil! They do terrible things to girls like me! And he's in my bedroom!"

After carefully analyzing the scene, it finally dawned upon the Lady. "*Ohhhh.*" she said at last. "Now I see." she snapped her fingers and James froze solid with his eyes glazed over. "No need to worry. He won't hurt you now."

Adelle remained on the opposite side of her bed, still eyeing James fearfully. "What do you mean? How do you know he won't hurt me?"

"Because I just cast a spell on him. Now the boy is under my full control. He will do anything I ask in the vain hope of receiving my approval. I could have him jump into a vat of acid if I felt like it, and he would gladly do it." She smiled. "It's a lot of fun. With some practice, you'll be able to do the same."

Adelle didn't really seem to be listening. In fact, she looked like she was going to be sick.

The Lady turned toward James. "Go out into the hall." she commanded, and he complied, his hands outstretched in front of him like a . . . well, like a zombie.

Adelle was feeling terrible. She could not get the image of a knife sticking out of a boy's stomach from her mind. Feeling woozy, she sat down on the bed.

The Lady Mediev walked across the room and stopped at an ornate, wooden cupboard. Taking a key from one of her pockets, she unlocked a door in the cupboard and lifted out a silver platter upon which were stacked a pile of what looked like pieces of charcoal.

"Here, try one of these!" said the Lady.

Adelle shivered. "Eww! What's that?"

"Why, they're Jillybons!" said the Lady. "It's all the rave in the City. Try one; they'll cheer you up in a trice!"

Adelle timidly took one and smelled it. It even *smelled* like charcoal. Or worse.

"Come on! Don't be a baby!" the Lady scolded. "Eat it!"

Adelle gathered her courage and shoved the object into her mouth. She nearly choked. It tasted worse than it smelled.

"That was terrible!" she moaned after finally swallowing. She was already feeling sick; the woman didn't have to make her feel worse!

"Well never mind then!" said the Lady Mediev, apparently offended. "I'll just take my leave. You're clearly over-tired, and need a good nap. And you won't ever have to worry about seeing that boy again. From now on you'll only meet boys that will treat you right."

Smiling condescendingly, she left the platter on the bedside, dimmed the lights, and left the room.

Adelle got up and went over to the door. It was locked! Fuming, she threw herself on the bed and imagined commanding *her* to jump into a vat of acid.

Outside the room, the Lady Mediev turned from the locked door to see James standing there patiently, awaiting her next command.

"Follow me." she said.

They walked through several hallways and into a large and slightly more rustic room that was in her study. The Lady sat down behind a desk while James remained standing in front of her. But she had barely sat down when James flung himself on the ground and lay there, gasping for breath.

The Lady sighed. "I was afraid that was going to happen. I knew from the moment I cast my spell that it was barely sticking and would fall off any moment."

James lifted himself to one knee. He was not accustomed to being weak. He couldn't remember a time where he had been weak. But here he was, striving for any hint of energy he could muster.

The Lady drummed her fingers on the desk, looking at him curiously. "All zombie children are enchanted. That's what separates them from motionless bodies. Many of my powers are based upon tapping into that enchantment. But this boy has another enchantment. One I have never seen before."

Her eyes narrowed.

"I don't think I like it."

By now James was feeling nearly back to normal and was finally able to stand. The Lady Mediev hardly seemed to pay him any attention, talking more to herself than anyone else.

"This enchantment does have a certain flair, a signature you could say, that I have seen before. A small part of me would like to study this new enchantment and learn its nature and where it came from, but the rest of me would rather just destroy the boy and move on to more important matters."

Suddenly the doors burst open and Fugue was standing before them. He was carrying a large musket and was loaded down with all sorts of bombs, daggers, and other implements of war.

"Sorry lady," said Fugue. "But we're gettin' outta' here!"

The Lady prepared to envelop the plucky creature in a deadly spell, but before she could finish, Fugue was dodging aside and Miss Bethany was charging into the room like a mad rhino. The Lady cast a flurry of spells at the seamstress turned nurse turned (?), but they simply bounced off. The women collided. The Lady Mediev was sent flying through the air and slammed into one of her bookcases, knocking from her both wind and consciousness.

"What better way to take out a sorceress than a broad who doesn't believe in such stuff?" said Fugue. "And they don't get much broader than this gal!"

Miss Bethany looked at James sternly. "Do you know how to do anything other than get yourself into trouble?"

"I've been trying to get someone out of trouble!" said James. "What are you doing here?"

"She's catering refreshment to the Lady's guests." said Fugue. "She and a bunch of dolls. I happened upon them in one of the hallways."

As if on cue, the four dolls skipped into the room. "It's that boy again! Did you find the princess?"

"Yes. She's in this house."

"Wonderful! What are you going to do now?"

Fugue, who had poked his head out of the doorway and was peering down each direction of the hall, hurriedly pulled back and slammed the door. "Get ourselves out of here!" he retorted. "The guards have finally caught up with us!"

He threw open the window and surveyed the alley below. Earlier that alley had been patrolled by several guards, but at the moment those guards were trying to break down the door behind them.

"But what about Adelle?" James demanded. "We can't leave without her."

The pounding on the door grew louder. "Well, we certainly can't leave with her." said Fugue. "Unless you can fight through a throng of heavily armed half-men and ogres."

A faint moaning came from the direction of the Lady Mediev. She was starting to come to. The occupants of the room couldn't see what was happening in the hall, but the ogres (who were slower and had been near the back of the pursuit) had finally managed to walk over the half-men (who were at the front and were rather pathetic when it came to breaking heavy objects). The door was promptly ripped off its hinges and hurled across the room.

Miss Bethany took in the situation. "Here. I'll make this easy." She grabbed James and jumped through the window. Her feet landed solidly on the alley with a cement-cracking thud. The dolls lightly dropped down beside her (being practically weightless had its advantages), while Fugue had to be a little more careful in his descent due to the number of explosives he was now packing.

In different circumstances there probably would have been several ogres crashing through the walls, but they had fervent orders from the Lady Mediev not to destroy her property (doors being a reasonable exception). Within moments, the group had slipped into the dwindling crowds outside the Manor and escaped.

*   *   *

After some time had passed, Adelle turned to look at the platter of Jillybons. She hadn't noticed before, but they had little faces, and all of them were looking at her.

"Eat Me!" each of them said, their chorus of voices hardly equaling a whisper.

Now that's unsettling, thought Adelle. *I just ate something that could be talking to me in my stomach!* They wiggled back and forth, begging for her to eat them.

She watched them for quite some time. She *was* rather hungry. But that Jillybon had tasted like, well, she didn't want to think about it.

The most disgusting thing in the world! She thought to herself, as she reached over and grabbed one. *It's probably poison, really,* she figured, as she put it in her mouth. *I'm positive that Mediev Lady is trying to kill me. She clearly hates me!* She ate another. After a time, she began to laugh a little. *Though he was very cute, for a zombie. And I suppose I was over-reacting.* She ate another, and cradled her head in her hands pensively. *I wonder exactly what it is that zombies do to girls like me? Maybe it's not so bad . . .*

She reached over to grab another, but her hand passed through air. She looked over to find the platter empty. Where had they all gone? There had been at least two dozen of them!

Adelle jumped off of the bed, careening with energy and a little dazed. She needed more Jillybons! She raced over to the cupboard and tried to open it, but it was locked. She put her ear against the cupboard door. From inside she could just hear the faintest sound of several high-pitched voices pleading to be eaten.

She had to get inside! Looking about her, she grabbed a small lamp and began to slam its base into one of the cabinet's doors. After several swings, the battered door caved in. Hurriedly, she pulled the pieces of door out of the way and looked inside.

More Jillybons! She quickly set to work, swallowing one after another. Every time she ate one, the little Jillybon would give a miniature shout of joy. But before long, they too were gone. She still couldn't say that she liked the taste, (they were frankly vile), but there was something about these Jillybons that was beyond taste. It was a sensation she had never experienced before.

And she needed more of it! Well, she couldn't see any more Jillybons here. She remembered the Lady Mediev saying that they were all the rave in the City. Surely there were shops and the like from which she could find more. But the door was locked. She was trapped, just like she was in the castle.

"I hate her!" Adelle whispered under her breath. *"We do too!"* she thought she heard a chorus of Jillybons concede from inside her stomach. She turned to look at the window, and then at her bed. Well, she had heard of it in stories. Why couldn't it work here ... She tore off all of the covers, tied them together, fastening one end to the bedpost. So far so good. Thankfully, the window wasn't locked. She opened it and looked outside. By then the crowds had finally dispersed and the street was deserted. After carefully tying the makeshift rope around her waist, she lowered herself out the window and down onto the moonlit streets below.

*   *   *

Mr. Mosspuddle had already been concerned the moment Fugue and James had jumped from the rooftop and into the crowded street, but as time passed and he still hadn't seen them return, he grew more and more anxious. The raven told him not to worry, and had even taken a nap, but Mr. Mosspuddle was not one to be so easily calmed.

Eventually James and Fugue did return. And with them were the four dolls. (Miss Bethany had immediately returned to the Happy Little Inn.)

"You're safe!" said Mr. Mosspuddle. "I was so worried!"

"There's still reason to be worried." said James. "We found Adelle, but we couldn't get her out. She's still in the Mediev Manor. She doesn't look like she's in immediate danger, but it's not a good place. Once we regroup we need to go back there."

"Yes, the sooner the better!" said Fugue. "There's more weapons I need to get from that place! Especially this *huge* gun the ogres had displayed in a back room. It was the most beautiful thing my eyes have ever beheld! It had four sets of four barrels—*sixteen barrels*—that revolve independently in some confusing manner that doesn't make any sense but that doesn't matter because however it works, it must unleash *utter chaos!* I have to have one! We need to find some means to bring it with us! Maybe a cart. Or we could hypnotize an ogre to carry it. Or a spell to give me ogre-sized muscles. That would help in the wielding of it."

"Finding weapons is not our top priority." said James. "We're here to rescue Adelle."

"Wait, wait, wait! You didn't see this gun! Once you see it, you'll realize how much easier rescuing Adelle will be when we're on the delivering end of it! I wish I knew what they called it! I can't keep refer to it as 'that really big gun'. That just wouldn't do it justice. It needs a *worthy* name. Well, since none are coming to me at the moment, I'll just call it the Hexadecagun."

While Mr. Mosspuddle, James and Fugue discussed their options, the raven's attention was drawn elsewhere: he was staring warily at the dolls.

"Who are these people accompanying you?" he asked James.

"Dolls I met earlier in the city." said James. "They own a teashop. They say they know Adelle, and would like to help us protect her. And they've invited us to stay at their inn."

"Dolls!" the raven exclaimed. "Don't you know *anything?* Talking dolls are *evil!* They are minions of Jakob Damond! Next thing you know they'll be brandishing knives and stabbing everything in sight!"

Mr. Mosspuddle hurried to their defense. "But I thought we'd already established that Fugue is not an evil toy, but a servant of good. Perhaps these fine ladies are as well!"

"That's right!" said Fugue. "Us toys can tell that sort of thing. I don't see any puppet strings of the toymaker on these dolls."

"We are no minions of the toymaker!" said the swan. "We are Princess Adelle's loyal playmates. We have enjoyed the presence of her company since she came into this world. Ask her yourself! She will vouch for our benevolence."

"Actually, that would be sort of tricky right now," said James. "But I think most of us are willing to give you the benefit of the doubt."

"Hurray for crazy demos!" said Fugue.

"Fine." said the raven. "I'll give them some trust. Just please don't let them get a hold of any sharp objects."

*   *   *

Ha! She was free once again! No stuck up lady was going to keep Adelle as her pet!

As she walked down the streets, Adelle could feel the Jillybons wriggling about her insides. It tickled. She grabbed her stomach and giggled. It was like having a bunch of friends playing with you even though you were alone.

She felt she would die if she didn't get more Jillybons.

As with most nights in the City of Orphans, there were few people out of doors. As Adelle wandered through the many twists and turns of the City, it had never felt so magical. (This was in part to the effect of the Jillybons.) Most of the people were attending parties at the various clubs, bars, and larger residences. All of these places were well lit and in full swing. But most of the shops were closed.

Adelle continued down one street after another. Every now and then someone would pass her way, but she did not want to be seen, and that desire was all it took for no one to notice her. At one point she passed by a little teashop. It didn't sell any Jillybons, but inside there were a number of quirky heroes discussing plans for rescuing a princess.

Adelle paused before a store window. There in the front there was an entire box of Jillybons on display. She put her face to the window. The Jillybons were calling to her. And I'm not speaking figuratively; they were literally calling her name. (By now everyone knew the princess). They pleaded and begged for her to eat them, and she hated not being able to.

Her hand slipped through the glass. Startled, she pulled it back and looked at her hand as though it were a foreign object. Her hand looked perfectly fine and normal. Cautiously, she reached it toward the window. Her hand passed right through it, sending ripples across the face of the glass. She was able to put the other hand through as well, and then her head.

She paused to consider her new position. The Jillybons were right within her reach. In the corner of her mind, a little voice cried that it would be wrong to take them. But look! She had passed clean through the window! It was meant to be! Maybe she was hallucinating. It didn't really matter to her.

She took the box of Jillybons. It passed through the window with her. She wanted to sit on the curb and eat them right then, but another voice inside her head (there were a lot of those in there at the moment) told her the proper thing to do in such a situation is to scurry off into some dark corner and eat them in secret.

She was just about to do this when she discovered that she was standing in front of the Lady Mediev.

"Well! I finally found you!" said the Lady.

Adelle was speechless. This was both because she was startled and because her faculties of speech were impaired at the moment.

The Lady Mediev eyed the box of Jillybons in Adelle's hands. "What mischief is this? I thought you didn't like Jillybons. Well, it is nice that your tastes have matured, but you had better put that back. Subjects tend to get uptight when they think their Ladies and Lords are stealing from them."

Adelle still didn't say anything. She wasn't completely coherent. After much coaxing, the Lady Mediev was able to persuade the princess to re-perform her window trick and return the Jillybons to their place in the front display. When that was finished, the Lady took out her watch.

"Look at the time! If you thought it was past your bedtime before, now it is really far gone! Next time you feel like escaping on a candy binge it would be polite for you to check with me first."

The Lady's words were somewhat misleading. She had many enchantments rigged inside Adelle's bedroom, and had known the moment of Adelle absence. Also, she could easily sense the various enchantments attached to Adelle and had no problem tracking her. In short, the Lady Mediev could have stopped Adelle at any time, and had only decided to wait as long as she had.

Adelle's condition was worsening. She was far beyond exhaustion and under the influence of about as many Jillybons as a little girl's stomach can hold. She slumped to the curb in a dizzy stupor. The Lady motioned to a half-man who was waiting in the shadows. The half-man stepped forward and lifted the girl over his shoulder. Then he carried her to a carriage that was waiting nearby and dropped her inside like a sack of potatoes. The Lady took the seat across from her, the half-man took the reins outside, and then they set off for home.

*   *   *

Meanwhile in the Happy Little Inn, the band of heroes was continuing their rescue plans.

"We need some means of getting closer to Adelle." said James. "We won't be able to rescue her from this place if we can't get near her. Or maybe if we can't free her right away, we can at least be close enough to protect her."

"I don't think that's going to be very easy right now." said Fugue. "Right now she seems to be a real hot item."

"We know something about that." said the dolls. "We pick up a lot of the gossip around the City."

James turned his attention to the dolls. "How frequently is Adelle by herself?"

"Aside when she sleeps? Hardly ever. Between school and shopping and parties the princess is constantly surrounded by people."

"And I'm sure when she's sleeping in her room is when that place will be the most guarded." said Fugue. "Especially after our little stunt this evening."

James groaned. "This City is doing a bang up job at keeping us from the princess!"

Fugue tapped his head pensively. "Maybe if we could blend in with the locals. Slip into the crowds around Adelle."

"Most of you are too cutesy to fit in with the local populace." said the raven. "You stick out like sore noses."

After the discussions wound down without reaching any solid conclusions, people started talking about heading to bed. Someone suggested they should keep watch in case anything tried to break into the inn. The dolls assured them that the building was perfectly safe, but no one really trusted the dolls' confidence in their friendly neighborhood. Fugue volunteered to perform the first shift. As he was sitting on the roof and enjoying the view, of the twilit City, the raven flew up and landed beside him all in a flurry.

"Curse you!" said the raven.

"What did I do now?" asked Fugue.

"I just spotted some doom ahead for you."

"Well, you don't look too pleased about it. Does some hideous fate await me?"

"No! It's all wrong! It's—it's, well, *happy!*"

"A happy doom?"

"Exactly! Doom isn't supposed to be happy! There's no such thing as happy doom!"

"What's going to happen to me?"

"Who cares? It's *happy!* I can't be going about doling out *happy* dooms to people! What kind of a Darke and Mysterious Raven would I be if I did a thing like that?"

"I think it would be rather jolly. People would start liking you."

"People aren't supposed to like me! People are supposed to run away and hide and beg not to hear what I have to give them! I am the messenger of fate, the harbinger of doom. If people like the prophecies I bring them they are insane!"

"It doesn't sound like the greatest way to make friends. Anyway, I thank you for giving me this prophecy. I wonder what sort of happy doom awaits me? I hope it involves a grand adventure!"

"Stop enjoying it! Prophecies of doom are not meant to be enjoyed!"

"Why not? Don't you ever have any prophecies for yourself?"

"Yes, of course. I'm not a hypocrite!"

"Well, name one."

"It was once prophesied that I would find myself in a stupid world full of stupid people, talking about stupid prophecies to a stupid person. That prophecy has now been fulfilled."

"Whoa. That's a trip!"

Meanwhile, downstairs James was checking in on Mr. Mosspuddle. The librarian had left their discussions early to resume his reading of Marloth.

"So what do you think of it so far?" James asked him.

The toad looked up from his reading; James had never seen him so happy. "This book is beyond anything I could have imagined! It combines hundreds of pieces of stories I have come across as if they were always meant to be connected in this manner! And it relies heavily upon the Theory of Dreams, a philosophy I have long wondered about."

"What's that?"

"The Theory of Dreams? It stipulates that the universe is comprised of many dreams within dreams, each stacked atop the other. The root dream is the most real one, and each progressive one is less and less real. When a person is sleeping, he loses track of the world around him and is living in a dream world. But when he awakes, he returns to the real world. So is the case with this stack of dreams. Whenever one of those dreams ends, the dream below it resumes."

The librarian halted and said, "I'm sorry, I could go on all night! How were the talks? Did you come to any agreement on what to do about Princess Adelle?"

"Nothing solid. But the discussion gave me an idea. I think I know how we can keep an eye on Adelle ..."

*   *   *

The next morning Ivy awoke to find that Adelle was not yet up and would not be coming with her to school but would instead arrive sometime later that day.

Adelle did finally appear around an hour before noon. She staggered into metageography class and sat down beside Ivy.

"You look terrible." whispered Ivy.

"I feel worse."

"What happened last night?"

"I don't want to talk about it."

"Then you're the only one here who isn't talking about it. Except of course the professor and that new kid."

"What new kid?"

Ivy motioned across the room. "I don't know where he came from. No one here recognizes him."

Adelle carelessly looked over and was suddenly jolted awake. Across the room, distinctly spaced from any of the other students, sat James.

The first thing that struck Adelle was how differently he looked from the other students. He did have that same pale complexion that so many of the other students prized, but beyond that, no one within the school had ever displayed so much contempt for their own appearance. How hadn't she noticed it before? Now she gawked at his shabby clothes that were slightly too large for his slight frame, his face and arms with their characteristic smears of dirt, and his virgin hair that had never known the touch of a comb.

"He's clearly from poorer society." Ivy continued. "Though he is kind of cute."

"I know who he is." said Adelle quietly.

"Who?"

"I'll tell you after class."

At the end of the day's classes James entered the hallways in search of Adelle. He was amazed at how mild the other zombie children were. He was accustomed to the constant fighting and debauchery that normally occurred in zombie child ranks. He figured high society school zombies must be more genteel. He was wrong. It was actually Adelle's presence that caused this effect. As long as she was present with her crown, the zombie children conducted themselves as respectable nobles in the royal court. They were still cruel and manipulative, but now they did so with good manners.

He eventually found her along one of the halls in the company of her usual friends. James approached the group cautiously. Very cautiously. He knew that if they wanted they could easily tear him to pieces. As he came within earshot he could hear them talking about Jakob Damond's Toye Shoppe. Apparently it had just appeared in the City and was scheduled to open its doors the next day.

James tried to blend in with the fringe of the crowd, but the moment he stepped near enough to be noticed everyone backed away and focused all their attention on him. Any conversation that had been going on abruptly ceased except for whispering near the back of the crowd. Ivy stepped forward and introduced herself. Then she asked him who he was.

"I'm James." said James.

"I've never seen you before." said Wendy. She looked at the other children. "Has anyone ever seen this kid?"

There was much shaking of heads and answers to the negative. Adelle was very quiet. Wendy turned back to James. "Doesn't look like anyone's seen you before. That's a little strange."

"I used to work for Deadwick." said James.

"*Ohhh!* One of *Deadwick's* thugs. That would explain the rags."

Bobby stepped into the center of attention. "*I* work for Deadwick." he reminded them calmly. Everyone seemed to suddenly grow smaller. After several moments, Ivy turned to Adelle and did her best to break the awkward silence.

"Anyhow, the gang is heading over to the Candy Castle for some Jillybons. We'll catch you later."

"Wait, I want to come too!" said Adelle.

"Really? That's capital! I hate for you to be left out. We won't even pressure you to eat one!"

"Actually, I'd love to have a few Jillybons." said Adelle.

James suddenly spoke up. "Are you joking? Jillybons are parasites! They'll suck the life out of you and drive you insane!"

Adelle looked at him in shock. "Nonsense! All the other children eat Jillybons, and they're just fine!"

"All the other children are dead!"

Adelle couldn't stop herself from laughing. "You'd like that, wouldn't you? If everyone was a zombie you'd be normal!"

Everyone, (except Osmand, who had no idea what was happening on any level), discerned this to be a good time to laugh with her.

"Besides, I've never felt more alive and alert in my life!"

"Wait, you've already eaten some?"

"Not that it's any of your business, but yes, I have."

"They're inside you right now? This can't be happening!"

"Is this bloke giving you trouble?" Bobby asked Adelle. His posture was very straight and at ease, yet it was clear that with one word he would grab James and snap him like a twig.

Adelle looked at James with concern. He *was* making her extremely uncomfortable, and he *was* a creature of undeath, and he *did* appear to be stalking her, but for some reason she still couldn't bear the thought of harming him. "No." she said at last. "He's not bothering me."

Some of the children made a few more witty comments about James and then the group set off for the Candy Castle, leaving James in the empty hallway.

James was fuming. What did he have to do to prove to this girl that he was on her side? He had come all this way to rescue a princess who didn't want his help; who didn't even see any danger. What was he thinking? Why was he putting himself through all of this? And then her new friends ... he didn't notice the personal remarks they made about him, but the fact that she would put her trust in a group of zombie children who would have no scruples in killing her, while she turned her back on the only zombie child with a conscience; the injustice stabbed at him like a dagger.

He debated about following after them, but he couldn't see any use in it. She had already eaten the Jillybons. She had already given herself over to the other children's influence. All he could do was make things worse. Even though he was better at reading books than reading people, he had still noticed how uncomfortable he had made her, and that grieved him. The last thing he wanted to do was make things worse. Yet as he reflected on everything he had done since his arrival at the City, all he had done was make things worse. Then again, he wouldn't have caused so many problems if she had just trusted him. But why would she? He *was* a zombie child. He *did* have desires to cause her harm. He would never forget his reflection in the mirror. He would never forget what his twisted heart was capable of. Who wouldn't flinch away from him?

He had originally planned to return to the Happy Little Inn after school, but now he had no desire for it. Feeling as black as black can get, he climbed up a nearby building and sat down on the roof, where he untied his book bag and took out the only book he had in it, Marloth. Then he opened it to a random page and began to read.

He read of how the good headmaster sacrificed his life to save his children. The children didn't ask him to save them. They didn't want him to. In fact, *they* were the ones who killed him. But he did it anyway because he loved them.

James pondered this for a long time. Then he rose to his feet, returned the book to its place in his satchel, and hurried back to the inn.

Once he had arrived and was in the main entryway, he located Mr. Mosspuddle and said to him with much urgency, "Do you know anything about Jillybons?"

"No. What are they?"

"They're a parasite that zombie children eat. Normally they do terrible stuff to people but they don't hurt zombies."

"Hmm. Do these Jillybons take residence within the stomach or intestines?"

"What? I don't know. I never ate them myself, I just saw the results of living people who did . . ."

"Have you tried fire berries? If these Jillybons do remain in the digestive tract then fire berries should do the trick. Fire berries are used to clean the stomach of all sorts of harmful things."

"Sounds good to me. Where can I find some?"

"Well, I'm sure some of the local shops carry them. You could probably start there."

James grabbed a few items and headed for the door.

"So what's happening?" asked the dolls.

"I don't have much time to talk right now. I'm going out into the city to look for some fire berries."

"Fire fairies? We know all about those! If you put one of them in a lamp, it can provide light for an entire village! And have you ever tried putting one in a pipe? Mr. Gingersmile did once, and it—"

"Berries, not fairies! *Fire berries!*"

"Fire berries? We know all about those too! They are used in some of the most exciting teas! For example, the—"

"I don't have time for this! I need to find some fire berries as soon as possible. It's for Adelle. It's very important that she gets them."

"For Princess Adelle?" said Mr. Mosspuddle. "Has she eaten these Jillybon things?"

"Yes." said James. "Already they are probably hurting her, and she doesn't even realize it."

"How dreadful!" said the dolls. "The princess must be saved! We will help you find these fire berries!"

"Really?"

"We have much experience shopping for rare ingredients. We will scour the city for these berries you seek!"

"And I will search for any more information about Jillybons." said Mr. Mosspuddle.

"Thank you." James said to everyone. And then they set out.

*   *   *

James arrived back at the inn around the same time as the dolls. Mr. Mosspuddle had already returned and had several new books he had acquired which spoke of all manner of candies, including Jillybons. The librarian was very eager to relate his findings to the others.

"These Jillybons definitely sound like a threat to Adelle's life. Even without the devouring of vital nutrients, the way these creatures alter one's judgment can alone be fatal. But the good news amidst my searching is that they do reside in the stomach, so fire berries are definitely a viable cure. Were you able to locate any?"

"No. Not a single one."

"And what about you?" he asked the dolls. "Have you found any fire berries?"

"We have searched high and low and in between, yet we cannot find any fire berries. Every shop is out of them."

"That's what I found too." said James.   He turned to Mr. Mosspuddle. "Are there any other places we could get fire berries?"

"Yes, there are, but none as practical. I know of fire berry groves, wizard markets, and the wishing well of fruit, but it would take a long journey to reach any of those places.   Our next best option would be the Library."

"I would like to buy a wizard." said Fugue.

"The Library has fire berries?" said James. "Why didn't you say that in the first place? Let's go get them!"

Mr. Mosspuddle looked apprehensive. "It's not that simple. The wizards will surely be antagonistic if any of us were to enter the Library. They think I sealed all of the doorways, but one remains, though it is only an entrance, not an exit. It would be a one-way trip into almost certain danger."

"So what you're saying is if we used that doorway we wouldn't be able to get back out?"

"Once inside the Library I would again have access to all of its books, and should be able to use them to make a new doorway, but that would take several days. I don't see any way that we could get the fire berries and return here in time."

"What about the raven?" said Fugue, "He was telling me how he's flown across all kinds of dimensions; maybe he could get the berries. Where is he now?"

"Right behind you." said the raven. He was perched on a cabinet in the corner of the room, and looking especially grumpy. "I was having a marvelous nap until a group of clowns burst in and woke me up."

The raven was going to provide further beratement, but James immediately began informing him of the situation. "Adelle is in trouble! She's eaten this candy called Jillybons and she—"

"I already heard!" said the raven. "And no, I can't do it. Yes, I can fly between dimensions, but there's rules to that, just as there's rules to moving around the physical world. For one thing, I can't pass through magical walls. If the wizards have the library sealed, then I would need a special portal just like anybody else. And besides, even if I were to phase into the library or any of those other fanciful locations, I can't carry things with me when I do that. The berries would just fall out of my beak. Now—if you don't mind—I'm going to get some sleep."

As the raven flew through the doorway in search of a more quiet part of the inn, the dolls wrung their stubby limbs in concern. (Except for Samantha, who was looking about for clowns.) Miss Perrywinkle was the most distraught of the group, and was on the verge of shedding felt tears. "Is Princess Adelle truly going to die?" she moaned. "Her life is in danger and we have exhausted all our options!"

"No," said James. "We still have that one-way door Mr. Mosspuddle spoke of. If we can't bring the fire berries to Adelle, we'll have to bring Adelle to the fire berries."

"That might work," said Mr. Mosspuddle, "But we still haven't addressed the problem of the wizards. Last I saw them they were very angry, and more paranoid than ever about people laying hand on the Library. Now there may be all sorts of invisible traps, or magical guardians, or even a real live wizard . . . or they might trust to the library being sealed and not have done a thing; they are very stingy with resources. In short, I won't know what to expect if we enter the Library."

James wasn't dissuaded. "If you don't know what to expect then there's no way to prepare for it. We'll just deal with that pickle when we come to it. Right now, I need to get Adelle."

"But she didn't respond well to you the last time. How will now be any different?"

"Desperate times call for desperate measures. So far I've been cautious. Now I'll do whatever it takes to get her to that library."

"Cool!" said Fugue. "I want to be a part of that!"

The librarian wrung his hands nervously. "I don't like any of this." he said quietly.

"Do you have a better idea?" James asked.

"No. I guess I don't."

"So are you with us on this?"

Mr. Mosspuddle hesitated. "Yes, I am. I will start work on opening the entrance to the Library. But please, James, be careful."

"Of course I will." said James, as he grabbed his gear and started for the door.

"And please be considerate of the princess." said Mr. Mosspuddle. "However she may act, she is surely not herself right now."

"Don't worry." said James as he and Fugue stepped into the streets.

*　　*　　*

Deadwick was waiting impatiently at a street corner not far from the Mediev Manor. He had scouts positioned all around the neighborhood and it had been some time since any of them had reported back to him. Something big was going down. He could feel it. He was about to set out to check on his scouts when one of them came rushing around the corner and nearly ran into him. Deadwick waited a moment for the zombie to catch his breath, remembered that he didn't have any breath, and said "Come on! Spit it out! What's happening?"

"I just came from the west side of the Mediev Manor!" the zombie gasped. While he didn't have functioning lungs, heavy breathing did help pull more energy from the distant zombie machine. "A boy and a dog creature just slipped into the house."

"Really? Now *that's* interesting. Tell the other kids to tighten their parameter around the house. And tell them I'll be in my spot on the west side of the Manor."

"Got it." said the boy, and he ran back up the street.

*   *   *

James and Fugue carefully made their way through the halls of the Mediev Manor. Fugue had already neutralized several guards. There didn't seem to be any immediate obstacles between them and Adelle's room. Assuming it still was Adelle's room. If she had been moved then things would become a *little* more complicated. They reached the door to the bedroom, which was locked, but that was easy to break. The intruders slipped into the room and were rewarded to find that it was still Adelle's place of residence.

Adelle looked so different than she had the day before. Instead of the exquisite image of youthful energy, she looked pale and weak, laying on her bed moaning. Though she seemed oblivious to her surroundings, she was coherent enough to notice their arrival.

"What are you doing here?" Adelle asked feebly.

James tried to speak in as soft and encouraging a voice as he could imagine. "We're here to help you. You're going to come with us to the Great Library."

"I don't want to go anywhere. I've been feeling so tired lately."

"That's probably just the Jillybons eating all the good stuff in your body." said Fugue absently.

Adelle giggled. "I'm nurturing them!"

Fugue, who had been moving from one window to another and keeping watch over the surrounding neighborhood, turned and said, "There are more groups of zombie children outside than there were when we were outside, and they are definitely staking the place.

And there's ogres and those half-men entering the Manor from the street. I don't know how much time we have before they find the guards missing."

James turned back to Adelle. "We need to get going!"

"But why? I just want to stay here and rest." and then she whispered "*I think it's mourning sickness.*"

"No, it's not. It's the Jillybons draining the life out of you."

Adelle sat up and looked at James fiercely. "Don't talk about my babies like that!"

James finally lost his cool. "We don't have time for this! I'm trying to rescue you! Right now you have a parasitic candy inside of you and if we don't kill it you will die!"

Adelle looked thoroughly frightened. She staggered to her feet so she could move further away from James. "I'm their mother! I won't let anyone harm them, and that includes you!"

"You're not their mother! You didn't make them! And that's not you talking, it's the Jillybons doing everything they can to protect themselves!"

Adelle began to tremble. "Stop saying terrible things like that! I'm already feeling sick, and now you're making me anxious! You say you want to help me but you keep making things worse!"

"Here," said Fugue, proffering her a glass. "This should calm your nerves."

"Thank you!" said Adelle, taking the glass, "at least *someone* cares about me." (casting a scornful look at James.)

She took a sip from the glass and fell to the floor unconscious.

"What did you give her?" James exclaimed.

Fugue shrugged. "Just a little something to make her more cooperative. Nothing poisonous as far as I know."

"But now she's out cold! What are we going to do with her?"

"Oh, don't worry. I brought a sack."

*　　*　　*

The Lady Mediev was sitting calmly in the parlor with Phyllis and Loury and a number of half-men when she suddenly jolted up as though she had stepped on a nail.

"She has escaped!" shrieked the Lady Mediev. All of the half-men turned to stare at her nervously. "You mean the girl?" One of them asked, twisting his cap in his hand.

"Yes, the girl!" Already she had risen to her feet and was crossing the room. "Summon the ogres and send them to the front streets. This is going to become *very* complicated."

At the same moment, Deadwick was sitting in a second-story room with a direct view of the Mediev Manor. He had one eye on the Manor and one eye on the card game he was playing with several half-men. Suddenly the head of one of his zombie children popped down from the top of the window.

"Two figures were just spotted moving along the rooftops! One of them was carrying a large sack!"

Deadwick sprang to his feet and threw his cards on the table. "The game is on!" he cried. He whipped out his gun, vaulted over the table, and followed the zombie child out the window and onto the rooftops.

*   *   *

Fugue and James were leaping from roof to roof when the raven dropped down and glided alongside them.

"Looks like half of the City is pursuing you right now." said the raven.

A bullet zinged past their heads and ricocheted off a nearby chimney.

"Tell me about it." said James.

The raven glanced back. "Who are those men in white coats chasing you?"

James didn't reply. Fugue just shrugged and said, "I think they want to put James in the loony bin or something."

"Well good for them!"

Fugue looked back and gave a sudden cry of euphoria. On the streets below, several ogres were riding a horseless carriage. On the back of the carriage was mounted a ginormous Hexadecagun, and with this, one of the ogres began to dismantle the rooftops the heroes were fleeing on.

"That is so cool!" Fugue shouted, as everything around him fell to pieces. Several bullets tore through James' flesh and caused him to momentarily stagger. He was not amused.

"We can't keep this up!" he groaned. He knew that if he took too much damage the zombie enchantment would lose hold of him and he would return to being a lifeless corpse, and he figured a similar rule applied to Fugue as well. A dozen pursuers could have been eluded by a few sharp turns, but there were far too many pursuers for that. They needed a more drastic escape.

"The only way we'll be able to lose these people is through the portal to the Library."

The raven ghosted as a flurry of bullets shot past him. "Right now? I don't know if the toad is ready yet. Nobody said anything about you hurrying back with an angry mob chasing you."

James ducked down as a zombie child lunged at him, missed, and fell into the street below. "Well now there is. Can you fly ahead and tell Mr. Mosspuddle to hurry?"

"Certainly. I can tell him you once again climbed into more trouble than a cesspit can fathom!"

The raven shot ahead and out of sight.

*   *   *

In the very center of the City of Orphans, there was an open square, and in the middle of this square, there was a well. At that moment a toad, a raven, and a number of dolls were gathered around it.

"There, it is ready." said Mr. Mosspuddle, looking down the well.

"It doesn't look any different than it did a moment ago." said Miss Perrywinkle. "Just as much black down there as ever. And I still don't see any water. What kind of well doesn't have water?"

"Though there isn't any visible difference from here, the well has changed." said the librarian. "It is now a doorway to the Great Library."

"It had better be the library down there! I wouldn't go down if it was still a regular well. The bottoms of wells are slimy and muddy!"

Mr. Mosspuddle thought about this and how, if someone had such an aversion to wells, they probably would not be happy with the Great Library either, but he decided not to say anything.

During this time, a sound had been slowly forming in the distance. It had been barely audible at first, but it had continued growing until now there was no mistaking the noise of dozens of pursuers rushing toward them. None of the individuals by the well said anything about it, but they were all apprehensively staring in the direction that the wall of sound was charging from.

Then James and Fugue appeared over the top of one of the roofs and wearily dropped down to the street level. Between them they were carrying a large, lumpy sack.

"Please don't tell me that's the princess." said Mr. Mosspuddle as they drew near.

"Okay, I won't." said Fugue.

Mr. Mosspuddle was about to say more when his attention was arrested by the front line of pursuers as they appeared over the crest of the surrounding buildings.

"Into the well!" he cried, and was the first to leap into its depths. As more and more malicious creatures rushed into the square, it did not take much coaxing to get the rest of the band throwing themselves down the well as well.

PART 3

Dear Sir,
I thank you for your advice, for it is based on truth, even if its motives are not. You would like me to remain in this state forever. But I am not going to oblige you.

I am a misshapen image of something far better than I. Until I fade from sight, I am obstructing the view. I must die, and all of this must pass away. But I am encouraged by the fact that after I fall into the earth, I will rise again as someone far better.

*As for your ledger, somehow you twisted this reality so that I destroyed my book. That is the ultimate of perversion and further reason why things cannot remain the way they are. This is **your** fantasy, and I am weary of being a part of it.*

Edward Tralvorkemen

* * *

Their journey to the Great Library involved a lot of falling and shouting and plunging into water and scrambling out of water.

Mr. Mosspuddle led them to the nearest shore, or at least the nearest thing to a shore; it was still submerged in half a foot of water. Once they had regained their footing, he pulled away a patch of vegetation from a wall beside the shaft, revealing a stone button which he promptly pushed. A fit of shaking and rumbling seized the library. This grew in magnitude until a barrage of rock and brick crashed through the shaft as it collapsed from the inside out. The impact caused a powerful wave of water to sweep past them, nearly carrying a random doll or two along with it. Once the water and dust had settled, all that remained of the shaft was a solid wall of rock.

"Now the last doorway is sealed." said Mr. Mosspuddle.

Fugue shook the sack vigorously and deposited a sleeping princess onto the damp ground.

"So she was in the sack." said the librarian. "Her condition looks even worse than I had thought." He set out into the aisles of books and soon returned with a book titled *Pigsy's Rare Fruits and Herbs*. He was also carrying a frying pan.

"Hold this!" said Mr. Mosspuddle, handing the frying pan to James. He then proceeded to frantically search through the book.

"Here it is!" said Mr. Mosspuddle, pointing at a certain page. "Hold the pan out." James did so. The librarian turned the book upside down and shook it over the pan. After several shakes, small glowing orange berries fell from the book's pages. The moment they touched the pan they began to sizzle and snap and before long, the berries dropped into the water and sunk out of sight.

James tilted the pan sideways and they both looked through it. The berries had bored glowing holes through its cast iron frame.

"I was afraid of that." the librarian murmured.

"What are we going to do now?" said Fugue.

"Tilt her head back and open her mouth!" was the librarian's reply. James hesitated but Fugue quickly obliged, grabbing a hold of Adelle's hair in one hand, her chin in the other, and then pulling each of them in opposite directions. Mr. Mosspuddle quickly lifted the book over Adelle and shook several fire berries down her throat. They watched as the orange glow traveled down her torso and then came the sound of a million little screams as a million little Jillybons were incinerated.

Adelle abruptly regained consciousness and jolted to a sitting position, coughing out billowy clouds of smoke. "What happened?" she wheezed miserably.

"Jillybons." said Fugue. "Little buggers were killing you, but we killed them first!"

Adelle moaned and fell back to the ground.

"Well don't thank us all at once." said Fugue.

James turned to the librarian. "They are all destroyed, aren't they?"

"I think so, though it will take some time to be sure. If an hour has passed and the fever hasn't left her then we should probably administer a few more fire berries. Right now we should give her some space and let her rest. That means getting out of her face." he added, pulling Fugue away from her, who had been staring down her open mouth curiously.

Mr. Mosspuddle looked back at the remains of the shaft they had come through. "I wonder if the other zombie children can still sense Princess Adelle even with the dimensional divide between us . . ."

"I'm afraid they probably can." said James.

"Well, either way, that door I just closed was the last entrance to this realm, so now your siblings will have a hard time getting in here even if they do know where she is."

"So that means we're safe?"

"That means we have a little time. Many powerful and determined forces are set on having this girl, and if they do locate her they will probably find some means of breaking into here."

"It's so dark and wet," said Mrs. Gingersmile, looking around the library disdainfully. "Where did all this water come from?" There was a lot of water. Streams of it were pouring down the bookshelves, and many parts of the floor were deep enough to swim in.

"I like the water," said Mr. Mosspuddle. "Nearly as much as I like books. The books don't mind the water. They're so full of magic the water just runs off of them. But the water *does* have a dampening effect on the books. It keeps them at a manageable level."

"Well, that may work for books and amphibians, but not for the rest of us." said Miss Perrywinkle. "I'd rather not stand around in this muck and gloom."

"And you shan't much longer." said the toad. "My living quarters are in the middle of the Library. It would be best if we got there before nightfall."

"What do you mean, *nightfall?*" asked Mrs. Gingersmile. "It's been night for several hours now!"

"Time works differently here." said Mr. Mosspuddle. "It oscillates at a different frequency."

"But what does the time of day really matter?" asked James. "It's already pretty dark in here."

"It's always dark here; that doesn't change. But most of the Library's more dangerous wildlife is nocturnal. I'm used to dealing with them, but now there is the safety of a much larger group to worry about, so the sooner we get to my house the better."

James looked at Adelle uncertainly. "She doesn't look well enough to walk. I think we should carry her."

Adelle, who had been looking practically unconscious, suddenly opened her eyes. "No! I don't want any of you to carry me!"

"That's not a problem." said Mr. Mosspuddle. "I'll summon my boat." He took a whistle from his coat pocket and blew on it, producing a noise reminiscent to a parrot biting itself. Before long, a small wooden boat arrived out of the darkness and stopped beside them.

"Here," Mr. Mosspuddle motioned from Adelle to the boat. "You can rest in here."

Adelle complied and laid herself down inside the boat. There was barely enough room for her.

"We are going to my lodgings," said Mr. Mosspuddle to the boat. "Keep close to us."

"I don't understand." said James. "That boat has neither paddle nor sails. How is it going to get Adelle to your lodgings?"

"It is very clever." said Mr. Mosspuddle.

And so they set out for the librarian's house. Mr. Mosspuddle led the way with Fugue beside him. The dolls went in the middle. Behind them trailed the boat that was carrying Adelle. The raven was also perched on top of it. James roamed back and forth amongst the party. Most of the ground along their course was submerged in water to some degree. Some of it was very deep. At some places there were narrow, wooden walkways constructed over the water. The group would walk on top of these while the boat would continue in the water beside them.

"So what do we do if we come across a wizard?" the swan asked them.

"If we come across danger, it will probably be some construct of a wizard, not a wizard himself." said Mr. Mosspuddle. "Wizards cannot react well to immediate threats. Magic requires a vast amount of energy; the more quickly a spell is prepared and cast, the more energy it demands. A wizard could cast twenty slow spells with the amount of energy required to cast a single instant spell. Thus, they prefer to work from a distance, relying on forethought and preparation to deal with opponents."

"That's right." said Fugue. "I've dealt with wizards before. Dangerous buggers, but get right up to them and you can punch 'em in the face!"

"Neither of which is likely to happen here." said the toad.

"So then what do we do if we come across a construct of a wizard?" the swan asked.

"We destroy it." said James.

"That's . . . convenient. And what of traps? What should we do about them?"

"Choose very carefully who is in the front." the raven called from behind them.

Either Fugue and Mr. Mosspuddle didn't hear him or wished to demonstrate their bravery, for they remained in the lead. James gradually fell back a few paces to ensure he could see the boat, which had some difficulty staying close to their path since it was restricted to the water. After some time, the dolls approached James and said to him, "We want to make certain that you clearly understand that you are not good enough for Adelle."

James halted abruptly. "Excuse me?" he said.

"We are simply pointing out the fact that Adelle is the living, breathing heir of Marloth while you are no more than a lowly zombie minion."

"I don't think I follow you."

"No, you aren't. We are following *you!* Very closely."

"Oh." said James. "Sure, I don't mind you tagging along."

"Good. You are open to accountability. Just don't forget your proper station in life."

"Wait, are we still on the same page?"

"You had better hope so."

Confused beyond hope, James continued down the aisle and did his best to lose the dolls. Up ahead he heard Fugue talking to Mr. Mosspuddle.

"And then we shoved her in the sack and took off through the window just as ogres were beating down the door! You should have seen us!"

"Yes, well," Mr. Mosspuddle coughed, and then spotted James. "James!" He said, motioning for the boy to join them. "Fugue was just telling me about what happened back at the Manor."

"I'm just glad that's behind us." said James.

"Well, that's sort of what I wanted to talk to you about. If what Fugue has been saying is anywhere near the truth, I think you need to apologize to the princess."

"*Apologize?* For what?"

"Did you lose your temper with her?"

"No. Maybe. I don't remember! I was focused on keeping her alive while she was delirious and spouting nonsense!"

"It sounds like I was correct. You should apologize to her at once!"

"Why? What would I say? 'I'm sorry for keeping you alive?'"

"No, tell her you are sorry for being unkind. For not being patient. For not considering that behind all the delirium and illusion she was still suffering from very real distress."

"Fine. I'll talk to her."

"Thank you. I appreciate that. And I'm sure she'll appreciate it as well."

James lingered back until the dolls had passed him and he was near the boat. But the raven was still there, and now the swan was there also, swimming beside the boat. The raven and the swan were discussing how pathetic creatures were that could not fly. Adelle was still lying on her back in the boat, though her eyes were open and she was looking upward thoughtfully. James didn't feel comfortable saying what was on his mind while there was other company around. He debated with himself as to whether or not he should ask the birds to give him a moment alone with Adelle, but he was not comfortable with that either. Finally, he just decided to go ahead and approached the boat.

"How are you doing?" he asked the princess.

Adelle sat up and looked at him in surprise. "A little better." she said.

James braced himself, and then said, "Look, I'm sorry for the way I treated you when you were sick. I wasn't kind."

The raven and the swan abruptly stopped their conversation, and eyed Adelle without turning their heads.

"It's alright. I hardly even remember it." she lied.

The eyes moved to James. "For whatever its worth, I was genuinely trying to help you. Those Jillybons *were* going to kill you."

Adelle's face paled a bit. "I'd rather not talk about it." she said quietly.

The raven and the swan resumed their conversation. James stood there for a short time and watched as the boat continued past him. He was in the process of sinking into deeper reveries when there was a sudden cry from up ahead. It sounded like Mr. Mosspuddle and it sounded something like, "My house! My *poor house!*"

James rushed forward past the boat and the dolls, and the raven darted alongside him. They caught up with the librarian and Fugue, who were standing before a clearing in the Library that was dry and composed of debris.

"This is where my house once rested!" wailed the toad. "Half of it above ground, half of it below!"

"It's still resting." said Fugue. "Just now it *is* the ground."

"I'm guessing the wizards didn't expect you'd be needing this any time soon." said the raven.

"This is devastating!" the librarian moaned. He slumped to the ground, covered his face with his webbed hands, and spoke no more for quite some time.

"Well, since there's no lodgings we might as well set up camp." said Fugue. "It looks like the remains of your house will make a wonderful campfire!"

*   *   *

Sometime later, the group was gathered around a roaring fire, dining on a meal the dolls and Fugue had concocted using what ingredients they could gather from books and local vegetation. Mr. Mosspuddle was still very miserable and unusually quiet. The dolls were filling Adelle in on the events that had led to her being there. James had just finished patching up the bullet holes in his body and was sitting back to reading Marloth. Fugue was trying to raise the spirits of the librarian, though with little success.

After some time, Adelle stood up and said "Now that we are all situated and together, I would like to discuss this matter of your kidnapping me."

"We didn't kidnap you! We rescued you!" said Fugue.

"Yes, well, you certainly keep saying that. But from what I can ascertain, you broke into my bedroom, drugged me, put me in a sack, carried me away in the night, and did all this while wielding guns and knives and who knows what sort of violent devices. Forgive my ignorance, but that sounds like kidnapping to *me*."

Fugue looked dismissive. "Anything can sound bad if you put it like that."

"We had to do something!" said James. "Otherwise those Jillybons would have killed you!"

"Well, if that truly was your main concern, I am now Jillybon free. Danger averted. I thank you, but that still leaves me here in the middle of nowhere with people who, regardless of their motive, did kidnap me. But that can be mended. If you return me to the Mediev Manor, I will put this whole incident behind me. And the sooner the better. One of the grandest balls of the year will be taking place at the Globe next week, and there are so many things I need to do beforehand!"

"We can't do that." said James. "The Lady Mediev is evil."

Adelle unconsciously reached up and touched the crown to make sure it was still on her head. It was. *But it wasn't working!* She *was* still feeling some of the disorientation of the Jillybons; perhaps their lingering effects were hindering her use of the crown. Very well then, she would just have to see how far she could go with classic diplomacy. Critiquing the Lady Mediev would be an easy concession that would gain some ground.

"I agree with you to a point," she said. "While I don't know that I would use the word *evil* to describe her, she is very arrogant and spiteful, and I was never entirely comfortable with being her guest. But I still need to return to the City. As another option, you could leave me in the charge of the toymaker, Jakob Damond. He is one of the kindest people I have ever met."

At this the raven exploded (figuratively), and repeated his lecture on how the title of "Toymaker" was a gross misnomer and how everything the toymaker did ended up in perversion.

Adelle was deeply offended. "I cannot listen idly while you slander Mr. Damond so! He is a good man, while you are arrogant and spiteful! In fact, you are just as unpleasant as the Lady Mediev!"

Now the raven was truly furious. "I am nothing like her! She bends and breaks truth to serve her own selfish ends. I stand by truth and defend it to the death!"

"If you can imagine that someone as compassionate as Jakob Damond is evil, then you and truth must be barely on speaking terms! Mr. Damond has been a lot nicer to me than any of *you*."

"That's all just a show," said James. "He just wants you to think that he cares for you."

"That's what you say, but there is no evidence. It's your word against his. But I will continue to be reasonable. If you really insist, then I don't have to go to the toymaker, or any other individual. You can return me to the City of Orphans and I will find my own way."

"We can't allow that either. The whole place is evil."

Adelle sighed. "Somehow I knew you were going to say that. Who and what isn't evil beyond you band of noble heroes?"

"I'm not noble." James murmured weakly.

There was a short pause and then Mrs. Gingersmile spoke up saying, "You boys have done enough talking. It's time to let us dolls convince Adelle."

Adelle wheeled about in surprise. "Convince me of what?"

"These aren't the only persons who think this world means you harm. On that point us dolls agree with them."

"You can't be serious!"

"We are no longer in the castle." said Mrs. Gingersmile. "Out here the people are raving mad and terribly uncivil. It is our solemn duty to protect you from the influence of such company."

"But what about our present company? They are outsiders to the castle!"

"That has not escaped our notice. We are watching them very closely." All of the dolls turned to stare at James suspiciously. James tried to shift the conversation back to Adelle.

"Whatever the case, the world is out to get you, and we are going to do everything in our power to keep you from it."

"So then I truly am your prisoner?"

"If that's what it takes, then Yes!"

"Wait! Stop!" said Mr. Mosspuddle. "Why are we being so antagonistic? Everyone here (except maybe the raven) is concerned for Princess Adelle's well-being. We're all agreed on that point. The only disagreement is over what is truly in her best interest. Now, at least for the time being there is no need to debate over whether the princess should be allowed to return to the City of Orphans or if she is our prisoner since, whether or not we were right in spiriting her away from that place, it is beyond any of our means to return her to the City at this time. For better or worse, she is stuck with us in this library. I think it unlikely that we will be able to stay safely hidden here indefinitely, and because of that, I will be searching for a means to get us outside the Library. But until then, Your Highness, this may be an opportunity for you to observe us, and perhaps you will see that we are not as bent on your harm as you think. And on our side, whatever wrong we may have done or are still doing, perhaps we will see that as well."

Adelle spent several moments pondering his words. "That was very well said. I will do as you say, and I will do my best to show all of you patience despite your uncouth actions. But let me ask you this: if there really are so many forces pursuing me, and it is only a matter of time before they find me, how are you planning on protecting me? Are you going to destroy everyone in the world who wants to cause me harm?"

"Egad!" said Fugue. "There would be no one left!"

"I don't think anyone here has figured out how to ultimately protect you." said the raven to Adelle.

"But we will," said James. "I know we will." Adelle was slightly annoyed by James' seemingly baseless confidence, but she held her peace.

With everything being said that any of them wanted to say, the conference dispersed. An hour later found the fire dying down and the band of adventurers preparing to sleep. Feeling forlorn and fragile, Adelle laid her head on a rolled up sweater and covered herself with a questionable blanket Fugue had dug up for her. She missed all of her friends in the City of Orphans, especially Ivy. Here in this dismal dungeon of books, with fractured misfits as her only company, she felt more isolated from the rest of the world than she had ever before.

*   *   *

The sun did not shine on Deadwick the goblin. The twisted forest he was scurrying through was far beyond the reach of daylight. The path he was moving through was the sort that is less trod and less known. Every now and then, he would glance back over his shoulder to make sure that no one was following him. Which was apparently a futile exercise, because he remained unaware of the dark and shadowy figure that trailed some distance behind him.

When the goblin reached the edge of the forest, he emerged at the foot of a low hill that rose above the withered treetops. At the top of the hill was constructed a church. Well, what once may have been a church. So many pilings and attachments had been hammered into it that it was next to impossible to distinguish any real walls.

The goblin made his way up the hill, zigzagging through the morass of tombstones which were scattered about the ground. The sense of danger and dread that hung about the place was so thick it was tangible, but the goblin did not notice. His mind was on business, as it always was. After a remarkably long climb, he finally reached the edge of the building where the front door stood.

Well, where the front door had once stood. If there still was a door, it had long since been entombed by all of the additions. Expecting as much, Deadwick began to circle the building in search of a possible entrance. While it was silent as the grave outside, a faint rumbling of commotion emanated from the surface of the building, as though the sound of tremendous activity was bursting inside the building, with only a hint of it managing to escape. Eventually he came to a thick, soot-stained window from which occasional blasts of warm light were issuing. Finding it locked, he tossed a rock through it. The action was immediately met with an eruption of sound that was so tangible a force, he half expected the shards of window to fly outward instead of in. Such volume would have murdered most ear drums, but it hardly fazed Deadwick. He climbed onto the sill and dropped inside.

No one noticed that a goblin had just shattered a window and climbed through. Everyone was too busy running about with boxes, wrestling with machinery, and arguing with everyone else. After taking all of this in, the goblin pushed his way through the chaos and found his way up the stairs. As he climbed, he left some of the din of machinery behind him.

On the second floor stood a man. He was hunched over a schematic of what looked to be some bizarre flying machine.

"Hey!" said the goblin. "Otto!"

The doctor briefly looked at the goblin and turned back to his work.

"Go away. There are no positions available. I have all of the workers I need."

"I'm not here to be hired," said Deadwick. "I already work for you! Remember me, the guy managing all these kiddies you keep churning out?"

The doctor looked at him again and then nodded wearily. "Oh ... you. If I remember right, you're what I would call a necessary evil."

Deadwick grinned. "You've got that right!"

The doctor sighed and once again returned to his work. "I heard you had the princess but she slipped through your grimy fingers. Why am I paying you if you can't do what I need you to do?"

"She slipped through a lot of people's fingers!" said Deadwick. "I hope you realize that I'm having to fight *way* too much of Marloth to get to her! Everyone is after her, and I mean *everyone!* But that's not the problem that brings me here. I could have brought the princess to you long ago except your kids keep going tipsy whenever she's around."

"What do you mean, *tipsy?*"

"One moment they are killing-machines and the next moment they are all giving her flowers and trying to impress her with stupid tricks. At least that's what the chaps do. The girls get even more petty and strange than usual. Some of the girls may kill her out of jealousy, but they would still have to fight through the rest of the kids and that would be a hopeless mess."

"That doesn't make any sense." said the doctor. "She should not be having that kind of effect on them."

"I think it has something to do with that crown she is wearing."

"And what scientific basis do you have to come up with such an outlandish idea?"

"Who cares about science? My gut tells me, and it's never wrong!"

"Well forgive me, but I hope I'm never led by the insides of a goblin."

"Fine then! If you're not going to listen to my gut and your science isn't giving you any answers, where else are you going to look?"

The doctor shook his head in frustration. "Science *is* going to provide me the answers, but its demands are growing heavier. I have so many questions, and the princess is the key to them. If I can somehow surmount these challenges and obtain her, I'll have all the answers I need. Answers to so many of those questions, particularly how to finish the crowning achievement of my inventions."

On the story below them rested his crowning achievement: a large boxish contraption bursting at the seams with gears, levers, gauges and every manner of technically mystifying apparatus conceivable by man. If you were to go to the Interdimensional Patent

Office and look up patent #4502935-308, you would find the following title: "A device for rehabilitating the expired physical entities of juvenile Homo sapiens."

Most people called it the Zombie Machine. It was the machine that maintained his entire army of undead children. And it was the children that made all of his experiments possible. His studies were phenomenally ambitious, and required a vast amount of manpower. Zombies had been the perfect tool. By now he had filled the world with his remarkable lab assistants, though most of them were only loosely under his control.

As can be imagined, the doctor was very paranoid when it came to his Zombie Machine, and he guarded it with a considerable array of hidden traps and scientifically enhanced hexes, not to mention the teams of zombie children that maintained his laboratory's operations and his own watchful eyes.

And yet somehow a creature managed to slip past all of those things. A creature wrapped in shadow and enigma. A creature more cunning than any invention the doctor would ever devise. In short, a monkey.

The monkey climbed to the top of the machine and eyed the obfuscated collection of controls like most other monkeys would look at a mountain of bananas. The machine hummed softly, as though beckoning for him to play with it. After studying the contraption for some time, he eagerly began to fiddle with its buttons and levers. With a few modifications and a strategically placed wrench, a small door slid open at the top of the machine and the monkey dropped inside.

He landed on a pile of papers that was far deeper than the size of the machine. Each of the papers looked like some sort of legal document and were attached to the rest of the machine through translucent wires. After rummaging through the papers for some time, he found the one he was looking for: the one with the word "James" signed on the bottom with big red letters. Taking a pen and notepad, he jotted down the identification number on the top of the document and climbed out of the machine. Once he had secured the door behind him, he climbed over to a panel with rows of numerical digits and entered in the number he had written down and then pressed a square button below the panel. With that, the machine made several creaking noises and then the word "James" floated up above the main control panel.

The monkey smiled wickedly. Grabbing hold of a dial on the main control panel, he twisted it all the way to the right until it snapped. Red warning lights began to flash.

* * *

Night descended upon the Library and everyone fell asleep. Everyone, that is, except for James. Zombies don't need sleep. They can become unconscious, but they get their energy from things like the Zombie Machine, not rest. Doctor Marrechian did have many of his children configured to nocturnally shut down to conserve energy and better coexist with the living adults of the world, but the children he sent with Deadwick were configured to be awake most of the time. James was one such zombie, so that the one who loved dreaming the most was the one who slept the least.

Throughout the night, James lay just beyond the edge of camp, staring up into nothingness. He tried and tried to remember his past, but it was a pale blur. No matter how hard he tried to fill his mind with different things, he could not stop thinking about Adelle. Protecting her was proving to be an epic feat, and was requiring a great deal of attention. He had poured so much thought into how to rescue her, thinking about her and her well-being had become habitual.

"James! Can you hear me James?"

"Leave me alone." said James, feeling cross. "I'm trying to think."

"Of course you are! That's why I'm here!"

James looked down and then jumped in shock. He was lying on a large mirror with his reflection waving up at him. Instantly he was on his feet.

"Get away from me!" He shouted. Not realizing his volume until the words were already out of his mouth, he shot a worried glance over to the camp, but no one seemed to have heard him.

"Now James, you know that's not possible!" said the mirror image. "You and I are one and the same."

"If you don't leave I'll tell the others!"

"Tell them what? They wouldn't be able to see me. They'd think you were crazy."

"I'm not crazy!"

"Of course I'm not. But enough of that. You're getting off on too many rabbit trails. We should be talking about our favorite subject."

James' decaying heart sank within him. "You don't mean—"

"Yes, Adelle! You finally found her! Isn't that wonderful! But that's not nearly as wonderful as the fact that she's sleeping just a few paces from this spot! Curled up under her little blanket without a shred of fear. She's all ours!"

"No she's not!" James stated, stalking away. He turned a corner to find himself standing before another mirror. His reflection was carrying a grungy knife and an eager grin.

"Look at her!" said the reflection. "Look at all that skin! You wouldn't have to kill her, just a few strokes on that canvas would be enough."

"It's never enough!" James shouted, and started to run away. But no matter how far he ran or which way he turned, he could not evade his reflection.

"You're just making things more difficult." said the reflection. "This is supposed to be fun! All you're doing is putting strain on the enchantment that is animating you. Stop fighting it!"

James was surprised to find that he was fatiguing. Zombies never tired! But he continued onward, expending just enough energy for a wearied "Never!"

But his reflection had not lost a drop of energy. "Admit it! You want to kill her!"

James collapsed to the ground. "Fine! You're right; I want to kill her! I'm a zombie! I want what every zombie in this world wants; to see her whimpering in pain! But that is the enchantment of the Zombie Machine. Ever since I found that book, I think I've become under the control of two enchantments. The second enchantment is from the author of this book, and it is deeper and better than anything I have ever known. When I think about this book and all that it says, I no longer want to see Adelle get hurt. I want to protect her. Protect her from everyone, and that includes me!"

For once the mirror image looked fearful. "Be careful, James! If you keep fighting yourself like this you'll tear us down the middle! Then the zombie enchantment will become mutated and we really will be crazy! Believe me, I don't want that to happen! I'm going to follow you wherever you go and make sure you see sense and follow your nature!"

James feebly rose to his feet.

"Fine then. Go ahead and follow me." he said, and he threw himself over a cliff.

*   *   *

Journal of Dr. Otto Marrechian - Entry #253

Today I finished a machine that determines the girl's location. It harnesses that mysterious ability of my children to sense her presence. It utilizes the principle of triangulation, though in a much more complex manner. I have placed children across dozens of different dimensions. My machine monitors how strongly each of them is aware of the princess and prints out detailed reports of its findings. I can then take that data and use it to calculate a rough idea of where she is. It isn't a very fast process since I still need to do all the calculations by hand, but I'd rather not spend hours automating a process that will be obsolete once I have her.

I just now finished my first run of this procedure and, assuming my calculations are correct, as of half an hour ago she was and probably still is in the Great Library.

The Great Library! That is no easy fortress to surmount! I've known for some time that the librarian of that place has been gradually destroying gateways to the Library. By now, I don't think there are any gateways left. But since I've known this for some time this is not a new problem for me. Killing the librarian or attempting to forcibly take control of the Library have never been viable options. The Library is an incredible source of power I can tap into, but it is also heavily dependent on the librarian. For the Library to be of any use to me he must continue doing his job unhindered. Thus, I did the only logical thing left for me to do: I published a book.

"A book? That's it! You really are a mad scientist!" said Deadwick when he heard of the doctor's plans.

"If madness is not being constrained by what holds others from greatness, then yes, I am mad." said the doctor. "But there is reason behind my actions. I know Mosspuddle's great weakness." He held up a book in his hand entitled "A Book without an Author" by Otto Marrechian. "There is something even more important to him than protecting his library: filling it with every book ever printed. He has a copy of my book sitting on a shelf somewhere in that vast expanse of literature. And it is no ordinary book. In each copy I have installed a microscopic device which can be remotely triggered to blow a hole through the fabric of reality, creating an interdimensional rift. A rift through which you and the children will be able to gain entrance into the Library."

"Say *what?*"

* * *

The next morning Adelle awoke to find the others already up and about. Fugue had managed to hunt down a collection of library flora and fauna and was using that to cook breakfast for everyone. Nearby the raven was conversing with the dolls, possibly about some doll-like doom that awaited them. (The dolls were very wide-eyed.)

Around that time Mr. Mosspuddle also returned from hunting, though the target of his effort had been books. He came into the camp looking harried and frequently glancing over his shoulder. Setting down his burden of books, he took out a handkerchief and began to furiously wipe his brow. There are few occupations more dangerous than that of librarian.

"Has anyone seen James?" asked Mr. Mosspuddle.

"Oh, he spent most of the night climbing up a cliff," said the swan. "He's almost finished. He should be here shortly."

Fugue looked up from his cooking in shock. "He's training without me? Drat! Why didn't he tell me! I've been needing to work on my game!" He kicked one of the toves in frustration. "All this lack of adventuring is making me lazy!"

"But haven't we been having an adventure?" said Samantha. "Aren't we in the middle of one right now?"

"Honey, if you call this an adventure, you ain't seen nothin' yet!"

As he spoke, James stumbled into the camp and slumped down against one of the bookshelves.

The librarian was amazed. "James! You look even more exhausted then I feel! How can this be? Isn't your energy source outside of you?"

"I don't know how I work. All I know is I'm tired."

"Well, what happened last night? The swan said something about climbing."

"I think it would be best if I didn't explain." said James. He tried to avoid meeting eyes with the librarian and noticed the raven staring at him intently. Somehow, James was sure the raven knew something about what James was facing. The raven seemed to know a lot of things he didn't say.

"I won't pry." said Mr. Mosspuddle and then, spotting a good subject to change to said, "Is that breakfast? I could use some sustenance!" He took the bowl that Fugue handed him and sat down by the fire. After taking a few bites, he said, "I can't shake the feeling that agents of the wizards will be arriving any moment. My house (or what's left of it) will be one of the first places they check. I think we should set out for other parts of the library soon."

While Mr. Mosspuddle and James discussed where in the library to move to, Adelle likewise sat down with a bowl of food. As she ate her breakfast it occurred to her that she no longer felt sick. In fact, she felt excellent. The Jillybons' effects must be waning. If they had been in some way dampening her abilities, maybe her abilities had now returned. She decided to experiment.

"This food is exquisite!" she said to Fugue. "Where did you learn to cook like this?"

"Adventuring," said Fugue. "For example, I learned how to use these spices from a Babylonian princess I helped rescue from an evil magi-demi-god-thing. Boy could she make a cup of coffee!"

"Do you frequently rescue princesses?"

"No, not a lot. You're the first in a long while."

"Well, I know I haven't done a good job of expressing it so far, but I really am grateful to you for rescuing me. It means a lot."

Fugue's smile broadened and he voiced a pathetic attempt at modesty. Adelle was gracious enough to feign acceptance of this token, and then said, "I can't wait until I get back to the City. It would mean *so* much to me to make it to the Ball! If I were to find a way back to the City, would you help me?"

"I would do everything in my power!" said Fugue.

Adelle had already been smiling on the outside, but now she was smiling on the inside as well. It was working again!

Once Adelle had finished her meal, she went to where Mr. Mosspuddle was sitting and in an innocent tone said, "Yesterday you spoke of finding a way out of the Library but that it would take some time. Are there any faster options you might have forgotten to mention?"

"Why yes, come to think of it, there were! Locked away in the deepest recesses of the Library there is a certain collection of books written by the wizard Ohm. They are powerful books, and can be used to open doorways very quickly. However, they are demonic and I would rather not consort with such devices. There is one other way, but it is not very reliable. Throughout the Library there are holes through the dimension the Library rests within. Most of these holes can be found in the outer rooms and passageways of this dimension, areas that are so old not even I know who built them or to what purpose. They are one-way holes: things can go out but cannot come in. And when something passes through them, there is no way of knowing where they will land. If a person were to fall through, they would most likely plummet to their death."

"But there is a chance of landing somewhere safe?"

"Yes, though it is a small one, and not something I would ever want to risk your life with."

"Then with all things considered, it sounds like the books of Ohm are our best option. You should find them right away."

"But as I've already said, they are demonic! If I take enough time I should be able to find a safer means."

"But it is imperative that I return to the City of Orphans as soon as possible!"

"Yes, yes. You are right. I will make all haste to locate the books of Ohm."

James watched Adelle in wonder. What she said made sense, and yet a part of him was screaming foul play. He found his focus shifting to the crown. *Where had he seen it before?*

Even though Mr. Mosspuddle had said he would immediately search for the books of Ohm, a subconscious part of his mind was against it, and looked for a way to counter it. At the thought of looking for books, Mr. Mosspuddle's mind drifted to the books he had just gathered, and began to monologue. "I am better at organizing books than wielding them." he said. "However, I have collected a few of the books I actually know how to utilize. Here, let me show you."

After rummaging through his bag, the toad pulled out a small booklet.

"You have probably never seen a book like this, for there is only it and one copy in the entire world, and I own them both. It was composed by the most brainlessly arrogant person to ever live in all of history. Because of this fact, this book has acquired several unique qualities that have more than once come in handy. For instance,"

He opened the book and flipped to a certain page. Suddenly, the book grew in size until it was well larger than the toad.

"Wow!" said Fugue. "How in the world did you do that?"

"It was the book's doing, not mine. Even though I cannot stress enough the insignificance of this book, we are currently witnessing its perceived self-image. It is so confident in its own value that it alters the reality around it and in effect makes itself larger. However, if you were to flip through its pages, you would find that there were no more words or insights added to it from this shift in reality. All that is affected is the book's physical size, for it lacks the imagination to give itself any real depth.

"But there's more." said the toad. He let go of the book and it remained hovering in the air. "Due to the incredibly obtuse nature of this book, once it is opened and affecting the world around it, its cover and binding are utterly immobile. If the entire world were to collapse upon it, we could safely rest beneath it. Its opinions are so preconceived and inconsiderate that nothing can affect it."

Fugue gave the book a push. It was like pushing a stone wall. "But if the book can't move, how do you close it?" he asked.

"The cover is immobile, but the pages can still move. All I have to do is flip to the index, which is the most pathetic piece of the book and lacks the self-confidence possessed by its other parts." The librarian did so and the book immediately deflated back into his hand. "Sometimes even the most misguided of creations can be a useful tool . . . as long as you never use them for their intended purposes."

"Like the books of Ohm?" asked Adelle.

"No." said Mr. Mosspuddle. "Conjuring a doorway is exactly the sort of thing they were made for." This was followed by a foreboding silence.

"But here," Mr. Mosspuddle continued, again reaching into his bag. "I can show you an example of a book that *is* good to use as it was intended . . ."

Adelle gently put her hand on his arm. "This is all very fascinating, but you can just as well demonstrate these wonders another time. Right now I think we are ready to begin searching for the books of Ohm."

"Yes. Of course! We will set out immediately. Just let me gather my things."

This doesn't make any sense, thought James. Once again, he found himself staring at the crown, trying to figure out where he had seen it. It taunted him. Him and his rotting memory. He tried to work his way backward. He had a vague recollection of an orphanage. And walking through the streets of a city with someone. They were going to some place. And then they were coming back from that place. And the person had something new . . .

And then it dawned upon him where he had first seen that crown. It all came together. Suddenly, James leaped forward and snatched the crown from her head.

"What are you doing? Give that back to me!" Adelle shouted. She threw herself at the crown but James dodged out of the way. "Give it back! You have no right to take that from me!"

"It's evil!" James said. "It's manipulating all of us. I'm sorry but you can't wear it anymore."

"You wicked little corpse! You said you wanted to protect me, but now your true colors come out! You just wanted my crown!"

"I don't want your stupid crown!"

"Well then why are you still holding on to it?"

James looked at the crown. "Good point." he said, and threw it out a window.

"No!" Adelle screamed, running over to the window. But it was too late. The crown had already disappeared into an endless oblivion of clouds and half-light. Adelle stood for some time in shock. When she finally turned around there were tears in her eyes.

"I hate you!" she shouted.

Suddenly there was a deep rumbling sound and everything began to shake. Vibrant colors began to shoot through the air and the world around them began to distort like a crinkling tapestry.

"What's happening!?!" James shouted.

"I haven't the slightest idea!" Mr. Mosspuddle shouted back.

*   *   *

At that same moment, on the roof of Otto Marrechian's laboratory, the doctor, Deadwick, and several zombie children were staring at the newly formed rift in time and space that was floating before them.

"What I don't understand," Deadwick was saying, "is if the explosion took place in the Library, what's part of the hole doing here?"

"Because this place is a magnet for that sort of thing. The explosion probably blew holes all over Marloth, and I was sure at least one of them would be in this dimension. I just didn't figure it would be on my roof."

They continued to stare at the rift. It was slowly moving around unstably.

"Is it safe?" asked Deadwick.

"By no means."

"And I'm supposed to go in it?"

"Yes!"

There was a pause.

"You don't pay me enough for this!"

*   *   *

After much commotion, the Library slowly settled down to its normal state.

"What was that?" Samantha asked.

"I already said I don't know!" growled Mr. Mosspuddle. "I've never seen or heard of anything like it."

"Where's Adelle?" James asked. Everyone looked around. She was nowhere in sight.

"Don't tell me she's gone!" James groaned. "Did anyone see her go?"

Head shaking all around.

"Well does anyone have any idea which way she went?"

"I don't know," said Fugue. "I was trying to avoid eye contact."

"Why are you asking?" said the raven. "You said you could sense where she was!"

"I could, but the awareness dimmed the moment I took the crown from her."

"Well maybe snatching that hood ornament wasn't the greatest idea."

"Wait," said James. "I think I can still feel something..."

"I was just trying to be considerate." Fugue muttered. "There was all that shouting and—"

"Quiet!" said James. He stood poised for several moments as though listening for something.

"I think I know where she is." He paused for another moment and then bolted down one of the aisles.

"Wait!" said Mr. Mosspuddle. "We're not ready yet!" but James had already disappeared.

Mr. Mosspuddle began to frantically gather together his books. "We need to keep together!" he told the others. "Whatever happened, it was most definitely magical, and the odds are it was not a pleasant sort of magic."

"Well I hope it does unpleasant things to that zombie!" said Miss Perrywinkle. "He threw away our mistress' crown! That's probably what caused all of this commotion!"

Mrs. Gingersmile nodded. "I knew he was a scoundrel."

"No he's not!" said Fugue. "He's going to rescue her!"

While the others argued about zombies and crowns, the raven flew to the top of one of the towering bookshelves to examine their surroundings. He could sense danger, and he had an idea what it was. As his razor-sharp eyes pierced through the murky gloom, he spotted what he had suspected several aisles away.

"We have visitors!" he shouted down to his companions.

There was a sound of rushing air and one of the bookcases exploded. Then another explosion lit a nearby aisle.

"What now?" cried Miss Perrywinkle.

"Ogres." said Fugue. "Their firing rockets. Though they aren't firing at us."

"How do you know that?"

"Because we're still alive."

In the distance could be heard cries and machinery and the sounds of death and destruction. A single zombie child rushed past them and was mowed down by machine gun fire.

The raven dropped back to ground level and shouted to the others "What are you waiting for? *Run!*"

*　　*　　*

Adelle ran blindly down one of the rickety pathways of wood that wound their way through the Library. Her emotions were turbulently fighting with each other: anger, hurt, loss, frustration, fear, disenchantment, but they were all united by self-pity.

Snap! One of the boards gave way below her foot, sending her falling through the pier and into the murky water below. The water there was deep, so deep that she was completely submerged. After several frantic moments of struggling she was able to push herself upward far enough for her head to break through the surface. Gasping for breath and clinging to one of the pilings, she tried to lift herself onto the pathway but found that impossible. She was not strong enough, and there was an inexplicable current trying to pull her downward.

She had to do something! Releasing her hold on the pilings, she lunged at the nearest board of the walkway. She caught it, but her hand slipped and she fell back down beneath the surface of the water.

It was getting harder to fight the current. Her limbs were growing weary and she was not breaking the surface as quickly as she had earlier. She was just starting to panic when James' outstretched hand pierced the water and motioned for her to grab on.

Adelle's immediate reaction was to avoid the hand. She didn't want anything to do with him. But that was quickly pushed aside by her increasing need for air. After a moment's deliberation, she took the proffered hand, deciding to begrudgingly accept his assistance and then give him a piece of her mind. With remarkable ease, she was lifted out of the water and set onto the pathway.

"I appreciate you helping me out of the water, but don't think that—"

Adelle stopped. It wasn't James at all. It was Bobby. "What are you doing here?" she said in surprise. She suddenly found herself very embarrassed, standing there soaked and bedraggled.

"At the moment I'm trying very hard not to get incinerated by ogres." was Bobby's reply. As if to illustrate his point, there was another explosion, this time as close as the end of the aisle. Books and wood flew everywhere.

"Come on!" said Bobby, taking her hand. "We've got to keep moving!"

* * *

As the heroes made their way through the Library, one of the dolls commented on how nice it was after all this time in the dark to finally see the sun rising again. Mr. Mosspuddle looked back.

"That's no sunrise!" he cried. "That's fire! They're destroying my Library!" Despite all of the dampness, somehow part of the Library had still managed to catch on fire.

"Better it than us." said Fugue, a sentiment the toad was slow to agree with.

"We can't keep up this pace!" Miss Perrywinkle moaned.

"*Ohhhh* no!" said Fugue. "You dolls are *not* going to slow us down!"

After some hasty debate, it was agreed that one of the dolls would ride in Fugue's pack, another in Mosspuddle's, and one would ride the raven. The swan did not need any assistance.

And so they continued on in this fashion. Periodically a zombie child would jump out at them and Fugue would blow it away with his firearm. This always had the awkward consequence (considering Fugue's lack of weight and the impressive force his weapon employed) of sending Fugue flying backwards and crashing into one thing or another, be it a bookcase, a fellow adventurer, or both.

Thankfully, both he and the doll mostly consisted of cloth so there was little harm done to them by these brief travels.

At one point they ducked into a stone corridor, made another turn, and nearly ran into an ogre. At first its back was turned to them, but on hearing their approach it rotated around to face them, revealing a massive Hexadecagun cradled in its beefy hands.

"They're everywhere!" shouted Samantha.

The ogre growled. The barrels of the gun began to spin as the ogre hefted it before him, aiming it at the hapless adventurers. Without a moment to loose, Mr. Mosspuddle threw the most obtuse book in the world open in front of them.

The book expanded just as the weapon began to discharge its rain of death. Bullets bounced and ricocheted down the corridor, but they were all deflected by the literary shield.

"This is getting exciting!" said Fugue.

*   *   *

The monkey frowned. The sensors he was observing had dropped several points within the past half hour. Something must have happened to weaken Adelle's aura. Now James would be milder. That wasn't good. This called for extreme measures.

Carefully he made his way back to the machine. But instead of climbing inside, he simply pushed a few buttons and adjusted a few levers. No more of this singling out zombies stuff; that could only go so far. It was time to pump up the juice for all of them.

*   *   *

Suddenly Bobby stopped and turned toward Adelle. Adelle likewise stopped and was puzzled by his sudden concentration on her. "Is everything all right?" she asked.

"Yes. Everything is fine." Adelle could feel his eyes as he looked her up and down. "Everything is perfect."

He was already standing next to her, but somehow he managed to step closer. Adelle's heart began to beat faster. He was about to say more but was interrupted as more children arrived.

"The princess!" they all gasped.

Bobby tried to restrain his anger. "Can't you give us a moment alone?"

"And what? Let you have all the fun? Not a chance!"

Bobby turned to face them and he looked ready to fight.

"Wait!" said Osmand. "If Deadwick finds out—"

Bobby cut him short. "Deadwick's not here. He doesn't know where we are, and he won't know what we do."

The children gave him murderous looks, but none of them took a step closer.

"Excuse me," said Adelle. "I'm a little out of the loop as to what everyone's talking about."

Bobby looked back at her and gave a reassuring smile. "Let's first get you further away from this war zone and then I'll show you everything."

*   *   *

James turned a corner and found himself in a room lined with mirrors. Mirrors! James had a lousy track record with those things. He turned to leave but could no longer find the doorway he had come through. He was completely surrounded by glass.

"Is this some kind of illusion?" he asked.

"I dunno." said his reflection. "I was kind of hoping you were the illusion."

*   *   *

The children hurried down one passageway after another and gradually left behind any hint of the activity going on in the more central parts of the Library. They were now in the older, abandoned sections of the Library dimension. Bobby led the way with Adelle close beside him. The other children followed a short distance behind. Though none of them wanted to acknowledge it, they were all afraid of him.

"You don't know how hard it is to be me." Bobby said suddenly to Adelle, not slowing his pace.

"What do you mean?" Adelle asked with great concern.

"So much is expected of me. I perform far beyond every other person in the world, and yet people eventually take that for granted. They don't realize that I have needs too. I push myself and endlessly sacrifice, and they give me so little in return."

"I had no idea!" said Adelle. "I thought you had everything you wanted."

Bobby looked at her again. "No." he said slowly. "Not everything."

There was a pause and then Bobby continued. "Sometimes I need to do their job for them. When they don't pay me, I need to take the payment from them. It's like I'm protecting them from themselves; making sure they do the right thing."

"I'm not sure I understand. Are you talking about *stealing?*"

"No. Certainly not. I can't steal anything that rightfully belongs to me, now can I?"

"No. I suppose you can't."

"Exactly. And I have certain needs that others have ignored. Needs that they don't want me to fill. But I feel like I am suffocating! They don't care about me!"

"I care about you!" said Adelle.

They stopped in a room constructed entirely out of old wood. Bobby turned to face Adelle.

"Do you care enough to help me?" he asked her. "Will you give me what I need?"

"I'll do anything for you!"

"Thank you." said Bobby. He grabbed Adelle's wrists tightly, twisted them behind her back, and lifted her off her feet and against the nearest wall. Adelle was so surprised it took her a moment to realize how much pain he was suddenly causing her.

"Stop it!" she exclaimed. "You're hurting me!"

The boy didn't seem to hear her. "Scream for me." he said.

"Bobby, what are you doing? Let go of me!"

"Just one scream." he said.

"No! Put me down this instant!"

He suddenly let go of her, and her feet slipped from under her so that her head slammed into the wall.

"You idiot!" she moaned, and was going to say more until she looked up and saw that he was now holding a knife.

"Where did you get that?" she demanded. "Put it away before you—"

He slashed her across the face. She was so shocked it took her a moment to even feel the pain. To feel the blood running down her cheeks.

"Scream!" Bobby commanded. Adelle began to tremble. She turned to the other children.

"Please! Somebody help me! He's lost his mind!"

The children didn't seem to hear her. Some of them stepped closer. All of them were watching with what could only be described as intent fascination. She noticed that many of them were also holding knives, and some had even nastier instruments.

Adelle screamed.

*   *   *

Suddenly James froze.

Crying. He could hear crying in the distance. It was a girl.

The reflection jumped up in excitement. "You heard that, didn't you! She's in pain! They're probably hurting her. You know what that means, don't you?"

"I should go save her?" James asked feebly.

"No! You should join them!"

James could feel his discipline waning. He needed help. Reaching into his knapsack, he rummaged for Marloth. It wasn't there! He must have left it with Mr. Mosspuddle! A fresh layer of fear began to creep over James, but he did his best to sound confident. "We've already been through this routine. I don't want to hurt her, and you can't make me."

Up to that point the reflection had been smiling, but suddenly the smile turned into a snarl. The reflection slammed its fist against the mirror.

"I want to hurt her, and if I want to hurt her then so do you!" He hit the mirror again.

It began to crack.

"What was that!" James blurted. The reflection smiled again and began to repeatedly beat against the mirror. "I'm coming out!" he said. More cracks appeared in the mirror.

"Stop it!" said James. "Leave me alone!"

The reflection continued his pounding with vicious enthusiasm. "Once I'm free there will be no more of these stupid fights. You'll be me again and finally get what you really want." A piece of glass hit the ground.

James was not sure where the voice came from, but he heard someone say, "Don't look at him!" James turned around to see the speaker, but the mirror was there instead.

"I can't!" he shouted. "I can't escape him! He was right all along: he is me! When I hear her in pain I want to increase it, and when he breaks loose I will too!"

"The reflection is the dead James. You have been given life. Embrace it!"

"But how?"

"By looking at me."

"But who are you? Where are you?"

"I'm standing right in front of you. But all you can see is that mirror. And Adelle in pain."

"Whoever you are out there talking to James" the reflection called out, "I suggest you run away before I break free. James is about to get violent!"

James cringed. "The mirror is giving way! I can feel him taking over me!"

"Look past the mirror!"

The reflection backed up for one final lunge.

"Mr. Tralvorkemen! I need you!"

The mirror shattered. Except that it shattered inward, not outward. Tralvorkemen stood where it had once stood, following through a powerful swing with an equally powerful axe. The reflection cowered in horror. Tralvorkemen raised the axe a second time and cut the reflection in two. The separate halves dissipated into a glittering fog of reflections that slowly faded into the surrounding darkness.

"I'm free!" said James.

"No, not yet." said Tralvorkemen. "Right now more evil is accumulated around you than has ever been before. The only thing keeping it at bay is me."

"Then what am I to do? I need to rescue Adelle!"

"Don't focus on her! That is exactly what they want. That is how they will get to you. Rescue her, yes, but don't look at her. Don't look at yourself. Don't look at the other children. Look at me! Look at Marloth!"

"But how can I help her if I'm not concentrating on her?"

"I will take care of that. The real question is: do you trust me?"

James hesitated and then said "Yes, I do."

"Then go." said Tralvorkemen. "Keep me in front of you and I will do the rest."

*　　*　　*

The monkey dizzily pushed away pieces of debris and put a hand to its head, trying to stop the spinning. It had been blown clear across the room. Smoke was billowing from the zombie machine. The machine was still functioning, but the control panel and a few other parts were in bits and pieces all over the room. Where had that surge of energy come from? The monkey would have investigated, but the sound of voices drew near. The monkey pulled itself to its feet and stumbled off. This looked like a good time to get out of there.

*　　*　　*

James ran. He ran faster than he had ever run in his life. He did not know his way through the Library, nor could he sense Adelle, and yet he knew he was heading straight toward her. He knew she was just inside the room in front of him. Without skipping a beat, James threw himself forward and burst through the rotting wall. Everyone in the room had just enough time to turn in surprise as he came hurtling across the room and past Bobby, knocking the boy off his feet. As James flew by, he caught a glimpse of Adelle. She had cuts all over her body and blood was dripping down her face and limbs. Her once beautiful clothes were now in tatters.

James didn't have much time to see her distress. He landed on the far corner of the room, sprung to his feet, and immediately engaged the group of zombie children. Bobby met him first and began to slash at him with lightning speed. James moved even faster. Nay, not faster, it was as though James already knew every move the boy was about to make—as though he had already moved out of the way before Bobby swung. Within two blinks of an eye, Bobby was on the ground stunned and James was taking on the rest of the group at once. They could not believe how fast he moved. Up to six attacks were leveled at him at once and yet he would find a position in space to avoid every one of them and at the same time retaliate with precise blows of his own. None had ever seen anything like it. James marveled, but not at himself. He marveled at the battle playing out before him; he felt like he was watching from a distance. He was not the one fighting. He was simply a channel, a channel through which an immeasurable power was flowing.

Bobby rose again and tried to attack James from behind. James ducked beneath the blow, grabbed the outstretched arm, and threw Bobby over his shoulder and across the room.

Meanwhile, Adelle was curled up against the adjacent wall, watching the fight with wide-eyed horror. She didn't know what to think. She forgot about how badly she was bleeding.

As she watched James struggling to keep the zombie children on one side of the room and her on the other, she saw several of the other children climbing up the walls and around the area of conflict.

"James, above you!" Adelle shouted.

James looked up just in time to see three more zombie children dropping down on top of him. It should be reiterated how nearly the entire room and surrounding structure was constructed from wood. In eons past it had probably been quite sturdy, but by the present time it had become little more than an aged, rotting carapace. When three zombie children landed in unison on James' head, the floor beneath finally said (with a creaking of splinters), "That's it, I'm out of here!" and dropped out of sight. This caused several of the zombie children to plummet through the floor, and then on through the floor beneath that, and then on into the endless oblivion beyond that. As for James, he was still grappling tightly with a handful of the zombie children, so that when the floor suddenly disappeared beneath him he found himself swinging at the end of a chain of zombie children, anchored by the few children who still had a floor beneath them.

Like a pendulum, James swung back and forth a few times, but he knew that wouldn't last long. Already most of the children not part of the inhuman chain were climbing down the wooden framework of the building so they could get a shot at James. One of them threw themselves at James and missed. That one disappeared through the floor below with a shower of splintered wood.

All of this was very challenging for James, for as more and more children gathered around the edges of the lower room, he was still struggling with the two zombie children who were holding him in the air. Each of them was holding him in one hand, and a knife in the other, and he was desperately trying to minimize the number of stabs he received from them while at the same time trying to stay out of the way of the oncoming children.

Up above, Adelle was just thinking about making her escape when Osmand suddenly loomed up behind her and pinned her against the wall. Osmand was not strong, even as a zombie, and normally Adelle may have had a chance at fighting him off. But with the loss of blood, it was all Adelle could do to remain conscious.

"Please, Osmand!" Adelle begged of him. "Please don't hurt me!"

"Oh, Adelle!" he hissed under his breath. "You always were such a tease! Always, *always* teasing! But I caught the signals. I know what you *really* wanted."

"I wanted you to know people cared for you! I wanted to be friends!"

Osmand didn't seem to hear, and didn't pause in his speech. "Teasing, teasing. You are *so* good at it! Both flaunting and demure, wanting to stay locked away, and wanting me to tear you open. Driving me insane to find out what's beneath your surface. Do *you* even know what is beneath your surface? Well now we can find out together ..."

Suddenly, a hand burst through the floor beneath them, grabbed Osmand by the foot, and yanked him through the floor.

Once she had regained a hint of breath, Adelle carefully bent down and peered over the edge of the broken floor. James was still dangling in a web of zombie children, grappling with Bobby and Osmand on either side.

Adelle did not have much time to watch. The remaining strip of floor she was kneeling on began to groan and shudder. Adelle clung to it tightly as though begging it not to abandon her, but it was too old to care anymore. With a stomach-dropping *crack,* the remaining floor disintegrated beneath her. James heard a cry and turned to watch the princess fly past him. He tried to reach out but he was held back by the undead lattice he was now a part of. Helplessly they watched as the other hurtled away into the distance, James disappearing far above and Adelle disappearing far below into the darkness that quickly enveloped her.

*   *   *

Marloth is a most difficult place to map. That is largely due to the ambivalent humor of its geography. In Marloth, points in space still have a spacial relationship to one another, though that relationship is better defined by ideas than coordinates. For example, somewhere just past disenchantment (and a little north of the Isle of Mute Salesmen), lies a particularly mysterious shore. No one knows its location, for it is very hard to find, and once found, it is very hard to keep found. It is the shore where all things that are lost or broken sooner or later are collected. Most of these things are lost for good reason: they are utter nonsense. This is the place where much of the incongruencies of Marloth are conveniently swept away, leaving behind the not-so-absurd bits for people to enjoy. If anything still alive were to ever set foot on this shore, all sorts of ridiculous and hard to comprehend ideas might leak out into the rest of Marloth. That is why it is best that such a place never be found, and is cloaked in oblivion. This shore has no name, because if it did it would be Forgotten.

It was here that Adelle found herself, lying face down in the sand.

She did not know how long she had been unconscious. It felt like years. She hurt all over, but she was surprised to find that she was not thinking about that. Nor was she thinking about how cold and wet she currently was. Nor was she thinking about how she missed her crown.

She was wondering where James was. Still a little dizzy, she pulled herself to her feet and discovered a whole new array of aches and pains. She touched her face and found that the blood had dried. She was sure she looked awful, but she didn't care about that. Despite her body's protests, she set out along the shore to see if she could find the zombie child.

Then she cupped her hands over her mouth to hold back a scream.

*   *   *

"Yes, I can imagine how fascinating some of these random objects would be to you, but we do not have time to stop and look at ... *curiosities.*" This was the librarian. He wanted to say *'garbage',* but he was sure the dolls would be offended by that.

The dolls did their best to communicate their opinion of the librarian through sour expressions and not-so-subtle whining, but they followed behind him as he led their search along the shoreline. Fugue was also with them, looking unusually haggard and in need of a nap. The raven was nowhere to be seen.

Eventually they came across the princess. She was sitting on an upside down bucket and staring vacantly out at the water.

"Princess Adelle!" the toad called out. If she heard him, she did not acknowledge it.

They hurried closer, and as they drew near, the librarian could tell that something had changed. Something had broken inside of the little girl before them. Not to mention the damage on the outside. All of them were shocked to see her condition. The wounds on her face would surely turn to scars if not attended to.

"Adelle! It's us!" cried Samantha.

Adelle finally noticed them and rose absently. "Hello." she said, not looking at anyone in particular.

"Don't get up. You're hurt!" said Mr. Mosspuddle, but she didn't resume her seat.

"I'm fine." she said.

"No, you are not! What happened? Where is James?"

"He's everywhere. Or at least he was."

"What do you mean? *What happened?*"

"I don't know what happened. The other children must have done it to him. He's—"

Adelle struggled to get the words out.

"He's in pieces. They were swept up on shore. It took me some time to realize they were him. I feel so sick."

She quivered and looked about to faint. Mr. Mosspuddle was at first taken aback by this news, but quickly recovered enough to reach out and gently keep her from falling.

"Can you take me to his remains?" he asked.

She nodded. "I've gathered them together. They are wrapped in a blanket."

She led them to a small cave that looked out over the beach. Sure enough, in the cave there was a bundled up blanket. Adelle turned her face away as Mr. Mosspuddle united the bundle and examined its contents.

"Yes, that is definitely James," said the librarian. "The connection between the Zombie Machine and James has been severed. This would happen whenever James' physical form deviated too far from his original definition in the machine."

"Is there anything that can be done?" asked Samantha.

"In theory, if we were to restore James close enough to his original form, the connection would automatically be reestablished. Then he would be back to his reanimated self."

The swan looked at the librarian warily. "How would you know so much about this Zombie Machine?"

"Because its general schematics are on public record at the Interdimensional Patent Office—a resource I have had many dealings with."

"That's good enough for me." said Mrs. Gingersmile. "What do we have to do to fix him?"

"Princess Adelle has already gathered the pieces together, and while they are in a terrible state, it looks like there is still enough of him intact. All that remains to be done is to actually sew the parts back together. I myself know little of sewing. Fugue, I am sure you are knowledgeable about such matters since you yourself are—well—basically a collection of stitches."

"Who me? I didn't make myself! All I do is go on adventures; how should I know anything about sewing?"

"Don't look at me!" said the swan. "I don't even have hands!"

"Ooh! Ooh!" said Samantha, raising her little hand in the air and jumping up and down. "Adelle knows how to sew! She was taught by Miss Bethany, the greatest seamstress in the land!"

Mr. Mosspuddle turned toward Adelle. "Is that true? Could you sew together James? *Would* you?"

Adelle looked down at the blanket of body parts. She could not help feeling the weight of James' sacrifice for her. He had been telling the truth; he really *did* want to protect her.

"I'll do it," she said. "I'll sew him back together."

After more discussion, it was noted that several items would be needed for the procedure, and so the party set out to search for those things. Adelle sat nearby the searching, looking like she was trying fight off sleep. As they scoured the debris, Fugue sidled over to Mr. Mosspuddle confidentially.

"What about the girl?" asked Fugue. "Should I tie her up so she doesn't run off again?"

"What? No!" said Mr. Mosspuddle. "Her heart seems to be softening! If at all possible, she should accompany us willingly. After all, she is the heir to the throne."

"Oh," said Fugue, clearly disappointed.

As the group looked for the needed items, Mr. Mosspuddle also located a few items that, along with one of his books, could be used to heal Adelle's wounds. After some time, Adelle felt her awareness returning and her attention clearing enough to ask the librarian how they had found her.

"With this," said Mr. Mosspuddle, holding up the book of Marloth. "In all the excitement, James left it with me. While most of the details of these stories are different from our present circumstances, there are many similarities. One of the stories in the book tells of a princess taking refuge on a shore, a shore that no one can remember. The story doesn't mention anyone like James, but it does tell of how a princess was found by a band of friends."

"That would be us!" said Samantha.

"Apparently this shore has an aura that causes everyone to eventually forget about it. There's never been any record of it in the Library, at least that I know about, because those records would also be forgotten. But somehow this book is able to override that magical property and tell of this shore. Though it does not give details for how to get here."

"Then how did you find it?"

Mr. Mosspuddle opened his mouth to reply and then closed it again. "I don't know. I forgot."

"What about all of you? What happened after I . . . left?"

Mr. Mosspuddle shuddered. "It was pandemonium! Ogres and zombie children and creatures I've never seen before all came out of nowhere! A massive battle ensued and there were explosions everywhere! Then—throwing out all concern for conserving energy—the wizards appeared and the carnage was escalated to an entirely new level! I still don't know how we were able to get away, but we did. Except for the raven: I don't know what happened to him. We got separated in the midst of the chaos. I hope he got out safely."

The librarian paused at this thought, and then added, "The wizards will undoubtedly hold a greater vigilance over the Library after that affair. That was probably the last I will ever see of my beloved Library."

"I am so sorry for you!" said Adelle. "I can only imagine how hard it must be for you!"

"My exile from the Library has been agonizing. But at the same time, there is a growing sense of freedom. It had never occurred to me how much time I've poured into a library that hardly anyone ever used. I spent most of my days reading about people living their lives, and it has only been since I was banished from the Library and caught up in this adventure that I began to truly live my own."

They continued searching for supplies, and after some time Adelle raised another question that had been bothering her. "Why are so many people after me? What do they hope to gain? Do they all just want me dead?"

"No, I think different forces want you for different reasons. I don't completely understand those reasons, but I have speculated much over what they could be. For one thing, you are of royal blood. People could be trying to gain control of the throne or destroy it. And some say that there are magical powers behind the royal line that can be harnessed. Then there is the fact that you are the last living child in the world. That means—"

"What? The *only* living child? *Everyone* else is dead?"

Mr. Mosspuddle suddenly realized that he probably should have eased into that information a little more softly. "Yes . . . you are. That is why you may be valuable to so many people. Some may want to wipe the world of living children, or use you because of it. The wizards speculated that since you are the last living child in a world of imagination, your dreams may have an amplified influence over reality, so that if someone could control your dreams they could control the world. Some of the wizards said there was evidence to suggest that this is all your dream, and we are just figments of your imagination."

"You make her sound like the most powerful person in the world!" said Mrs. Gingersmile, who was just within hearing distance.

The librarian shook his head. "All of these theories could be wrong. As I was perusing Marloth today it made a very good point: evil is not sane. It could very well be that Adelle is simply an ordinary little girl and this world wants to corrupt her simply because it is evil. In the end, that is all the reason it needs."

* * *

Deadwick sat in one corner, tending to his wounds. The doctor was sitting at his desk looking over a pile of notes and mechanical devices.

"Why do I even listen to you?" Deadwick was grumbling.

"I said that the rift would create holes all over Marloth—I just hadn't anticipated people so quickly sending forces through those holes. You have to understand that the odds of such a thing happening were absurdly low."

"You never told me there were any odds! I was worried about going through the portal; I didn't know I should've been worried about what was on the other side! It was hell back there! I was nearly blown to pieces a dozen times over! And that hole is still there! At any moment we could have an army of ogres coming down on us!"

"Actually, the opening in this dimension isn't on the roof anymore; it's been moving around. At the moment it is in the basement. I am not regretting my decision to make a way into the Library, though I have to admit: that rift is becoming a nuisance."

"Can't you seal it?"

"No, I can't. At least, I haven't figured out a way yet."

"Seems pretty stupid blowing open a back door to your evil lair."

The doctor threw up his hands in frustration. "There was no way to predict exactly how the explosion would work! I did what I had to do and I'll live with the consequences. I've set up temporary measures to act as a bandage until I can determine a more permanent solution." He motioned the goblin to a nearby workbench upon which there was a giant, stony hand.

"This is an ogre's hand. It must have been extremely difficult to sever from its owner but somehow my children managed it. Since then I have been performing experiments on it and recently developed a serum that quickly spreads throughout an ogre's tissue and deconstructs it. Very deadly stuff. I have a dozen syringes filled with the chemical and can give these to my children during key situations."

"The kids don't need chemicals to take an ogre down! They just need numbers. About five kids per ogre should do it."

"That's true, and most of the time that is sufficient. But there are occasional situations, such as the guarding of that rift, where I'd like to ensure that any ogre who steps through will be neutralized swiftly and with little fuss. This is my home we're talking about, and I'd like to avoid walls getting blown up and bullets shooting out of the floor below me."

*   *   *

James looked around him. Everything was fuzzy and unnaturally bright, as if the room itself was glistening. As his vision began to come into focus, he identified the room he was in as the orphanage infirmary. He was lying in bed with his face bandaged. Mr. Tralvorkemen was sitting on a chair next to the bed and reading a book.

"You're awake." said Mr. Tralvorkemen. "How do you feel?"

"Dead. I'm dreaming, aren't I?"

Mr. Tralvorkemen put the book down. "Yes. You are."

James tried to think. "The last thing I remember I was fighting dozens of zombie children."

Mr. Tralvorkemen nodded. "You were protecting Adelle from them."

James tried to leap from the bed and fell on his back from the strain. "Adelle! Is she safe?" Tralvorkemen put his hand on James' shoulder.

"Adelle is safe. For now. She's sewing you back together as we speak."

James relaxed, at least as much as was ever possible for him. It didn't even occur to him to ask why he was in need of any sewing. His mind was still centered on the events at the Library.

"I saw you there!" he said suddenly. "You saved me! If it wasn't for you I would have ..."

James stopped. He couldn't finish his sentence. He began to choke up. "I am so sorry! Look at what I've become! It's all my fault! You gave me everything, and I threw it all away! And I blamed you for it!"

"I gladly took the blame. It was the only way to save you."

James dissolved into tears, and the headmaster put his arms around him. After some time, the mourning subsided, and Mr. Tralvorkemen took a handkerchief and wiped the tears from James eyes. Then he rose and said, "It is a beautiful day. We do not have much time, but it would be nice to enjoy the weather while we are here. Come take a walk with me around the orphanage."

James looked up. He felt weak and was afraid that he would not have the strength to stand, but Mr. Tralvorkemen helped him to his feet and he was surprised to find that he could now walk with ease. In fact, he almost felt as though he were gliding. He followed Mr. Tralvorkemen out into the hall, down the stairs, and into the living room.

Several children were there, sound asleep on the furniture. James recognized Nivana on one couch, and Millamer on the floor. Catherine was curled up in Mr. Tralvorkemen's armchair. James turned to the headmaster.

"Why is it that zombie children want to harm Adelle so badly? I understand we're animated by evil magic, but why so much focus on Adelle? Why not move on to other things?"

"That involves your purpose. Do you remember the knight?"

"What knight? The one from Marloth."

"Yes. The one who rescued the princess. Do you remember what happened whenever the princess was endangered?"

"He was magically filled with increased energy and determination! He did not always have the energy; it only appeared when he needed it."

"Precisely. We are in a twisted version of that same story. Like the knight, you have increased energy when Adelle is in distress so that you can protect her. But unlike the knight, your zombie nature cares nothing for that end goal of protection. All it cares about is the thrill. Adelle gets hurt, the zombie nature grows in energy, and it seeks to cause her more pain, thus generating more energy, until the princess is ultimately dead. Your zombie enchantment is still drawn to the princess, but no longer to save her. As with most everything in this world, the end is severed from the means."

"But that's not my only enchantment, is it? There's another one. A good one! It's what makes me want to protect her!"

"You are correct. The other is *my* enchantment. It is a conduit between this story and the original. It connects you to what you were meant to be."

They continued through the front door and out into the yard. It was a beautiful day. The sun was shining and birds were flying about happily. The flowers in the garden were just beginning to bloom. But all of this only extended to the boundaries of the orphanage. Beyond the walls, the city looked dark and colorless. Curious,

James walked over to the wall and looked through a small opening in the gate.

Outside, the city was a smoldering shell of its former self. Through the waves of smoke he could make out the blackened remains of buildings and coaches. Bodies were strewn across the street. Hideous monsters roamed the carnage. Some of those monsters were zombie children. One of them spotted James through the gate and looked straight at him.

James bolted away from the opening and hurried back to the headmaster's side. "Why would Otto make such things?" James asked him. "Why would he make us evil?"

"He did not intend for you to be evil. He thought he could harness evil without being tainted by it. He was wrong. He doesn't like creating murderers, but he counts that a small price to pay for his work."

"*A small price?* What could be worth so much death and destruction? Why is he doing all of this?"

"He wants to be me." said Tralvorkemen. "I think you of all people can relate."

It hurt to acknowledge it, but James could relate. He had not simply tried to imitate Tralvorkemen, he had tried to replace him.

They continued back into the house and ascended to the roof. From there James could better see the crumbling world beyond the orphanage. The children's dreams of leaving the orphanage and setting out into the world seemed silly now.

"I have one more question." said James. "Couldn't you have stopped me? Couldn't you have prevented all of this tragedy?"

Tralvorkemen sighed. "James, I can't adequately answer that. The real me has all the answers, but I am not the real me, only a pale shadow of who I am."

"I don't understand. You are Mr. Tralvorkemen, aren't you?"

"I *am* Edward Tralvorkemen, but I am also an incomplete translation. All you've seen of me has been incomplete and distorted. But you *have* been given a means of seeing the real me."

Tralvorkemen motioned downward. James looked and for the first time noticed that he was holding Marloth in his hands.

"That book you are holding, it is one hundred percent pure and genuine. If you want to know the real me, read that book." As he spoke, the light grew diffuse and sounds became distant. The headmaster rose to his feet.

"This dream is coming to an end, but we will meet again, and when we do, I will be more real. The closer you get to the original story, the clearer I become. As for what you see before you, I'm a fading memory of a past you never knew you had."

And then everything blurred.

*   *   *

James sat up dizzily and looked around. He was in a cave. Mr. Mosspuddle was sitting nearby, surrounded by open books and shifting his gaze from one to the next. Then he noticed James.

"You're awake, and alive!" said the toad. "Or, at least sort of alive. I'm sure you have so many questions."

James was still very disoriented. "Adelle." was all he managed to say.

"She's safe. And nearby. She had several injuries, but with the help of the swan and one of my books we were able to heal them. Her scars are nearly gone, and will completely fade with time. You, however—your injuries were much more severe."

"That doesn't matter." said James. "I'm used to injury."

"Not like this! We found you in pieces! You were as lifeless as a doornail. But Princess Adelle gathered them and sewed them together again. There *were* a few bits missing so we had to substitute cloth and other random materials to fill the gaps."

Fugue appeared and joined in updating updated about what had happened the past few days. But James wasn't very concerned about what he had missed except for one person.

"Where is Adelle now?"

Adelle was sitting on the rocky slope above the cave and gazing out over the water. She had been doing a lot of that lately. Her mind was a washing machine of thoughts. As she was thus employed one of those thoughts materialized as it stepped out of the cave below her and looked around. Her heart leapt within her. He was alive! Then another of the thoughts she had been struggling with rose to the surface: what if she had made a mistake? Had she reanimated a hero or a monster?

Before she knew it, James had spotted her and was climbing up the slope to where she was sitting. What should she do? If she had been rescued by a truly living boy and he had sustained injury in the process and yet had lived through it, she would have thrown her arms around him, but this was a little more complicated. As he approached, she decided to receive him with cool reserve, a thing she had never been very good at.

"Thank you for putting me back together." James said when he arrived beside her.

Adelle didn't look up. "You make it sound like Humpty Dumpty—I mean . . . you're welcome."

James sat down nearby and asked her how she was doing.

"Terrible!" Adelle replied miserably. "Mr. Mosspuddle informed me that I'm the only living child left in this world! All the other children are zombies! I feel so alone! But who am I kidding? I've always been alone—I've just spent my life trying to distract myself from seeing it."

James wanted to say something comforting, but he wasn't very good at that sort of thing. Instead, he just stood there awkwardly. It was Adelle who continued the conversation.

"James, why did they want to hurt me?"

"It's their nature. Seeing others in pain gives them more energy."

"Are all zombie children like that?"

James clenched his teeth, hating his sense of honesty. "Yes." he said.

"Do you want to hurt me?" Despite her question, she did not look scared.

"No!" James said quickly. "I mean—yes, but mostly no! I *am* enchanted by an evil spell, like all zombie children, but I also have another enchantment—a *good* one. The enchantments are battling over which can control me, and the good one is winning."

Adelle didn't look convinced.

"It's Mr. Tralvorkemen," James continued. "He somehow enchanted me through his book. When I read his stories of epic heroes, I want to be like them; more like him. But the longer I am away from the book, the fairytales fade and I start to become more . . . like the way I was."

There was a long pause that Adelle did not bother to fill. James finally continued. "As long as I have the book, the good enchantment will be strong and everything should be alright. I'll protect you from the other children."

Adelle stood up in frustration. "I am grateful for you rescuing me from those zombies; really, I am. But I am so tired of needing to be protected! Of being helpless all the time! Mr. Mosspuddle has been telling me about how this whole zombie thing works; about how your strength and agility is determined by magic instead of things like muscles. Apparently even a little zombie girl half my age could pick me up and throw me across the room! I'm pathetic!"

Once again, James was not sure what to say.

Adelle rose to her feet with determination. "I am going to try very hard to forget about all of this blackness, if even for just a little while. Look, there are the dolls further down the beach. Maybe they will cheer me up."

She set off in their direction. James did not follow her. He remained there for some time, once again feeling the weight of his own inability. How could a creature of evil like him give her any good? Yes, he had just rescued her, but he had been a razor's breadth away from doing the opposite. He could not escape the images of all the things he had done to other children like her.

But inside him loomed a guilt even larger than the pain of his career as an undead minion. The more he read Marloth, the more clearly he remembered the orphanage and what he had done there. Part of him told him that Mr. Tralvorkemen had taken care of everything, and that he no longer needed to worry about the past, but James was unable to fully embrace that idea. He was still being driven forward by the guilt of his mistakes. No matter how hard he tried, he could not shake the feeling that somehow this entire fallen world was his fault.

*　　*　　*

When Adelle met up with the dolls, they were busy organizing the debris into different piles and from these piles constructing some form of building.

"What are you doing?" Adelle asked them.

"Making a house." said Mrs. Gingersmile. "You should help us! This is something you will have to learn one day when you have a husband and children of your own. Every good wife and mother knows how to be a housemaker."

At this Adelle's countenance fell. "I don't want to be a mother anymore." All four dolls looked up in shock.

"How can you say such a thing?" Mrs. Gingersmile scolded her.

"Because now I know what it's really like. To have someone that just takes and takes from you."

"Is this about the Jillybons?" the swan asked her. "Because a baby is completely different from a Jillybon."

"How so? Is it less demanding? Is it less greedy?"

"It's not about greed, but need!" said Mrs. Gingersmile. "Babies are helpless! They need their mothers!"

"Jillybons are just as helpless. They need people like me to suck the life out of!"

"Children are precious gifts from above! We were *made* to care for them. We were never meant to care for Jillybons."

"I don't know if I agree with that, but even if there is *technically* a difference between children and Jillybons, they don't *feel* any different."

The swan considered for a few moments. "Feelings aren't always true. Look at us dolls; are we evil?"

"No. You may not be perfect, but you certainly aren't evil."

"That's what most people used to believe. But the toymaker corrupted so many playthings and gave them such a reputation that now people automatically assume I and my sisters here are likewise evil. We did not do anything to gain this reputation. Jakob Damond imposed it on us."

"I am sorry for you and your situation, but what does that have to do with Jillybons?"

"You are viewing children the same way other people view us: harboring feelings that we did not create; associating evils with us that we were never involved with."

"I respect your opinions, but once again, one of the noblest people I have met is being vilified by people who can't possibly know much about him. Am I to believe that you too are suddenly experts on philosophy and morality?"

Mrs. Gingersmile shook her head. "We may not know much about books and magic and philosophy, and maybe we don't know that much about Jakob Damond, but one thing we dolls know about is motherhood. Motherhood is about Love. That means giving to your child without expecting anything from them in return. That is *beautiful*."

"I'm sorry, but even if children are better than Jillybons, I can't see what is so beautiful about giving everything you have to someone who doesn't give anything in return."

That was the last straw for Miss Perrywinkle; her temper snapped like a twig. "Young lady, it is time *somebody* told it to you straight: you are more selfish than any child I have *ever* met! All you speak of is what you want and what people can give you! You are the *real Jillybon!*"

The effect of this speech was like dunking Adelle's head in freezing water. Her heart was cut to the quick. With water filling her eyes she fled from their presence. After this the dolls debated amongst themselves as to whether Miss Perrywinkle had been too harsh, and while all of them to some degree believed that Adelle had needed that message, even Miss Perrywinkle admitted she had spoken more out of anger than kindness, and was determined to make things right.

Sometime later Miss Perrywinkle found Adelle curled up in a corner of the beach in much distress. Miss Perry climbed beside the girl and put her stubby arms around her tenderly.

"I'm sorry, dearie! I shouldn't have spoken so! You are a good person; I have seen you act selflessly on many occasions!"

"No! What you said before was true! I *am* selfish! Wretchedly selfish! I am so ashamed of myself, I hardly know who I am anymore!" Adelle sighed. "I still want to be a mother. No that's not it exactly—I *want* myself to want to be a mother, but I can't shake away this ugliness I feel toward it. I fear my sense of motherhood may be forever tainted!"

"Oh dearie! What you need is to fill your head with good things. That City filled it with so much bad." She considered for several moments. "That book James has, you should read it. Mr. Mosspuddle has read a number of its stories to us. They are good stories."

"I don't think bedtime stories are going to fix me," said Adelle.

"You should give it a try. It has stories about women. About mothers. Mothers that love their children and make great sacrifices for all the people they care for. You know some of the stories; your mother told them to you."

At the mention of her mother Adelle felt a new pang in her heart. She was not sure if it was loneliness, guilt, or the resurfacing of doubts about whether her mother had ever truly loved her. She wished she had done more to be certain of that. She was sure there were more questions she could have asked. For the first time she felt her heart longing to return to the castle and secure her mother's love for her.

*   *   *

Eventually it began to rain and James returned to the cave. He found Mr. Mosspuddle and Fugue much as he had left them.

"I don't think all of your talking to Adelle about zombie children is helping." said James. Mr. Mosspuddle looked up from his research in bewilderment.

"She's the princess! I can't hold information from her! And even if she wasn't of royal blood, I can't help it. She's been asking me so many questions, and when someone asks me a question I have to answer it!"

"I'll have to remember that."

"Besides, I think she has a right to know about the things that are threatening her life."

It was then that he noticed the rain outside.

"Where are the dolls?" he said. "They're going to soak like sponges if they don't return to the cave soon. And Princess Adelle could catch a cold."

"Maybe they like getting wet," said Fugue.

As they were speaking, Samantha appeared at the front of the cave. She was carrying a large umbrella.

"Hello!" she said. "I'm here to inform you that you are all invited to our new inn—unless you would rather spend your time in this damp, dingy bachelor pit."

After much puzzlement and wonder, the three heroes dropped whatever it was they had been doing and followed her into the rain.

It was difficult to see through the downpour but there appeared to be a building down the shore.

"What is that?" said the librarian, pointing at the structure.

"That's our new inn," said the doll. "We built it today. Do you like it?"

As they drew nearer to the inn they could see that it was a cute, three-story building that was elevated from the ground and boasted a porch that looked out over the water. They climbed the short flight of stairs up to the porch. The front door was opened by Miss Perrywinkle.

"Good evening good sirs!" she said, ushering them inside. Once she had taken their coats, she asked them if they would like to buy some tea."

The librarian stood there for a moment in surprise before acquiescing with. "I suppose I would. What kinds of tea do you have?"

"Oh, we only have one kind at the present," said Samantha. "It's our shoreside special!"

"Very well, I'll have the special."

"Good choice! That will cost you five kisses."

"Oh," said Mr. Mosspuddle, thinking she was referring to candy. "I don't have any of that with me."

"That's all right," said Mrs. Gingersmile. "We'll put it on your line of credit."

"Thank you." said Mr. Mosspuddle, though he was not entirely sure what she meant.

"Your tea will be ready in a few minutes." said Miss Perrywinkle. James and Fugue were also asked if they would like tea. James strongly declined while Fugue asked if they offered it in gallon mugs.

Towels were provided for the guests to dry themselves. As they were doing so, the swan came down and scolded the other dolls for charging the librarian.

"These are our guests, and fellow adventurers! Of course we are providing both tea and dinner without charge! Please everyone, have a seat!"

There was a long table along the front wall. Around the table was a wide variety of chairs that had been collected from the shore. Mr. Mosspuddle sat down in a chair with a back that was far taller than he was.

"Where's Adelle?" James asked.

"She's upstairs." said Mrs. Gingersmile. "She should be down shortly."

They were not long seated when there came a rapping at the front door. Miss Perrywinkle opened it and in flew the raven. Despite his general lack of friendliness in the past, the group was happy to see him.

"Mr. Raven!" said Samantha. "What a pleasant surprise! Where have you been all this time?"

"I've been trying to stay alive," said the raven. "Something I never had to worry much about until I fell in with this lot."

"Well, we are glad to have your company!" said the swan. "Would you like some tea?"

The raven said he would and settled at one end of the table.

Next Mrs. Gingersmile asked what they would like to eat. James rolled his eyes as Mr. Mosspuddle asked what there was to eat.

"Crumpets." said James.

"How did you know?" said Samantha, greatly impressed. "Did you use your dead person powers to divine the menu?"

James assured them that it was nothing so supernatural.

Before long the drinks and warm crumpets were served. Fugue unpocketed a small bottle of "tonic" he had found in the wreckage and administered a dose of this into his mug of tea. (It was a large dose for a large mug.) Then he searched around for some meat and cheese and made himself a hefty crumpet sandwich. After a couple requests, the dolls were able to provide some additional items of food that weren't on the menu.

They had just begun to dine when Adelle came down the stairs. She was unusually distant and only half-aware of her surroundings.

The moment the librarian noticed she was in their presence, he hopped to his feet and offered her a chair saying, "How is your royal highness faring?" This brought her somewhat to the present. Mr. Mosspuddle was the only person she had met outside of the castle that had a healthy respect for royalty.

She told him she was a little distracted, but not unwell, and then took a seat. After the dolls had served her food and drink and taken their own seats at the table, Mr. Mosspuddle spoke up.

"Now that we are all gathered here I think this would be a good time to discuss our future course of action."

"But what about the girly folk?" said Fugue loudly under his breath and motioning at them with his thumb. "They'll hear everything we say . . ."

"Yes," said Mr. Mosspuddle. "That was sort of what I just said. Whether formally or informally, the dolls have become a part of our band, and they have proved themselves very useful. As for Princess Adelle, she is our superior and has more right to be a part of these proceedings than any of us."

Since no one voiced any dissension on that point, Mr. Mosspuddle proceeded by addressing Adelle. "Earlier you disagreed that there were forces set on causing you harm. Do you still hold that position?"

Adelle unconsciously reached up and touched the line across her cheek. "No. I very much agree that those children back there wanted to kill me. But I don't agree that every force you claim is against me. The toymaker is still my friend."

This caused much interjection from many parties, but the toad did his best to calm everyone's tempers.

"Regardless of the toymaker's intentions, I think we are all agreed that *someone* malevolent is after the princess. I fear it is only a matter of time before the forces seeking her will track her down to where we are now. I'd rather not wait for that."

"But where do you think you'll take her?" said the raven. "This place is evil—that place evil. Everywhere we turn someone seems out to get her. You can't keep running forever."

Mr. Mosspuddle sighed. "As much as I have been trying to ignore that fact, we seem unable to escape it. It is not enough to run from the evil. We need something good to run toward. And I do not know where to turn."

There was a pause as everyone mulled on this, except for James. He already knew what he wanted to do. He had known for a while.

"We need to find the orphanage."

All eyes fell on James.

"What orphanage?" said Miss Perrywinkle.

James reached into his pack, took out Marloth, and placed it on the center of the table. "The orphanage of Edward Tralvorkemen. It's a sanctuary."

"But everyone in the City said that he was a wicked man!" Adelle felt obligated to point out.

"Do you believe that he is?" asked Mr. Mosspuddle.

"I do not know what to think of him." said Adelle. "He seems to be more of a legend than a man."

Mr. Mosspuddle picked up the book in the middle of the table and held it reverently before them.

"Despite its being titled a collection of fairytales, I have never seen a book that so closely corresponded with reality as does this one. The more I read it the more everything makes sense. At this present point in time, I would trust it more than any other piece of literature. If Marloth says that Edward Tralvorkemen exists, and that he is a good man, and that his orphanage is a place of safety, then I believe the orphanage is where we should go."

"Sounds great!" said Fugue. "Let's do it!"

Everyone else expressed their agreement with this course of action except for Adelle, who said nothing one way or the other. This did not escape Mr. Mosspuddle's notice and he asked her what she thought.

"I suppose I don't have much choice in the matter either way," said Adelle. "If you go to the orphanage then I go too."

Mr. Mosspuddle was not completely satisfied with that response, but decided it best to move on.

"So to the orphanage it is then. That leaves us with the matter of actually finding that place; I have no idea where it is."

"It's in a city." said James. "Though I don't know what the name of the city is."

"That's not much to work with," said the swan. "Do you know how to get to this city?"

"I might. Whatever the city was, that's where I came from when I got on the train."

"You mean the train that took us to the City of Orphans?" asked Mr. Mosspuddle.

"Yes. If we could trace its path, we should be able to find the city with the orphanage. Where did you get on the train?"

"I have no idea." said the toad, "I didn't enter it in any formal sense. The wizards banished me from the Library, and the next thing I knew I was on the train. But surely there are other ways of getting on the train. In theory all we should have to do is find a train station and ride the train back to this city we are looking for."

After further discussion, it was decided that the librarian's plan would be adopted and that they would leave the following morning on their quest for the orphanage. After they were finished working out the details for the next day and their upcoming journey, Mr. Mosspuddle thanked the dolls for their hospitality, took Marloth and went upstairs to scour it for any clues regarding the location of the orphanage and the city it resided in

An inn wouldn't be an inn without places to sleep, and the dolls had made certain that their inn had plenty of rooms for everyone. The boys were provided rooms on the third story while the girls quarters were on the second story.

One by one, people began to head up to bed until the only two people still at the table were James and Adelle. Adelle felt bad about how she had responded to him earlier. She could see that he had been trying to raise her spirits. After smoothing things out to some degree, she asked him a question that had long been bouncing around in her mind.

"Do zombie children feel pain?"

"I do."

"Yes, but you're weird. What about everyone else?"

James thought about the other children. The sorts of masochistic acts they performed. The children of wealthy families were known to do unspeakable things to each other and then pay for expensive magics to restore their flesh—no needle and thread for them. At one point it had somehow made sense to James, but now he could not understand any of it.

"The others don't feel any pain." James said.

"That would be so wonderful! To no longer feel any pain!"

"I want to feel the pain. I want to feel it because I know it is *real.*"

"That is definitely weird. How about this: I don't like pain, and you seem to revel in it, so I'll keep my eyes open for some way of giving you all of mine."

James came very close to smiling at her, but he was too absorbed by the weight of the subject. She didn't realize how willing he would be to do what she joked about. He looked out into the distance and reflected on his past.

"I didn't used to feel any pain. On the outside I was having fun. But deep down there was a fear that I was living a lie and that sooner or later it would all catch up with me. I think all zombie children have that. We don't want to look beyond our little zombie world because somehow we know that if there is anything beyond this, it's Hell. Judgment Day. Doom."

"I think that's just you," said Adelle. "You seem to be drawn to most everything morbid and depressing."

"No, that's not true. I love reading Marloth, and Marloth is full of hope. It says that there is a world beyond this one, and that it is something wonderful. Something worth looking forward to."

"But that totally contradicts what you just said about the outside world being hell!"

"I think it's both. In Marloth there are characters who never see the beauty of reality, and to them reality is hell. But to the characters that do see its beauty, the ones who have felt and tasted it, they want more."

Adelle pondered this. "I find it curious that the little mad boy with his book of fairytales would be so adamant about reality."

"I believe the fairytales are real and the world is a fairytale." said James. "Naturally, the world wants me mad."

*   *   *

Ivy was growing increasingly upset. Not a single boy had yet asked her to the ball. Normally she was having to turn them down right and left. In desperation, she took the initiative and begun asking boys if they would take her to the ball, and so far all of them had responded that they were holding out for a chance to be Princess Adelle's partner. And no one had seen the princess in over a week! Boys that used to drool over Ivy didn't even notice her anymore.

But boys weren't the only issue. It was with people in general. Within a remarkably short period of time, Ivy had gone from being considered one of the most attractive, clever, and influential girls in Marloth to simply being "Adelle's friend".

"Oh yeah! I know her! I can't recall her name, but she used to hang around the princess a lot."

Deep down, Ivy had hoped that Adelle's disappearance would result in things slowly returning to normal. But instead, the princess had been elevated to the status of legend. The papers were throwing around all sorts of theories as to what could have happened to Adelle and where she could be, and discussing those theories seemed to be the great new pastime for everyone in the City. Ivy was sick of it! Even her mother could talk of little else than retrieving Adelle to the Manor.

*   *   *

The next morning Adelle arose early and walked along the beach. The sun was just rising and a few of its rays managed to cut through the clouds. The light from the rays bounced off of the water, creating glittering ripples of gold. It was very soothing to behold.

It was also very brisk. Adelle was wrapped in a jacket and she could see her breath wafting in front of her as though her spirit was slowly escaping her body.

As she was walking along the shore, Adelle felt a sudden inclination to stop, pause, and turn. There, nestled in the midst of the random debris that surrounded her, was the crown. Her breath froze. A torrent of conflicting emotions passed through her. She was about to bend down when she heard a sound above her.

Adelle looked up. And nearly gasped. The raven was sitting on a perch nearby. He was looking at her critically.

"You may have the others fooled, but not me."

Adelle quickly straightened. "What do you mean?"

"All of these people pursuing you do not understand what they are dealing with. They think that there is an enchantment around you and that it is protecting you from them."

"Me? Enchanted? I think I would know if I was enchanted!"

"Oh, you are. They've got that part right. It's the latter part they have wrong: the enchantment is not protecting you from them, it's protecting you from yourself."

"From me?"

"Of course! Do you really think you are as innocent and good as so many people have portrayed you to be? That's not innocence darling, it's naiveté. No, you are just as twisted as the rest of this world, you're simply being held back by the enchantment."

Adelle was taken aback. "I can't believe you just said that! That's cruel even for you!"

For the first time in their conversation the raven finally acknowledged the crown, motioning at it with his head. "Why don't you pick it up?"

Adelle followed his gaze to the thing her heart desired. But she didn't move.

"Do you know much about demonic devices?" the raven asked her.

"No." she replied. "I can't say that I do, or that I would ever want to."

"That's curious, considering how you are intimately acquainted with one."

"I suppose you mean the crown? I have never felt so good as when I wore it. How could it be evil?"

"All of Jakob Damond's toys are demonic, and as with all things demonic, they are pure evil. But things aren't always what they seem, and that is especially the case with demonic devices. They look attractive. They look beneficial. They appear to offer the user so many good things. But in reality they have nothing to give. All they do is take. Take and take and take until there is nothing left. A person tries to use one of these devices, but in the end it is the device that uses them." The raven paused to reload and then said, "You've already experienced this with the Jillybons."

Adelle cringed at even the mention of them. She looked down at the crown with growing confusion.

"If you ignore everything you have witnessed, pick up that crown, and put it back on your head, then that means the enchantment is virtually gone. But if you walk away now and leave the crown behind you, then know that the enchantment is the only thing that could cause you to do that."

"Because the crown is evil and so am I?"

"Do you have a better explanation? I don't know any other sort that would want to manipulate the hearts of everyone around her including her friends."

Adelle stomped her foot in frustration. "It's not like that! You don't know what it's like! If anything scary comes along you just up and fly away or become all ghostlike. Nothing can touch you! But me, I'm just a little girl! There is so much in this world that wants nothing more than to harm me, and by myself there is nothing I can do about it. I am so vulnerable! Don't you see? If I am ever going to survive, that crown is my only hope."

The raven was deeply sobered by this. While he did not agree with everything she said, neither could he simply discount it. After much inner wrestling he finally said, "I don't normally talk about this, but I think I need to explain something to you. You said you were not sure if Edward Tralvorkemen was a legend? I can assure you he is very real. I have known him for a long time. It is from him that I have the ability to move between dimensions, and I have used that ability to run many errands for him.

"Yet things are not the way they once were, for we had a falling out of sorts. There were things he promised to do that I waited and waited for, and he never did them. He said I should have patience, but my patience ran out. I still run errands for him from time to time, but I don't see him as ideally as I used to.

"But with that said, I would still put my trust in him more than anyone else in Marloth. And whether or not you trust him, he is looking out for you. I do not understand his reasons, but he has determined to protect you, and to do so in a very indirect manner. That group back there, they may be a pitiful lot, but every one of them would give their life to protect you.

"But you can't have both them and the crown. Right now you are wavering in the middle, wishing to have both, but eventually you are going to have to make a decision: who are you going to choose, Jakob Damond and his magical toys or Edward Tralvorkemen and his lowly band of heroes?"

Adelle looked at the crown, and then at the inn. After a long, agonizing pause, she pulled the shawl tighter around her and headed back toward the inn.

The raven looked relieved. He followed her back to the inn, and as they went, he said one thing more.

"There are things even I fear," he said to her. "Your toymaker is one of them."

*   *   *

While the Lady Mediev was attending a formal evening party she happened upon Jakob Damond. He was holding a glass of wine in one hand and entertaining multiple guests with his fantastic stories. Curious, the Lady approached him from behind.

"Why, if it isn't Jakob Damond in the flesh! I didn't think you were the socialite."

Damond turned to look at her and smiled as usual. "And if it isn't the Lady Mediev, likewise in her flesh! Actually, I love parties. I just usually attend wilder ones."

The Lady made some witty comment about toys and wild parties.

"Which reminds me," said the toymaker, almost blushing, "there is something I would like to ask you. In private."

The Lady raised an eyebrow. "A private conversation with Jakob Damond? How could I resist?"

The toymaker excused himself from his audience and started walking beside the Lady. As they walked the toymaker took a few sips from his wine and then said, "I would like to make you a proposition."

"A proposition! How intriguing. What sort of proposition?"

"If you were to do me a small favor, I could tell you—not right away but sometime in the near future—where Adelle is going to be."

"What! You know where she is?"

"I didn't say that. But I did say you are a very handsome and clever woman."

The Lady eyed him suspiciously. "And what favor would I need to perform in return? Am I properly dressed for it?"

The toymaker maintained his steady smile. "That you would leave Adelle and her entourage alone. At least for now."

"And why would I ever do that?"

The toymaker took another sip from his wine. "Because you are making them agitated. Causing discomfort when what you *should* be doing is making them happy."

"Happy? *Happy?* That is the *opposite* of what I should be doing! I want control of Adelle, and for that she needs to be broken. Since she first arrived at the City of Orphans I have been patiently deconstructing her, and with much success. More than most people realize."

"Yes, yes. You get a pat on the back for that. But breaking her will not accomplish anything by itself. Someone is helping her. Someone with considerable powers. Neither you nor I nor anybody else is going to make much progress toward acquiring Adelle until that help is undermined. And the best way to do that is to give her and that band of heroes something they are presently lacking. Something that, once they possess, will be their undoing."

"What, despair? Apathy? A spell to render them senseless?"

"No. What they need is self-confidence. And that is a need we are going to fill."

*   *   *

Once again, the lair of Doctor Otto Marrechian found a monkey sneaking into its core and tinkering with the recently repaired zombie machine. Except now he wasn't turning up the juice, he was turning it down. For now.

Part 6

Dear Sir,

It has come to my attention that you are still alive. I must say, that is an impressive trick. You may think me worried that you have returned, but you need not worry about me. From what I hear, you are hardly more than a ghost. I am not afraid of ghosts.

You were right about one thing: everything did pass away. But that turned out to be hardly a loss for me. With the passing of that dimension I have gotten my book back. And now I have made copies. Your death was in vain.

There have also been rumors of you wanting to end this world as well. That simply will not do. I don't appreciate your obsession with destroying worlds, and it is my duty to prevent you from destroying this one.

Hoping you see reason,
Jakob Damond

*   *   *

Deep within the farthest reaches of the most devious of minds, there was a room. It was a narrow, dingy room, with a tall ceiling and only the faintest hint of light. Within this room, there was a little boy. He was just waking up and wondering *what in the world was he doing there again!*

He was not awake long when the door opened and in stepped a man he had never seen before.

"Hello." said the man. "I am Doctor Norris. How are you feeling today, James?"

"Dead." said James. "I'm dreaming, aren't I?"

"No, though you have been. You managed to escape the Asylum and were found several days later in a ditch. You were oblivious to your surroundings and muttering endless gibberish. My assistant has been documenting much of what you spoke during your delirium. You certainly have a fantastic imagination."

"What happened to Doctor Hurley?"

"After the debacle with his 'new miracle drug', your previous physician was relieved from his post. Indefinitely."

"And what about the nurse? The one who assisted him?"

"Oh, her? She was fired." The man did not seem at all concerned about this.

James glared at him. "What do you want with me?"

"Not much, really. I am going to document your condition and then leave you alone. Since my assistant has already recorded what your unconscious state is like, all that remains is to observe how you are when you are awake."

The doctor pulled a book from his coat pocket and began to peruse it curiously.

"So tell me, James, has anyone gone out of their way to preserve your life?"

"Why do people keep asking me that?"

The doctor was starting to lose his calm. "You've asked enough questions for the moment, James. Now it's time for me to ask a few questions. Has anyone gone out of their way to preserve your life? Yes or no."

"My friends have my back, but no one has gone out of their way to keep me alive that I know of. So no."

"Thank you. Next question: Who would you—"

"What is that book in your hand?"

"What, this? Oh, this is my assistant's notebook documenting your case."

James recognized the book. "No it isn't!" he cried. "It's from Jakob Damond's Toye Shoppe! That's the book I wrote! It's *evil!* You have to destroy it!"

"James, listen very carefully. This is my assistant's book. It is what he's been using to take notes."

"No! I'd recognize that book anywhere! I can feel its taint! I can hear it calling to me to write more in it!"

The doctor rose to his feet. "I think it would be best to resume these questions at another time." he said, and left a fuming James behind him.

Outside the cell stood his assistant, who had been listening to the conversation. The doctor sighed. "We need to quickly finish this case and get away from it as soon as possible! It is astounding how this boy's delusion is capable of sucking in everything around him and making it part of the fantasy. This boy has ended too many careers, and mine won't be one of them."

As they walked away, the assistant asked him why he asked the boy if anyone had tried to preserve his life.

"I was trying to more precisely diagnose the type of psychosis he has. When the mind has fragmented into multiple pieces, those pieces sometimes become cognitive of their own illusory state. They become aware that without both the delusion and the patient they will cease to exist. Thus they become a parasite, trying not only to preserve the delusion, but the delusion's owner as well."

"But this patient doesn't have any such pieces bent on protecting his life?"

"There doesn't seem to be. Whatever this delusion is, it doesn't seem to care about his life. It's almost as if James' delusion isn't dependent upon James."

"But that can't be possible!"

"No, it can't. Yet I don't know any other way to account for these circumstances. I don't like it. The sooner we leave this case behind us, the better."

*   *   *

With the departure of the doctor, the room was once again dark. As James sat there, he noticed something different about the adjacent wall. Despite the blackness of the room, there was a faint point of light coming from beyond that wall. The light was slowly growing in size and strength. When it grew bright enough to start adding illumination to the room James jumped back in horror. Once again, the adjacent wall was a giant mirror!

But then he discerned what the light was and his nerves relaxed. It was a lantern, held by someone on the other side of the mirror. And that someone was Fugue. He was walking toward the mirror. Following both alongside and behind him were the raven, Mr. Mosspuddle, the dolls, and Adelle. They reached the mirror and touched it curiously. James could see them opening their mouths as though speaking to one another, but he could not hear any sound.

After some deliberation, Fugue whipped out his firearm and blasted the mirror into oblivion. James ducked as he was showered by bits of glass. When he straightened, he saw his friends climbing down from the mirror. The room quickly became very crowded.

"So this is where you live," said the raven. "It looks like the typical bachelor pad."

"What's happening?" James asked them.

"We've just arrived to break you out of this place." Adelle replied smugly. "Now it's *your* turn to be rescued!"

"But how did I get here?"

"Don't you remember?" said Mrs. Gingersmile. "You were apprehended by the men in white coats!"

"No. I don't remember anything like that."

"They were at the train station." said Miss Perrywinkle.

"What train station? We haven't reached one yet."

"Yes we did. We reached it yesterday!"

"How come I don't remember any of that?"

Mr. Mosspuddle scratched his nonexistent chin in contempla-tion. "When the men grabbed you they stuck you with a syringe and you passed out. Maybe whatever they gave you damaged your already tenuous memory. What is the last thing you remember?"

"Clearly? Leaving the Shoreside Inn. From there everything gets fuzzy."

"Then you missed a lot!" said Mrs. Gingersmile. "After we left the shore we traveled to the nearest train station. It took us several days and we had many adventures on the way. When we arrived at the station, we asked about the city that we don't know its name, and they said they didn't know of the train stopping at any such city. Then a group of men in white coats appeared and started chasing us."

"And that's when I got the idea to let them capture you." said Fugue.

"That was your *idea*?"

"Yeah, I think I asked you first. Then I assisted you in getting spotted, and they did the rest. Whatever the case, it was a better idea than that silly train one."

"And how was that *better*?"

"Because once they captured you they took you to the Asylum."

"And how was that *better*?"

"Because the Asylum is in the city we've been looking for. The one with the orphanage."

Understanding dawned upon James. The idea made a Fugueish sort of sense. Sort of.

"Then how did *you* get here?" he asked them.

"Don't mind us," said Fugue as he blasted the lock from the door and it swung open. "We're just in your head."

"I am most certainly *not*." said Adelle indignantly, and then, "It's dark out there."

Sure enough, it was just as dark outside the room as it had been within.

"While you all debate how one or the other of us got here, I'll be scouting the area." said the raven, and he flew through the doorway.

Everyone continued to peer through the black doorway. It was very foreboding.

"I'm going to close this ..." said Samantha as she pushed the door closed. It didn't latch since there was a big hole where the latch had been,

"It's too dark here." said Mrs. Gingersmile. "Do we have more lanterns?"

"I have another one." said Fugue.

"Then let us have it on at once!" said Mrs. Gingersmile.

Fugue lit the second lantern and handed it to her. She beamed happily and the dolls began to make shadow puppets on the wall. Some time passed, and then the raven returned, popping through the hole in the door.

"I flew all over the building. It appears to be deserted; I didn't see a single soul."

After some procedural debate and quips, they stepped out of the cell and into the hallway beyond it. Both sides of the hall were lined with rows of similar cells. Most of the doors to these were open. As they passed one cell after another, each one proved empty. No people. No other visible lights than the two lanterns they carried.

The swan peered into one of the empty cells. "There must be a lot of mad people running around." she said.

"As if that's new." said the raven. "But wherever they went, none of them are still here."

Fugue nodded. "With how easy it was for James and I to escape this place, I figured those doctors were running out of patients."

Adelle spotted something smeared across the walls and stepped back in revulsion. "What is that? Is that blood? It's all over the walls!"

James stepped closer and examined the nearest wall. "Yes, that is definitely blood."

Mr. Mosspuddle rubbed his chin in further contemplation. "I wonder who it belonged to? Did something attack the patients, or did the patients escape and attack everyone else?"

"Oh, let's please not dwell on that!" said Samantha.

James pulled out one of his daggers. "Whatever the case, there is definitely something dangerous around here, or at least there was. We'd best assume it's still here. I'll take the front, and Fugue, you can take the rear. Mr. Mosspuddle, if you have any books that could help us in a fight, I suggest you have them ready."

"We can read too, you know." said Adelle.

"What do you mean?" asked Mr. Mosspuddle.

"You aren't the only one who can use those books. The dolls and I can too."

"Yes, but books are very dangerous! If they aren't used properly they—"

"I know that! You've already meticulously shown us how to use many of them. I trust you weren't just doing that for fun."

The librarian sighed. Reaching into his bag, he pulled out a book.

"Do you remember me talking about this book?" he asked.

"Yes. It is one of the acclaimed Books of Nature. They are among the most well written and easy to use books in print. This is the first volume: Geology."

Mr. Mosspuddle was impressed. "Very good. The ease of this book makes it well suited for beginners, and since it consumes physical energy instead of magical energy, you won't need any additional power sources to use it."

He searched through its contents until he came to a certain page and then handed the book to Adelle. "I recommend this section on sedimentary rock. It can be used to hurl rocks at high velocities. That will draw a fair amount of energy from you, so pause between uses to check how fatigued you are. If you push yourself too far you will lose consciousness."

"And what about us?" said Samantha.

The librarian sighed again. "Can you actually read?"

"Of course we can!" said Miss Perrywinkle. "And watch your tone! I'm probably older than you are, young man."

"I am neither young, nor a man," said Mr. Mosspuddle. "But I am reasonable. The Book of Geology requires a fair amount of energy to use, so you dolls can read along with Princess Adelle and supplement her flow of energy with your own. I'm guessing you dolls don't have any physical energy to bestow, but this book has a conversion table that can utilize magical energy at a reduced rate. You'll find that in Appendix C."

"I don't need a book." said the swan. "I will scout ahead with the raven."

They continued on their way. As they crept through the halls of the Asylum, James was haunted by repeated glimpses of what looked like a book on the ground, but every time he drew closer there would be nothing there. He was not sure what book he thought he was seeing, but he had an uneasy suspicion that it was a writing book from Jakob Damond's Toye Shoppe.

Eventually they reached the main doorway and stepped out into the city. It looked as desolate and forsaken as the Asylum. There didn't appear to have been a fire, and yet all the buildings had an ashen tone as though all the color had been burned out of them."

"Funny," said the raven. "I don't remember bringing any doom to this place."

James looked down one street and then another. "I've only been here once, and it was all a blur then. Now it's a blurred blur. Some parts of this city I think I can still remember, but not this one. If we explore a bit we should come across a street I'm familiar with."

So they set off, heading down one random avenue after another. As they were traversing the deserted streets Adelle looked like she was debating inwardly about something, and then finally she drew closer to James and said to him, "So you don't remember anything from the past few days?"

"No . . . well, not much."

Adelle weighed this for a moment. "Do you remember anything between you and me?"

"No. Should I?"

"No—no!" said Adelle, quickly looking away. "It's no big deal. Nothing worth remembering," though her face contradicted her words.

After wandering about the city for some time, James stopped in the middle of an intersection.

"This corner looks familiar." said James. "But I'm turned around. I'm not sure which way is which."

As James wracked his brains and the others waited for inspiration to strike him (like a brick), a ragged-looking man appeared on the scene. He was the first sign of life (aside for their own lively selves) that they had seen in that city. The clothes on his wiry frame were tattered and singed. He stood some distance from them and stared at them strangely until someone in the party called out to him, at which point he walked toward them with a hunched, writhing gait.

"Strangers. Strangers. Probably dangerous," the man muttered to himself, though he didn't look afraid of them.

"What happened here?" Mr. Mosspuddle asked him.

"I sees things. All kinds of things."

"Yes." said the raven. "Haven't we all. But did you see what happened to this city?"

"I saw you two!" said the man, motioning between James and Adelle. "You were walkin' this 'ere way some weeks ago."

Adelle looked startled. "I'm sorry, but you must have me mistaken for someone else. I've never been here before."

"'Twas you! 'Twas you! There's no question o' that! 'Twas the dead o' night and I sees you two passin' by!"

Mr. Mosspuddle looked at Adelle curiously. "Is that possible?" he asked.

"Of course not! This man is clearly mad or inebriated, or both! Why would you—"

"Did we have a crown and a book?" James asked the man.

The man scratched his head for a moment, and then shook it. "No. I don' recall you havin' such things."

"And which way were we going?"

The man pointed up the street.

"Thank you." said James and then, pointing in the opposite direction, he said. "We go that way."

He set off down the street and the rest soon followed, though the swan turned back and asked the man if he would accompany them. The man adamantly refused and said he was going anywhere but that direction, and that he needed to find his work. (He had once been a carpenter.) Reluctantly the band of adventurers left him behind.

The further they progressed down the road, the more confident James became that they were going the right way. As they continued, the raven swooped down and glanced around them uneasily.

"There is something out there." said the raven. "Many things. But they are eluding me."

The dolls shivered.

"Maybe we should have questioned that gentleman more," said Mr. Mosspuddle, though none of them had really wanted to speak with him longer than they had.

Suddenly there came a warlike squeal and out of the shadows jumped several little humanoid creatures armed with a variety of primitive weapons.

James and Fugue were the first to react and quickly engaged them in combat. The creatures swore the most vile profanities but, thankfully for the females, their high pitched little voices were practically unintelligible. Their attack was fierce, but James and Fugue managed to deflect their blows and deliver several of their own. After receiving several injuries, the things turned around and disappeared back into the shadows.

"Good heavens! What were those little devils?" said Miss Perrywinkle, once they were gone.

"Goblikins." said Fugue, wiping his sword on the ground. "They're like goblins but smaller."

Mr. Mosspuddle turned toward the raven. "Well, it looks like we found your mystery creatures."

The raven shook his head. "Those weren't what I was sensing. If I had caught a glimpse of a goblikin moving around, I would have known it was a goblikin."

"Well thankfully no one was hurt." said the swan.

Fugue was perplexed. "Goblikins are cowards, not formidable fighters. I don't know why they attacked us. They looked afraid of us before we even met swords."

"I don't think we're going to find out anything more standing here," said James. "It's almost nighttime. We need to keep moving."

Night was approaching quickly. There were no stars or moon visible, nor were there any streetlights or any other form of city light. It looked like it was going to be a very dark night.

Finally, they came to the waterway alongside which the orphanage had been built. As they drew near, James grew increasingly excited and ran toward the gates that stood before the property.

But James was soon disappointed. The front gates were the only part that still stood. Where James had expected to find the orphanage there was instead an empty plot of land. Empty, that is, except for staggered rows of tombstones. James was dumbfounded.

"I don't understand! The orphanage should be right here! Everything else around it looks just the same!"

"It looks like a graveyard to me." said Mrs. Gingersmile.

"Well it wasn't! I don't know where those things came from, but they didn't use to be here!"

The raven dropped down into the middle of the graveyard and looked about curiously. "Most of these graves are empty. Looks like they've been dug up."

The others entered the graveyard as well. In the middle of the lot there was a weathered looking monument made from stone and marble. Adelle stopped in front of this and examined it curiously.

"This bears resemblance to the work of craftsmen that have served my family for generations," she said. "Castle Elington is full of artwork just like it." She stepped closer to a plaque on the monument and tried to make out the inscription, but it was nearly illegible.

The others began to look at each other nervously.

"Well, whatever this place is, it's not the orphanage," said Mr. Mosspuddle. "Perhaps it is somewhere else around this city."

"This was where it was!" said James.

"Either way, it's not here now and this is definitely not a safe place to tarry."

"Just one minute . . ." said Adelle. "I'm trying to read this inscription. I think this is a royal tomb."

Mr. Mosspuddle grabbed her arm. "We need to keep moving."

"Wait! I can just make it out. It says . . ."

And then she gasped. Everyone turned around to look at her. She fell backwards and began to quiver.

"My parents!" she shrieked hysterically. "Those are my parents!"

Mr. Mosspuddle hurried to smooth things over. "Surely there must be some mistake. You're parents are in fine health, and whenever they do pass away they won't be buried in the middle of an unknown city like this."

"But this tombstone, it looks so authentic! It even has the royal seal perfectly carved into its surface!"

"It's probably an illusion." said the librarian.

"Your parents are dead." said the raven. "We already knew it."

"Don't say that!" said Mr. Mosspuddle.

"But it's true!" said the raven. "We can't all stand around here pretending we didn't know! We did!"

"*What?*" said Adelle, looking about ready to fall to pieces.

"Don't listen to him!" said Mr. Mosspuddle. "He's just trying to be spiteful!"

Adelle stopped listening to any of them. She simply curled up and grew very quiet. As the rest of the group considered what to do next, their attention was diverted by a sudden cry from down the street. It was hard to tell if it was an expression of anguish or perverted glee.

"What was that?" asked a nervous Mrs. Gingersmile.

"Trouble." said Fugue. "We need to get going."

"But what about the orphanage?" said James.

"What about it?" said the raven. "Do you want us to remain here longer and ensure that there isn't an orphanage hiding behind one of these tombstones? It's not here! Can you admit that?"

"*Yes!*" said James. "I *do* see it! It's just that my memory seemed so clear about this. My mind's rarely clear about anything, it felt special to have such a vivid memory. I don't understand how I got it wrong."

"Maybe your memory isn't wrong," said Mr. Mosspuddle. "Maybe the orphanage burned to the ground. Maybe they replaced it with a graveyard."

Samantha gasped. "Maybe these are the graves of all the orphans! Maybe this graveyard is haunted!"

"Maybe we should do less speculating and more moving somewhere that isn't here." said the raven."

"How about this," said James. "I could climb up the nearest building and get a better view of what's happening. Maybe all of this will make more sense from a different angle."

"It's worth a try," said Fugue. "I say we all go up."

"Agreed!" said Miss Perrywinkle. "This graveyard makes my cloth crawl!"

It was as they were starting to leave that Mr. Mosspuddle noticed Adelle. She was crouched in front of the tomb with the book of Geology open on her knees. She was not reading about sedimentary rock. She was reading a much more advanced passage about mining and tunnels and the excavation of earth. Suddenly, the ground began to shake, until the stone slab in front of the tombstone erupted in waves of dirt as though the ground was being rapidly dug up from the inside out. Within moments the motion subsided, leaving a gaping hole. Adelle discarded the book and dropped out of sight.

The others were frozen in place, not knowing what to do. Mr. Mosspuddle was the most astonished. His gaze was fixed on the book lying on the edge of the hole. James was the first to gather himself. Without a word, he dropped in after her.

At the bottom of the hole, James found Adelle kneeling beside a coffin so large it could house multiple people. She was trying to raise the lid but she was so fatigued from the immense use of magic that she was unable to lift it. She looked up at James with tears in her eyes.

"Did you know? *Do* you know? Who is it? Who is inside this coffin?"

James hesitated, and then he gripped the lid and threw it aside. Inside the coffin were two decomposing bodies. On the left was that of a woman, mangled and disfigured nearly beyond recognition. On the right was the corpse of a man so full of incisions and holes that it truly was beyond recognition.

Adelle broke down. She fell back against one side of the hole, sobbing and screaming and repeating over and over, "It's them! It's them!"

Her grieving was soon interrupted by cries from above. Samantha poked her head over the edge of the hole and shouted down to them, "Goblikins! They're back! Just thought I'd let you know." James wasted no time in grabbing hold of Adelle and pulling her out of the grave.

Goblikins were surrounding the graveyard. They were making a fierce display, hopping about and waving their little weapons, but most of them were not brave enough or frenzied enough for a full-on attack.

Adelle didn't want to deal with this right now. She just wanted to curl up in a ball and cry. But somehow she managed to lift herself to her feet.

Suddenly a handful of the goblikins charged forward, running past Fugue and focusing their attack on Mrs. Gingersmile. Fugue and James jumped back to protect the doll, but they were not able to intercept all of the attackers. One of the goblikins made it to the doll and dove at the lamp she was holding, knocking it from her hand just before James ran the creature through with his knife. Two more goblikins charged Mr. Mosspuddle, who barely had enough time to read his book and send the creatures flying backwards through the air.

"What are they trying to do?" James wondered aloud.

In his haste to banish the goblikins, the librarian had dropped his lamp. Fugue looked at the lamp resting on the ground. Understanding dawned upon him.

"There's shades out there!" Fugue shouted. "The goblikins are working with them!"

James looked out into the darkness fearfully. "What are you talking about?"

Fugue began to charge one side of the wall of goblikins. "Quick! We have to get out of here!" The heroes had no choice but to follow Fugue as he slashed a hole through the goblikins' ranks. The cowardly creatures scattered before his wild attack, but soon regrouped and gave chase to the fleeing adventurers.

"What is going on?" Mr. Mosspuddle called ahead.

"The goblikins are gunning for our lights!" said Fugue. "It's the classic arrangement. Shades get some weaker creatures to take out the lights, and then the shades swoop in."

They turned a corner and ran into another group of goblikins.

"Take the alley to your right!" the raven called to them from above, and they quickly followed his lead.

"What are shades?" asked one of the dolls.

"Creatures of pure darkness. Shades are nearly impossible to kill with physical weapons. Light is their main weakness. Faint light aggravates them, stronger light hurts them, and bright light kills them."

"There's more goblikins coming toward you from the front!" the raven warned them.

James frantically looked around them. "In here!" he shouted as he kicked open a door alongside the alley. The group hurried inside and slammed the door behind them.

They found themselves in a small bedroom. Fugue rushed to the next door, opened it, and led them deeper into the house. As they hurried through, they could hear the sounds of shattering windows pursuing them from other regions of the building.

"They're coming up behind us!" said Mrs. Gingersmile.

"Keep going." said Fugue, as he slipped back to guard the rear. James and Mr. Mosspuddle led the front of the group while the females were in the middle.

They came out of a long hallway and into another room when Mr. Mosspuddle was suddenly tripped by an unseen goblikin. He crashed to the floor and the lamp he was carrying shattered. The only other lanterns were being carried by Mrs. Gingersmile and Adelle near the back of the line. Two more goblikins dropped down from their hiding places and shut the door to the room, cutting the party in half and sending the room into complete darkness.

Darkness! They had to do something fast! James tried to think. The lantern was broken. There had to be flammable liquid on the floor. He reached into his pack and took out a matchbook. He quickly lit one of the matches and threw it toward where he figured the middle of the room was.

The floor burst into flame and the room was filled with light. For a brief moment James saw four shadowy figures before they dissolved into nothingness. At the same time, Mr. Mosspuddle's clothes caught on fire, but with James' help the flames were extinguished before any harm could be done.

The door behind them burst open and the rest of the party appeared, sending the goblikins fleeing through various holes in the walls and windows.

"What happened?" said Fugue. "Are you all right?"

"We're fine." said James. "Let's keep moving."

They hurried through the front door and back into the streets. One of the two remaining lamps changed hands from Mrs. Gingersmile to Mr. Mosspuddle.

"This way!" the raven called to them, and they ran after him.

As the group rushed down one street after another, they drew near a darkened corner where several shades were preparing a bomb. This was not a bomb of metal, but of magic; a device that would extinguish every light within throwing distance. Shades cannot create such things, so it was probably some device they had stolen from a wizard. As they were intently listening to the approaching heroes, the shades did not notice a creature sneak up behind them and deposit a bomb of its own. They did notice when the creature scurried away, but by then it was too late. Windows shattered and bricks crumbled as the street was consumed in a ball of light.

The heroes came to an abrupt halt. The street to their left had just exploded.

"What was that?" cried several people at once.

"I can't tell from here," said the raven, "But let's go this way instead."

After following him up and down several streets, they came to a long avenue at the end of which was the train station. They made a dash for the station, but as they did so goblikins began leaping out at them from the surrounding buildings.

"Make sure your lights are protecting each other!" said the raven. "There are shades just beyond the range of your lamps."

But that was easier said than done. The goblikins were growing desperate. James and Fugue were having to divert all of their attention to fending off the goblikins, but no longer were the goblikins retreating like they had before. One of the goblikins reached Adelle and began to stab at her with a little spear. She barely managed to dodge the attack, but in doing so the lamp she was holding was swung about at such an angle that her torso cast a shadow over the back of the party. There was still just enough light in that region to make out a pitch-black figure suddenly flying toward them. Adelle screamed for the dolls to look out. The figure stretched out a long scythelike limb and swung at them. The dolls dodged out of the way but Samantha wasn't fast enough. Her torso was sliced in half.

"Ow! My body!" Samantha moaned.

The moment Adelle was able to, she swung the lamp around and aimed it at the dolls. There was a hideous shriek and the shade was thrown backward as though hit by a cannon ball. Samantha's two halves were quickly gathered up and after much more struggle, the band finally reached the train station.

"Tickets, please." said the steward. The raven had already procured tickets, and gave them to the steward. The gates opened and the party hastened through. The goblikins tried to follow after them, but the gates had already closed.

"Tickets, please." said the steward. The goblikins were at a loss.

A monkey handed him a ticket and scurried onto the train.

* * *

The first stage of their train ride was very quiet. The band of weary adventurers had found an empty car near the back of the train, and there they were tending their wounds and regaining their wits. Adelle sat in one corner of the car, struggling to channel her concentration into repairing Samantha. She didn't want to do it. She didn't want to do anything. She felt so empty, she wished she could just lean back and let emptiness submerge her. But she continued with her work, and once she finished sewing Samantha back into one piece, she had her wish.

"Thank you!" said the doll, hopping up and looking at the seam around her middle. "But I do have a considerable scar now. Oh well, if anyone asks I'll just say I had a C-section."

Adelle didn't hear her; she had already sunk back into her seat and was looking through the window vacantly.

James sat on the other side of the car where the rest of the party was. He was very disappointed about not finding the orphanage. He had thought they were so close. He had thought they would be in the orphanage at that very moment. But then he looked over at Adelle and his discouragement paled compared to what she had to be going through. He could still cling to a hope that they would find the orphanage, but there didn't seem to be any hope that her parents would come to back life, except possibly as bloodthirsty zombies.

James rose from his seat and walked over to where she was sitting. She didn't seem to have noticed him. He gathered his courage and said to her, "I know how you must feel. If it's any consolation, Mr. Tralvorkemen—"

Adelle suddenly turned on him angrily. "You don't know how I feel! No one does! Everyone else in this world is either stuck up adults, lifeless zombies, or fairytale creatures with two-dimensional personalities! I feel more alone than ever."

James shrank back and returned to the other side of the car. Adelle could see the hurt in his face and hated herself for it, but she felt powerless to make anything right. Powerless to be nice or sweet or pretty or any of the things people were always expecting from her. All of the hardship, all of the horrors of the past several days seemed to be converging on her all at once. And one thought rose to the top of them.

"I'm an orphan." she whispered breathlessly.

The rest of the group watched her with growing concern. Even the raven looked sobered by her condition.

"Adelle looks very tired." said Miss Perrywinkle.

"Tired?" said Mr. Mosspuddle. "She should be in a coma! Did you see the spell she cast to excavate that tomb? She couldn't have spent more than a few minutes preparing it. I myself am not capable of that level of magic, and a veteran wizard would have devoted at least half an hour to perform such a feat. She must have an unnatural store of energy to channel, and remarkable intuition to execute such complexity without any practice."

"Then she must be really good at magic!"

"Yes," said the librarian. "She must be." He did not say all he was thinking. Why so many people wanted to control her was starting to make more sense. He had no idea what was the source of her power, or the depth of it, or if she knew herself, and he hoped she didn't. Mr. Mosspuddle was still concerned for Adelle, but no longer in quite the same way. He hated to admit it, but he could no longer look over at the trembling little girl on the other side of the cab without feeling a tinge of fear.

"Adelle has been surrounded by so much unpleasantness," said the swan. "She needs something to take her mind off of all the ugly things. Something fun and happy."

"She should go to the ball!" said Samantha.

"Yeah, that would be fun and happy," said the raven. "If your idea of fun and happy is getting tortured and killed by undead children! We already had this conversation! The ball is in the Globe, and the Globe is in the City of Orphans. That's the last place in Marloth we are ever going to take her."

There was a pause, and then Mr. Mosspuddle spoke up. "Is it really less safe than anywhere else we've been? We keep imagining that the next turn will be safer than the last, only to discover all new dangers. If the entire world is truly seeking her harm, perhaps the safest place to be would be the last place they would look."

James frowned. "I could see sneaking her into the City and keeping her hidden. The most dangerous of our pursuers probably aren't even in the City at this point—they are out on the hunt. But the ball is a different matter. The Globe will be swarming with zombie children. We can't possibly hide her from that!"

"She could wear a disguise," suggested the swan.

"That just might work!" said Fugue, turning to James "After all, you said you can't sense her presence anymore, so I bet they can't either!"

"How would we disguise her? By now she has the most well known face in Marloth!"

"I can take care of that," said Fugue. "I am the master of disguise!"

"Really?" said Samantha.

"Didn't you know?" said the raven. "He's actually a dwarf."

Fugue scrutinized Adelle with the eye of a trained whatever-he-thought-he-was. "With the right makeup, hair dye, and some of my secret techniques, I could make her look like any other zombie girl. Her own mother wouldn't recognize her. Whoops!" (This was from Miss Perrywinkle kicking him in the shin.)

James wasn't convinced. "I still don't like it. If something went wrong we wouldn't be there to protect her."

"Well of course at least one of us would accompany her."

James did not yet see where this was going. "But I don't think any of us could go to the ball without being spotted."

"You could go."

"No, I couldn't. There have been too many times where I have fought for Adelle in public sight."

"Yeah, that's not really a problem. Nobody ever notices you."

James didn't know how to respond to that.

"Besides, if you're that worried, you could put on a fake beard or something."

"A what?"

"He doesn't need a beard." said the raven. "If you were to take a bath and put on a new set of clothes, not even we would recognize you."

It was decided that since James was the one who would be accompanying her, he would be the one to present the scheme to her. Adelle's heart was instantly warmed at the thought of the ball, especially after giving up all hope of it, though one detail did bother her.

"A disguise? But it wouldn't be the same! If I go in disguise then no one will know who I am. That's part of the thrill of going to a ball! Being known. Having friends. Being popular."

"Being *popular?*"

"Don't say that like it's a bad thing! There's nothing wrong with being liked. Before you dragged me down this rabbit hole, I was held in high esteem by most everyone. Isn't that worth something?"

"I'll never know." said James.

Adelle looked at the grimy little mad boy and suddenly felt ashamed. Few people knew James, and few of those liked him. "I'm sorry. The ball would still mean a lot to me even with a disguise."

"That's good." said James.

Adelle smiled. "And besides, you'll know who I am. That's what matters most."

That went right over James' head.

*　　*　　*

As the days passed and the public frenzy to know Princess Adelle's whereabouts increased, so did Ivy's jealousy. And her outspokenness. The Lady watched this development in her daughter with interest. The more she observed Ivy's bitterness toward Adelle and turned it over in her own mind, all of her maternal instincts rose to the occasion (and the surface). She recognized this growing bitterness in her daughter as an object of considerable potential and so began to carefully nurture it.

When the time of the ball drew near and the Lady Mediev felt that the fruit was ripe for the picking, she informed Ivy that she had strong reason to believe that Adelle would be returning to the City, and early enough to attend the ball. This cast Ivy into a wretched mood.

"That *would* happen, wouldn't it? Just when I thought she couldn't take anything more from me, she takes the ball from me too! I hate my life!"

"Is that any way for a Mediev to talk? Have I taught you nothing? You don't have to be the victim here. So far you've been playing by her rules. It's time you started playing by mine."

"What do you mean?"

"I have a plan. A plan that, if you play along, will reverse your respective positions and leave Adelle carrying all the jealousy she left you to bear."

*   *   *

The band of adventurers arrived in the City on the eve of the ball. At the train station, Mr. Mosspuddle procured a coach as a discreet and expedient method of traveling to the Happy Little Inn. It was a tight fit, but the entire group managed to pile into the cab. Adelle looked out through the coach window at the buildings and streets that passed by. She found it strange that even though she had not resided in the City for long, it held so many memories for her, and even though it had not been long since she had disappeared from its view, it felt like years since she had last been there. She was also surprised that the longing to return had greatly diminished from the time she had first found herself in the library. Returning to the City in time for the ball didn't make her as happy as she had thought it would. She didn't know if she would ever be happy again.

They arrived at the Inn without incident. There they were gruffly greeted by Miss Bethany. Adelle had mixed feelings about being reunited with her old nurse. Once again, the dolls provided the group with food and lodging, though the dolls were very tired and quickly went to bed after dinner, and the rest of the group soon followed. Except Mr. Mosspuddle. He stayed up through the night pouring through Marloth, trying to discover the location of the orphanage.

The next morning Adelle descended to the main room to find Miss Bethany busy preparing breakfast. From a booth in the corner of the room came the faint sound of snoring where Mr. Mosspuddle was slumped forward with his head propped on his books. Adelle felt out of place and was about to return upstairs when Miss Bethany said something to her, and before Adelle realized it she was in the midst of an earnest conversation with the seamstress.

Miss Bethany was a simple, straightforward person. She did not often speak, but when she did, she spoke her mind. As Adelle gushed all of the events and emotions she had experienced since she had left the castle, she was surprised at how consoling Miss Bethany's remarks were to her. Miss Bethany was not easily distracted by extraneous details, and had a way of presenting things in a manner that was both simple and obvious. Adelle had never been able to see it before, but for the first time she realized that Miss Bethany really did care for her, even if it was in a subdued fashion. Before long, Adelle found herself working alongside the woman in preparing breakfast.

When Adelle reached the part of her story where she had discovered the tomb of her parents, she found it particularly hard to proceed.

"Now I'll never know if my parent's loved me." she said.

"Of course your parents loved you! There's no question about that. Sure, their love wasn't perfect. Sure, they loved other things that they probably shouldn't have, but don't throw the princess out with the bath water!"*

Adelle said that she was encouraged by this, but that it still wasn't the same as hearing it from her parents. Or even seeing them again. She would never see them again.

"I'm an orphan." Adelle sighed.

"Look, missy, I'm an orphan too. Never knew my parents. Don't know what they thought of me. But there is someone who does care for me, and for you too. Someone who cares for you more than your parents ever could. One day he will come back, and then you'll see for yourself."

For a moment Miss Bethany almost looked distant. "I've been waiting my entire life for that day."

---

*A maxim she had learned from experience.

They talked for some time more. By the time the rest of the company came downstairs, and the toad was awakened, and everyone was sitting down to breakfast, Adelle was feeling very encouraged. She was beginning to imagine that she could be happy again. Perhaps she could even enjoy the Ball. The meal itself was the most elaborate they had eaten so far during their journey. Miss Bethany was a marvelous cook, and provided a very well rounded selection of dishes for the hungry adventurers.

After breakfast many of the group set to work creating a proper disguise for Adelle. They wanted it to be both attractive and yet different enough from her natural appearance to protect her from detection.

After much of the morning passed by, Adelle finally stepped out into the main room modeling her new look. Everyone agreed it was stunning. Along with a new dress, her hair had been dyed black and her face made up in a way that, while maintaining her natural beauty, did change her identity. Now she looked like a very pretty zombie child. Adelle was very pleased with the feedback both her dress and disguise received, and then she glanced over at James.

"You do have another change of clothes, don't you?"

"No."

"Then you'll have to get one."

"But I like my clothes! We've been through a lot together."

"I'm happy for the both of you, but you can't go to a ball looking like that!"

"Why not? Are there magical traps? Will lasers shoot out and obliterate me?"

The dispute would have escalated except the librarian pulled James aside and did his best to explain how much it would mean to Adelle if he made this concession for her, and after much convincing, James finally agreed, though he did not pretend to understand.

At this point Mr. Mosspuddle longed to return to his studying, but he felt a nagging fear that he was the only person in the group who could properly assist James in a young man's proper attire. After much inner debate, he found himself volunteering to take James shopping. The ladies thought that was a splendid idea, and so before either of them knew it, James and Mr. Mosspuddle were scouring the streets for a suitable suit. What they both hoped would be a short affair turned into a major ordeal. After a few hours passed, Mr. Mosspuddle concluded that James was cursed. Nothing seemed to fit him. Nothing seemed to look right. Good clothes simply fled from his presence. But as the sun began to wane and all hope was nearly lost, they happened upon a set of clothes that had both the right taste and right dimensions. It was also far more expensive than anything Mr. Mosspuddle had considered paying, but by then he was desperate, and handed over his money as though he was not long for this world. With their prize in hand, they made haste for the inn.

The price of time and money was not in vain. When James finally stepped into the central room of the inn after washing and putting on his new clothes, the group was amazed. In a way he looked very different, and in a way he looked just the same. Mr. Mosspuddle had managed to find clothes that were similar to what James had already been wearing before, but aside for being new, they were subtly more slick and stylish. He was still the same rag-tag James, but now it was an idealized, poster perfect rag-tag.

Adelle was speechless. Once again she found herself standing in the presence of a boy and feeling very inadequate. Part of her hated that feeling, and yet part of her reveled in it.

James looked around for Fugue, but the fellow was nowhere in sight. He was about to ask where Fugue had gone when he heard a gruff, deepish voice say behind him, "I'm ready to embark when you are." James turned around.

Fugue was wearing a beard. And a toupee.

"That's great, Fugue. But someone's going to need to keep watch over the rest of the group while we're gone."

Fugue didn't immediately reply, but instead took off his glasses and wiped them with a handkerchief as a scholarly manner of thinking. (He was also wearing small, thick-rimmed glasses.)

"We don't need anybody to watch us!" said the dolls. "We were taking care of ourselves long before you came along."

"Yes, but things have changed. Too many people are searching for us, and there's a chance they may have already found this place. Fugue is the best person to get you out of danger if it comes."

"What the boy says is true," said Fugue, still trying to sound as though he had a deep voice. "I will stay with the womenfolk."

James looked over at Mr. Mosspuddle. The moment they had returned from shopping the toad had resumed his study of Marloth. Aside for his brief nap and the shopping excursion, Mr. Mosspuddle had been busy with his research since they had arrived at the Inn. After some deliberation, James approached the librarian and asked if he could borrow Marloth for the evening.

Mr. Mosspuddle looked up in exasperation. "I keep having to set aside my studying! If we are ever to find the orphanage then I need to finish translating this passage!"

"But I haven't read any Marloth today. You've had it for hours."

Mr. Mosspuddle sighed. "You're right; we need to share. How about this: I could copy all of the pages I need right now into my notebook. Then you could take the book for the rest of the evening."

"How long would it take you to copy them?"

"Well, there are several pages and I'd want to be very careful that I transcribed them with perfect accuracy. Maybe half an hour. Maybe an hour. It's hard to say."

"You know what, it's all right; you don't have to copy anything. I've never felt as clear headed and free from the zombie nature as I do today. It must be due to my extra reading while we were on the train. I should be good for a long while. I'll go right now with Adelle and read up on Marloth when we get back."

*   *   *

Evening came and the two children set off for the Globe. That was where most everyone was going. It was one of the largest buildings in the world, and this night it needed that for the volume of people it was being expected to hold. It was also the most well lit building in the world—the light passing through its outer glass walls and ceiling made it a beacon of light to the rest of the City. It was the same with the sound. The Globe had an enchanted sense of acoustics that allowed its sound to travel remarkable distances with a minimal amount of decay. Echoes of laughter and music saturated the entire City.

Flying over the city was the raven, keeping an eye on the two children and the area surrounding them. He was trying very hard to ignore the fearful suspicion that he might be harboring some affection for them.

Despite the crowds of people that were being ushered into the Globe, there was still a degree of exclusivity to the event, and while by her beauty and dress alone Adelle would have probably been allowed into the Globe, the exact opposite applied to James, who, even with his new clothes and attempt at bathing, still looked like a street urchin. Because of this and a desire to avoid as much attention as possible, they chose an alternative means of entry. Adelle had been to the Globe a few times with Ivy, and from Ivy she had learned of a little known back door. Armed with this knowledge, and James' eagerness to render unconscious any half-men attempting to be guards, they made their way into the Globe. The raven did not go inside, but instead circled the building and maintained a steady vigil on all its entrances.

While the outside of the Globe was beautiful, that was nothing compared to standing inside it. It was like being inside a towering diamond. Adelle was breathless. She had been impressed by it before, but that was nothing compared to what it looked like now.

Light came to life and reverberated around them, bouncing off of the glass walls and tile floor. It was like walking through heaven.

As they made their way through the crowds, Adelle caught a glimpse of Wendy and Sandwich, and she saw someone in the distance that might have been Harris. None of them recognized her, thankfully, though she had to restrain herself from calling out to them. There was something haunting about seeing them again from this new perspective. Adelle kept glancing around her in the hope of spotting Ivy, but so far she was disappointed. She dearly missed Ivy.

They reached the central ballroom and stood there for a moment, looking at the spacious architecture and the bustle of people surrounding them. Adelle was soaking every facet of it into her. Angelic music was wafting down from the heights, and already many people were dancing in the center. Adelle waited for a few moments. Then she turned to James.

"Well aren't you going to ask me to dance?"

"What?"

"It isn't proper for the lady to ask the gentleman to dance. He has to ask her."

"Dance?"

"Why of course! That is why you came with me, isn't it?"

James was staggered. "I—well, I . . . *yes*, that's it. That's why we're here. Exactly what you said."

Adelle looked at him patiently. James gathered his resolve.

"Will you dance with me?" he asked her.

Adelle clasped her hands together. "Why, I'd love to!"

And they danced. James had never done such a thing before, but he had inhuman coordination and learned quickly. As for Adelle, she had been trained by experts since she was old enough to walk. They weaved around the other couples like a smooth breeze on ice. With every change of music Adelle would gasp and say, "Oh, I *love* this song!" Time passed by quickly.

"Oh, James! It's just like a dream!"

"Yes, but whose dream is it?"

Adelle leaned her head on his shoulder and began to cry. All the joy and excitement still mixed with the pain of losing her mother and father. The flood of emotions washed over her. James was at a loss as to what to do. No one seemed to have noticed her, and they continued through the motions of dancing, though her movements had become somewhat limp. James tilted his head to look at her. In a way she was the most beautiful when she was in distress. She was the most alive. The most real. James' mind began to wonder. He began to think of—

Suddenly he tore himself away from her. Adelle nearly fell over and dizzily looked up in amazement. James paused for a moment, staring at her in horror, and then he turned and ran out of the ballroom. He ducked behind a dark corner and stood there with his back to the wall, gasping for breath. It was not long before Adelle came running up.

"What is going on?" she demanded, trying to pull herself together.

James held out his hand to keep her back. "Don't get too close to me!"

"Why? What's the matter? Is it something I did?"

"It's my zombie nature! It's waking up! I am such an idiot! I should never have left Marloth behind. I need to get Marloth!"

"But James, can't we have at least one more dance? We've come all this way and—"

"Do you want me to hurt you?" he shouted.

Adelle cowered back. "No." she whispered.

"Well I want to!" he said, and then hit himself. "I shouldn't have said that! I wouldn't normally say that. I'm not myself. At least I'm not the self I want to be. Don't you see we need to go?"

"Fine, we'll go!" Adelle said, clearly upset and still a little teary. "Just let me get my things."

James waited for her in the hallway. Time passed. He didn't think it should take so long for someone to gather their things.

James didn't notice it the first time it entered the hall. That was because of the music. There was a large, arched doorway that connected the hallway to the main ballroom, through which swelled a great deal of warm light and warm music. The music was very loud; so loud that it drowned it out.

The second time it was stronger, strong enough to make itself known over the music, and that was when it first caught his attention, though he dismissed it as his imagination. But once he was listening for it there was no questioning the third time. That time he heard it clearly—it was a cry for help.

James bolted down the hall and up a flight of stairs, tracking the reverberating cry to its source. He finally turned a corner into a large, open room with four zombie children in the center of it. One of them was Ivy.

The others were huddled around her and stabbing her repeatedly.

James did not hesitate but charged into their midst. With the advantage of surprise, he slammed one to the ground, kicked the second across the room, and began to punch the third. To his surprise the child pulled back and ran away. Quickly, James turned to face the other two, only to find that they too were running away. Not knowing what to make of it, he turned his attention toward Ivy. She was in a wretched condition. She was a pincushion of knives and was bent over and struggling for consciousness.

"Don't worry!" he said, running over to her. "They ran off." Carefully, he reached behind her and pulled a knife from her back.

"Thank you," she said. And then she suddenly threw her arms around him and kissed him.

James was so stunned by this it took him a moment to react, and when he did he was even more surprised to find how hard it was for him to disengage. He suddenly felt a very strong desire to return that knife where he had found it. But the good enchantment was still wielding some influence and he finally pushed her back. When he did he noticed something to his left. He turned and felt his soul sink into the ground below him.

It was Adelle. She was staring at them, horrified.

"Adelle!" he exclaimed. "It's not what it, don't—"

Adelle's heart broke in two. She turned around and ran out of the hall. James watched in shock as she disappeared around the corner. He pushed himself away from Ivy and threw the knife to the ground. "I'm so stupid!" he said. "Stupid, stupid, *stupid!*"

He turned to run after Adelle, and then looked back at Ivy. It takes a lot to slay a zombie, but she was so torn open that she was barely conscious. While his zombie nature was regaining ground, the good enchantment inside him was still there, and it did not want him to leave Ivy in her plight. He chafed at that. He wanted to race after Adelle. But the good enchantment pointed out that in his present state he would only put Adelle in danger. It also noted that the raven had said he would be patrolling the outside of the Globe and it was likely that he would see her and give pursuit. James thought that was a weak possibility, and didn't want to rely on it. The zombie nature told him that he could handle it. That he could pursue Adelle and restrain his zombie nature enough not to hurt her. The good enchantment disagreed. For once he was angry with it. He tried to fight it, but the good enchantment would not let him go his own way. Surprising both himself and Ivy, he returned to assist her.

"Aren't you going to go after your girl?" she asked.

"What? After Adelle? No, I can't. I've totally screwed up. If I followed her now I would just be putting her in danger. And I can't leave you here. Those boys really messed you up; you need help too."

Ivy was speechless.

"There," James said, after a few minutes. "The knives are out. I can carry you to some place where you can get patched up."

Ivy was tempted to oblige him, but she said, "No, I can walk."

James looked uncertain about that, but he helped her to her feet. "Someone should escort you home," he said. "In case those boys come back."

"They won't bother me anymore." she said, and felt a tinge of guilt over her certainty.

James desperately wanted to go after Adelle, and he knew he needed to find Marloth. But the good enchantment said he wasn't done yet. "I shouldn't take that chance," he said, and he assisted her down the stairway. Her feet were unsteady and she *did* need his arm to maintain her balance. James made certain to take paths less tread and, fortunately, they did not come across any other children. After they had gone for a little way, Ivy asked him, "What did you mean when you said you would be putting Adelle in danger?"

"Danger from me." said James. "I don't have Marloth, and it has been too long since I read it. The good enchantment is wearing thin, and I can feel my zombie nature growing stronger. I'm glad those boys ran away. Even with that brief fighting I started to feel the old thrill of violence returning. I wanted to pummel them. To hurt things."

"Well what's wrong with that? You're a zombie! That's what all zombies do; they hurt things. If you really want, you can hurt me."

For a moment James let go of her. "No! I don't want to do that! I mean, the zombie part of me does, but not the good part!"

"What *good part*? We're evil! We don't *have* good parts!"

"Edward Tralvorkemen gave me a good enchantment. With it I can be kind and selfless and all sorts of things that zombie children aren't supposed to be. I was a new person. I didn't want to hurt anyone anymore. But like I said, that's wearing out and if I don't read Marloth soon I'll become the old James again. Marloth is the only thing that strengthens the good enchantment."

Ivy was beginning to understand. "So you can't help Adelle until you read Marloth?"

"Yes." said James.

It was Ivy's turn to let go. "Look, I'm feeling a little better already. And I can see my house in the distance. Don't let me keep you any longer. You need to find Marloth as soon as you can."

"But—"

"Look, James, maybe you have some good enchantment, but I don't! I'm evil! I don't deserve your help!"

"I'm not sure what you mean. You're the nicest zombie child I've met."

Ivy couldn't bear the weight anymore. "Don't you see? This was all a setup! I was supposed to get you away from Adelle and push her over the edge. She was the only real friend I ever had, and I betrayed her! That's the kind of person I am! I have no heart. I have no soul. And it's too late to fix that. Now leave me! Help the only girl who can still be saved."

James stood there stunned. It took him a long time to catch up to all she had said. Then he sadly nodded. "Each moment it's getting harder to fight my zombie nature. I really had better get to Marloth soon." Slowly, he went to return to the inn. But before he left he looked back and said, "They would have said it was too late for me. But it wasn't. It's never too late."

*   *   *

Adelle rushed blindly forward, her emotions tearing her apart from the inside out. She felt so inadequate. And she felt so jealous of Ivy. James could freely hurt Ivy without worrying about killing her. And the way most zombie children were deadened to pain, Ivy would probably enjoy it. But he was deathly afraid of hurting Adelle, and he avoided her because of it. For the first time, Adelle saw his desire to cause pain as a need. James had a need and she was not able to fill it. Only a zombie could.

"I hate my life!" she exclaimed bitterly. She wanted him to want her. But as long as she had something to lose, he never would.

Then she noticed something at her feet. Not all that glitters is gold, but this object did both. It was the crown. Gingerly, she reached down and picked it out of the snow. She had forgotten how beautiful it was. A small part of her mind told her to drop it.

Told her to throw it away. That she was traveling down a terrible path of no return. But the rest of her mind told her she didn't care anymore. She placed the crown once more upon her head.

That's when she made up her mind. She knew what she had to do.

*   *   *

When James returned to where he had left the inn, it wasn't there anymore. "Drat." James said to himself. It had moved again. He didn't have time for this!

With no methodical option available, he began to randomly race about the City in the hope of catching a glimpse of the inn.

*   *   *

Confused and tired, Ivy returned home. Phyllis and Loury were supposed to be there, but they had snuck out to the Ball. All the servants seemed to be out as well, leaving the Manor empty. This suited Ivy's mood just fine. She went upstairs to her room, took off her tattered clothes, washed and patched up the various gouges in her figure, and put on a new dress. When she went downstairs, her mother had just returned from the ball to pick up some items she had forgotten.

"There you are, Ivy! I'd been wondering where you had gone to."

"I was just changing into something new." said Ivy.

"Decided to put something on to match your mood? I just saw Adelle running off in tears. You must be feeling pretty good right now."

"No, I'm not."

"Thankfully everything went according to plan. In fact, things went even better than I could have imagined! Adelle is completely separated from those guttersnipes, out of her wits, and ripe for the picking."

Ivy wasn't paying her any attention. She was still marveling. "He didn't hurt me. He wanted it but he didn't take it. I've never seen anything like that."

"You mean that milksop trying to play the hero? No need to worry about being spurned by a little mad boy. He can have his prissy princess when we're done with her."

"You don't get it, do you? He didn't spurn me, he showed me respect!"

"Nonsense. Any male who doesn't want something from you is useless. Respect is about being in control."

"No, it isn't! For a moment he saw me like he sees her: as someone in need. I think he genuinely wanted to help me, and you know what, I *liked* that!"

"Ivy! I'm disappointed with you! If you continue down that path you'll be nothing but a limp rag. If you had experienced everything I've been through, you would know how foolish it is to rely upon any man who isn't wrapped around your little finger. There's a lot more you still have to learn before you reach my station in life."

"Your station? I don't want your station! I don't want to be anything like you! I *hate* you!"

"Well, that's some progress. I was starting to worry that you didn't have any backbone."

Ivy screamed in frustration and stormed out of the room.

*   *   *

James was at his wits end. He had been running about the City of Orphans for what felt like hours. He was getting nowhere, but he didn't know what else to do. He had no book, no comrades, and no clue where to search. He paused at a street corner to think. He had the terrible feeling that important events were taking place all around and he was missing every one of them.

The corner he stood on was located upon a hillside and provided an excellent view of the City. It was from there that James noticed how the Globe was no longer the only distinct source of light in the City. An orange glow was rising several blocks from it, and quickly growing in magnitude. Apprehensively, James decided to rush toward the glow.

When he arrived at the site, his fears proved true. The inn was the source of the glow, for it was engulfed in a pillar of flames. All around were crowds of zombie children, eagerly watching the blaze and dancing around madly. Nothing excites zombie children like destruction.

As James peered around a corner, preparing for something drastic like fighting the crowd and rushing into the burning building, someone gently grabbed his shoulder. With one move he pulled a knife from his sleeve and turned to face the person behind him.

It was Ivy.

"Reconsidering my offer to stick those back in me, are you?" she said, looking at the knife at her throat. James quickly lowered the weapon, but he didn't put it away. "I need to rescue my friends," he said, and turned to charge toward the building.

"Wait!" she said, grabbing his shoulder again. "You're friends aren't in there. They've already been taken away. To Otto Marrechian's factory."

"How do you know?"

"Because everyone is talking about it. Deadwick marched them straight through the Globe."

"And why would he do that?"

"Most people don't know, but there is a portal inside the Globe that leads to Otto's place. It appeared a few days ago, and mother has been doing her best to hide it. She's been trying to use it to fight her way into Otto's factory, but so far Otto has kept her at bay.

Deadwick was really cocky to parade through the ball like that, but he knows that most of the children are on his side. Some of the children who work for my mother helped him get past the traps and illusions she set to guard the portal. When I arrived back at the Globe, everyone was talking about how Deadwick had captured those people at a nearby inn and set it on fire. I figured I would find you here."

James pondered this information and then Ivy continued. "I can show you where the portal is, though I have no idea what to expect on the other side. My mother has been sending all sorts of creatures through the portal and none of them have returned. But it is the only way I know of to Otto's lair."

"Then to the Globe it is." said James.

*   *   *

At that moment, on the edge of the building that was both laboratory and factory, both the center of research and industry, Mr. Mosspuddle was being escorted into the study of Doctor Otto Marrechian.

This was not the first time they had met. When Doctor Marrechian had been more accepted by the Wizard's Council there had been several occasions that had brought them into each other's company. Mr. Mosspuddle remembered the doctor to be a surprisingly talkative man for someone who spent most of his time cloistered away, and the doctor remembered Mr. Mosspuddle to be an amiable chap who would agree with anything to avoid a dispute.

After their initial greetings, the doctor paced back and forth for a few moments and then began. "I was skeptical of the rumors. It was said that the custodian of the Great Library had joined with a band of rogues. That they had kidnapped the princess. That they were wandering all over Marloth and causing no end of confusion. When I discovered that the princess was concealed in the Great

Library, there was still some hope that they had done so against your will, but it was a small hope. By then I had figured the rumors probably were true. Now I have the final confirmation standing before me, and yet I still find it hard to believe."

"I find it all a little hard to believe myself."

Doctor Marrechian almost smiled and then turned toward one of the zombie children who was attending the librarian. "You confiscated his books, correct?" The child nodded and lifted up a sack she was holding. "Did he happen to have a book named 'Marloth'?"

The zombie child reached into the sack and took out Marloth.

"Marvelous! After all this time, I finally have custody of that book. No, I don't want to touch it; put it on my desk." The zombie did so.

Mr. Mosspuddle looked at the doctor curiously. "So you acknowledge that it has power?"

"If it has power, it is the power of madness. It carries madness like a rat carries a plague. My curiosity is begging to read it, and someday I may devise a means of exploring it indirectly so as to avoid its influence, but I might not."

"It's only madness if it is a lie. But if it is true, then the nature of its power is not madness, but enlightenment."

"We could spend all night asserting whether its power is good or ill, but without evidence we are simply trading air."

"Agreed, and as it happens, I do have evidence for my case. We are standing in the middle of it. By means of this world, I have seen Marloth's power demonstrated."

"Aside for making people fools, what demonstration do you speak of? I heard how Message opened the book, tested it and found it wanting. Message was designed to have exceptional discernment of magical properties. I should know: I was one of the key architects behind its construction."

"Message works from an unquestioned assumption, that if a book has an effect, it would be a limited effect. But what if that wasn't the case? What if that book affected everything; what if it was affecting the entire world right now? There would be no way to distinguish it! No contrast between where the effect began and where it ended!"

"There has never been a book with that broad of an influence! It is impossible!"

"You mean you haven't discerned a book with that kind of power. If there was such a book, all of your methods and all of the wizards' methods would be insufficient to measure it."

"I don't recall you ever being this argumentative," growled the doctor.

"These aren't my arguments. I acquired them from the book. By now I've read Marloth so much it is in my bloodstream. While the specifics of the book are different from the specifics of this world, the general patterns are the same. It has a scene similar to the one we are in right now, where two people are debating the importance of Marloth. One of the characters is even a doctor. We are reenacting that scene right now. We are in the story."

The doctor slammed his fist on the desk. "I refuse to believe I am a character in a book! There is simply no proof!"

"Your only thought of proof is things you can measure with your instruments! But there are proofs beyond your tools!"

"Enough! I can take no more of your nonsense. The reason I called you here was to offer to restore you to your position at the Great Library, but now I see you are utterly lost to reason!"

"I've spent nearly my entire existence poring over books, yet I discovered that there is only one that really matters. I'm done being a librarian. That life is behind me now."

"Then this has been a waste of time!" the doctor shouted. He furiously motioned toward the children standing in the doorway. "Get him out of my sight! And then silence him for good! Silence the lot of them!"

*   *   *

As James and Ivy were heading toward the Globe, the raven dropped down from the sky and rested beside them. He looked sullen. So sullen in fact, that he did not immediately initiate dialogue, but sat there coldly.

"Where's Adelle?" James asked.

"I lost her." said the raven, and left it at that.

"Lost her? How?"

The raven looked at James as if hoping the boy would lose interest, and then replied, "She told me to leave. And I left."

James was stunned. "This is Adelle we're talking about, right? You actually obeyed her?"

The raven began to jerk his head back and forth angrily. "She must have cast a spell on me! I didn't realize what had happened until she was already out of my sight."

"How could she have done that?"

"I don't know! It's all a blur! All I know is that I should never have bothered helping her! She's nothing but trouble. All girls are trouble!"

It was then that he noticed Ivy.

"What is she doing here?" he shrieked.

This was when Ivy spoke up. "Otto has captured your friends, and I—"

"They're not my friends."

"—And I am leading James to a portal in the Globe that can take him to Otto's factory." Ivy finished in annoyance.

"Wow." said the raven. "That smells so much like a trap the fumes are nauseating."

"I trust her." said James.

"Yes, well, you have a thing for pretty faces." said the raven.

"And apparently so do you." said Ivy. The raven grew very quiet.

"You don't have to come," said James. "I trust Ivy, and I'm going with her to the Globe."

The raven grumbled low enough to avoid being understood and followed after them.

*   *   *

There was a knock at the door of Otto Marrechian's fortress. Which was a bit awkward because the door was boarded up. But the children didn't mind. They didn't even hear it amidst all the bustle and industry.

Suddenly there was a girl standing in their midst. She was dressed completely in black and gray and wore a crown upon her head. Though she was not tall she seemed to be looking down at all of them.

"I'm here to speak with Doctor Otto Marrechian." she said.

"Who are you? How did you find this place?"

She focused her attention on the nearest child. "Take me to Doctor Marrechian."

Murder flashed across the child's eyes, but it did not retaliate. None of them did. Normally they would have just quartered her then and there for the fun of it, yet they didn't. Begrudgingly, the child stepped forward and led the girl through the crowd of stunned laborers. As they walked through the factory the girl felt a sense that she had been there before, but she thought little of it. Eventually the child led her up a winding staircase and into the doctor's study.

Otto looked up in surprise. "Who are you?" he exclaimed.

"Do you not know me? I am Princess Adelle, Daughter Heir of Marloth."

Otto nearly dropped his spectacles in even greater surprise. "It *is* you! Standing right here in front of me! I didn't recognize you!"

"I hear you have expended a great deal of energy and resources into trying to bring me here. Well, here I am."

The doctor was still struggling to catch up. "Somehow I thought you were younger."

"Is that any way to address your future queen?"

"No, I just—"

"I did not come to listen to the Great Otto Marrechian babble. I have a job for you . . ."

*　　*　　*

When Ivy returned to the Globe, the party was still in full swing. No one seemed to pay attention to the zombie boy and raven trailing behind her. They didn't seem to notice Ivy either. It was the first time she saw a reason to appreciate her loss of popularity.

After leading the two heroes through several crowds, they finally reached a less populated region of the Globe and stopped before a dead end. Ivy put her hands to the wall and after poking and prodding it in several places it slid aside to reveal a secret passage beyond it. The passage was round in shape and pitch dark except for a faint rainbow of color that could be seen at the far end of it.

"Wait right here," she said, and she disappeared into the darkness. After several minutes, she returned and, after lighting a lamp, told them to follow her.

"My mother has all sorts of magical traps, and I just disabled them," she explained as they traveled down the passage. At the passage's end was a swirling vortex of color and magic.

"There it is." said Ivy. "Now hurry. I need to reset my mother's traps and return to the ball before anyone notices."

"Thank you for helping us," said James, and he stepped through the rift. The raven, however, lingered behind for a few more words.

"I suppose these circumstances aren't coincidence, because it so happens that I have a message for you."

"Oh, yes, I know: you're the bird that flies around telling people horrid things. Well make it quick; I don't have much time."

"No, you don't. What I have to tell you is the same perplexing message I brought to the boy who just left us. Despite your being dead, somehow you are going to die again. I don't expect you to believe me. No one ever—"

"How long do I have?"

The raven was surprised. "I can't say for sure, but I sense the end of this whole business is drawing near. I doubt you have beyond the night."

Ivy nodded. "Thank you. I'm glad to know my demise in advance. There are things I want to do before I go."

She did not sound angry or upset. She did not sound afraid. She sounded tired, like someone who does not cry because they have run out of tears. But there was also a hint of peace. She looked like she *wanted* to die. She paused for a moment in consideration, thanked the raven again, and moved down the passageway. The raven cringed inside. His job was getting harder. It had been easier when everyone had just hated him.

*   *   *

For a moment that felt like years, James was surrounded by flashes of color and sound. The next moment he was standing in the basement of Otto Marrechian's fortress.

From the ceiling above him he could hear the rhythmic clattering of heavy machinery, both low pitched 'thunks' and high pitched 'clinks'. There was a single doorway leading out of the room and up a winding stairway.

The room was strewn with the dismembered remains of zombie children, and in the middle of the room there was a large pile of dust and weaponry. The raven soon appeared beside him.

"Some party." said the raven. "I wonder what's with all the metal and dirt?"

James began digging through the dust. "It's ogre equipment. I'm guessing this was once an ogre. Maybe several of them."

"The only thing I know of that can turn ogres to dust is wizards," said the raven.

James picked up a syringe from the floor and looked at it curiously. "Otto is a wizard of sorts," he said absently. He placed the syringe back on the floor. Then, after pulling a few grenades from the debris and tucking them into his satchel, he and the raven headed up the stairs. The stairway led them to a large room filled with gears and pulleys.

There were scores of zombie children running from one place to another and looking very busy. No one noticed the newcomers. A group of zombie children, many of them armed with syringes, filed down the staircase James and the raven had just come from.

"I'm going to explore the place and find out what I can." said the raven, darting up another flight of stairs. James did his best to blend in with the other zombie children and set off down the nearest corridor.

Ever since he had stepped through the portal, James had felt a strange sensation. It was similar to what he had felt when he had sensed Adelle's presence, but this sensation was stronger and it couldn't have been Adelle. Her aura had been warm and comforting. This felt cold and malicious. James chose his path carefully. Whatever it was he was sensing, he wanted to avoid it.

* * *

"What?" said the doctor. "But that will make everything so much more difficult! Not to say that your request is a new idea for me—I have been prepared for that possibility from the beginning. Somehow you *are* in the book of contracts, and you would be a candidate. But still, it would be a considerable inconvenience and I'd rather avoid it."

"You know what, at this point I'm not really concerned about inconveniencing you." said Adelle. "I *am* the future Queen of Marloth."

"Yes, you are."

"Address me as 'Your majesty.'"

"Yes, your majesty."

"Good." Adelle walked over to the window. "Now to the question of how to do it. I've been thinking that the tower would make a good departure."

"Yes." said the doctor. "But if so, your majesty should give me the crown to hold for you. Otherwise it would probably get broken."

"No! You're not taking my crown! Never mind, I won't go that way. I'll use a more stable means."

"Well, you're going to have to trust me with that crown sooner or later."

"Maybe so, but not until I absolutely have to."

"That doesn't make any sense. If you're—"

"The crown stays!" she shouted.

"Yes, your majesty."

*   *   *

James had not realized how big the factory really was. It was a fiendish labyrinth of twists and additions that spit in the face of geometry. The dolls must have been horrified at its structure, for it did not simply lack aesthetic taste, it was a living, breathing attack against it. There were places where doors were used as parts of walls, not to provide a doorway, but simply because they had been the most ready material at hand. The floors and walls were rarely level and some were close to diagonal. Stairs were infrequent. Instead, the zombie children climbed ladders, chains, and machinery to ascend or descend the levels of the factory, while a limited number of rickety elevators existed solely for the doctor's use.

Despite the daunting schema, James somehow had an easy time predicting its layout. He could not remember if he had been there in his earlier zombie days, but he figured he must have since much of the building was familiar to him.

As he was skirting a hallway on the outer edge of the factory, he came across a zombie boy who actually paid attention to him.

"What are you doing here?" said the boy. "This is a restricted area!"

"Sorry," said James. "I must've gotten turned around."

The boy examined him more carefully. "I've never seen you before. Who are you?"

"I'm new here." said James.

The zombie wasn't buying it. "I would have been informed of anyone who—Ahhh!"

James lifted him off his feet and hurled him through the nearest window. As with every other window in the factory, this one was boarded up, so the boards exploded outward as the zombie child crashed through them.

James had not expected what was on the other side of the window. Beyond it there was no landscape or clouds. There was no sun or moon. There was nothing but a swirl of colors, just like the portal he had passed through.

"Pretty wild, isn't it?" James straightened to see the raven landing beside him.

"What's going on?" asked James.

"I don't know how it happened, but that's portal space out there. Otto's factory has been completely displaced from spatial reality. Step outside of this building and you could wind up anywhere in the world."

James took this in stride. "So have you found anything on the others?"

"Yes. They aren't here anymore. I didn't see it myself, but from all of the talk I picked up around here, it sounds like they escaped."

"Good for them! How did they escape?"

"I think they stepped outside."

Oh. James looked back at the window. "So then they could be anywhere in Marloth?"

"That's about the gist of it. But not the book. I saw it in Otto's study. It was on his desk."

"Where's his study?"

"Follow me."

*   *   *

Mr. Mosspuddle continued to examine their predicament. He, Fugue, the dolls, and Miss Bethany were stranded on a narrow plateau of marble rising high above the clouds.

"What a pretty view!" said one of the dolls.

The librarian wasn't enjoying the view. Neither was Fugue. "We need to get back to the action!" he exclaimed, and then turning to Mr. Mosspuddle, "You're the smartest fellow here. How are we to get off this place?"

The librarian threw up his webbed hands in frustration. "I don't know! I'm trying to think of a solution, but I'm no wizard. I'm not an expert at wielding books, and most of the books I did have were lost in our series of adventures."

The few books he had left were neatly arranged on the ground before him. He carefully gazed from one to the next.

"I told James I would take care of the womenfolk!" said Fugue. "I can't let him down!"

"Actually, we aren't in any danger at the moment." said Mrs. Gingersmile.

"And it sounds like you want us to go back *to* the danger." the swan added.

The cloth animal kicked a pebble and made some noncommittal comment.

Suddenly there was a cry and everyone turned to see Mr. Mosspuddle hopping up and down excitedly. "I have it! I have it!" he shouted. Taking one of the world's most obtuse books, he held it over the edge of the plateau and opened it. The book grew to the bloated size of its own self-importance and rested in mid air. The librarian gave a short laugh, gathered the rest of his things, and hopped onto the book.

"Come on!" he said, motioning for the others to join him. Not fully understanding his idea but having nothing better to do, they likewise climbed onto the book. Then the librarian opened the second copy of the world's most obtuse book just beyond the edge of the first one. It likewise expanded and remained fixed in the air.

"Now climb over to that book!" he said. Once they were all across, he closed the first book, carried it to the other side of the second, and opened it again.

"See what I'm doing?" said the librarian. "We're using these books like a person walks down the street: one foot after the other. It's brilliant!"

"Yes," said Fugue. "This is going to take forever."

*　　*　　*

Deadwick was receiving more and more reports of fights breaking out around the factory. A fight every now and then was nothing remarkable amongst zombie children, but this sudden concentration of them was raising the goblin's suspicion. As he was on his way to investigate one of these fights he passed Doctor Marrechian. The doctor stopped him to ask if he had recently seen Adelle.

"No. Have you already misplaced your princess?"

"Not exactly . . . I'm certain she's still in the laboratory. At least, I hope she is. Oh, what if she isn't? What if she has left me? It's all my fault, really. She didn't like any of the choices I was presenting to her so she said she was going to find a better one. At the time I thought she meant a better method that I could implement. But what if she meant a whole different approach entirely? One that didn't involve me! This is so frustrating! I didn't even get a chance to finish telling her all of my ideas!"

"I think you're making this way too complicated," said Deadwick. "Though hey, what else do you do?"

"This is not my choice! She's an idealist, and wants everything to be perfect. I'm having a hard time finding a solution that meets all of her expectations. She has many demands, the strongest of them being that whatever method we use does not dislodge the crown from her head."

"So she wants to—*Crown?* She has a crown? *The* crown?"

"I think so. It looks like the one her mother used to wear, except paler."

"And she's actually *wearing* it? Why didn't you take it from her?"

"Because she didn't want me to. How could I go against her wishes?"

Deadwick looked at him in astonishment. "She has you under her spell! You'll do whatever she tells you no matter how stupid it is!"

"I am under no spell."

"That's exactly what you would say if you *were* under a spell. Spells are sneaky."

"Well if you're so worried then why don't you go and shoot her? She'd probably appreciate it." "No way! I'm not going anywhere near her!"

*   *   *

James peered around the doorway into Otto's study. There was no one in sight. He motioned to the raven and they ducked inside. The raven landed on the desk. There was no book on it.

"It's gone!" he exclaimed. "It was here not more than ten minutes ago!"

James did a quick scan of the room. There were a few books lying around but nothing like Marloth. He began to frantically dig through drawers and piles of paper.

"I'm not very well suited for this form of searching," said the raven. "Perhaps I should continue scouring the factory for any more information. And if the book has been moved I may catch a glimpse of it."

"Thank you." said James, and the raven flew from the room.

Sometime later, James finally concluded that Marloth must be elsewhere. He hurried out of the study and down a winding passageway. He was not sure where he was going; he just knew he had to keep moving. The place was crawling with zombie children and he had already had to fight off several of them.

James rounded a corner and nearly bumped into Doctor Otto Marrechian. They both stood there for some time, staring at each other in surprise. Finally, James exclaimed:

"Doctor Hurley? *You're* Otto Marrechian?"

The doctor scrambled to find a good response. "This isn't what it looks like! You are in the middle of a delusion, and you have dragged your idea of me into it! None of this is real! You are really back in the Asylum and—"

"Oh shut up! I'm not buying that 'it's all a delusion' stuff anymore."

"Fine." said the doctor. "Maybe this isn't a delusion. But you're still mad."

"And so are you."

"Fair enough."

"But I haven't come for my sanity to be tested."

"Oh, you'd be surprised how such tests can sneak up on you. But yes, I think I know why you are here."

"Good. Tell me where it is."

"It? Don't you mean *her*?"

"It. I've come for Marloth. Where is it?"

"You mean that book that's caused no end of trouble? I thought you were here to rescue the princess."

"Adelle? She's here?"

"Yes, she's here. She came willingly."

"What is she doing here?"

"At the moment? Probably dying."

*   *   *

Adelle could not believe how disorganized the laboratory was. Children were running everywhere and she could not get a straight answer from any of them as to what was going on. As she patrolled the winding corridors in search of any intelligence, she finally came across a person who was actually able to provide some useful information. It was Deadwick. They nearly bumped into each other turning a corner, and before the goblin could retreat he had once again under her magical charm.

"The doctor is looking for you," said Deadwick.

"As I am for him!" she said. "What is going on here? This place is turning into a riot!"

"A troublemaker slipped into the factory. We're trying to find and dismember him, but so far he has eluded us. At one point we almost had him cornered in the East wing but he had planted a bomb that took out seven of my kids. That little bugger is going to pay!"

The goblin stood there a moment stewing and then said, "Anyhow, the doctor is worried about you. He's afraid that something might happen to you."

"Why? Not even you and your army of zombie children can hurt me now, what is there left for me to fear?"

"It's not that. He's not afraid you'll get hurt. It's that you might change your mind—leave the factory and choose someone else, especially now that . . ." The goblin trailed off.

"What do you mean? Speak plainly!"

Deadwick actually shuffled his feet and looked at her sheepishly. "It's the guy I mentioned. He's ... that zombie kid with the crazy book."

Adelle's eyes widened. "James is here?" She looked off into the distance wistfully.

"I want him to do it."

*   *   *

James was in a quandary. As he was in the midst of madly dodging the pursuit of one zombie child after another, he was at the same time struggling with whether to find Adelle or get as far away from her as possible.

The question was answered for him when he stepped out onto a walkway that rose over and behind the central room of the laboratory, the room which held the zombie machine. The zombie machine itself was stationed against the wall directly below the walkway James was crossing. James had nearly reached the other side and passed into the next room when he stopped in his tracks. In the middle of the room was Adelle. James could not believe his eyes. "The crown? She has it ... *again?*"

But there wasn't time to worry about that. A zombie child was rushing toward Adelle and swinging an axe. Without a moment to loose, James dropped down atop of the child and the two entered into a fierce struggle that finally ended with James hurling the other through an opening in the floor. The child fell several stories and crashed into a collection of machinery below. James pocketed his knives and turned to Adelle. She looked so different from when he had last seen her at the Globe. It's as if the zombie child disguise had taken on a life of its own and made her look far more grim and terrifying than any zombie. He had no idea what was going on, but he suspected it had something to do with the object on her head.

"What are you doing with that crown!" he exclaimed. "Don't you remember it's evil?"

For a moment Adelle had almost smiled, but it quickly disappeared. "Are we *really* here again? Are you going to throw my crown out a window like you did last time? Dash my feelings against the rocks? Make me cry? You'd like that, wouldn't you?"

"Yes—I mean, no! I mean . . . you are kind of attractive when you're . . ."

James felt something in his hand and looked at it. He was holding one of his knives. That was strange. He didn't remember taking it out of its sheath. He looked around to see if there were any mirrors materializing nearby, but there didn't appear to be. Then again, his reflection didn't really need to be there—Adelle was already doing the reflection's job. James tried to focus.

"It's been too long since I've read Marloth," he said. "The good enchantment is wearing thin. I need to find Marloth so I can restore it."

"Oh, Marloth. Yes, it's somewhere around here."

"You know where Marloth is?"

"Maybe . . ." Adelle said flippantly.

"Where is it?" he demanded.

"I'm not going to tell you."

"Adelle, listen to me! My zombie nature is taking over! If I don't read Marloth soon, I will kill you. I'm trying to get away from you but I don't have that much control anymore! If you won't tell me where Marloth is then please get away from me! I'm trying to fight it but I can't fight it much longer: I want to kill you!"

"I know. I want you to. And I'm staying right here until you do it."

"What? Why are you doing this?"

"I can't take the pain anymore. I want to be a zombie like the rest of you."

"But what about the hell? The Judgment Day? All of the evil that a zombie child does facing them on the world beyond this world?"

"I'm not sure there is such a thing."

"There is!"

"Maybe so, maybe not. It's a chance I'm willing to take. James, this isn't just for me, it's for you too! When I am dead, I will have more to offer you. You will be free to hurt me without any guilt. I know that's what you want."

James reached out and grabbed her by the throat. "Stop tempting me!" he shouted. Despite the restriction on her throat, Adelle still managed to say, "Looks like your zombie nature is kicking in."

James was horrified and quickly let go of her. Okay, that's not what happened. He *tried* to let go of her. But he couldn't.

It was then that the doctor stepped into the room, followed by Deadwick.

"So there you are," said the doctor. "I see you two are working out your differences."

Deadwick snickered. "Maybe we should give them some privacy."

James was trembling as he slowly found himself shifting into position with his knife hand outstretched behind him, ready to strike.

"What are you waiting for?" Adelle pleaded. "Please stop the pain!"

"Yes, hurry it up!" said the doctor. "We haven't got all day!"

But to James all of their talk was becoming a distant clattering. Every drop of his concentration had been sucked from the room and into the unseen battle being waged within him. "One more time," James whispered. "Please help me just one more time." Slowly, painfully, his left hand fought itself free from Adelle's throat and awkwardly worked its way up to the satchel slung over his back. As if with a mind of its own, his hand took out the bomb.

"What are you doing?" the doctor demanded. "You can't be resisting! You have nothing to resist with!"

James did not say a word. He simply pulled back the bomb, took one last look at Adelle, and hurled the device into the zombie machine.

The room was enveloped by sound and light.

It was some time before anyone stirred. The doctor was first, pulling himself from the debris and turning to look at his machine. In its place was nothing but a hole that extended across much of the floor and wall. He was horror-stricken.

"My machine! My children! All destroyed in an instant! Why? *Why?!?*"

Adelle likewise rose to her feet. She seemed to be unharmed, though disoriented. The goblin also was just then standing. From an upper window, the raven watched solemnly. Adelle looked at the ground nearby where there was a crumpled glint of gold. A flying brick had just missed her head and clipped the crown from her temple. Now the crown was a mangled mass lying on the floor. There was no way it would ever fit on her head again.

Then she spotted James. He was lying on the floor in a motionless heap, his vacant eyes staring up at the ceiling. "James!" she shouted, and rushed over to him, trying desperately to revive him but to no effect. She burst into tears over the still body that had once called itself James.

"Sometimes I hate being right." said the raven, and flew away.

"This is all her fault!" said Deadwick. He drew his firearm and pointed it at Adelle but the doctor stepped between them.

"Oh no you don't!" said Otto. "I can build another zombie machine, but until then she is of no use to me dead. I hate her and that boy for what they've done, but we still need her. Now lock her upstairs until I can figure out how to fix this mess we're in."

For a moment Deadwick looked like he was going to cast the doctor aside and shoot her anyway, but after much glaring he begrudgingly holstered his weapon.

Adelle didn't hear any of this. The world around her and James had dissolved into a fuzzy haze. She couldn't take her eyes off of the body lying in front of her. This wasn't what she had wanted! She hadn't wanted to hurt him—she had wanted to join him! This wasn't supposed to happen!

Something grabbed a hold of her and began to pull her away from James. She screamed and kicked, but could not fend off the force that dragged her away from James until he had disappeared around a corner.

James was lifeless! What had she done? What had she been thinking? But wait, what if he wasn't completely gone? She should have checked his pulse. No, on second thought, he had probably never had a pulse.

This was silly! He had never really been alive! He had only ever been a puppet of the machine! And yet, if that was all it was, then why had she wanted to be just like him? It suddenly felt so foolish.

Then the something let go of her and she heard a door close and lock behind her. Gradually she slipped from her reverie and became aware of her surroundings. She was in a wide, dingy room with a low ceiling and a dusty atmosphere. It was crammed with tons of forgotten miscellany, mostly things that were shades of brown like cardboard boxes and wooden furniture. There was very little floor space left to walk on. While she did not forget about what had just happened to her and James and her guilt continued to play in part of her mind, her natural curiosity was triggered enough for her to begin to stumble through the piles of endless stuff and see what oddities she might find.

It wasn't long before she came across a tall, framed object that she surmised might be a painting, but it was so caked in dust that she could not say for sure. She took a rag that was lying nearby and wiped away a portion of the dust. Hmm. It looked like a painting of the room she was in. No, that wasn't right. It was a mirror.

She wiped away another swath and saw a little girl looking back at her. Black lines ran down her face where the tears had traced their paths. She looked wretched.

She wiped away more of the dirt until she could see her entire figure in the mirror, a stroke of gray before a background of brown. She hadn't realized how much of her skin was unclothed. She looked around and found a shawl just about her own size. After shaking most of the dust off, she wrapped it around her. She also removed the stuffed animals from her dress and tossed them aside. Then she took another look at the mirror. Even though now she looked a little frumpy, she was more decent. Then she took the rag and began to wipe the paint from her face. Without water it was hard to remove. She had to scrape her skin to get the stuff off, and even then she was not able to remove all of it. But when she was done she looked more like ordinary Adelle.

Then she spotted through the reflection that the book was laying not far behind her. Turning around, she went over to the book and picked it up. Yes, this was it; the book James was always carrying around. She sat down and opened it. Most of the languages she did not recognize, but after some scanning she found passages written in a language she was familiar with. Throughout her childhood she had heard so many fairytales. Now for the first time she began to read where they had come from.

*   *   *

On a distant cliff a man was looking out over Marloth. The raven flew up and landed beside him.

"She betrayed us!" the raven exclaimed. "I knew she would! I knew it, I knew it, I knew it! Why did I ever trust her?"

The man looked at the raven gravely. "You're not really disappointed, are you?"

"Of course I am! How could I not be?"

"Because you *wanted* her to fail you."

The raven jerked his head back and forth a few times. "Okay. Maybe a little."

"None of this is really about trusting Adelle. Your complaint is with me. The real question is: do you trust me?"

"For the most part."

"That's not trusting. If you trusted me, you would not have given up on Adelle. I told you I was going to save her."

"And you haven't! It's too late now! She's corrupted to the core!"

The man sighed. "I think you should go back and help her."

"Aren't you listening to me? Haven't you seen what's happening? She's already corrupted! James is destroyed! Jakob Damond is coming to get her, and she'll play right into his hands! It's too late now!"

Again the man looked gravely at the raven. "It's never too late."

*   *   *

When Deadwick returned to where he had left the doctor, he found him searching the debris frantically.

"She's locked up." said Deadwick. "How soon before I get my army of kiddies back?"

"I don't know. One of the most important components has been destroyed, and it will not be easy to replace. I'm not even sure if there is another like it."

He took out a pen and paper and began to write. Once finished, he proffered the note to Deadwick, saying, "These are directions to a certain toyshop. I need you to go there and ask for a book of contracts. He'll know what you mean."

Deadwick looked at the note in Otto's hand. "You know, I'm really not in the mood for errands right now."

"Then your army of zombie children will have to wait!"

Sighing, Deadwick took the note, started to move toward the exit, and then abruptly stopped. There was an ogre filling the doorway. The doorway was huge and yet the ogre barely fit.

"The portal!" Deadwick shouted at Otto. "It's not guarded anymore!" He whipped out his firearm but already a second ogre had shambled through the doorway on the other side of the room. Deadwick took a step back and lowered his weapon. Things like a goblin with a gun were nothing compared to the destruction two fully equipped ogres could unleash.

"Don't worry," said the Lady Mediev as she entered the room accompanied by several half-men. "I didn't use your precious hole in reality; that thing is gone. I came through the front door." She noticed James' body lying on the ground. "Wow." she said. "That is such a relief. He is finally dead—er."

"What do you mean, '*gone*'?" said Otto.

The Lady looked up and glared at him. "You know exactly what I mean! Blowing holes in reality is one thing, but ruining my ballroom, *that* is unacceptable!"

"What in the world are you talking about?"

"Don't play games with me! I want you and your filth out of my ballroom this instant!"

The doctor was so confused by these words that he was not sure what to say. But Deadwick didn't need to understand people to argue. "We're not in your stupid ballroom!" he growled.

"That's right. Why don't you look outside and then tell me that again?"

Both the goblin and the doctor went to the nearest window and looked through. Beyond it they could see the spacious interior of the Globe. Hundreds of youthful bodies were strewn across the floor. The goblin uttered many foul oaths of amazement.

"I must say, I had no idea that so many of my patrons were your science experiments." the Lady Mediev noted.

"What happened?" the doctor wondered aloud, still gaping through the window.

"I don't know what happened! It was *your* hole! It's gone and now your ugly laboratory is in the middle of the Globe. My beautiful ballroom! It's now mixed with your doghouse like two works of clay that have been smashed together. And the clay is still moving around."

The doctor launched into a stream of scientific theories as to what could be happening, all of which meant nothing to the Lady. As she scanned the room, she noticed the mangled crown on the ground. "You mentioned that you had someone locked up. Who is it?"

The doctor paused, first in anger at being interrupted, and then in consideration of how to answer. "It was a zombie girl who mis-behaved." he said at last.

"Yes, and with what looks like your zombie machine scattered around the room, it's more important than ever to keep those little zombies locked away."

Deadwick glared at Otto. The doctor had never been very good at inventing stories. The Lady turned to Deadwick.

"Bring Adelle to me."

Deadwick did his best to look innocent. (A travesty indeed.) "The princess? I don't know what you're talking about."

"I sensed Adelle's aura earlier at the ball but I never managed to catch sight of her. Now I sense it again. Go and fetch her. Quickly."

Deadwick looked at the doctor, looked at the ogres, and then looked at the Lady. Mumbling more oaths, he jogged up the stair-case. It was not long before he returned with Adelle. She was carrying the book with her. The doctor was about to say something about that, but then he looked at the Lady and changed his mind.

"Hello, Adelle." said the Lady Mediev. "It's been too long since we last met. Would it have hurt you to at least write once or twice while you were having adventures?"

Adelle was very quiet.

"A little shell shocked, are we? Well, a ball will fix you up. Though that will have to wait for a moment. Before we can settle down and have some fun, we need to deal with the other people."

"What other people?" said the doctor.

"In the other building. I'm going to inform whoever is inside it that they also need to leave my Globe. Come along—we'll all go together. I'm a little leery of leaving you two out of my sight."

So the Lady, the ogres, Otto, Deadwick, and Adelle all walked out through the front door of the factory.

As they stepped out into the Globe, Adelle was able to see for the first time the rows of bodies stretched out across the dance floor. It was very still, though there were more half-men and other bizarre creatures than there had been during the ball. They were patrolling the grounds warily, as if expecting trouble.

But none of that held the group's attention for long, for their focus quickly drifted to the tower at the other end of the ballroom, its peak rising through the crystal ceiling of the Globe and far into the sky above.

"It appeared at the same time as Otto's factory," said the Lady in explanation. "I don't know where it came from, and I don't really care. I'm going to march over there and tell its owner the same thing I told Otto."

As they crossed the ballroom, one of the bodies caught Adelle's eye, just as her heart caught in her throat.

"Look! It's Ivy!"

The Lady hardly even glanced in the direction Adelle was pointing. "That's not Ivy. That's a lifeless zombie. Ivy is at home throwing a tantrum."

Adelle continued to look back at the body as they walked past. She was struck with a pang of guilt as she thought about how angry she had been at Ivy. She would have turned back, but the Lady had a tight grip on her arm and forced her to continue marching forward.

They finally arrived at the front door of the tower. It was an elegant door, with an elegant knocker that looked like it was shaped from candy canes. The Lady took hold of the knocker and gave the door several violent raps. There was a long pause. Everyone stood around and waited.

"Perhaps no one is home." said the doctor.

"I think I briefly saw a light upstairs." said Adelle.

It wasn't too much longer before there came the sound of bolts and levers being unfastened. There must have been several locks involved. They made a melodic tune as the door was methodically unlocked.

The door was answered by a monkey.

There was a lengthy space of time where everyone stared at the monkey and it stared at all of them. The monkey waited expectantly. It was not about to be the first to speak.

"I demand to speak with the owner of this edifice." said the Lady Mediev. The monkey gave no reply, but nodded its head and ushered the group inside.

The interior of the tower was arrayed in the most luxurious fashion. Every detail bespoke of wealth and extravagance. The monkey led them up through long halls and winding staircases, and as they progressed they passed many displays and showcases of different toys. Each of the toys had a plaque beneath it that contained both a date and a title. Some of the toys Adelle had seen before. One of them Adelle had to stop in front of. It was a crown. *The* crown. It was as dazzling as ever. She leaned against the glass that encased it and could feel the longing rising in her heart, but that was quickly replaced by a flood of guilt. She recoiled from the glass, loathing her own selfishness, and hurried to catch up with the others.

Eventually, after far too many stairs and hallways, they finally arrived at a cozy drawing room. Directly in front of them was a large window that presented a magnificent view of the City. The light from the City mingled with the light from the fire which played gently in the hearth to their right. Before this fire there was a large armchair, and sitting in the armchair was none other than Jakob Damond, the Toymaker.

He was staring attentively at the clock over the mantle as they entered. It was the Eleventh Hour, and he knew it. But then he seamlessly buried his musing and rose to greet his guests.

"Welcome to my winter house!" he said warmly.

"It's you!" cried Deadwick. "You're the guy from the castle!"

The others were surprised to find themselves in the house of Jakob Damond as well, and a little nervous. Especially Adelle. Her eyes were being opened to the fact that, despite his warm demeanor, he was a very dangerous man. But then again, she was presently *surrounded* by some of the most dangerous people in Marloth.

"And you are that goblin that keeps trying to get ahead but keeps getting the short end of the stick," Damond replied to the goblin. "Yet I was right, wasn't I? You did manage to finally acquire the girl; though she turned out to be a bit more than you bargained for, eh?"

He thought this a grand joke, and gave Adelle a knowing look as though to imply all sorts of scandalous exploits. Adelle considered running for the door, but she figured she probably wouldn't get very far.

Jakob Damond motioned for them to take a seat in the plush chairs clustered near the fireplace. Deadwick did not like the idea of sitting down in the midst of such company, but the others complied. The Lady was just about to sit down when a half-man entered the room and handed her a note. She told him not to bother her, but still glanced at the note impatiently. Her countenance immediately changed. She asked if this was a joke. He said he didn't know. She asked who had written it. He said he didn't know that either. She asked him where he had gotten it. The half-man told her. Now the Lady looked very agitated. She absently dropped the note, begged her leave, and hurried out of the room. Curious, Adelle went over and picked up the note from the floor.

I'm sorry, Mother. I know I was a disappointment to you. I tried to redeem myself. I tried to redeem the mistake that was my existence, but I never succeeded. I'm sorry I said I hated you. I don't hate you. I'm grateful for all the good things you gave me and all the clever things you taught me.

I have to go now. I may never see you again, but I hope that I will. I hope there is more to this world than what I see. I hope what the little mad boy says is true.

Your loving daughter,
Ivy

Adelle was breathless. She quickly stuffed the paper into her pocket.

"Well that was sudden." said the toymaker. "I hope no one else is planning on fleeing our party."

The monkey, who had also taken a seat, gave a wicked grin.

"I see you have Edward's book with you." said Jakob Damond, pointing at the item in Adelle's hands. She wished she had some means of concealing it, but she didn't.

"I haven't seen that book in a long, long time," he added, with almost a hint of nostalgia.

"So you are familiar with it?" said the doctor, "I should warn you, it is a very dangerous book."

"Yes, it is," said Jakob Damond. "It is Edward's primary means of haunting me."

"You mean Edward Tralvorkemen? I wondered if you had heard of him, considering your trade."

Jakob Damond stared into the fire as though seeing an ancient struggle retold in its crisscrossing flames. "I am not referring to the Edward you are thinking of. The man you knew was a struggling headmaster. The man I speak of is a deadly sorcerer. If you have ever seen 'Deminox Farinoi', it contains a striking depiction of the fiend that is not far from the truth. Many times I have received the brunt of his mischief. Today he dealt me a particularly low blow—with one stroke he wiped out my entire customer base! It is a sad event, but hope is not lost; I can still fix everything." He turned toward the doctor. "I can restore your zombie machine."

Otto's countenance brightened. "That just so happens to be what I wanted to ask you," he said. "My book of contracts was destroyed."

"Yes, I know. But do not fear; I have another. In fact, I have a copy upstairs. *I* am not a fledgling businessman; I know how to protect my assets." He gave the doctor a peculiar look. It was hard to discern whether it was one of amusement or admonishment. Then he turned to Adelle.

"Wouldn't you like that? To have the machine restored again? Then all of your friends would be alive again. Even that one little boy, the scruffy one. What was his name . . . ah yes, *James*. I'm sure he'd be happy to see you again!"

Adelle tried to make herself as small and invisible as possible.

"But before I can do anything like that, there is a matter that must first be attended to. Edward needs to be dealt with once and for all. And for that I need you to do something."

Adelle looked up at him in surprise.

The toymaker rose to his feet and motioned for Adelle to follow him over to the window and away from the others. She timidly obeyed. The doctor was puzzled by this request, while Deadwick watched the toymaker suspiciously. As Adelle drew near, the toymaker whispered to her, "If you help me I will give you everything your heart desires. The throne. The boy. Eternal youth. You name it. I can even give you a certain piece of headwear I know you want so very much."

Adelle backed away from him. She felt it was time to declare her position. "I don't want your crown. In fact, I don't want anything from you. I'm sorry, but I don't trust you anymore. If you really are as kind as you claim to be, you'll let me leave this place." She started edging her way toward the door. The toymaker followed suit.

"But you don't understand!" he said, no longer whispering. "Everything I've done—everything I am doing; I'm trying to save the world! Edward wants to destroy it! But his power is limited as long as he is kept out of it. He has managed to enter it to a limited degree from time to time, but not enough to destroy it. He has been trying to use you to get him into this world completely, but—thankfully for us all—so far you have not obliged him."

"Can I leave?"

"Yes, you can. Right after you perform a tiny little favor for me and the rest of the world. Destroy that book."

Adelle looked at Marloth in surprise. "But why?"

"Because that book is Edward's only means of entering this world. Once that book is destroyed, the eternal safety of this world will be assured. Then the world will go on and on forever. Unfortunately, that book is not an easy thing to get rid of. There is only one person in the world who can destroy it. Do you know who that someone is?"

Adelle had a good idea, but she didn't say anything.

"I'll give you a clue. Her name starts with 'A.'"

"A what?"

"An 'A'!"

There was a long pause.

"Here's another clue: she *loves* toys."

Adelle remained very quiet.

"Ohhh, and I'm sure you'll guess it with this one: she's a princess! And she's gorgeous!"

More silence.

"And she's a stubborn little *****!" he snapped. "Okay, so you can't guess it! She's you! You! You're the only one who can destroy it! And if you don't, this whole world will end very, very soon!"

By now he, Otto Marrechian, and the monkey were all on their feet. The toymaker seemed to have forgotten their presence. All his attention was on Adelle.

"Do you want this all to end? Everything you know to suddenly and permanently cease?"

"No."

"Then throw that book into the fire."

Adelle stared at the fire, and then at the book. "No." she said.

"And why not?"

"Because I think you're lying. Or at least not telling the whole truth."

"But I *am* telling the truth! What do I have to do to convince you?"

"I'm sorry, but I don't think there is any way you can."

The toymaker put his fists on his hips and looked at her with feigned annoyance. "Adelle! You are being terribly naughty! Do you *want* everyone to die?"

Deadwick looked sad. "I don't want to die."

"I don't want to die either." said Otto.

The monkey looked like it was going to cry.

Adelle felt her resolve waiver, but something held her firm. The toymaker waited several more minutes and finally sighed.

"So is that the end of it, then? You absolutely are not going to oblige me this one little thing?"

"No, I won't."

The toymaker suddenly smiled. "Actually, you will! You see, there's more than one way to make a girl play with fire. If you're going to be naughty and not care whether we live or die, then we might as well go all the way and make you even *naughtier*." He motioned to the monkey who quickly raced out of the room. In a few moments it returned with a large platter of what looked like lumps of coal.

"Jillybons!" Adelle moaned.

"Yes, Jillybons! You were so much fun when you had a couple pounds of these little guys inside of you!"

"No! I'm never eating that filth again!"

Jakob Damond turned to the others. "Could you be so kind as to restrain the princess?" The doctor held back, but Deadwick and the monkey grinned in unison. And lunged forward. She tried to dodge out of the way but Deadwick caught one of her arms while the monkey latched onto her hair. She tried to pull free but she was like a doll in their grasp. Deadwick jerked her toward him and grabbed her other arm, at the same time pinning her feet under his. The monkey pulled her head back violently by the hair. He was bobbing up and down like a furry priest swinging from the chain of a church bell. In all the scuffle Marloth was dropped on the floor.

"Maybe I *am* lying," said the toymaker, as he grabbed several Jillybons and moved toward the struggling little girl. "But even if I am, truth means very little in a world of *Fantasy!*"

"Don't do this!" she begged, just before he violently crammed a handful of Jillybons into her mouth.

"You'll thank me in a minute," he said, as he plugged her nose and clamped his hands over her mouth, strangling a noiseless scream.

Convulsively, Adelle threw all of her weight backwards, kicking the platter of Jillybons into the air. The platter slammed into the side of Jakob Damond's head, sending Jillybons flying in all directions. The toymaker lost his balance, and his grip. Deadwick lost his balance, and his grip. Adelle fell to the floor, spitting out Jillybons. Before anyone could realize what was happening, she was on her feet and had snatched the book. Deadwick swung at her but she ducked beneath the blow. As she ran for the door, he swung at her again and this time connected with her head, knocking her off her feet. She flew several feet through the air and violently landed on the ground across the room. Yet through all of this she did not let go of the book, and awkwardly rose to her feet to find that she had landed right beside the doorway, which she scurried through.

"Stop her!" Otto shouted, and then as it occurred to him, "But don't kill her!"

Deadwick ran out of the room and took out his gun. He was through with this. He had spared her life far too many times; this girl needed to die. But once he stepped through the door his movement was hindered by a crowd of toys that were likewise taking pursuit.

The doctor turned to Jakob Damond. "So all this time you've been interested in the princess simply to destroy that book?"

"No. I have a million things I want to do with her. But I can't do any of those if Edward messes everything up, now can I?"

Adelle was racing down the zigzagging staircase when the wall beside her exploded, showering her with bits of marble. She glanced up to see the toys cascading down the staircase after her and Deadwick above them, lowering his massive firearm and pulling out a second, smaller pistol from his belt.

She reached the bottom of the stairs and nearly ran into several half-men, all of them armed with various weapons designed to skewer and bludgeon people. Adelle jumped backwards to avoid a swing from one of them. Another blast from Deadwick's gun could be heard from above, missing Adelle's head by a hand's breadth and piercing the chest of a half-man.

Suddenly Fugue crashed into the fray like a cannonball dropped into a pond. With his sword rapidly thrusting in every direction he made an opening through the group of half-men that Adelle rushed through. Once she was past them, Fugue vaulted over the half-men as the toys reached the bottom of the stairs and collided into them.

Mr. Mosspuddle was also there, randomly throwing open books and causing endless chaos. So were the dolls. They did not fight but their dancing around caused a little distraction amongst the forces of evil.

Then there was Miss Bethany. She did not have any weapons. She did not have any magic. She didn't need any. She was a Force of Nature. Everyone avoided her like a hurricane, and for similar reasons.

Another volley was fired, this time hitting Adelle's torso. She fell to her knees with a stifled cry. Horrified, Fugue and the librarian pulled back from their fighting and lifted her off of the floor.

Mr. Mosspuddle threw down one of his books. It hit the floor and flew open. A gray fog began to issue from its pages and slowly spread across the ballroom. Within the cover of this book-generated shroud the heroes slipped through the mob.

After much confusion and running about, one of the monsters managed to find the book and close it, causing the fog to quickly disperse. Once the hunters realized their quarry was no longer in sight, orders were shouted to search the Globe for the princess.

It wasn't long before Miss Bethany was spotted charging up and down the halls, knocking over everyone that did not leap out of her way. Some of the monsters gave pursuit, but it was evident that Adelle was not with her, so most of the creatures avoided her and looked elsewhere for the princess.

Amid the flood of search parties, one group of evil toys entered a room near the back of the Globe. The room was empty except for a bed that rested in the far corner. It was a bed that at one time must have been quite elegant but was now rather decrepit and looked as though it had not been used in centuries. Its posts were tarnished, its headboard moldy, and the fabric of its pillows and linens were a faded brown.

The toys were not intelligent enough to look under the bed. They were only designed to walk around and kill things. After a quick scan of the room, they proceeded on to the next room.

Underneath the bed was the band of misfits. Once the room was vacated, they climbed out from the bed, being extra careful of Adelle and her injuries.

Fugue went over to the door, which had been left open a crack, and carefully closed it. "What do we do now?" he asked.

Adelle gasped for breath. "I need to get back to the laboratory."

Mr. Mosspuddle wrung his webbed hands nervously. "I'm not sure where that is from here, and I have no idea how we could get there unseen."

It was then that the raven flew into the room from an upper window and swooped down to land beside them.

"What is going on?" he exclaimed, and then noticed Adelle. He hadn't expected to see her there. He had thought she would be with the toymaker and destroying the book. Instead, here she was in the most miserable condition. The side of her face was bleeding and starting to swell. Her dress was torn and blood was seeping out her side. But she was still clinging to the book. It was still intact. Painfully, Adelle lifted herself to her feet.

"I have to make things right," she said. "I have to get to James. It's what Mr. Tralvorkemen would want me to do."

The raven was stunned.

"Do you know the way to the laboratory from here?" Mr. Mosspuddle asked him.

"Yes," said the raven absently, all of his attention on Adelle.

Monstrous cries of impatience could be heard echoing through the hallways. Fugue made some comment about more monsters searching the room at any moment. The librarian was growing restless. He turned to the raven in exasperation.

"What are you waiting for? Are you going to help the princess or not?"

There was a long pause, and then the raven spoke,

"What princess? I don't see any princess. All I see is a queen."

*   *   *

The forces of darkness continued to search for the princess, but they could not find her. The leaders of the forces began to speculate that she may have slipped from the Globe and out into the City. They began expanding the radius of their hunting to include the immediate neighborhood.

Suddenly there was a cry that someone had found her. The cry was carried by more and more minions until the entire Globe was filled by creatures running toward the source of the discovery.

The purveyor of this cry was the raven, who was hiding at the far end of the Globe.

Mr. Mosspuddle peered out into the ballroom. There were still creatures dotted here and there, but none of their focus was on the doorway of the laboratory or any of the paths to that location. Carefully, the group of heroes made their way out into the ballroom. They were more than halfway to their destination when they were spotted by a monkey. The monkey made a tremendous commotion that drew everyone's attention to the center of the ballroom. No longer benefiting from caution, the heroes bolted for the doorway. Throughout the Globe, fell beings began changing direction away from the raven and toward the other side of the Globe. But the raven had bought them enough time. The adventurers managed to slip through the doors of the laboratory just before the first of the pursuers got to them.

The doors were large and very solid. Fugue and several of the others leaned against the doors, trying to do anything they could to keep them from opening. But more and more fiends were gathering on the other side.

"We'll hold them off as long as we can!" Fugue said to Adelle. "But that probably won't be very long. Whatever you are going to do, you'd better hurry!"

Adelle hated to leave them in such a dire position, but she knew she had to. Thanking them once again for their sacrifice, she stumbled down the corridor and left the chaos and warfare behind her.

It was surprisingly quiet inside Doctor Marrechian's laboratory. The walls must have been remarkably thick to block out so much sound. She made her way toward the room where the zombie machine had once resided. She entered the room and looked about apprehensively. There was James where she had left him, lying on his back with his limbs splayed out.

She bent down over his still form. "I don't know if you can hear me," she said. "But I want to say I'm sorry. I wish I could take back so many of the things I have done." She paused for several moments, and then sat down. "I don't know if this will do you any good, but it's the only thing I know left to do." Carefully, she opened the book.

As the rest of the occupants of the Globe were trying to break down the door to what had once been Otto Marrechian's laboratory, they were suddenly stopped by a sound that echoed through every room and every hall of the building. It was the voice of a little girl. Her voice was quivering and weak, struggling to breathe. There was no introduction. She began to read.

She read of a wonderful fairytale world, full of adventures and happy endings. Of beautiful landscapes and fascinating creatures. Of a noble headmaster who protected his children from the darkness and loved them dearly. And how the headmaster gave his life to save them all.

"What is that nauseating sound?"

"It sounds like a little girl. What is she saying?"

"It is dreadful, whatever it is. Make her stop!"

"But where is it coming from?"

"The Globe has a sound system! Could it be coming from that?"

"That's right! Someone should turn it off!"

There was much scurrying and frantic chatter. After some time of this, someone said, "Will someone turn off the Globe's sound?!?"

"We just did that! But it didn't work. So we severed the wires. And then we tore down the speakers. None of it worked. We have done everything we can think of but that girl's voice keeps coming!"

Eventually she did stop. She had to stop. The right side of her face was so swollen she could no longer see through the eye on that side, and she felt guilty the way her blood and tears were dripping onto the pages. Before long the loss of blood finally caught up with her and she collapsed beside James.

*   *   *

Dear Sir,

You are neglecting to look beyond the surface. In this dream your book of contracts remains intact, but in the dream that dreams this dream your book is destroyed, and that is what matters. All of your contracts have been made void.

*You say you want to keep this world going forever? But how are you to do that? What are you going to add to extend it? You cannot create pages. You cannot create anything. With or without my opposition, you have no means of perpetuating this dream. The end **will come.***

There is also the matter of compensation. You have taken every-thing from me except what matters most: you can never take away who I am, and that is your undoing. I acknowledge that even in this present dream I am still an imperfect reflection, but I am now far more accurate a rendition then I was before, and growing more precise by the minute.   Soon I will return for what is mine.   All that has been taken, it shall be restored.

Edward Tralvorkemen

*　　*　　*

James groggily opened his eyes and looked around.   He had just been dreaming he was in the orphanage infirmary, and Mr. Tralvorkemen was removing the bandages from his face. But now he was in the mostly deserted laboratory of Doctor Otto Marrechian.

At the same time, Adelle regained consciousness.   Her body didn't hurt anymore. The blood was gone. She propped herself up on one elbow and it was then that she noticed him.

"James!" she cried out with joy.   She sprang up and wrapped her arms around him. "You're alive! You're alive! I am *so* sorry! Will you ever forgive me?"

"For what?"

"For too many things, the worst of them being making you destroy the zombie machine!"

"Look, I needed to destroy that thing one way or the other.   You just showed me that I had to."

"Really?   But still, so much of what I did was wrong.   Will you forgive me?"

"Yes!   Of course I forgive you!"

Then the depth of the situation hit her and she stepped back to look at him in amazement. "But how is this possible? The zombie machine is destroyed! How are you still moving?"

"The zombie machine is not what is animating me. Mr. Tralvorkemen is. I can feel his enchantment working through me stronger than ever before. He's *here*."

*　　*　　*

I would like now to paint a picture for you. A slowly moving picture. First, there is a room. A huge room with ceilings so high that you have to look upwards to see where the walls end. A room so vast it could hold legions of people. And it is: from wall to wall it is filled with legions of evil. A seemingly endless variety of deformed creatures bent on harm. All of their attention is focused on the far end of the room where there is a doorway. A doorway that is also quite large and yet still dwarfed by the overall scale of the room.

The crowd is trying to gain entrance through the doorway, but the doors will not open. They try force: fists, clubs, guns, bombs, but to no avail. They try magic and all sorts of dark arts, but the doors do not budge, causing their incantations to look like nonsense. The maker of the doors is there and even he is puzzled; he had made them to be ordinary doors and he says there had never been anything special about them.

The crowd is growing chaotic. Its unsated drive to get through the doorway is threatening to turn against itself.

Near the edge of the crowd there is one creature that does not belong there. It is a raven. It has a resigned and morbid look upon its countenance. It is being held by a clever looking man who, despite the growing tension surrounding him, looks calm and confident.

Suddenly the doors burst open, throwing the nearest minions deeper into the crowd and hitting the walls on either side with a deafening thud as the knobs and knockers are embedded into the mortar.

And this is the zenith of the picture: out of the doorway steps a man. He has a tall frame. While his appearance is simple, he carries with him a regal dignity. He stands before the creatures without any acknowledgment of their hostility nor the discrepancy of numbers between him and them.

Someone from the crowd calls out, asking who he is. He says he is Edward Tralvorkemen. A doctor in the audience pipes up, saying that he had once been friends with Tralvorkemen, and that this was not that man. The doctor says that Tralvorkemen is dead. The man who calls himself Tralvorkemen says that truly the doctor had once been a friend, but had since turned his back on him. The man also says that he had died and yet is alive, and that the doctor should be used to such things.

In the midst of this exchange, the raven manages to escape the clever man's hold and fly upward, shouting several times that this is indeed Edward Tralvorkemen before settling on a window ledge far above the crowd.

The crowd doesn't really care who this man is. They tell him to move aside or they will kill him. He says he will not allow them through the doorway.

The crowd finds this amusing. They begin to laugh and deride him using crude language. They gloat about the perverse things they will do to the princess. Except for the clever looking man. He doesn't say anything. He just takes a few steps back, turns around, and runs like a madman.

Despite all of their words, no one has yet taken a step forward. Instead, someone asks the man standing in front of the doorway what he is doing there. He says that he has come for many things, one of them being his children. They ask, "Who are your children?" He says, "I will show you."

And here is the most amazing part of the picture. The man who calls himself Tralvorkemen is gesturing. There is a burst of light. Light so intense and blinding it casts shadows clear across the room. The light gradually fades, and one of the zombie children is standing in its place. It looks about in wonder. The crowd looks at it in wonder. It no longer looks like a zombie. Its skin is whole and new.

There is another flash. And another. Children begin to rise up in the midst of the crowd. One of the half-men, growing in fear, raises his sword and attempts to cleave the nearest child in two. The child takes the sword away from the half-man. More flashes of light. More children lifted to their feet. They look happy, as though finally waking from a long bad dream. The legions begin to panic. Some of them start to fight. Some of them start to flee. The man who calls himself Tralvorkemen rushes into the crowd. A boy and a girl and several fairytale creatures are running out of the doorway and eagerly following behind the man. More children are coming to life. The swarming mass of fleeing monsters and pursuing children begins to slowly acquire momentum and move up the stairs. They cascade and crash upward like water rebelling against gravity, rising along progressively higher levels of the building. Along the wall of the stairway there is a sign that says, "The End is nearly upon us!" Monsters are leaping out of windows and screaming and occasionally turning to fight only to be submerged by the upward surging force of children. In their midst are the freed prisoners, running alongside the headmaster and shouting enthusiastically.

The building itself is very tall, but eventually the people reach its pinnacle. The top floor does not have much in the way of walls. It simply has beams of wood shooting up to the roof. There is an explosion of minions as they pour out of the top floor like a fountain. The fountain continues until there are no minions left.

The forces of darkness are no longer to be seen. Now all that remains in the building are the headmaster, the band of adventurers, and hundreds of children. The children are all gathering around Tralvorkemen, every one of them trying to get close enough to embrace him all at once. Adelle is in the crowd. As she looks around she spots Ivy standing in wonder. Tears fill Adelle's eyes. She calls out. Ivy sees her and runs toward her. They hug each other tightly. Miss Bethany is dancing around with a child on each of her shoulders. Nearby, Fugue is talking to the dolls and says to them, "Now *that* was an adventure!"

They are all very happy. So happy, there are no words sufficient to express how happy they are. What can I say? The best I can do is this: for the first time ever, the little boy who rarely spoke and never smiled, smiled.

Then Tralvorkemen motioned for everyone to listen, and the hundreds of voices gradually quieted to hear him speak. "We don't have much time, so I will be quick. This is a time of rejoicing, but don't think the fight is over. On the contrary, it has only just begun. Today another hole was bored through the dark sky, letting in more light. Letting in more reality. But there is still much reality being obscured. There are still many souls out there who are enslaved by evil. You must fight that evil. You must fight it with reality.

"But that is not the only fight you will face. You are still dead, and there is a void in your souls because of it. Right now my magic is filling that void, but some of you have already seen how the enchantment requires upkeep or it will shrink. The zombie machine was simply a conduit for forces which still exist, forces that have other means of taking control of you. When my enchantment on you weakens it will leave room for those forces to fill. The rest of your life will be a fight to keep that enchantment strong. But now our time has run out."

Already things were starting to become blurry. Sounds grew echoey and distant. "What is happening?" exclaimed Adelle.

She could barely make out what Tralvorkemen said, but it sounded something like, "Don't worry. We'll meet again."

"What?" said James.

And then they awoke.

The End

Awake O sleeper

And arise from the dead

And Christ will shine upon you

-From an ancient text written

by a man named Paul